T0162623

Divinity

Divinity

christian rodriguez

DIVINITY

iUniverse books may be ordered through booksellers or by contacting:

iUniverse
1663 Liberty Drive
Bloomington, IN 47403
www.iuniverse.com
1-800-Authors (1-800-288-4677)

Because of the dynamic nature of the Internet, any web addresses or
links contained in this book may have changed since publication and
may no longer be valid. The views expressed in this work are solely those
of the author and do not necessarily reflect the views of the publisher,
and the publisher hereby disclaims any responsibility for them.

Any people depicted in stock imagery provided by Thinkstock are models,
and such images are being used for illustrative purposes only.
Certain stock imagery © Thinkstock.

ISBN: 978-1-4917-9799-0 (sc)
ISBN: 978-1-4917-9800-3 (e)

Library of Congress Control Number: 2016908165

Print information available on the last page.

iUniverse rev. date: 05/18/2016

Dedication

in loving memory of **James Scott Jr.,** You might not be with us but in our hearts, forever you'll stay

The Spiral pool

"the spiral pool is where all the Divinity gathers, from there the Divinity swirls like a spiral pool. This is what truly shifts the divine energy; or Divinity to access their true inner energy or hidden potential. Drawing in the positive energy like air to an AC unit, swirling and mixing it with the divine body to explode into the phenomenal creation that is the Miraclelytes."

The Shrine

"the combination of the heart and the soul of a Miraclelyte. The battery to this non stop warrior of light, a positive energy - driven source that needs recharge like a person needs sleep; only going dim when needing to recharge again, this source of energy gives strength to the Spiral Pool to do its function of circulating the Divinity in the body. Even with the Spiral Pool completely destroyed, as long as the Shrine is intact the Miraclelyte will continue to forge on. However this being the heart and soul of the body it is also the biggest weakness that needs the most protecting."

Divinity

"this is Divinity in it's unleashed form, once activated one's individual strength or abilities begin to reveal themselves with Divinity like the fire underneath the cooking pot. Once unleashed Divinity starts to enhance a person's attributes immediately, truly the greatest weapon to the Miraclelytes."

"the external and activation of Divinity causes and influx of energy. This is the form it takes once tapped into and activated for the use of the owner"

Welcome To Our World

Divinity

Life may be a tiny bit different from both what you and I were taught, what is life truly? Who are we as humans? And more important who really is God? Something I always asked...when I used to be of the world you are reading this from. I found the answers, more like they found me. The answers to all three of these questions might surprise you, they might shock you, they might even change the way you look at life itself. Or you might even stop listening the moment I begin to scratch the system that programmed you, to reject any outside ideas either way I-...I – hold on just one quick moment I'll be right back.

Meanwhile, "I'm... so scared I hear noises under my bed- I tell Mommy and Daddy but they don't listen! *Gasp* I heard it again please God help me I hide under my blankets but I-I-I have nowhere to go... I feel it breathing on me... he's a big scary monster with big teeth and sharp fingers... he says he wants me... that he loves little girls they make perfect wives – I don't want to be married – I'm only four! – He says that if I don't marry him he will eat me – like all the other girls. My mommy told me if he doesn't stop that I should pray to God because he will hear me.

Please God I'm so scared – I don't want to die or be married... he's pulling back the sheets....God please!!! HELP ME!!!"

Four year old Felicity Chaves is too innocent to know that she is being haunted by a demon. A diabolical creature that takes young girls as his wives and devours them, he terrorizes them until they give in out of fear. His kind is one of the reasons for the missing children. A truly malevolent force that was forged in the flames, it is to be eternally bound to... Or is it? Its purpose and others of this category is no other than to destroy this world. Completely ominous that they take pleasure in destroying something as pure as a child's innocence that could only be constructed by a devil... or could it? This freak of nature standing in front of Felicity's bed at seven feet tall, but in Felicity's frightful eyes he probably looks twenty or more, with jet black, rough, crackly and crispy skin rougher than crocodile's. Its fangs hanging out like a saber tooth, blood and saliva trailing off the tips of its anxious lips as its slender tongue swished back and forth. Horns coming off its forehead curving up towards the roof, it had a strong muscular upper body like it was a human but it was covered with black fur, its lower half was that of a pair of goat legs. With a pointed tail swinging left to right like an excited pet his face looking exactly like a goat full of rage and pure evil with blood leaking out his eyes like tears.

Felicity stunned with fear as he panted heavily; making the most terrifying pattern of breathing that Felicity has ever heard. Felicity was in the farthest corner of her bed, tucked into a ball pulling her feet away from the monster. The demon was slowly pulling his body across the bed in an attempt to reach her. His long, twisted, curled black claws coming closer and closer to Felicity. Screaming at the top of her lungs, but it was like her room's walls were made of concrete. Nobody could hear her. Nobody could save her. She backed up against the wall trying to get away but there was nowhere to go, the demon hissing as he reached out to grab her feet and pull her towards him but just as the demon lunged Felicity screamed as loud as her lungs would allow "*GOD HELP ME!!!*"

Just then in that very instant the demon was in midair as it leaped towards Felicity like a lion pouncing on an injured gazelle. Something fell from the sky right on the demon's back, landing on him as if an anvil had smashed through the roof, crushing his back. He roared in pain and Felicity's beds bent as if it had lots of children were jumping on it. Felicity covered her ears and shut her eyes. Continuing to scream in distress and fear just then the demon was launched from Felicity's room like he was shot out of a catapult. The demon wrecked a hole right through Felicity's left wall flying out into the middle of the street lying on his back with drywall all over his ashy skin like lotion. He shook his head left to right trying to recover from the haziness.

Felicity heard the sound of the demon snarling from afar so she began to slowly pulling her hands down from her face. She was expecting an even bigger monster to be standing right in front of her. Opening her eyes, she did not see an even bigger juggernaut but someone sitting at the edge of her bed concealed with a shining white hooded robe glistening as if it we're made from the stars that decorated the night. Felicity thought for a second that it might've been the tooth fairy. But then she realized it couldn't be, still frightened knowing if they we're friend or foe Felicity backed away slowly pushing herself back up into the corner. Then hearing the calmest, soothing and inviting voice that cradled her as it spoke, the shrouded figure from sitting at the edge of her bed. "Sorry Father could not be here so I am gonna try to fill Daddy's shoes" confidence like fire radiating off a burning building, by the texture and deepness of the voice Felicity could tell it was a man, Felicity curiously scooted an inch forward but no more curiosity coursing throughout her entire body as she couldn't help but ask "God is your Dad?" The figure had his head pointed towards her but the hood completely shaded his face, shadows like a mask concealing every inch of his identity. No matter how hard Felicity squinted to try to see at least one facial feature he responded "yeah he's your Father too you know he's everyone's Father and everyone is his children I – umm... you'll understand when you're older but I want you to know something...-"

The figure stood up off the bed and then pulled his hood off his head, suddenly a light shot through the gaping hole in the wall as if the moon we're shining a spotlight. Felicity now able to fully see his face Felicity instantly thinking he was her prince charming, her knight in shining armor sent to save her; she thought he was absolutely gorgeous.

Having wild spiky blue, a jungle that had thick strands of royal blue instead of vines, hair that blazed the most fearsome dark sky - blue flame, His eyes a scorching bright blue; a perfect window view to the depths of his soul, his skin crystal clear, flawless, without a blemish, like having personal grounds keepers to make his facial features impeccable. Smiling to show his pearly white teeth, even his thin precision cut eyebrows we're the same community of blue. Standing up, now the robe curtaining out to reveal a slab of rock hard abdominals, there is no buying this six pack at any corner store. Arms rippled like a pond during a violent tremor, every possible muscle fiber was sculpted out front and center; his biceps half the size of Felicity's head, his shoulders sturdy enough to carry Felicity and her entire bed set upon. Felicity now wondering why his "boobs" we're bigger than her mommy's, his body was the type that they bring into a chiseler's officer pointed at him and demanded "we want the Zeus statue to look like this!" Although he was wearing a hooded cape that was bright enough to be the light house on the shore line so ships don't crash, he was pretty plain other than that wearing a pair of jeans that had a unique tone of navy that you would really have to stare at and cock your head to the side for a minute to confirm it was really navy. With a blue belt, the same tone as his hair I'll have you know, lazily slipped through only some of the pouches not really able to properly do its job; oh but the shoe lace, also the same blue family, was for some reason in every loop and hole to hold up his pants and his belt more like support? I don't understand kid's fashion today. Lastly were his high-tops, skinny shoes that went up to the bottom of his shins although I don't understand it I can't deny they look great! Mainly go ahead and guess... that's right blue with black like a hype cheerleader in the back chiming in and out of the patterns on the side.

Felicity couldn't put her finger on it but seeing his face and seeing him she started to let it go releasing the tension in her tightly curled body. She definitely started to feel warmer as she scooted closer and closer to him, but above everything she felt safe. The man then squatted to eye level, a six foot tower of muscle crunching himself to a child's size as he pointed at the middle of her chest "you have a heart and soul, you must make them strong because they will never steer you wrong. Follow whatever your heart tells you, God gave it to you to be your compass whenever you feel lost, and your soul so you can always be with him. He is with you it might not seem like it but he is... it's just times are hard right now for everyone including him, I need you to do me a favor will you try your hardest to do this for me?"

Felicity absolutely trusting him to not even think of steering her wrong nodding yes almost instantly. Felicity felt a slight tap on her head as the man's hand gently rested on her hair he then spoke "keep your heart pure, one day your heart will bring you to God. It is brighter than gold and more valuable than any diamond, never sell your soul or let it become dark, because you might lose your way – but just looking at you... I can tell you're a smart kid. When the time comes you'll always know what to do – I believe in you Felicity."

As the man got up and began to walk towards the massive hole in the wall Felicity shouted after him "Wait!! How you know my name?!" The man stopped and turned his head half to the side to call over his shoulder to her "I know a lot of things... I am not like you, your Mommy or Daddy I am a bit different... I would *love to tell you what I am but maybe that would be a better story for when you're older. All you need to know is that where ever evil is I am gonna be there to kick its ass! Damn! I forgot you're like four – shit! I did it again!" The man nervously covering his mouth to stop anymore cuss words from leaking out he started over as if nothing happened.*

"What I mean is – just think of me as one of your guardians, now excuse me I'm gonna make sure Mr. Tall, light and handsome on opposite day over there, never bothers you again!" As the oh so mysterious man began to walk towards the tunnel he made in her wall Felicity was by his side as she swiped his hand quicker than a pro pick pocket starving for his next meal. She looked up at him with eyes puppies wish they had, the man's hand being firmly squeezed in between both of hers. Her heart leaking into her voice as she asked "what is you name?"

The mysterious man looking down at her like a teacher proud of his student, a master proud of his disciple, like a father proud of his daughter Felicity even continuing "so you come again I member you" the man looking like he was trying to retain his happiness. Smirking at her "my name is Azuru" fully satisfied with getting with what she wanted nodding with glee as she walked back over to her bed to let Azuru get down to business. Azuru nodding his last grin as he gave her one glance from the side turning away once he seen she was safely on the bed.

His mood flipping like a light switch now being engulfed by seriousness and anger he began to pass through the wrecking ball sized hole. The wall began to regenerate itself like a construction crew working so fast they we're invisible, fixing the wall in milliseconds Felicity's eyes as wide as her sockets would allow her before they fell out, mouth almost hitting the floor as all she saw what was left of the hole was a dent big enough to get a window of Azuru's hand looking like he had just finished snapping. A mere moment later it was like the hole was never there and Felicity whispered to herself "Zazuru"

Azuru stood outside in the dead of night with the demon, standing on its hind legs, it's back hunched, and fangs bared the most furious look on its face as it shook away the drywall. His blood red pupils just said they wanted to rip Azuru apart slowly as Azuru was still in Felicity's yard walking over to the demon.

Stepping over Felicity's unicorn themed tricycle that was left lying around, Azuru's hands we're in his pockets his back a slouching posture and his face shaded by shadows; as he aimed it towards the ground the gruesome beast standing completely still not panting, flinching, shaking, or trembling. Like a tiger so motionless it makes its prey try to feel as if it's not there before it pounces. Azuru now on the black asphalt picking his head up to look at the demon as he exhaled upwards to blow the tips of his hair in frustration, the demon began to grind its teeth together, seeing that look on Azuru that expression so clear even a blind man could clearly recognize it. Practically being shouted by Azuru's eyes the longer the demon stared into them; he was drowning in boredom

The demon absolutely infuriated what was this man?! Some over privileged child forced to do chores?! How dare he not take him seriously Azuru's lips began moving as soon as the first word came out "I-" the demon dashed than lightning strikes thrusting his claws forward to Azuru's face. But even faster than him while still being able to remain statue – still, Azuru caught the demon's claw like a master catching a fly with his hand, Azuru having about as much stress as a kid who just left school to go on his summer break, merely holding back the entirety of the demon's claws that looked fearsome enough to slash through iron genders. Only two fingers we're needed from Azuru his index and thumb pinching the palm of the claw the demon trying to pull back or pull away. It felt like it was stuck in tar or quicksand Azuru continued now that outburst had been silenced

"I – do not like being interrupted – I am just gonna let you know that right now it will be some handy info that will save you *a lot of pain. –" the demon roaring in defiance only to screech in pain a moment later, Azuru had tightened his pinch on the claw like the adjustable roll on a wrench. Shaking his head in disappointment as he said "what did I just get done telling you dumbass? I'ma let you know right now, I'm not a four year – old girl so I might put up a much better fight... just a little bit." Just then in a flash it felt like a sledgehammer traveled all the way from hell, with the speed of a meteorite to uppercut him in the jaw. A violent throbbing on top of feeling like the entire world was spinning and it couldn't even feel the ground it took a minute to regain itself only to come to realization that it was kicked in the air. It even felt its own putrid black, dense, disgusting sewage looking blood splattered all over its face while high in the air. Among the last moments the demon was able to regain recovery and land on its feet, panting from the impact looking from across the street to see Azuru slowly pulling his right leg down. A smirk started to break out from Azuru's face that escalated enormously into bursting out laughing. As he said "I was kidding about the little bit part you're straight up gonna get wrecked! ...and you're looking at the one man demolition crew...-"*

Azuru then whispered to himself "damn gotta write that down what did you guys think?" Azuru is now forward like some newbie no nothing actor, looking at the camera still going as he said "don't worry I got more watch! Hey! Dracula's bumpkin of a rejected cousin! Are you feeling like a man then pull up your big boy pants and let's do this!! But do me a favor please be gentle, it's my first time... in the last 15 minutes –"Azuru looking at the camera again with one of those arrogant smuck smiles his finger and thumb under his chin as he said "what do you guys think?"

He then waited for a response like someone was actually giving their opinion, Azuru then exaggeratedly_scoffed with a hint of repulse "TRY HARD?! Well I think you're not trying hard enough! Excuse me Mr. Sir or Madam who has a set of buttocks that hates to work, I'm gonna kick this thing's ass like, insert badass simile here it's up for the reader to decide but even they know this thing is gonna die!" The demon with bullet speed so fast no human eye would be able to catch it was already in front of Azuru with his right claw cocked back ready to impale his face with his five miniature spears. Azuru staring up at him like the demon was his mother talking Azuru's head off about what he did wrong today! Azuru's head tilted to the side as his eyes were just so unable to concentrate on the "threat" in front of him suddenly Azuru's entire body lit up. His eyes flashing with life as he shouted "oh shit!" Ducking and rolling his head unintentionally under the demon's claw as he tried to stab him in the face.

Now looking down toward his pants digging deep like he was looking for gold. As he continued his sentence "almost forgot" pulling out a miniature notepad from his back pocket a pen was inside the tin spirals that held it together. "Now what did I say again you're gonna straight up get wrecked! And...what?"

The demon was so shocked and taken back that it had no idea what to do, this is the first time it ever came across a situation like this where the opponent was so stupid to take his eyes off the battle right in front of them or he considered it so harmless that he needed to pass the time somehow, you be the judge, but the rage overtaking the demon. It snarled and spoke with complete frustration and irritation spewed out from the words of his weird language **"WHO ERAD UOY!!! OD TON NRUT RUOY SEYE MORF EM!!!"** (How dare you do not turn your eyes from me). Now using his left arm to swing a vicious claw to try to dig right through Azuru's brain but only getting a handful of air. Azuru simply tilted his head to the right not taking his eyes off the page as he spoke to himself still trying to jog his memory "What was the line agaaaain?! What did I say dammit! It waaaaasss – IT WAS WHAT?!!"

The demon so hot boiled at Azuru's lack of attention it just wanted to rip out his skull from his body right then and there. Its arms blurring out as he shot them at Azuru like a wave of machine gun bullets, each one with Azuru's forehead for the mark; all of the demon's steel- like, razor edge fingers pointed forward to form a knife formation, the demon going so fast it looked like he just grew six more arms just to deal with Azuru. Still not a single scrape on Azuru's face as he bobbed, weaved, tilted, swung, tucked and rolled his head with such ease and 10 times slower than the speed the demon was going; only making him go faster by how frustrated he was getting by his inability to land a single mark on Azuru, no matter how hard he tried.

Azuru still trying to wrap his brain around what he just said moments ago " hmm it was something like I am the wrecking crew – nah it wouldn't be that, come on it's me I am much more clever than that okay okay okay. Ittttttttttttt might have been something like I am gonna wreck you worse than a demolition crew?? Nah! It wasn't that either! –"Just as Azuru was battling with himself, the demon roared absolutely losing it now trying to bring down his right claw like a sledgehammer being brought down to crush pebbles. But still without even a single glance Azuru seen it coming with eyes he wasn't using, anticipated with the mind that was already preoccupied. Sending an axe kick up to bounce the demon's claw back with such strong recoil it looked like it almost broke the demon's arm; screeching slightly with a hint of pain Azuru concentrating on the only thing that truly deserved his attention "No no for sure I think I got it this time I will wreck you like... I wrecked your mom! NO!! That's not it either – how would that work by the way? Hey! Mr. Halloween mask for a face! Is satan your mom and dad or what the hell?!... ha did you see what I did there?!"

The demon tried to crush Azuru's head in between his massive claws like smashing two coconuts together. Azuru still not even taking his eyes off of his notepad ducking quicker than moles in every single whack- a- mole game; the demon swiping a whole lot of air suddenly screeching at the top of his lungs as he felt that an anvil fell on his left foot. Looking down from his roar that he released into the sky, to see Azuru's right foot smashed firmly on top of his foot, just as he was about to slash Azuru's face right off, Azuru merely shoved his right shoulder into the demon Azuru then continued his self_conversation "maybe I surprised myself and went a poetic route... nah! I hate poetry a person think its soooooo nice because it's written fancy and uses big words. Let's be honest nobody really knows what the hell they are saying! We just don't want to look stupid even though it's too confusing for self expression"

The demon felt like he was tackled by a humongous heavy weight line backer, when he fell his bone snapped like a twig. The demon violently and fiercely snarling clutching its leg trying to make the pain go away, Azuru then kicked it punting it halfway down the road. To Azuru that fearsome display of power was like a child kicking a rock that was in his way; as the demon was withering in pain practically a block away, spewing out sewage colored blood from his mouth. Azuru was still pondering WHAT DID HE JUST SAY?!?! "Dammit it was only like a minute ago how can I forget?!... Well what can you do when every word you speak deserves to be engraved in gold as the world's catch phrase – that's why I carry my hand dandy writing book!!"

Stumbling and shaking as the demon fought against gravity to stand panting with evil intentions racing through its mind it then shouted "**I LLIW PANS RUOY ENIPS EKIL A GIWT! I LLIW HSURC RUOY LLUKS NEEWTEBNI YM YTHGIM SWALC!! I LLIW KNIRD NOPU RUOY DOOLB!! I! LLIW TSAEF NOPU RUOY DOOLB!! I! LLIW TSAEF NOPU RUOY TRAEH!! UOY LLIW EID EREH!!!!** "(I will snap your spine like a twig! I will crush your skull in between my mighty claws! I will drink upon your blood! I will feast upon your heart you, will die here!)

Azuru sighing like his boss just wouldn't get off his ass no matter how hard he tried to imagine he wasn't there. So Azuru finally took his eyes off his notepad to look up at the riled up and aggressive demon that was just oozing blood lust. Even too *lazy to put full effort into a sarcastic response Azuru drug his feet with his voice. "Oh my gentle God! Please, please please! Save me! Won't you save me from this demon! Who is so original with his threats "eat my heart out" yeah I never heard that being born in the 70's. If only! ...If only!!! I had some sort of training to combat this incredible adversary! ...well I guess I should write my farewells, I had a good run but my time has come! but may I have one last request before you brutally butcher me and sell my body to the black market or whatever demons do?...-" The demon starting to get used to Azuru's personality there was no way that any of this could be real if it had eyebrows the demon would have definitely raised them by now. But back to Azuru's Oscar winning performance "can I - this might be asking too much but can I... give you this shoe? ... -"Azuru then pointed at his right shoe the demon then had a look of bewilderment,*

Not losing an ounce of anger this was probably some sort of trick "yeah so can I give you this shoe as a testament of passing on my will?... don't worry though I'll go ahead and give it to you allow me to hand it over to you! -"Azuru then began walking over to the demon his shoulders swaying forward with his body, as his peaceful grin began to get more and more boiled. Escalating like lava building up from a dormant volcano dominance radiating off of Azuru like a stomach turning cologne. With each step he took towards the demon, a new shiver appeared in the demon's body as he attempted to take steps back. That is when he realized that this man was drilling fear into him like a dentist into a patient's molars. He made the demon actually forget for a moment who the actual demon was here

Azuru's fists tightening so hard you could hear his skin squeak, teeth grinding together, every step he took broke the pavement. His voice didn't even match his wrathful expression sounding as if he was a friendly neighbor aggressively trying to offer him cookies "here! TAKE. MY. SHOE!" the demon starting to become more and more apprehensive as he became closer even taking the measurement as jumping a length back. "Ooooooh! Please don't back away YOU'RE GONNA HURT MY FEELINGS!!!"

The demon cringing at the image of this monstrosity walking towards him do people like him really exist? Is this really a game of cat and mouse? Azuru, still driving his intimidation into the demon like the crash test cars driving straight into a brick wall. "You're pretty tough talk from all the way over there, problem is I couldn't hear that well!!-" Azuru sounding as his teeth were grinding harder than Tony Hawk grinding his skate board against a rail_" DO ME ANOTHER FAVOR AND TELL ME AGAIN JUST WHAT YOU'RE GONNA DO!!" The demon couldn't even take his eyes off of Azuru coming forward like a nuclear warhead with legs. The demon was absolutely silent you could hear his shaking louder than anything, Azuru scoffing shaking his head worse than all his disappointed teachers in high school, "silent! Exactly what I thought! Because I'm not a helpless little girl, because I am not a weak or frail human, believe me when I say I AM NOTHING LIKE YOU HAVE EVER FACED BEFORE!!! NOW ALLOW ME TO GIVE YOU MY SHOE!!! – Funny thing about my shoe though, is that it can only be accepted through a hole! And since the top one is busy doing a lot of talking I guess I have to use the other one –"

A sadistic mischievous smirk came over Azuru's face just spelling out trouble without having to use a single letter, how he was able to keep a straight face as he asked this question is beyond me "Ready?!"

The demon's blood eyes widened with absolute shock and in panic and a manner like he wasn't thinking shouting as loud as his voice could carry him **"YATS YAWA MORF EM!!"** (Stay away from me!!) Azuru chuckling as he watched the demon's cheeks puff up with air then saying without a care in the world "yeah I have a problem with authority I have a syndrome called "rebellion syndrome" where I have to do the exact opposite of whatever people I have no respect for tell me so...-"Just then the flames began to howl, like wolves in the night, from inside the demon's mouth as *some it spread to his cheeks as he was just about to release it Azuru still not the least bit worried, hands in both pockets as he walked forward with his back hunched over. Suddenly Azuru then came to a stop as he saw a humongous cluster of flames rolled into a bay sun; it was as big as the roundabout on this street. Azuru's eyes locked on this baby meteor and would not wander anywhere else. Azuru then said "Holy Shit!" With eyes star struck right before the ball of fire swallowed him whole like a person being taken by a tsunami*

The demon huffing and puffing with fire still burning on the side of its cheeks, acting like perspiring sweat glands the demon was even unknown that it had. That amount of power locked inside a huge weight lifted off its shoulders not having to deal with that nuisance any longer, still that look in his eyes still haunted his mind he could've truly been formidable he made the demon dig deep inside to call upon power it never knew existed. The demon began watching its work at hand, those dazzling flames work its magic, and it couldn't help but get some pride from it all as the furious embers burned, growled, snarled, howled and roared. The flames then without any warning blew out like a miniature hurricane just strolling through or more like it was an already melting birthday candle to reveal an unharmed, unscathed, without a scratch absolutely flawless Azuru standing in the eye of the storm. With his eyes closed and the most calm and collected look on his face his lips an "O" shape looking like air had just done escaping, so much causality was radiating off Azuru. His body relaxed, his muscles loose, his left leg pulled up so his foot was balanced onto his tip toes. Azuru couldn't be more vulnerable if he put his weak spot on a sign with directions.

Both hands in his pockets and he paid no attention to his opponent in front of him who so awe stricken he was shaking. Azuru finally spoke as his eyes shot open with precision targeting almost looking through the demons as he said "I remembered what it was" then within the blink that the demon instinctively took Azuru was already in the demon's face. He traveled half a block within a millisecond he was so fast he could beat lightning in a race, and that is with a head start included. Azuru's arms cocked back and at his sides, chest pushed forward knees bent, a sadistic smirk on Azuru's face – sorry I am just going through the checklist before Azuru sticks his boot so far up the demon's ass he has a size 12 replacing a vital organ. Azuru then spoke with a tone like he was holding back the immense, intense, incredible, excitement, but it was like a twig replacing the entire hover dam. Soooo not too well "you're straight up gonna get wrecked!" Azuru then jabbed three times at the demon's chest first off: so fast they almost looked connected to the same damn punch. Second: Azuru didn't even use his fist he snapped his fingers and the impact of the snap hit the demon's chest, Azuru never touched the demon. Finally third: a blue flamed flare the size of a humongous softball mashed the demon in the chest at the mere snap of Azuru's fingers every time down to the millisecond. Azuru then swung his right hand for an overhand right - ...snap? That collided into the demon's jaw also launched him forward like an entire team of beefy meat headed foot ball players tackled him all at once.

His body somersaulting, flipping head over heels more than an Olympic acrobatics, finally coming to a crashing halt thanks to the lamp post that he broke in half with his skull, Bone cracking and popping as he struggled to get up the flames still burning furiously on his face and chest. The demon snarled to violently pat it out but it still kept on burning, like its hand would pass right through the fire. It's vision instantly zig zagged all over looking for Azuru as it remembered hit wasn't anywhere close to being out of the woods yet. A voice was heard behind the demon penetrating it, it was so close with so much fierce confidence and strength behind it "and you're looking at the one man demolition crew!"

The demon turning his head against his better judgment, and being controlled by fear like strings on a puppet turning to face Azuru, who was standing above him like the clearly superior warrior that he was carrying himself as. The moonlight shining down as the light of righteousness accompanying the brave knight on his path to justice; the demon stared up and down every single inch of Azuru, eyes traveling faster than a well played tennis game, he was just invincible, unstoppable just unfathomable amount of power taking human form. The more and more it realized this it began to question itself *"YHW MA I GNINOITSEUQ OHW EHT RETSNOM SI EREH?!"* (Why am I questioning who the monster is here?!) Azuru then shouted "ALLOW ME TO GIVE YOU MY SHOE!!!" Azuru then picked up his right leg like the big hitter on a kickball team, but before his foot even made contact with the demon's burning face, a hurricane of blue the size of a giant human engulfed Azuru armoring his kick. As he catapulted the demon up into the sky high enough to see the entire neighborhood, the demon screaming in agony a whole new multitude of burning smashing pain that consumed its entire body, that mysterious blue fire now spreading like a disease onto the demon covering half of his face, ribcage, chest and upper thighs. The demon didn't know how to react to his bones being crushed even tinier that potato chip particles or the fire on his body that burned him quicker than paper that was oiled with gasoline.

Azuru just following him with his eyes, slowly lifting his head as the demon climbed up higher into the midnight sky decorating it like the countless number of stars that followed the moon. A mischievous grin growing from ear to ear as Azuru simply lifted one finger from his hands that was crossed over his chest. In his typical boredom stance, suddenly the demon abruptly stopped flying upwards being completely stood still and standing completely straight stiff. The blazing blue flames crackling and out crying, eating away the skin of the demon, finally lowering his finger to lay it back down on his arm. The demon came crashing down as fast as Azuru's finger, splashing a cloud of dust as soon as he impacted. Azuru began shaking his head in disappointment, as he spoke to himself in a whispered tone.

"Damn I was gonna explain to the audience how I could do that but you're probably unconscious *sigh* WHATEVER! For kicks and giggles let's just pretend you're shaking it off right now..... annnnnd go! –"Azuru then spoke with a triumphant tone even though the whole situation was just plain sad it was like a comedian laughing at his own jokes. "How was I able to do that you ask?! Well my grotesque, hideous, face not even a mother could love, looking like a foot for a face - having friend, I will tell you! Those flames that are turning your body into a roasted pig, are my flames, they don't go out unless my energy runs out, I die,which will never happen haha, orrrrrr Telilian Grace feels like like letting you go – what?! Who is Telilian Grace you ask?! Well my dumb, brain dead, idiotic, moronic, absolute definition of stupid friend, I will tell you! He is my partner in crime he lives inside my shrine and we have a deal to share this body, he is allowed to come out and play,if he's not being a pain in the ass, sometimes and in exchange he lets me borrow his energy; his fiery being burns anything that I deem evil. It absolutely will not burn the innocent, huh? ...How is this all possible?! Well like all rich children's fathers *rich boy voice* Daddy gave it to me uhuhuhuh (hahaha) my soul was scanned and identified and based on my soul Telilian Grace was the best of many partners suited for me. Took a while but we finally have an understanding and yeah I kick so much ass my boot has bruises! Okay that it? Anymore questions Mr. Anime villain?"

The dust now started to clear to show that the demon was hunched over heavily panting looking to be in excruciating pain on top of the crater that it smashed into the asphalt. It's black horrendous blood splattered and splotched all over it as it struggled to a shaky stand, Azuru then put his hands back into his pockets as he began strolling over to the demon, the demon panting like an asthmatic child who was forced to run the mile, trying to catch his breath like a dog trying to catch his tail, as Azuru got closer and closer to him with each step the demon who was shaking, trembling, convulsing and quavering. Fear had now poured into it surging through it like electricity through a light bulb; biting down on its fearsome rows of meat shredding teeth as it refused to be a victim, with shadows oozing and leaking from its claws like a fresh coat of paint; the demon then slammed its hands onto the ground like a pair of thunderous sledgehammers. Immediately following up with this earth – shattering declaration was a flare up of dark toned fire that outlined the edges of the cul-de-sac; cutting off the entering road and only leaving this creature and its tormentor with an even more massive tormenting ego

the shadows beginning to come it's aid, just as a farmer doing his dinner call for his pigs to come in and get the grub they all moved into to it. Going from body - less shapes and shades that we're collected from objects, homes, shapes and sizes from all sorts in this ring of death that this demonic fiend conjured up; beginning to rise up and gain the stature and bodies that they lacked rising up from the shadows and convulsing their new builds into shape. Azuru's eyes gently bouncing its line of vision across each evolving what used to be blob of darkness, scoffing up a "that's some heavy artillery tex and by heavy, I mean flimsy, and by flimsy I mean shitty and by shitty I mean these paper creatures will be dead within seconds so don't test me boy! Cause I'll pass with flying colors!"

The bodies of the night now solidifying themselves already becoming bigger than daddy who gave them life, they certainly grow up fast don't they? Buff, bulky a muscular darkened body with shadow as their skin tone, the first demon was the template to their birth that they followed; the hairy goat legs, the robust fit among fit upper bodies, curving horns and bleeding eyeballs with a somehow dusk tone to them than the original.

The demon pointing at Azuru like a person behind the one - way glass telling the police officer which one stole its purse, the shadow bodies diverting their eyes to the one that their master wanted dead with clear hater and disgust in its voice

"YM NERDLIHC! I KSA FO UOY OT LLIK EHT ENO OHW SERAD YFED SU! OG OG DNA EKAT SIH LUOS ROF EHT KRAD DROL!!"(My children! I ask of you to kill the one who dares defy us! Go go and take his soul for the dark lord!!) Now the big clumping feet began to march and to head towards the single Azuru like a sane mind in an insane asylum

Arms crossed over his chest just turning his head side to side to see the wave of enemies closing in like tide coming into the shore line. Azuru just forcing out a sigh not very happy about his predicament having to get the last word before the circling crowd of enraged shadow beasts swallowed him whole "okay but do you go guys mind if I make myself more comfortable before you guys send me to my "grave?" - Cool thanks" The fire that enclosed the cul-de-sac off from the rest of the world in an attempt to put Azuru through their shadow world dramatization, was blown out and replaced with much more fierce, taller, wilder, and more roaring blue flames that even lit up the ground with a blue tint.

Azuru just feeling absolutely at home here, now showing them what hell truly looked like. Azuru with a big D shaped smile on his face "so what do you think boys? Remind you guys of home?? If you want I can torment you guys eternally to make it feel even more like home!!" All of the newborn shadow monsters looking back at their mother like a pack of calves without direction, to which the demon just reappointed them back to who their enemy was; this somehow giving them their confidence and now cocking back and loading their claws, flames starting to gather up from their mouths like gurgling water, now their hind legs moved in unison all rushing to Azuru.

Azuru simply looking around to see he was surrounded, cornered at every inch; but above all his smile never dampened only growing more anxious and spewing excitement "okay boys I am gonna go all out for you guys!" Azuru now picking up his arms, unfolding them from his chest, with his fists still clutched tightly "I want you all to feel the-"but as soon as Azuru flung *his hands open in enthusiasm, each and every shadow imploded being blown to absolute particles like if an entire house fell onto each and every one of them at the same exact time. Azuru left to stand alone with a circle of black ooze splattered all over the floor, feeling bad about the massacre he unleashed completely unintentionally onto his unsuspecting opponents all he could fall back on was an apologetic "damn! I hate it when that happens, sometimes all the epicness in my body just rushes out you know? Badass problems!! – What can you do though? Win some you lose some!"*

Before the demon could calm his shivers an attempt to bend down to pick up its jaw from the floor it was given no time with a knee driven deep into its face like its frontal mug was a garage for this powerful knee cap traveling at the speed of a sports car. The pressure that shot through its body to send it gliding over the air, feeling like a hurricane packed inside as it was bashed against his face. Heading to the blue wall of fire that was almost as high as the street lights beside it, almost about to bullet on through until the demon was swung with such poise and control, able to swerve away from like a last minute detour sign. The wind buffeting his face making it almost impossible to see what was yanking his chain, with his face being almost crushed it almost didn't notice the blue blazes smoking all over its facial surface that is when the pieces fell together. A blurry tall blue blob was all the demon could pull out in its deteriorating vision as it was going to who knows where, Azuru had this monstrosity on a string line of fire that was twined around the same, right face – bashing knee, Azuru with his right leg yanked up was still just swaying the thing in a slow pendulum.

Out of the blue Azuru snapped and threw his body into a complete spin, whiplashing the demon that was along for the ride, Azuru then dropping his right leg, that was poised as high as could be, to the ground with authority. The demon then following the motion like the "slow one" in the group of friends that was cracking jokes, slamming right into the concrete to implant an outline of it body into the ground.

Azuru putting down his leg like he was sheathing his blade once again growing bored from the demon, which just ended up as a ball of hot air, both metaphorically and sometimes literally. Surprisingly where Azuru thought that this putrid creature would stay down, he heard groaning and growling from the hole that was just designed into the ground by Azuru's demolishing expertise.

Now seeing the demon beginning to raise forcing his body to recuperate and now spewing out a ball of fire half the size of the first one he fired out. Azuru without even looking quickly stepped to the side so fast the demon didn't see his feet shuffle, all he was able to catch was Azuru perfectly out of harm's way and still advancing to him. Azuru then said in such a calm collected mater "go ahead and use your hellfire, shoot all the spit wads made from flames at me!" The demon jumping back to create as much distance between them as he could it then began to belch, wrench, and gag as Azuru still made his way to him. The demon now sounding like he was violently choking, Azuru still not even giving him the benefit of his attention Azuru then said with the same tone "go ahead and shoot your acid stomach bile at me!" Just then vomit shot out from the demon's mouth like a frog's tongue except it didn't retract back. Like a missile flying at Azuru once again Azuru using his bullet speed step to move out of the way not even looking up to see what direction it was coming from.

Sizzling the street sounding better than bacon bubbling up the black top like no blow torch could, Azuru then said as he still continued to pursue the demon that was fed up at this point. Dashing so fast within seconds he was standing over Azuru, towering the already intimidating statured six – foot figure, "you can even use your soul breaker on me" not one single ounce of fear was coming off Azuru actually inviting the danger into his home. Its claws glowing a fearsome black and red but dripping a truly ominous aura trailing down its claws as a pentagram glowed on the back of each claw. Trying to smoosh Azuru's skull in between its massive blade - like a trash compacter that ice cubes the gigantic piles of trash. Azuru simply rolled his neck underneath the demon's incoming right claw while easily holding up the demon just with his right index finger stopping it dead like a concrete wall. Continuing his sentence Azuru utterly unphased by the demon's failed attempts at trying to harm or vanquish him

"Do whatever attacks your demonic powers are able to produce at your current level – but I will tell you one thing – both you and I know one very important thing about yourself! We both know you aren't a fighter; you're a coward who only manipulates and preys on the weak, so your skill level only needs to be above human strength. Because believe a guy who takes down your brethren, who are the size of mountains, as warm up for their boss, it's safe to speak when I say I know what I'm talking about and –"Azuru suddenly pausing to focus on inflicting pain, his finger quicker than any man made bullet on earth left the demon's claw to stop defending for the moment, a split moment later the demon felt as if a wrecking ball was just dropped down from the sky onto his arm; the bone connecting to his shoulder not only dislocating from its socket but shattering it beyond repair.

Body shaking as the demon's head creaked to the left to look at exactly what is causing it this unbelievable amount of pain. The demon was completely breath taken to see Azuru's right index finger on top of its left shoulder but before it could even release a sheer shriek of absolute utter agony, Azuru slammed his index finger down onto the demon's right shoulder to now give him matching particle sized shoulder bone matter. He then flicked both of the demon's knee caps all with his index finger, all under a millisecond keep in mind; the demon's body fell over like a pine tree a victim of their natural enemies: the lumberjacks.

Spasming and squirming in pain as it screeched and screamed in torment, Azuru now finding the perfect time to finish his sentence stomping his foot onto the demon's chest to sort of smother the demon's wails; putting his entire body on that knee as he rested his arms on top of it and arched his back to lean on top of them. He picked up the conversation like it was never dropped in the first place, and to Azuru it probably wasn't, "you sure are the child of Satan aren't you? With 6 twisted powerful uncles, and I thought rednecks had messed up families. You pick on the weak and defenseless instill fear into, like how I instill fear into you! Young girls who are still learning, I know Felicity isn't the only girl I know there are more girls you tormented! There is so much evil in the world it is hard to keep track of all of you, especially as the years go by I see you pet goats trying to put your plan into action. But ever since 1995 this team, which now I'm now in charge of! Has been making things difficult for you haven't we? 18 years huh?! Hahahaha I'm one hell of a monkey wrench! Well enough crowd informing subtle chit chat I am going to reclaim those four girl's souls - I can feel them swirling around inside you it disgusts me!"

Azuru now began to drive his foot deeper into the demon's gut, blood squirting out of his mouth like a pumping well. Azuru's face turned into the sheer definition of rage, replacing whatever picture was in the dictionary before to depict it, Azuru's stance completely shifted, his arms wrenched at his sides, teeth grinding, face rippled like tidal waves after an earthquake, eyes a portal gateway to all the pain that is about to come as his tone was just oozing wrath.

"Demons in general make me sick, but there are very special types that fall into a very special category in my heart! They are above the false light, the fallen angels, your creators, even the system! So on a day where I need something to keep me going, something to give me enough anger to rip encyclopedias like wet tissues, to make people see there is no such thing as Earthquakes I was just shadow boxing!!, TO WIPE OUT A POPULATION OF DEMONS LIKE I WAS SEARCHING FOR OIL!! I JUST THINK OF YOU WASTES OF LIFE! You tormented these little girls, put them through their own version of hell, cut their lives short and destroyed their destinies SO NOW HOW DOES IT FEEL TO BE HELPLESS!?! TO FEEL WEAK AND USELESS AND NOTHING YOU WILL EVER DO WILL CHANGE ANY OF IT!!!"

It was like the aftermath of a volcano erupting Azuru trying to calm himself trying to regain his composure. But that was like trying to swim after a fish that jumped off your boat back into the sea "...now if you don't mind GIVE THEM BACK!!!" Azuru then drove his palm down into the demon's gut a river of pure white energy glistening with silver, gold, and crystal rushing out from his mouth like rapids. Only to spew out four orbs that at first just hovered over the ground rolling without direction in place but suddenly the orbs began to unravel.

Like a rose finally beginning to bloom the souls grew up outwards expanding like a tree branching out. A see through entity, without legs just the tails of the gown floated inches off the floor, meanwhile their chests we're pushing forward as their arms spread in a "T" fashion their heads gently leaning on their shoulders, as the middle of their tiny chests illuminated like tiny suns. Staying in this pose for a couple seconds before finally releasing with a relaxing exhale, the poor dears began looking around not knowing up from down or worse what even happened to them, Azuru was shaking his head in absolute disappointment. Like an experienced elder judging how much a waste this was then spoke with a bit of rage still lingering "well I can still see your faces so that must mean you weren't in him for long... - I guess that's what really matters." This was true although their own soul's glowing white aura coated them like a dress they we're almost invisible except for their distinct features.

Azuru could barely make out the skin colors, but he could see as clear as day that one of the girls had very rosy cheeks and wavy long brown hair, another had the most beautiful sight guiders he had ever seen on a person. He also noticed her thick curly black hair; the other features on the other girls were still able to be picked out. According to Azuru he came just in time the reflection of their appearance in the soul indicated how long they have been without their body to anchor them to Earth.

Souls without a body can be corrupted they can be turned into damned souls, at that point be under demonic control and there is almost no coming back from that, curiosity that was like slick on an eel, a question arose from one of the little girls " what are you talking about mister?" Azuru cringed for a moment saying to himself in his head "I have probably said it to myself I don't know how many times, that I can take everything hell throws at me... - but this has to be the hardest part of the job... telling a child that they died it just never gets easier for me."

Just then one of the little girls screamed like bloody murder that is probably what was going on all over again in her delicate mind. All she could say was "it's him!! –I- I –it's him again!" As the rest of the girls all turned their attention to the floored demon, who struggled under Azuru's foot like a mouse ever so desperately trying to get away from beneath the cat's claw. At first terrified shrieks filled the night sky and Azuru sucked up his urge to turn away, his eyes closed shut and his lips quivered, his teeth were grinding so violently. The noise didn't bother him at all; all that was going through his mind was "they have gone through so much" he had to swallow his own emotions like swallowing a brick as he disguised his anguish, so the little girls wouldn't be the least bit terrified.

Cracking a smile was like a ferocious lion purring, as the king brushed up against a feeble human's leg. "There's nothing to be scared of... I promise you, you won't ever see this thing again -" Azuru then picked up a medium sized pebble. He held it in the middle of his palm, as the moments passed it began to glow, illuminating like a casual flash light, but all the light pulsed towards the pebble. Being gravitated by it, almost like it was feeding it – until suddenly the pebble popped into the typical baby winged angel that you would see in churches, funerals, hospitals or even nurseries. Smoothed skinned, curly haired, tan toned, beautiful pools of sight to view the world in, lying belly flat with his hands holding up his head and his legs kicked gently in the air. His wings flapped so delicately as well, Azuru then raised his hand holding this fragile piece of art, closer to his mouth as he spoke into it. Like it was some sort of warlike - talkie "Grace Reaper pick up, setting marker immediately."

Azuru then crushed that poor innocent essence of God's artistry in between his diabolic fingers. But when he relaxed his hand to open his palm, the frame of the angel was still intact but now radiating the most golden gold ever to be seen on Earth's surface. Azuru then gently laid it down, the baby angel's light spread to the sky replacing even the brightest searchlights on the planet.

The little girls were simply in awe, of course they wanted to ask what was going on, how was he doing this, who was he, why is the light from the former statue glistening the same color as their skin tone, silver, crystal, gold, yellow, white and dim shades of the rest of the other colors of the world. All they could do was watch the most beautiful thing in their lives takes place right before their eyes. There was no time to talk; the clouds above them began to part like a giant was opening the curtains to his bedroom. In the middle of the now gaped clouds was, from the little girl's current stand point seemed to be a star coming to Earth, the brightest star too, the kind that shows up first in the jet black blanket that is the night, the ones that every child wishes upon once they see, but as the luminous and lambent star came closer and closer to them within moments it seemed that it traveled miles without any sign of even disturbing the air resonating or tremendous speed or push. It was like it was simply strolling with it coming closer, the girls began to see a figure that looked like a person that was double maybe triple the size of Azuru. The girls thought he was an absolute tower; they now began to recognize that the shining that they saw was her aura that even from a far burned so bright that it gave her the appearance of a star.

They saw her body waved like hair in the wind her shimmering silver and crystal V- necked robe was in the same fashion as the little girls, this looked to be her skin. Her dress was much longer than theirs that seemed to even play the part of her legs, her face looking so pure, innocent, warm, loving, caring, faithful, trustworthy all wrapped into one. The little girls just stared and watched like a queen was stepping in front of them, a hood covering half of her head so they couldn't see the back of her hair that trailed down her shoulders to her chest seeming to have midnight galaxy inside of her hair. Sparkling and twinkling even though it was the blackest night black that there could ever be now standing before them a sky scrapper to Azuru's three storied building, not even touching the ground.

All the little girls looked up at her as if she was the statue of liberty was standing right next to them, and this was their first time visiting; she spoke in a tone that just pushed the most peaceful wave inside the girls that put their tiny little hearts at ease filling their souls with tranquility. They instantly ignited with warmth that could never be doused "was this immediate enough Azuru?" The most beautiful and enchanting smile came over the magnificent, glorious being even making each of the girls laugh, as much fear that was hammered into them by this demon, it was instantly broken by this beyond elegant being. Everyone now taking light of this, except Azuru and the demon, Azuru_remaining quiet while the demon shivering in fear as it stared up at the majestic presence before him even speaking with a tone like his soul was in pain. "Yes thank you you're Graciousness" laughter spout out from the Grace Reaper as she said "lighten your burden Azuru your soul will dull if you center yourself around the negativity of this world, and – call me "Grace" or "Gracie". Anything you are an imaginative soul craft me a name"

The little girls giggling in unison as the Grace Reaper continued to tease Azuru, he sighed as he tried to pick himself up from his slumped state. Not sighing but simply replying "I will get on that your Graciousness and this is a bad time I just need a minute or two to perk up. I swear I'll be fine" "then swear that is more like you!" Laughing at her own joke even got Azuru to smirk a bit, but while one of the little girls was giggling moving her hand over her mouth she noticed her scintillating skin.

Reminding her completely of all her curiosity she forgot due to the extraordinary and beautiful Grace Reaper that had her at a loss for words. The little girl raising her hand as she called out "Ms. Gracie!" The Grace Reaper pointing to her as she said "yes go on" the little girl while looking at herself "why am I all shiny? What happened to me? How did I get here?" Azuru then turning his head to the side as he looked at the Grace Reaper pointing for her to leave the Grace Reaper responding with glee "All wonderful inquiries of ponder I will explain as we go children we must now take our leave."

The little girls then realized that they didn't even notice the Grace Reaper's blanket that she scarfed over one shoulder in one instantaneous moment the blanket turned into a flock of doves that beamed all the colors that make up a galaxy. An entire universe made up in their feathers, beaks, talons, and so on as they flew a circle around the little girls until they became a solid ring. That illuminated every single color spectrum to ever exist, the Grace Reaper grabbed a piece with her left arm that she rung around to her right side going around her completely. It then took control itself to connect itself together from the tugged piece that gaped away from completion connecting like railroad tracks. It was finished the twisted ribbon was complete, each in a circle that was always flowing, always moving forward; one of the children analytical enough to ask "what is this Ms. Gracie?" The Grace Reaper answering like she had been a teacher for years "this is to make sure you are with me on our way to our final resting place

– so you won't get lost, or stolen, no one can harm you in here other than yourselves now off we go on the way I will tell you all is needed to be learned."

They took off the ground like a beautiful bald eagle taking flight; Azuru didn't even turn his head to watch the infinity sign floating away. He knew they would absolutely be fine only putting up his index finger and middle finger as a gesture for good bye, the demon then began screeching in appall flailing his claws to try to reach out for them, but with Azuru's foot anchoring him like gravity holding every single human onto planet Earth. It was virtually impossible but that didn't stop the monster from screaming "ON! YM SLRIG!! EMOC KCAB OT EM EREHW ERA UOY GNIOG THIW YM SEVIW?! EMOC KCAB DNA EVIG EM EFIL!! UOY HCTIB!! GNIRB -"(No! My girls!! Come back to me, where are you going with my wives?! Come back and give me life!! You bitch!! Bring –)

The demon then began oozing his sewage blood from his blasphemous mouth. Screaming harder than a rich girl who broke a nail and doubling in pitch, by the moment the ground beginning to crack around it. Slowly crushing it underneath it as if a wrecking ball was being set down on the fragile street, the demon using all of the power he posed only to creak his neck forward to see how deep Azuru's foot was being driven into its stomach. It violently shook as it picked up its head to stare up at the absolutely livid Azuru; his face just said his anger's boiling point was only beginning; it was just at the bottom of the ladder going to start climbing. Azuru was like grinding together two cogs that didn't match, looking as if they were to start spew sparks the anger soaking into each word that he spoke like water to starving plant.

"YOUR GIRLS... YOUR GIRLS!?!? TELL ME WHAT HAVE YOU DONE FOR THEM?!!? I KNOW THEY HAVE ONLY TWO FATHERS AND YOU STOLE THEM FROM BOTH!!! -" Azuru putting his whole body behind his single foot instantly creating a crater shaking the Earth with a single step, blood gushing out of the demon as he screamed silently in the most agonizing state of pain that left it breathless. Azuru picking up right where he left off

"TAKING THE LIVES OF THE INNOCENCE OH YEAH YOU'RE SO BAD MAN, A SEVEN FOOT SACK OF SHIT PICKING ON GIRLS WHO ARE TERIFFIED OF YOUR PRESSENCE. YEAH MAN THOSE STEEL BALLS OF YOURS MUST DRAG ON THE FLOOR!! – I take the most pleasure in ridding this beautiful world of your horrible existence. You will no longer corrupt anyone anymore... feel flames that burn hotter than hell!" Azuru then threw a ball of his blazing blue flames onto the demon like he was spilling a drink on him; Telilian Grace spread quicker than scratching the chicken pox, every inch of the demon was being devoured by the torrid gases. The demon squirmed as much as its broken body would let it flopping up and down, rolling around as it tried to put itself out. But it was withering and chipping away already, might as well been a slab of fresh meat on the grill, screaming so high its lungs probably burst. Azuru was just staring over it eyes void of emotion he wasn't taking pleasure, excited for revenge, feeling bad for it, or even angry anymore he just didn't care.

All he did was watch as his arms and legs began to crackle into dust. Its violent struggling slowly came to a stop as it lied straight on its back; cracks began snapping throughout its entire body. As if someone threw a baseball at a mirror, cracks began spreading and opening all over its body until its arms began to burst into dust. Turning into absolute grime made from his body, the rest of its body began to follow up till it was only a torso, oh how hard the demon had fallen only 20% of its former self, and a head blanketed by Telilian Grace's flames. The demon had the nerve to stare into Azuru's unsympathetic eyes with its own filled with mercy and sorrow Azuru could see the desperation in its eyes screaming out for him. Azuru merely scoffed and snapped his_fingers and the little fire rushed like a rapid river from the demon's torso to the head instantly converting it into a pile of ashes. Like the rest of its body Azuru then walked over to the hunk of dirt picking up a rock on his way over, tightly squeezing it in his hand as he stood in front of the crispy demon remains.

A golden luminance radiated from his hand by the time he squatted down it was a jar the size of Azuru's hand and he used it to scoop it inside. Azuru spoke with such a spiteful tone as he said_" I bet you that is the look those little girls gave you, well you know what they say 'do onto others as you want done onto you' – hmmm in hindsight if everyone followed that rule Earth would probably be a better place." Azuru then began screwing on the lid, on the front of the jar engraved in silver in a plaque was the phrase "Azuru slain demon #85,079 demon type: pet goat stage: primal"

Azuru then put the jar inside his large pockets, in the back of his pants because the front we're the pockets he already had his hands in. Walking with a slouching fashion back towards Felicity's house as he had his back turned towards all the destruction he caused.

Before he hopped over Felicity's fence he stopped, snapped his fingers and kept on walking; it was like a magical broom in one foul sweep. Brushing away all the debris and havoc that was wreaked here, in a couple of moments all the craters that we're engraved in the street, the lamppost that looked like it was karate chopped by a giant, all the asphalt that was turned to tar by the burning flames and the burning flames themselves going out like Azuru turned off the domestic fire with a knob. All repaired like minutes before the fight even started, walking to the wall he cannoned the demon through earlier and passed right through it like Azuru's body was made of smoke, the walls rippling like a stone being dropped into a pool.

Azuru startling Felicity as she screamed pointing frantically, thoughts racing too fast for her mouth to capture into words;

all that jumbled out of her mouth was "y-y-you – you wall -w-h – how ghost!" Azuru not thinking much of what he just did it was basically was like walking through an open door to him, nothing special he even asked with a witty tone "I just beat a demon with my bare hands, threw him through your wall, fixed it without even touching it, and the thing that has your tongue tied in a knot is that I walked through a wall? You certainly are an odd child"

Felicity then running up to Azuru to hug him wrapping her arms tightly around his legs Azuru then shouted with confusion " your emotions are just on roulette wheel aren't they?!" Felicity looked up to Azuru and with a pondered expression on her face asked "what a roulette wheel Zazuru?" Azuru's eyebrows twitching, the urge to correct her but he simply pulled out his fake laugh; as he hammered his words down so they we're nice, soft, and gentle toned. Even overexerting a smile to mask his irritation but in the end just creeping out Felicity

"It's Azuru! But anyways you never have to be afraid ever again Felicity he is gone and now you have me" Azuru then crouched down to meet eye level with Felicity as he continued "all you have to do is remember what I told you "keep your heart pure" always believe in what's right, remember that God is here he hears you so don't give up on him push forward and don't worry about the path you are on because I will be right here-" Azuru then touched the outside of Felicity's heart with his index finger. Felicity's smile went ear to ear as she said with excitement "no matter where you at all I have to do is call you and you come?!" Azuru looking slightly taken back and a bit nervous as he tried to delicately disarm this bomb that was bound to blow up on him.

"Well... I don't know about that – I have to go on important missions, I also have a team to lead so I might not be able to" Felicity now wearing a childish frown as she said " but you said 'I will be right here!!' A slight irritation came over Azuru's face as he said out loud and slightly shaky "yeah I know but... umm I didn't mean it I just wanted to sound cool, and mission accomplished, I won over the crowd and got my award, that's all anyone cares about anyways right?!" Felicity then retorted very maturely "My daddy always says to 'mean what you say and say what you mean' and daddy is always right" Azuru getting even more flustered inside his head "I already get my ass chewed out by Emily for 'supposedly being cold hearted, cruel and hotheaded' then next time that old lady shouldn't be mad dogging me! 'Oh I can't see I'm blind and have asthma and diabetes' you gotta back up your talk old lady! – oh yeah I don't need a four year old telling me how to do my job too!"

Azuru showing a completely_different side as he spoke to Felicity "yeah I know I'll stop" meanwhile Azuru was laughing at his own statement in his mind snickering as he uttered "how do you get out of trouble because of a lie? ....shower a mountain of even MORE LIES!!!!" Felicity then gave Azuru a suspicious eye "promise?" Azuru in a frantic frenzy in his mind declared "dammit what do I do now?! She's trapped me like a fish in the bowl! I can't give up my will of wanting to do whatever I want!! What am I gonna tell Serenity when we actually go out on a date – maybe, kind of, sort – probably would never happen – but what if!!! What will I tell her? Oh excuse me Serenity, but I have a date with a four - year old little girl and I just cannot be late! – please, please don't make me do this!!"

Azuru giving a fake and hollow smile as he responded "how 'bout one thing at a time? How about I come whenever you call me and if I am doing something then I will try to make it later on?" Felicity then held out her pinky and Azuru's eyes suddenly got so wide. In his mind he had a voice stunned by astonishment as he said "My God.... I'm doomed" Azuru not being able to resist wrapping his pinky around Felicity's. Azuru smiling on the outside crying on the inside "goodbye freedom" Felicity continued "you have to come whenever I call you okay?!" Azuru said in his mind "you're the real demon." Azuru smiled so plastic he could be the new ken model for Barbie, so hollow you could knock and almost get a sound out of it he said out loud "okay." Felicity then hugged Azuru and Azuru's smile once again became genuine as he said to himself "moments like this make the job worth it". As much as Azuru didn't want to let go he had to slowly release Felicity, saying "it's time for me to go now"

Azuru's skin began to gradually turn to gold, glistening silver, glowing crystal and shining white spreading to his entire body like a virus. From the tips of his fingers all the way down to his feet, illuminating like a golden statue glazing like he had thousands of flashlights inside his body; Felicity half shielding her face as she took a few steps back, watching the spectacle right before her. Azuru waving goodbye as his lambent transformation took place then swiftly Azuru shot through Felicity's roof in the form of a beam and quicker than a Gatling gun bullet. The darkness returned to Felicity's room and once again she was all alone she leisurely put her hand down from her face and just stared at the spot that Azuru was at last. Felicity then turned around to climb back into her bed getting snug inside the blankets and closed her eyes; but before finally going into a peaceful sleep she whispered "Zazuru." The door to her bedroom gently creaked open a small crack so two heads could pop in and two whispers were heard in the night, "see I told you she is fine you're over here having a heart attack" "well I just wanted to be sure, I could have sworn I heard a voice or something." The door ever so delicately shutting once again so the shadows could return.

Shoes were somehow inconceivably walking on top of the clouds, treating like the puffs of air that formed a sea of white, like it was just a normal sidewalk. A voice was heard, as in the distance a ball of light the size of a pyramid like a star right in front of this person only miles away getting bigger and lustrous with each step that is taken towards it. "So like I was saying it is completely up to you! You can believe everything you see and hear and join our army of awakened reborn souls –"just then the tomb sized shining star was finally close enough that the light almost parallel to folding out or expanding the blinding florescence. Became the aura of an even more breath taking, amazing, majestic awe inspiring establishment; it seemed to be a kingdom with an entire country surrounded within its walls even cities that went past the eyes could see the entire kingdom, sparkling every square inch of this monumental palace on a galactic level completely towering over any man made master piece on Earth. Energy rising up from it like steam on a cooking dish, the buildings looking to be made from something completely naked and ignored by the human eye; Spirit and aura, to take a semi solidified form in this place, in unison this unparalleled kingdom ignites brighter than the brightest constellation. Burning a sight in the midnight sky for all to see, like a candle being held next to the sun, the casual shoes continued to trek towards the astonishing – striking region the clouds began to part like sand on a beach. Becoming irrelevant once in the water, and the pair of feet were still walking on solid ground that was underneath the clouds the entire time. The shoes click clacking against the ground itself a luminous brighter than neon white shining a blinding jet black that had golden galaxies, quasars, planets comets and moons engraved inside the floor that all moved actively like the ground was just a giant telescope. The stars gleaming noble silver looking just like the view that a regular person would have gazing up at the sky at night; the entire universe was embossed inside of this ground, or maybe this kingdom where ever it may be was high above the universe. The highest step on the ladder that not even the universe could climb, the voice continued as it came closer to the front entrance of this grand temple of sacredness.

"You can go ahead and deny any of this, find your proof to prove us wrong, hide behind your leaders and what they tell you to make sure you don't wet your bed at night. Hate us, criticize us, forsake us, mock us, betray us, you can even try to kill us, do whatever the system demands from you so you can keep it alive with your soul. But no matter if you believe every single word the people above you, tell you without question, and you're perfectly fine being their puppet, then fine go ahead you guys deserve each other. But if every day of your life questions keep piling up and multiplying by the second, you know in your heart and soul something isn't right and you want to know the raw, unaltered, mind shattering truth; then you first have to start by opening the first door... your mind... either way whatever path you choose from here on in is up to you makes no difference to me and my team regardless we will free you all... just the one who picked the first choice are in for a rude awakening. If you're brave enough to turn the page then pull up your big boy pants and let's do this!"

The back of a rippled, defined, beyond masculine man was now standing in front of a statue that was as big as a three storied house. And as wide as a barn, his blue wild spiky hair blowing with the wind from the clouds as he slowly turned his head back to look with a grin on his face. "My name is Azuru and welcome to our world" as Azuru put out his right hand for grabs inviting anyone willing to step forward.

Make yourself
at Home

Azuru now gliding through the kingdom that he dragged everyone brave enough into soaring like an eagle that was treasured by the people. Gliding through the clouds like he owned this entire gracious kingdom; a pair of blue wings big enough to trail down Azuru's towering six foot body ending at his calves. Also big enough to support a stack of muscle like Azuru, just spewing out flames as he went, like the women spraying free samples of horrible perfume at the mall sooooo very obnoxiously. Azuru twisting and spiraling in the sky, flipping head over heel as he landed perfectly on marvelous silver tile looking rooftops, that which Azuru leaped off the ledge as soon as he reached it.

Corkscrewing back into flight, drifting over the buildings that we're shaped like a donut a giant circle with a gap in the middle; then the mysterious buildings that we're crafted like a flower. Pedals and everything some buildings had some truly strange shapes to them some we're shaped like soda cans and pyramids. Others we're skyscrapers and rainbow formed establishments, Azuru the little dare devil he is flew towards buildings that we're shaped like rings even came in a set of three. Being a speck in comparison of course Azuru had no trouble flying right through them but still! He could have walked away no one told him to fly right into them *sigh* this kid man. But as Azuru free roamed through the clean, open, free sky he began to ponder something "hmm why did I start my sentence off with "hmm"? Damn thinking clichés! Also wonder where everybody is at? Sifu usually finds me somehow and greets me when I come back from a mission. Ms. Neko Neko Cat Lady usually gives me a cat shaped pie or something as soon as she sees me; YEAHH!!! Usually tries to shoot me and misses... or at least that's what I make him think haha I burn his rubber bullets so he'll feel bad hahaha I wonder if everyone is having a meeting? Eh its cool I wouldn't be Azuru if I didn't show up late."

Just then Azuru within a split second kicked his flight to the next level. Squatting his legs like the Olympic swimmers when they are about to kick off the wall. Once Azuru sprung forward he left a blazing blue torch of jet stream behind him; the entire city becoming a blur of lines but to Azuru, who was ever so casually dodging buildings leaning to the right, to the left, spinning, jumping, to dash across a rooftop and back to instant transportation. Until Azuru flipped himself into a ball right in mid – air to spin as much as one would before landing swiftly on one knee.

Picking his head up from the direction of the ground to a humongous titanic sized door, all this glistening golden and silver majestic door needed was a pair of arms and legs to start destroying cities. Azuru dusted himself off as he began to walk towards the gargantuan door inserting his hands in his pockets as he complained "not even Norman the man who loves this door is here?! This door is his life! – What else does he have?! Nothin'!! I mean I'm not judging a man can do whatever he wants to his door... but I wanted to tell him how I beat him with just my finger...- hmm can't help but to think that I told him this story before – well I know he would loved to hear it anyway it doesn't have any doors involved but it does have me so he should love it."

Just as Azuru was a foot away from the door it seemed like he would need an entire army of Azurus to push it open. Azuru though, didn't even take his hands out of his pockets just continued to walk forward in his typical slouching position just as it looked like Azuru was going to slam his lips right onto Norman's woman Azuru passed right through it like it was a hologram. Or just a figment of Azuru's imagination, but Azuru paid it no mind not even giving an explanation just continued down this illuminating hallway that glimmered like the floor was encrusted with diamonds. The hallway was long like the hall of a dungeon, except the walls were a luminous white and every inch of this hallway looked to be smoother than cream sparkling from every nook and cranny of the ground.

Azuru finally reached the end of the hall only to see a head of hair. He thought he recognized along with the face and awkward spying skills Azuru was trying not to make it obvious that he could see their head poking out from around the corner creeping up on him. Azuru was analyzing his movements and shaking his head as he hid his grin and pointed his face downwards to play the clueless role. Azuru said to himself as he snickered "Angelo ruins it in 3....2.....1" just then a voice broke the silence like a bulldozer trying to get inside a china shop. "FRIENDS!! I SPOTTED HIM!! HE IS COMING TOWARDS US!! I TELL HIM ABOUT THE SURPRISE NOW?!" he then casually walked around the corner.

A shushing and cautious voice angrily retorted "SHUT UP HE'LL HEAR YOU!!" The first spasmodic voice a bit confused not understanding the concept at all responded "but how is he supposed to know our surprise for him?!" another irritated voice now tried to enforce the hushing. By now Azuru was already walking towards their direction down the hall hearing every single "secret" conversation "IDIOT! THE WHOLE THING ABOUT A SURPRISE IS THAT HE DOES NOT KNOW!!" Azuru so desperately trying to hold in his laughter but it was like a guy trying to hold in his farts. It is virtually impossible without letting little ones out here and there that is exactly what Azuru was releasing as little snickers.

The first awkward voice sounding absolutely appalled and repulsed by the definition of surprise. "THAT IS DISHONEST TO TRICK OUR FRIEND! THERE SHALL BE JUSTICE! JUSTICE!!!" A muffling sound began being heard behind the door. Azuru currently stood in front of the door like they were trying to stuff a sock into a microphone. An agitated voice then said "whoever picked Angelo to be "ninja" is fired!" a smart aleck insight voice then injected "I told you he swallowed a microphone when he was a baby!"

Only to be met with an irritated retort lashing back due to no support "SHUT UP RYKER!" Azuru smiling as he shook his head. Now looking at the door he recognized it upon glance he then questioned himself "I wonder why they picked our conference room for a surprise for me and I wonder what the surprise is for anyway it can't be national Azuru day already."He then placed his hand on the knob of the door and wiggled it dramatically to give the ones who are supposed to be surprising him a heads up. All he heard was a wave of shushes and murmuring "he's coming" "he's here" even a "did I feed my fichus...yeah I think I did, I'll be home soon jerry" for some odd reason.

And lastly like the stupid elephant entering the room Angelo's microphone sound wave he calls his voice exercising his lungs seeming to almost shake the walls as he shouted out " DON'T DO IT AZURU IT'S A TRAP RUN AWAY IT'S INJUSTICE!" Azuru gave them a couple moments to do whatever they had to quiet him down. Then let out a sigh as he said to himself "Angelo this is why I don't take you onto missions that require stealth... or intelligence and because you're annoying, and I wanna help whoever you're fighting kick the crap outta you haha"

Now Azuru finally deciding to twist the knob he walked into a room full of shadows. All this suspicion curling Azuru's eyebrows, as he snapped his fingers and his blue flame emitting from his finger tips like a torch lighting the way in a cave. All Azuru saw was a concert amount of bodies clustered inside the room Azuru then said out loud "what the hell?!" That is the moment that the lights flashed on to reveal every single familiar faces as they screamed in unison "SURPRISE!!...sort of" everyone scratching their heads in embarrassment as each of their heads began to glare at a single person who was tied up wrist to ankles with duct tape over his mouth. You could still hear the muffled "Justice!" Azuru chuckling a bit "no don't worry I'm still surprised I have no idea what this surprise is for did I break the record in kicking ass and taking names? Because I am pretty good at doing that" Laughter spread through the entire crowd

Which gave him the creeps, pulling his head back a bit as he scrunched one side of his face and raised one eyebrow shaking slightly in displeasure "stop it everyone you're getting lipstick on my ass!" Laughter and a parade of guffaws shot out from the crowd, enough knee slaps to make a rap beat, even the shy ones snickered. Azuru rolling his eyes as he couldn't help but laugh with them he then felt a hand rest onto his shoulder, he then creaked his neck to the right over his shoulder to see three people behind him.

One a very tall slender young man with what looked like to be an iron rectangle over his eyes, a serious energy to him but even he still cracked a smile on a face. A black coat that paved a way down to his calves, outlined white the sleeves of this coat we're ripped off but he wore a gray long sleeve underneath that went only to the forearms. On his forearms themselves were black metal cuffs along with his usual attire his black leather pants with tears making breathing room for his knees his neon snow white combat boots the most unusual thing on this so intense man. Straying away from his two associates who were dressed in white when it comes to fashion next to this man was a gentle and soft spoken woman. Who had this calm alluring aura to her a smile that had its own glow to it as it formed half a circle, so smooth and silk looking caramel toned skin and honey dipped curly hair to match. A very frilly white miniskirt was worn on her petite body, but below that white outlined black shin guards and track boots. The woman standing next to her looking to be a very fierce statured woman; black short hair combed to the left side of her head, lines cut so precise looking like her barber used a laser. Not caring too much about her appearance, dressed in a simple white tank top that gleamed like a supernova, plain tight black jeans, some low topped all black shoes with white shoe laces. The only thing that really stuck out was her fingerless mixed martial arts style gloves that had golden glossy streams with silver and gray sprinkled on, running down her knuckles.

The stick thin man then said correcting Azuru's guess "they're here to celebrate your second anniversary being leader and all the progress that you've made. Since your first year you brought in 800 new souls to help us wake up the world in the entire 18 years that is more than when the team even first existed." Azuru trying to pipe the man down by flapping his hand in the air with his head pointed excited towards the crowd wearing a mischievous smile on his face "shush! Poyoyo watch this they love me I am taking advantage now! I don't know how long this is gonna last – hey! Guys wanna hear a joke? -" Of course a huge tide of nods rushed through the entire masses Azuru clearing his throat before he threw out the opener to his wisecrack. "Angelo is the strongest on the team" Azuru with a face like a successful rapper that just dropped the microphone after metaphorically dropping his verse on them. Just sitting back and watching the bursting of joyous clamoring. Some bending over clutching their stomachs as their abs cramped up, some couldn't hold themselves up as their legs gave up on them on their hands and knees. Some had some fearsome thick stream of tears pouring down their faces. Angelo using his entire body to leap up and down in a single motion; his face just showing his rage and fury

Azuru looking over to the trio to see the expression on their faces. witnessing an array of monsters being made right I front of their very own eyes Azuru's smirk getting more and more troublesome by the increase of laughter Azuru then said with confidence just dripping off him "watch me bring it home!"

"Guys! Now what's the deal with airline food?!" just like Azuru spoke a forbidden passage in front of the village elders or swearing right in front of innocent and porous children. Now everyone switched like the flip of an on/off turner one man calling out "that's not nice they try very hard to make that food you should at least be grateful!" a woman in that same cluster also called out "Yeah Azuru! They work extremely hard to keep their passengers safe and happy it is a full time day care basically it's not as easy as you are bashing them for!" Ms. Neko Neko Cat Lady, a sweet tiny orange – haired a bit goofy looking but adorable above all old lady, been found in this crowd and even she had something to say "they let me bring aboard not everywhere let's me take my cat!" You know what Azuru?! I am with them they work to the nubs of their bone even if you cut them down that isn't gonna stop them from being the best they can be they will – "KEEP DOING YOUR JOB OR I WILL GET MORGAN FREEMAN'S NUMBER I SWARE THIS IS NOT A THREAT BT A PROMISE!" geeze why don't you just rob me of my freedom to have an opinion why don't you?! You guys don't pay me anyways "and Ms. Neko Neko Cat Lady you don't have to take your cats everywhere just a suggestion!" Ms. Neko Neko Cat Lady definitely not appreciating that comment retorting with such venom. "A stupid suggestion"

Azuru completely taken by surprise she just seemed so nice and pure, Azuru still not losing his mischievous smile. Turning his head over to the trio and smirked with a bit of arrogance as he said "yeah as you could tell Poyoyo (Pollo but Azuru likes to call him Poi yo – yo) I truly am amazing and all of you would be lost without me." Everyone in unison took a moment to groan in annoyance as their own palms met their forehead in one gigantic sounding single clap. The man called Poyoyo by Azuru shaking his head in disagreement as he inquired "first off it's POYOYO! (Pollo!) "Azuru interrupting as soon as he could find a space to squeeze in his two cents "really?!Then why do you spell it like that? Like you're even confusing our readers! You should spell it like Pollo or something - that's like my name having a big O'le fatass Q in the middle and expecting people not to pronounce the Qu – uh!"

Poyoyo seeing no winning or benefit from arguing with Azuru so he just moved on from that topic. "Second! A little humility would do you well Azuru!" Azuru with his arms crossed over his chest rolled his eyes and responded with a feet dragged upon tone, "okay... my team helped out a little bit - I guess but I did 99.9% of the work" "Azuru that is basically everything what did everyone else do then?" "just think of more things for me to do" Poyoyo just chuckling seeing no way out from Azuru's cage that is his over confidence, just putting out his hand for a horizontal slap before going down so Azuru could pound the top of his fist.

The woman in the middle standing next to Poyoyo very bubbly jumping as she said "because of your hard work we now have over 2,500 people with us that's amazing! That means 800 for Poyoyo and his squadron of fighters! 800 for yours truly, Ms. Honey Bee and my lovely Divinity Carriers so we can lend support. Finally 800 for Ms. Minerva so she can do research on all of the demons, the fallen excreta, all that good stuff because of you and your team's hard work." Azuru slipping on his mischievous grin once again as he replied "thanks for the exposition Honey Bee you get all that reader? Also thank you very much I see why they call you honey Bee it's because you're so sweet!...."

Azuru waiting for a waterfall of applause and a wave of laughter, but the only attention he got was from the crickets who were giving their full undivided attention to Azuru. After a few moments he was able to squeeze out a chuckle from Minerva who responded "stop trying Azuru we don't pay you to be a comedian! - you would be unemployed if we did." Azuru retorting with full intensity "it's not my fault my jokes are too advanced for you guys and you guys don't pay me at all! – Hey that's a lot of divinity leaking from your hands, what? Lost to the wet paper bag again?! I swear you two just cannot get along, but I'm telling you for your safety Minny! He is gonna kill you one day!"

Minerva's fighting mug began to peek as her inner savage began to surface through a wicked smile. "Get a nosebleed and jump into a shark tank!" Azuru replying so coolly and ever so calm "nah I already had my morning swim with the frenzy but thanks for thinking of me." Now Minerva was the one who switched the shoes that contained the entire cool "only just frenzy? I mean that sounds right for a rook. I train with a pack of T – rexes but you should go your own pace wouldn't want you to get hurt." Azuru still as cool as an ice sculpture that had the dry ice steam radiating off it " when I said frenzy I was referring to a group of adult megalodons but still T – rexes that's adorable do they squeak when they "roar?!"

Minerva clenching her teeth as she had finally had it with Azuru a rapid twitch appearing under her left eye as she sounded like the beasts she fought. "SOUNDS TO ME THAT YOU STILL HAVEN'T SEEN A REAL BEAST YET YOU WANNA COME WITH ME AND I'LL SHOW YOU ONE?!" Minerva now in her fighting stance fists parallel across from each other as they we're held in front of her face her right foot pike in front to take the lead while the left foot squared up onto her tippy toes, bouncing up and down with each passing moment. Azuru sliding his hands into his pockets as he stepped towards her; with a smile begging for chaos still spewing gasoline for the burning inferno that took the form of fighting words. "Yeah will you show me where I can find one?"

A fouled up growl climbed out from Minerva's throat as she stepped to Azuru but as soon as she came within a foot of Azuru

Honey Bee already had her arms wrapped around her. Pulling her back as she faced the opposite direction and Poyoyo blocked Azuru's path like a bouncer's big meaty arm at the hottest club in town. But Poyoyo wasn't using his arm he used a hilt from a sword to hold Azuru in his path he pulled this hilt from within his black coat. Poyoyo taken back and appalled couldn't keep the shock out of his tone as much as people couldn't keep the popcorn out of their teeth once gorging the bucket down. "Azuru! You would hit a woman?!" Azuru walking in place as he tried to move forward but Poyoyo's hilt like a toll booth arm "no! I never would hit a woman but they're over here screaming about equal rights! "Minerva dragging Honey Bee at glacier speed while attempting to move towards Azuru "THAT'S BECAUSE YOU'RE A PRETTY PRINCESS AND YOU DON'T WANNA RUIN THAT FACE! DON'T TRY TO ALL OF A SUDDEN ACT LIKE A GENTLEMEN!!"

Azuru like a magnet trying to move closer but an obstacle would not let him pass so he just stood where he was. "BULL! MY GRANDMA DIDN'T BEAT ME DIRECTIONLESS WITH A CHANCLA FOR NOTHING SHE ENGRAVED THAT LESSON INTO ME!!" Minerva obliviously missing the point and wouldn't be able to find it with a microscope scoffing "THAT'S IT?!" Azuru instantly outraged like Minerva finally found Azuru's button and bashed it in with a sledgehammer. "TE VOY A REVENTAR TU CICO! (*I am going to bust your muzzle open*) WELCOME TO MY CHILDHOOD!!"

Honey Bee on the verge of just of releasing Minerva tossing out the idea like a quarter back's last ditch effort to make a touch down at the goal line. "h-hey Azuru –y-you should –en-enjoy your party you can fight Mi-Minerva an-ytime!"

Azuru then suddenly stopped to creak his head back and see that the entire crowd was watching the whole thing take place, like a bunch of creepy peeping toms. More importantly Azuru was getting the bigger picture that basically everyone was here.

The Valiant squadron: that all had varied looks depending on personalities but somewhat revolving around armor. Moderately similar to the style of knight armor but to much more smoother curves, it was like the sheets of metal we're Taylor made for these combatants. Their muscles rippled right through each appendage slot except for the helmet, the arm, forearm, leg, chest, back all we're like an extra layer of skin so tight knit but still breathable and of course flexible. Some warriors wore the helmets and no other coverage of divine metal, some just wore the protective covering for the arms and legs, others only wore the front and back to cover their chests. All different strokes for different folks but none the less they still came from the same clan and all without hesitation would lay down their lives for this family.

The completely different uniformed faction right next to them that looked a whole lot less armored, looking to be dressed only in what made them feel comfortable, flexible, or aerodynamic they we're designed to be fast speed is their main goal anything that weighs them down should be discarded. A lot of unitard, track type and light fabric being worn with or without wins again completely optional but whatever would give them the boost so they can give the Valients or Research more; cures and chants, evacuations anything that the team was not prepared for. Home base sends them down to Earth with, fighting not being their best strong suit; they will try to get in and out like revolving doors but will lend support if needed. A good amount of them have rings around their arms and ankles like they we're slipped on, the amount differed some had just one per appendage, but others had three or four per each. This is very important these rings we're a dull yellow now, but if needed for a light speed boost the user only needs to fill it with Divinity and double their speed

"HOLD UP!! HOLD UP!! HOLD UP!!" umm what- what is it Azuru? Why are you all of the sudden interrupting like you went to film school and are the director of this masterpiece that

I put together!_"FIRST AND FOREMOST! I WOULD NEVER WASTE MY MONEY ON FILM SCHOOL! - THE WAY FILMS ARE COMING TODAY LITERALLY ALL I HAVE TO DO IS TAKE A DUMP IN A FILM REEL AND THERE YOU GO MOVIE OF THE YEAR! NOW YOU JUST INVEST IN THE SEQUALS AND MERCHANDISE! SPEAKING OF **PROPER** STORY TELLING!! YOU KEEP THROWING DIVINITY OUT THERE LIKE IT'S FREE SAMPLES AND YOU GET PAID OFF COMMISSIONS!! WITHOUT PROPERLY EXPLAIN TO THE READER WHAT THE HELL DIVINITY IS!! I BET THEY ARE JUST THINKING 'why does he keep on saying the title? Do they use the show as energy? Are they milking the series already?!' No! Okay in short Divinity for us Miraclelytes or reborn humans, Divinity to us is even more important than blood for you guys. Because yes we can lose a lot more Divinity than you guys can blood, - it takes the absolute last drop of Divinity or damage to an important vital organ for us to fade into oblivion. Yeah even though we we're reborn again we can still die but that's a whoooooooooooooole other topic that hopefully I'm not explaining, cause damn I can't carry the whole show! Even though I am – oh anyways! Let me show you what Divinity looks like and what it is, because it is a physical substance like blood that flows through us...-"Azuru why are you biting your thumb? "- Shut up I'm still explaining! See? It is like a tiny ball of light bout the size of a peach fuzz hair and it is actually physically and not so liquidy like how blood is splattering around and what not. Now see – oh well you can't really see but in your mind visualize this golden ball of luminance slowly fading a gray and begin to ash away into the air, this is because if it is not inside of our bodies or being put to use by us then it starts to disappear this is how we lose Divinity.

The amount of Divinity we lose our strength, power and energy is also affected until we basically run out by over using it or taking too much damage. But Divinity courses through our veins and with it we can do so much: heal wounds, give a power increase, create a pure force field, become the formula for miracles, break curses, it can give the awakened sight, cleanse people's souls, banish demons, so on and so on. Divinity is the essence of Spirit, the awakened energy that was instilled in us since the day we are born and the more divinity that is alive and well, more power is put into that person's soul and strength. Everyone has divinity inside them its whether they want to embrace it by recognizing, finding, understanding and loving Father, that it is unlocked. Humans who have activated their divinity are just different from regular humans. Because it is what connects people to the universe they we're created in and the greater power among them. Well back to your explanation Mr. Narrator listen I am not gonna bail you out every single time you cannot tell a story right! This is a freebee don't let it happen again or I swear I will replace you with a guy who stutters is that u-u-under-r-rstood?"

Yes yes oh great and mighty master.....anyways! As I was saying before I was rudely interrupted those are the carriers and speed is their deadliest weapon. They can enforce it with divinity and still use it for any combat situation that they might run into. Gathered in a bunch next to them was the recon development now this was truly the mix matched group. Some of them wearing the most common casual clothing, some of them disguised as military soldiers from all over the world, teachers, doctors, they had more variation that a party mix chip bag. Able to take the form of any desired animal on Earth to further smokescreen their efforts on digging up information, even the form of a pure, invisible to the naked eye, spirit is within reach – risky due to demon and fallen angel's sense of spirituality but still in their arsenal of options. Their main goal is to blend in to find out what is happening on the ground to report back. When it comes to combat they are the middle men, their fighting skills aren't what put them in this faction; it is the ability to completely camouflage themselves into enemy lines. But if they are found out while trying to scoop up

Intel they have to be able to get themselves out of the mess with at least decent combat ability or distance to call down a warrior squad for back up. Anything that Azuru and his team and the warriors, that risk their existence on the front lines, know today is because of this group; they studied them and reported back to home base with the information about demons, the fallen angels, the false light, and any threats to them.

That is just foreign expedition half of the research there is also a domestic experimental side as well. Where they test the properties of divinity, demonic blood and treasures found on Earth brought back to the safe haven. Every faction does it's part one not being greater than the other every day being a battle, but one step closer to their million mile journey to their goal of freeing the people of the world.

Azuru and his team we're the general leading their army to the front line, and all of his comrades looking at their heroic leader. Each and every person inside this room and,even those who could not attend because evil never sleeps, have seen him grow from a rough rugged, hard headed, aggressive, stubborn, amateur to a now rough, rugged, hard headed, aggressive, stubborn professional. Who is just fine with all the lives on his shoulders wearing all of their trust like his favorite shirt; hope, love, faith, loyalty and passion shining in the pupils of each person as they looked up at Azuru like he was the monument that have never seen before. Azuru then dropping Minerva like a bad habit as he said "you're right Hon my people are waiting on me I will give them what they came here for a whole lot of Azuru!"

Just as Azuru was about to walk off into his crowd of adoring fans and admirers, He remembered something a certain feeling that bungee corded him from walking away completely. Hanging on just by the strings of a sudden impulse as he said "I looked throughout the entire crowd and I didn't see Sifu he off somewhere?" Poyoyo picking up the inquiry like a pin point rebound "yeah he said something about checking on a "very important place that once could not be reached." Azuru's face looking like a ghost within a moment traveled through his entire body spiraling down his spine just before exiting. Concerned and worried about Azuru's lightning fast distress that he quickly tried to conceal; Poyoyo, Honey Bee, and Minerva all looking at each other before Poyoyo asked "everything okay Azuru?" Azuru now reclaiming himself his pride too strong for him to show any emotion that wasn't arrogance, so he was collected but still had a hint of uncertainty in his voice as he walked from them "think about it... Sifu is going himself....to check something out this should be pretty eye brow raising" leaving the trio to dwell on this factual thinking that left a chill in each of their spines.

as he walked away shouting this without turning his head just before the wave scooped him up, pats on the back, hugs engulfing his body, handshakes, inside jokes, laughter, and such acts of comradery absolutely surrounded Azuru. Azuru knew every single person by first name basis and had a different unique and genuine reaction to every single person; having a special individual relationship with each person. For instance while he was shaking hands and making a group of people laugh and exchanging greetings through hand contact, however they

Azuru was trekking on route to his crowd, cheering as if Azuru was the main artist walking on stage. With his head down bobbing with each step, hands firmly dug into his pockets, and back cane – slouched. Minerva just remembering as Azuru was about to be swallowed whole by the abyss that was the people who cherished him, calling after him "oh Azuru! Forgot to tell you thanks for leaving me your boy Passion! Ever since you dropped him off a year ago our Intel process and recon mission success rate has gone up 70%! He really is workin' his ass off he's vice Captain now but if I'm not careful he might be the commander of the Recon Force!" Azuru simply throwing up his index and middle finger "told you the dude is a beast!"

felt comfortable, before Azuru's hands fully went down it shot up like a bouncing betty land mine. Azuru tightly clutched his fist too like he trapped something inside it was so fast his inner circle was filled with gasps and awes they couldn't even see it coming. Azuru then called over "nice try YEAH! But you're gonna have to be faster than that!"

A flood of heads turned to the direction Azuru's voice was aimed to see a boy typical adolescent height, with bright crimson spiked mullet that trailed smoothly down his neck, dressed in a timeless outfit definitely enough space to move around in his tan toned clothing. A black short sleeve with a brown hooded vest, a pair of golden glasses with red bull's eyes engraved in the middle, tan baggy and roomy shorts and some actually up to date high - tops shoes.

A boy was aiming his pistol with a front grip on the rail beneath the barrel, the butt of the gun pushed into his shoulder as he looked through the scope only seeing Azuru's face. But there was something off about his "gun" not actually looking like a gun the top of the rail and the barrel itself was like the half pipe at a skate park open for the public to see. As the rubber pellet darted faster than the speed of sight YEAH guffawing as Azuru reduced his ammunition to mere ash with the blue dazzling flames flared onto his hand even shouting with an upbeat response "YEAAAAAAHHH! YOU GOTTA ADMIT THOUGH MY AIM WAS ONNNNN POINT!!!"

throwing the thumbs up to Azuru as he put his weapon away Azuru with such smug and arrogance " yeah now all you have to do is get past my impenetrable defenses, lightning fast speed, and beyond supersonic instinctive movement...good luck with that." All this did not discourage YEAH one bit still keeping his thumb in the air statue still his optimism holding it up high and in place suddenly a screeching "Jeffrey can beat you!"

Azuru not even needing to turn his head to respond to this "You're off your rocker Ms. Neko! Also Jeffrey is a horrible name for a cat! – I know a sprinkle is a cliché name but don't you think it has a better ring to it?! " Ms. Neko holding her orange pelted pal like he had challenged Azuru and was waiting for him to accept her pride and joy being held up like the rising sun by the arm pits. This is a prime example how well Azuru knew them like his own thoughts before he thought of them. Some people would be bending over clutching their stomach with only a few exchanges of words, other times he just stood there so egotistic with his arms crossed over his chest as the others struggled to hold back their comrade charging at Azuru. Some he danced with, arm wrestled with, shared battle stories with, sang with, continued their famous inside jokes or things they once talked about before. Just not leaving a single person alone or disappointed by the fact Azuru skipped them.

Azuru then began looking around for his team jumping up to stick his head over the crowd only to see a small group bickering at the way back wall of the room. Azuru then turned back to his fellow party goers who we're fully engulfed by the festive spirit dancing, laughing, hugging, storytelling, wrestling, just feeling so free without the weight of the world crushing their shoulders. So Azuru decided to use this time to take flight, walking over to the group he spotted earlier. Only a 16th of the way there and he could hear the arguing and squabbling; a smile just broke out on Azuru's face like bad acne as he got closer and closer.

A woman in the middle of the group with a clipboard in her hands definitely conveying the impression that she knew more than anyone in this room, doing more than what she was actually doing, even more capable to do what needed to be done by herself. The team like sharks as soon as they see blood in the water five on one side four on the other. All trying to close in on her but each argument starting comment shut down like they we're late on their electricity bill.

She was like an octopus handling all nine comments calmly at once, this girl although she looked sweet as cotton candy iced with fluffy foamy whip crème swirled on top of that with caramel, sprinkled with a cup of sugar finally topped off with a cherry... dipped in chocolate. VERY SWEET HAVE YOU COME ACROSS THE POINT YET?!

She was also very assertive, this young woman standing an average 5'4 was no butt to a joke – she did dress in unique attire. Like she was brought up in a different era separate from modern times; wearing a dazzlingly glossy silver hooded cape, being indoors she had the hood off. A shield strapped over her shoulder covering her backside like a back pack – a fiery hot red and white emblem imbedded in the metal of the shield. A heart taking up 80% of the triangular shield, inside of the heart was the sign of infinity also sporting a shoulder strapless white frilled top that had a leather looking material (the way this girl looks it's probably not real she wouldn't want to hurt those cows.) tied around the top of the ribcage. Red and gray stripes raced down from the belt line that marked the start rushed all the way down to the bottom of her shirt that ended in a pyramid shaped gap, the size of a full index and middle finger spread length. Another red belt was tied across her waist, but this one was not merely for design like the previous one. This one was to help hold up her paper thin, but sharper than any witty comeback, sword the scabbard did have some ties wrapped around her hips. Just for enforced assurance, a red belt also held it up her lightweight blade a gleaming red. The cross guards two arrows shooting outward almost as sharp as the blade, on the head of the rain guard was yet another heart but engraved in gold her jet black skirt was probably the only normal thing she was outfitting. Her feet happened to be protected by some fearsome sturdy, reliable and doubtless mighty pair of shin high mud toned combat boots. Her hair the same jet black as her skirt except for the blue tips at her banes and tips of her French braided tail that came over her left shoulder; the same glow as her alluring and mesmerizing eyes. Her face the type to break all the guy's necks as they turn as many degrees they can to at least get a glimpse of her and they can die happy – so drop dead to speak. Again looking sweet but this sugar – coated little gum drop had a pinch of salt to her as she stood her ground against those animals, that tried to rip her limb from limb.

"WHY DID YOU SEND ANGELO OF ALL PEOPLE?!" "Because Zandra, he was begging so close in my ear he was piercing the opposite ear drum... - still trying to see if there was any harm done to my brain, so forgive my less than better judgment due to a certain someone's let's say "intense enthusiasm". But next time you try battling him off see if you can beat my time kay kay? – kay kay!" a body that was covered in ropes hopping as high as a toddler off the ground and every time he reached eye contact with this young woman she would responded "no you're still in time out." "Yeah Emily also I wanted to talk to you about my reality television show – Now hear me out hear me out!! Ok... so someone from the recon division follows me right? Annnnnd broadcasts all of my wacky antics and sentimental moments on screen. We send it to Earth and make millions because there is no other show like it! I even have the name: it's gonna be called "this just... goat serious!!" badass right?!"

The only professional amongst a bunch of grown children spoke once again "shut up Ryker like I told you before absolutely not! Also no Angelo you are still in time out!" Emily statues herself against the wave of complaints groaning and griping; Emily then held her clipboard towards the girl closest to her and with a smug look on her face "here Zandra if you think you can handle it you can be in charge of Angelo, I will let you borrow my clipboard to write down his actions and improvements and progress." The bellyaching vanishing like disappearing ink as soon as the responsibility was given to the one called Zandra. Her face turning almost pasty as she looked at Angelo hopping up and down at Emily's feet like a dog excited to see their owner return home. With each leap Angelo only was met with a "no" every single time.

Zandra then pushed the tablet back towards Emily responding with a vigorous and proud excuse "I am no one's babysitter!" Once again the one known as Ryker jumping into the conversation like an eavesdropper. "No wait hold on though Emily I didn't explain the goat part yet! It's because the goat was gonna be my partner I was gonna be the loose cannon cop and he was gonna be the only cool headed one to keep me in line make sense now?" Only to be shot down by Emily's heat seeking debate destroyer. "Ryker I said to shut it you know we do not work with anything goat related I know you are doing this just to piss me off so knock it off! And well I am the baby sitter for all of you that includes Azuru! Just let me know if you think you can fill my shoes better than me...- no still in time out." Zandra filling her cheeks with air like a squirrel storing acorns for winter, pouting her lip as frustration emanated off of her.

At first glance she doesn't at all look or even begin to resemble how hot headed and opinionative that she really is – best not to judge a book by its cover. Especially when you're looking at Azuru's team, she was simply dressed but it was her and the essence of her that made the outfit luminance like a mountain of gold. A plain button up white t – shirt a gap between the shirt and white belted skirt, which traveled halfway down to her thighs, revealing coke bottle hips and a poppy little belly button all that was left to her outfit was her shin high long black socks and white high top shoes. A petite figure to her but it was her essence, her being, which she was as a person that made this set of fabrics much more than just that, luscious, silky lustrous, lavender tinted long, lengthy, heaping mass of hair. Trailing off at her buttocks parts rested delicately on her shoulders the rest flowing down her back; her eyes burning a fierce purple lighter than her hair, such full peach toned lips that could drop men to their knees merely puckering them. Her face similar to medusa she is able to make men lose their minds upon first glance, except melts their heart instead of turning them to stone.

The jester right behind Zandra inserted his "stack of gold" once again "or we could reverse the roles the goat could be the loose cannon cop and I be the calm one to keep him in line…. Until the plot twist reveals that I am actually worse than him! – Why are they not funding me?! Like seriously I could make movies off this! A trilogy! Prequels that will be shitty and have horrible dialogue and not make sense if you start putting things together, also I am gonna put a character that no one likes and force him upon the crowd and make sure that the people love him even though they hate him tenfold in the forced process….I will then make sequels that continue the originals, Emily are you writing any of this down?" The plot being too convoluted like certain movies that the man known as Ryker pulled the idea from

Emily was writing but not a single word as she flipped her tablet to show her finished mater piece, as gleeful as a child as she kicked her professionalism to the side, with an ear to ear smile "No I got lost right after "reverse" so I thought to myself hmm what can I do while he is talking because this should be a while and then it came to me! I made you into a pony!" a picture of the gallant Ryker converted into another species his clothes where his skin of the poorly two dimensional character his hair was the mane and it personally resembled a kindergartener drawing it last minute to turn in their piece. She then said "nope still not yet Angelo" to the hopping Angelo as she showed Ryker who took a close inspection. Examining the piece he took in all the factors the coloring, line art, and all around design as he scratched his chin saying as he further took in the artwork "hmm you know what you should have drawn…is a goat, me riding it…with glasses on, an explosion erupting behind us…tattoos because tattoos are a clear showcase of badass, and fedoras because all the greats wore fedoras." Emily's palm met her forehead as she took a moment to tuck under her arm pit even with eyes closed_Emily still kept saying "no.....nope.....no.....nuh uh"

This clown named Ryker looked like he only acted like a fool besides looking mature. To be in his late 20's or so, he was the type of look that if he we're to cock his head at an angle and smile with those bright white teeth of his he could get away with pretty much anything. His face is almost as chiseled out as a statue, a ton of masculinity radiating off him enough to make a grown woman back to a school girl crushing over a boy in school. His features are developed like a rose that has had time to bloom, a distinguished type of handsome to him; but he dresses like he was still a rebellious youngster in his young buck years trapped in a grown and sophisticated body. For instance wearing a gray sleeveless shirt underneath a shadow black also torn off sleeves, sewn hooded jacket so you could see all the ripping, defined, hunk sculpted muscles in his shoulders, biceps triceps, and forearms. So tight knit and irresistible making the girls bites their lips before they tackle him down. Also navy blue fitted jeans with rips at the knees and black mixed with white high-tops on his feet having neat shaggy space black hair... neat shaggy? - You are all saying to yourselves yes you heard right and there is only room for one invisible voice here thank you! Ahem lastly the originator for all of Ryker's manipulation and sly escape from any trouble that faces him, his big ponds of darling sharp gray, he could cause a litter of puppies and a daycare full of babies to be completely ignored and neglected by his enticing tantalizing and most of all hypnotizing twin lagoons that ladies would just get lost in. Even with an atlas of the universe and the best satellite gps known to man they could still not find their way.

Emily taking her hand away from her head to still shake in disagreement, even had a growing weary tone to her as she asked for more punishment. "Okay whose next? Anyone else want to share their displeasure with my blunder?......no not happening

Angelo" a man with a graceful presence, an old soul a wise spirit gendering to be at least in his 60's with the amount of wrinkles, gray stripped into his shadow black hair but he seemed to have age like fine wine. Although having his fair share of age spots, skin folding, and age spots; this did not diminish his youthful spirit or his golden aura this energy that just vibrated off him. At first glance it is just automatic to come to the conclusion that he is from a completely different time than everyone else. Dark navy blue very roomy and slack like pants continuing his attire was a white tipped with gray sleeveless shirt that had a gray shirt underneath also sleeveless. The white shirt was a button up v –neck, the last accessory to decorate his arms we're the white gleaming hand wraps that we're tightly bound across his fists. A large blue belt, the size of a full adult's hand, was wrapped around his waist, another shade of blue this time coating a large scarf (that sure is a lot of large things you wearing there guy... you okay downstairs?) that was tied around his neck and the last form of his uniform he wore was the headband that was tied across his forehead, it was a noble silver that had the image of the earth drawn on it shining a vibrant gold.

His shaggy hair folding over the headband almost like the headband was a dam that wasn't high enough to hold back this wave of black water. Speaking of water his eyes sparkling like the most crystal clearest waters in the world, a beautiful glowing blue with all this elegance of course he was gonna look great for his age. First question here in the ladies' heads is what did he look like in his prime? Arms crossed over his chest with eyes closed as he shook his head in displeasure "it's definitely was not one of your best decisions." Slipped out from his lips, standing a bit behind Emily was a figure that towered over her but by the position of his stance, rubbing the back of his head like he was the one who was embarrassed. He looked to be a gentle giant just not nearly as stacked as Azuru, trying to put shirts on him was like trying to put sardines in a can.

Big smile on this titan's face now this man looked to be the black sheep of the bunch and by the sight of his dressings he looked like he seen more animals than talked to people- no bust seriously this guy stuck out like a sore thumb....a green thumb that is!..... You guys probably pissed your pants laughing I just know it. But to give him some credit other than looking like the hired help to cattle the barn animals, he does look like he knows what he's doing on that barnyard he does have the tan that is like a reference on a job application.

The skin tone looking to be misplaced as it clashed with his golden locks but the young man took what he was handed with stride as his hair shined like the sun that he worked to the bone under as it beamed down on his skin and gave him his new color. A button up denim jean jacket over a red and blue checkered plaid shirt underneath the denim jacket was open and unbuttoned but the plaid shirt was closed off also sporting off a pair of dark navy blue jeans. This young man also wore a pair of reliable tough, sturdy, and everlasting pair of boots that seemed to have gold melted down to form the base color or at least spit shined with Divinity. The last thing to top off this unusual placement for a character was the hat that was nesting on his bushy head full of graduated long blond locks of hair. His golden curls of thread – like clumps of hair, his face combined with his stature made him seem like he could only do good – like big muscular men we're only built to do lift, toss and slam and flip human beings in the same fashion he looked like he wasn't capable of cruelty. He was meant to be kind, generous, warm and loving the benevolence just shined from his twin pools that we're his eyes, smiling to show his pearly millimeter perfect bright teeth. Still brushing the back of his head up and down as he said "for being the supervisor of this team you forgot for a moment that Angelo was"

Giving the capital "d" flipped upside down type smile as he laughed Emily simply rolling her eyes with a slight smirk. Letting out an exhale "well Kenjin maybe it was unwise to not express your thoughts on this also.... Enough time with Angelo will make anyone unwise – Duke I am your overseer and am on the same level as Azuru when it comes to authority. I rank higher it's just – I completely underestimated him when you guys when you said he was that bad! I just thought you all we're over exaggerating and – no!"

Just then a click clacking slowly approached Emily and the others coming in towards them in such a cool and calm manner compared to the other savage beasts on the team. Practically breathing fire at Emily good thing Emily kept a cool mind and her fire proof - everything! While being roasted on the hot seat. One foot so harmonious and curvaceous radiates grace as the foot was gently put in front of the other. Making walking a true blessing that graced by merely part taking in it, the most beautiful poise that a person could ever walk. The alluring and angelic presence of this woman such long slender legs that no matter how well you knew yourself you will get lost in, strong and firm as well as toned but being on the soft and caressing side also. Her body being the type to inspire the glass bottles having that hour glass frames her hips looking mighty solid as solid as Azuru's biceps – more or less. Her beauty causing aches and pains in the heart of every man having males practically crawling at her feet, but she looked to be bored of their lust and desire. Or maybe she's grown tired of only being focused on because of her appearance; but just every part of her was sculpted to be enticing. How could one not fall in love with her upon first sight?! I have the best chance of being with her by the way just letting you guys know – I am the narrator I can make it happen! – I mean umm back to her.

Her arms and hands looking so slim and delicate – being barely above the level of petite but she wouldn't be wearing black fingerless gloves if they we're too delicate to be of use to her. Sporting homage on her shoulder a plaster of master pieces on her left shoulder and on the corners of her collar bones near her neck; a flock of peacock feathers flourished from her forearm an entanglement of clouds, fire, and memorable significant pieces that glowed on her body as they we're carved in. Her entire body was just flawlessly molded only leading up to the finale that just closed the sold out show the most elegant piece of the puzzle, the originator of all these men on the ground as a result for falling head over heels for her . Her just herself beyond gorgeous, beyond beautiful, beyond stunning and breath taking just no words could describe the refinement of her face that had captivated the hearts of nearly all men who lay eyes upon her. Lips so full, juicy, tantalizing so smoothly caressed with a bright red lipstick. All those who desired her smacked their own pair of lips in the air or bit upon them as they imagined that her lips we're right in front of them so spiral pool – wrenching.

A blemish less, silky smooth flawless soft texture and clear face, eye liner and shadowing only adding to her already perfect beauty. Her teal or lazy green colored eyes piercing everyone's sight upon the slightest glance, at the same time pulling you into her world like a gravitational ray with those marvelous vision trail blazers. Jet black hair glistened like the moonlight on shadow filled dusk, trailing off to the bottom of her shoulders her hair itself not wavy in the least bit but more combed and tamed to one side over her right eye nice and neat. Her outfit she was currently making history with as they recorded how beautiful she looked today in the history books a licorice black shoulder – less strap zip up top. The front of the outfit ended above the breasts wearing a belt filled with holes to mark the end of her top, the type of material for the lower half was an onyx toned silky and creamy looking type of fabric that we're cut off at the shins - how long they truly were was a mystery due to her shoes being in the way. Looking if it fell off of the boot tree or sprouted from a branch of that type of boot fashion, the pair scaled up to her shins but glimpsing further they didn't resemble combat boots but heels that covered the foot completely. Only appearing that the heel of the shoe was strengthened by having a block instead of that flimsy tower being made solely for battle, seemingly like she was cat walking up to the rest of the group.

Her opinion being voiced to join the group of other thoughts and inquires "well if I may" Emily inviting her right in with entrance gesture and a kind "the floor is yours serenity." Serenity doing an adorable and shrine twisting curtsy that sent a wave of men flopping and flipping around like a tsunami hitting the shores hearts, drool, and awhs! Everywhere, and nothing but an equal sized flood of women slipping their foreheads and shaking in absolute disappointment to the supposed men... so nothing new right ZING!

Serenity continued in her respectable declaration "to be fair for Emily; we all know how Angelo is, and none of us added our two cents!" Nothing but boos and jeering heard from the team as they completely disagreed with Serenity's statement but at the same time being quieted down by Emily with a water gun that had labeled "team misbehavior." Each of the team hissing and swiping at Emily before they began licking themselves like the pussies they were (pun intended of course) Serenity also continued "but to be fair to us we all know how Angelo is you and you know each of us like the back of your hand, you know Ryker never pays attention! Zandra is almost as hot headed as Azuru and Azuru – well he is just a four year old stuffed into a 24 year olds body. So you should know just how umm, persistent Angelo can be and there isn't a cure for his umm... different attributes but we are hard working on one. –"

Azuru and Ryker at the back of the room in lab coats and for some reason big white beards that took up half of their lower face, both holding clip boards as they stared down at some object on a table. Ryker speaking in a high pitched and much exaggerated old German native man accent "untz Doctor Azuru it's seems zat ve finally have broken down ze mechanism and it's quirks....lederhosen!"

Azuru looking down at the object only to gently drift his head up towards the roof only to painfully bring his head back down, biting his lip and shaking in frustration as now tears trailed down his face and his face was the most compelling focus right now vacuuming you your vision in his eyes especially taking the spotlight but pushing the audience back a bit so he was able to place his glasses on. Only to slam them onto the table as he screamed in absolute agony "I can't believe that lazy piece of shit beat the streak! Him of all people!!" Ryker patting him on the back in an attempt to comfort him as he poured sympathy onto him as well "I know I know! Zis just doesn't get any easier! Vut I believe today ve will crack ze code... Hasselhoff!" Finally getting a look at the object that was getting the rise up of emotions from these brave men. Sitting on the table so dastardly, so diabolic that not even the most genuine minds could wrap their heads around this conception or how it worked.

A white rectangular figure of doom! Having a circular hole.... of doom! A square hole of even more despair and even more doom! Lastly and of course the most ominous the triangle hole containing the most dooms to ever exist ever! .... DOOM!! Everyone knows triangles are the most dangerous aren't I right pyramid people? I'M WATCHING YOU PYRAMID PEOPLE!! YOU AREN'T WATCHING ME! ME YOU! YOU NO ME!! Anyways enough of my paranoid insanity, right beside this ironically very nicely decorated rectangle of terror was three shapes a can, a square, and a triangle. Ryker then said "vee have concluded zat ze circular van goes into ze circular hole, ze square van goes into ze square hole etcetera etcetera but! Ze circular van cannot go into ze.... Triangle van!! Bratwurst! Sausage!!" Azuru then rolling up his sleeves as he stared menacingly at the demonic contraption "oh it doesn't eh?! Who the hell you think you are eh?! Cleopatra?! Cause you're not! You never will be!! You won't even be Cleopatra's fat cousin!! It's not about what you want not Azuru thing it's about what Azuru wants! Like it or not that's how it always will be!!... Eh!" Ryker inserted as he was scribbling down to his clipboard "as zew can see the threats also have no e-ffect even Azuru's fearsome Cleopatra insults do absolutely nothing!" Azuru full of rage picked up the can shaped circle and slammed it on top of the triangle cracking the rims a bit as he tried to crush the can inside of the triangle but it didn't work no matter how many times Azuru tried.

It wasn't going to go in, Azuru grinding his teeth as he slammed the can with the force of a thousand suns – however much that is "GO IN YOU SON OF A WHORE!!!!" For an instant almost seeming like the whole entire world was going against a pyramid a world that was being pushed by Azuru... remember this it will probably be important later. Cracking, chipping and spitting began creaking and squeaking out from the object. Ryker then screamed like the entire world was falling apart "OH NO YOU DESTROYED IT!!.... ZE SCORPIONS!!" An eruption of epic proportions imploded right before their very eyes when the dust cleared and all was done the circle was inside of the triangular hole that was now forced to be a circle. Azuru now standing beside Ryker both writing on their clipboards as Ryker declared "Vat an astounding turn out!" Azuru nodding his head as he also wrote random things down ending his conclusion with "eh" and now back to Serenity as she proved her point "needless to say without having the test results you should know what we all have on our team." Now switching as quick as the "on" button for the lights the team began wooing, cheering, clapping and whooping as they lifted serenity up throwing her up in celebration screaming "hey –oh – hey – oh – hey – oh – hey – oh –hey –oh – hey!" Emily just pinching the bridge of her nose with her index and thumb letting out an exhausted sigh; "of course" only hearing a stern and simple "it was a bad move that's it!"

Emily actually chuckling at how blunt it was looking over her shoulder with a giggly response "just that simple huh Eminent?" A strict simple nod came from a man standing a five foot eight inches arms crossed over his chest as he was very plainly wall flowering this party. Tough, rugged, macho, hard as nails, hard boiled weren't even close on the manly scale to describe the humongous piece of masculinity, besides the gun holstered on his leg by belts and buckles over sleek black, blend into shadow, pants on the miniature packs that held all the ammunition he needed was strapped onto a clip on belt. That also had its connection to what seemed to look like suspender straps and he was wearing a black undergarment because at the pectoral area the shirt split into a tan color with a much thicker material that had Eminent's abdominals and pectorals carved out. Maybe the suspender straps we're actually overall straps and this was an overall jumpsuit oh wow! ....this is about as interesting as Eminent gets sorry folks "that's because Eminent sucks!" Please! Azuru I am trying to narrate this.... Creature? If you will?! "If I will? If I will insult him again, Is that what you we're trying to insist? In a heartbeat to answer your stupid question – Eminent sucks so bad that they should name a vacuum brand off him, for credibility! Ohhhhh!!!!" hahaha not going to lie that was good while Azuru jumped into his crowd of followers to catch him Eminent was – oh wow he looks pretty pissed.

Okay okay calm down I didn't even get to talk about your mando cool black fingerless fighting gloves. Or your totally rad blood red Mohawk reminiscence of its war origin or your blood colored eyes to match your Mohawk see now you're starting to cool off see?! Didn't I tell you I was getting to the good parts - yeah show that vibrant smile of yours – relax no need to get so worked up now let's talk about how much your face just oozes machoness_"talk about his tutu and how he likes to be called Queen sprinkle puff while on the battlefield or how he hits all the bad guys with his magic wand and sharing of his feelings! – So they just laugh themselves to death!!-" AZURU seriously man you're gonna get me killed! He is literally turning red "eh he can't do anything to me sucks to be you though! On a scale of one to ten he br-"

a miracle from the heavens saving my life as Emily pulled Azuru away by the ear as she lectured him on the way "what did I tell you about speaking negatively about people?! – I told you don't say anything at all if you don't have anything nice to say! – I understand that you never shut up and that would be impossible for you but-"Emily beginning to trail off as she drug him as far as she could from me and Eminent. Where Azuru could do no harm but like a desperate coyote he tried to chew his own ear off or at least stuff napkins he found on the floor into one of his ears okay now Eminent nothing he said was true! Both you and I know that! But let's tell the audience and possible fans that! He has a chin looking like it could have been sculpted from iron. His eyes, once opening from sleep, look like they we're designed specially to guide Eminent to the kill zone. Even without his eyes they could see that the end was Eminent! ...Name drop you like what I did there?

No? Okay! Whatever mission he is has a 100% chance of success and just know where ever he goes the end is Eminent...I did the name drop again – did you like it that time? – I CAN LIVE OH THANK YOU KIND SIR!! Umm – hey look Emily!

Emily was walking in front of Eminent with her clip board as she looked over a very quiet and hush-up pair that was sort of backed away from the rest of the group Emily then looked at the tall slender one first "what about you two? Have any comments of the matter? Come on I need the feedback Angel why don't you go first then Maximus" the noiseless little angel who seemed to wander away from his savage and diabolic comrades a truly gentle soul. Even an eyeless person could tell by first glance, his aura just made you want to be better his aura and energy so kind, so loving, warm, embracing and just so innocent. Not a single ulterior motive, dark thoughts or just ounce of negativity existed in this circle of purity. He has a humane and meek soul, if ever there were one, his cheeks puffed up as he pouted his lips and peddled his right foot back and forth like he was trying to kick an imaginary can.

His hands tucked into his pockets as he slouched his back speaking with a spiteful and juvenile tone like a child holding a grudge – actually that is exactly how this was. "I wanted to go instead of Angelo". Emily smirking as she squeezed Angel's feelings, that he wasn't planning on sharing, out of him. Emily having a talent for bringing out the best in people she was able to lure angel out of his shell she simply replied 'did you tell me that you wanted to go?" Emily at the back of her mind very satisfied as she consulted herself. "This is a huge improvement compared to how he was before now he is sharing how he feels he used to just whisper what was wrong to Azuru and he would take care of it somehow." Angel so childish as he said "yes!" with an upset tone Emily responding so appropriately her maturing not wearing off one bit no matter who she dealt with "well I didn't hear you did you say it loud enough?" Angel once again replying with his same upset typed tone "yes!" It seemed more like he was hurt than angry, a recollection of what happened a good ten minutes before the entire party started

The guests from the valiant, recon, and analysis divisions running around like a bunch of ants that lost their way to the ant hole. Somewhere setting up the decorations by streaming a cloud along the roof and letting it leave a trail of crystal and silver lingering dust that glistened like smashed diamonds remains. Some we're doing role call to make sure all the right people we're here and that enough infantry was still on the ground patrolling for some reason a man walked in with a completely blue painted donkey. It for some other strange reason that probably makes sense in some parallel universe the Mohawk spiked up from the tail all the way to the top of its head having it on a leash the man exclaimed excitedly. "Okay guys! I brought the blue donkey!"

Forehead slaps, nose - bridge squeezing, and sighing all around from everyone as they proclaimed to his failure "Bobby it is not that kind of party!" "Man what are you thinking?!" "Sometimes man! Seriously wondering what's going on in that brain of yours!" Bobby and his donkey both had their heads down with their smashed happiness as they walked back from where they crawled out from

On the flipside of the party towards the back wall where the group basically is now, Emily had everyone gathered while looking down at her clip board; she then asked "so Angelo went off to do whatever he does when he is alone, don't really want to find out so who wants to go because no way in hell am I letting him go" everyone staying almost completely silent. Eyes wandering about to see who was going to volunteer to go Angel in the absolute back trembling as he gulped heart beating like a drummer in a metal band the anticipation fueling his race track heart. Saliva almost turning into dust his mouth was so dry but he made a declaration to himself "I'm gonna do it...I'm gonna tell her I want to go!!"

Angel took a moment to close his eyes take a deep breath held it in his chest for a moment or two only to push it up and out. Ready, determined, iron – willed without a hint of doubt or negativity as he whispered as loud as his lungs would allow him "I-I wanna go." But Eminent accidentally coughed so loud it completely masked and camouflaged Angel's brave announcement that shook the heavens at its core had been disregarded as rerun news. His shrine dropped to his stomach his head was aimed at the ground as he spaced out in his own thoughts "she didn't hear me?! How could she not?! I was practically screaming?! Now the gloves are off... and neatly folded I am gonna have to really bust my lungs on this one!" Angel taking a short confidence – building breath like he was ready to take on this entire room full of people with his hands tied behind his back! With the fire of perseverance and courage igniting his heart this time he was really ready "I-I w-would like to go!" but the randomness and unpredictability of Ryker yelling "Potatoes!" Then going back to staring into nothing completely disrupting the erupting volcano that was Angel Emily paying more attention to Ryker as she didn't even pick up her eyes to respond to Ryker already built up to be a natural as she brushed off "yes thank you for that contribution Ryker anyone else have any vegetable to add or anything of that sort? Maybe we could volunteer if we aren't doing anything? Do I have any takers?" Angel was still in the shadows as Emily encouraged everyone by forcing the title on them "anyone? Nobody wants to be the angel of good news?"

Angel cringing to himself "she even said my name this is destiny!" He thought so strongly in his head this was it "third's time the charm" really was the case here, as the energy inside steadily building like molten lava ready to erupt. His roar conjuring peddling inside his lungs as Angel was steadily preparing himself to unleash the outcry to impact everyone but just as he exhaled, all of the oxygen through his nose ready to rampage like a bull. Before he could even open his mouth a blue flash appeared right in front of Emily and shouted twice as loud as Angel could even dream of shouting. "HOW COULD YOU BETRAY ME EMILY?! I ONLY WAS GONE A COUPLE OF MINUTES AT MY QUARTERS TO ICK THE PERFECT WARRIOR'S OUTIFIT AND YOU TRY TO GIVE AWAY MY POSITION THAT YOU PROMISED ME!!!! HAVE YOU NO SHAME EMILY?!?!" Emily pressing her hand against her cranium as she said "no it apparently disappeared with my eardrums pieces of my mind and my sanity – ah –oh! This is what it feels like to be in front of a megaphone point blank! Plus you took too long and he is already here in the city making his way to the tower I was trying to give the job to someone else but I suppose you we're the man born for the job now get in the hallway already or I'll have someone else go instead!"

Angelo walking past Emily and towards the front door as he ranted on "this is the worst injustice I have ever seen my own leader and team going against me it's mutiny! The worst kind of mutiny... mutinous mutiny!" Before exiting Angelo gave one glance to everyone who was counting on his warning call to get the perfect surprise on Azuru. Looking over the horizon of hopeful eyes it seemed that Angelo truly understood how important this was to them but then shouting at ear popping volume "JUSTICE"

Sliding his legs apart simultaneously as he pointed up towards the even further heavens with his index finger. Just before slamming the door and leaving Eminent chuckling just before "told you haha" Duke laughing in amazement "as true as the cows coming home" Eminent then punched Duke in the arm he softly rubbed his arm afterwards.

Still wearing that unfading smile, the whole entire time no one ever noticed Angel in the corner of the room with his own private black cloud over him as his knees touched his chin his arms hugging his legs together as gloom completely cradled his words instilled in them like jelly in a donut. "He was so loud! It's like he swallowed a microphone or something! – There is no competing with that." Now current events once again taking over the time frame Emily put the clip board underneath her armpit as she placed her hands on her hips. "You need to really try to speak up or no one will hear you! – how do you expect for people to know how you feel?!" Angel's feelings just getting more hurt than they already were Emily having good intentions but doing more harm than anything.

As Angel's upset expression slowly shifted to soft sorrow that Angel was desperately trying to hide. Emily read him like a best - selling book (something my beloved fans should make this into just saying just saying) despite his efforts, Emily delicately shaking her head as she made her way towards Angel who was still peddling his foot with his lip pouting out trying not to look at Emily. Stepping right into his range of vision even though it was pointed towards the floor as Emily inserted herself. "You need to assert yourself better it isn't rude to tell people how you feel and it isn't bad to speak louder than others either! Speak up for yourself!" Angel not too keen on being told what's wrong he aimed his sight back towards the ground Emily's boots he only thing he saw of Emily. Two fingers gently lifting up his chin like how Emily is lifting up his spirits looking him directly in the eyes without a hint of a break and with compassion just flooding out "another thing I promise I will try my best to hear you if you're going to speak up for yourself."His pouting lip being pulled in as his frown began flipping to a creaking smile, Emily putting out a hand for an agreement that Angel took without hesitation.

Squeezing with all the love that he felt, afterwards Emily held out her arms eagle - spread as she asked a wonderful and shrine warming question. "Would it be okay if I gave you a hug?" Angel's smile stretching from one side to the other side of his face, like a child being brought into a toy store and being told "you can take anything you want!" Tightly wrapping his arms around Emily – I mean who wouldn't hug this gentle soul?!

Skin tight light blue jeans, some casual black shoes with white shoe laces, and a red shirt underneath a gray button up cardigan sweater. A red and black checkered scarf tied around his neck like a noose, light brown hair styled to a single forward spike his skin so light looked like a ghost scared him right out of his skin and this was all that was left. Light blue aura colored eyes, sky eyes basically, making everyone wanting to just dive into – he was just such a delicate soul how could you not treat him as such?! Emily released from his snap jaw of a hug laughing as she felt better knowing she was able to finally one of her team mates just to make sure though "better" Angel gave a satisfying nod with his smile shining like the sun on a beautiful sunset. Emily smiling as she caught Angel's smile like the cold that was going around "okay...now how are you doing Maximus you're also very quiet" Emily now standing in front of a stack of muscles that was stuffed into a very formal black business suit. This tower of intimidation looked like he was waiting for his executives to show up for their meeting any minute now, the double chested button up with a blue tie tucked in a white long sleeve polo shirt underneath.

Everything that wasn't the jacket was neatly tucked inside of his belt, his black slacks and black plain Jane working shoes he went the whole nine yards. Forget that he went the whole end zone to end zone! Having a stocky body like thick clumps of defined and concrete muscle hard to believe it was being held back by the flimsy threads he was wearing. Seemed like one slight scratch of his nose he would tear everything and would end up in his underwear in one second flat, he had the look of an average man – meaning he looked like he wouldn't be caught dead in these but looks can be deceiving. Messy, puffy dark brown hair with big dark mud puddles of vision to match; a very iron chinned type of masculinity his face being chiseled out he would be no doubt terrifying if he wasn't so calm and tamed standing with his hands so neatly tucked behind his back as he patiently waited for his turn. Nodding his head in acknowledgment speaking so civil and proper as he said "no nothing out of place on my side" an eyebrow rising from Emily's questioning expression. She even asked again to be sure "really? – I mean this doesn't have to be just about the Angelo thing it can be about anything – where is Angelo by the way? – ah anyways anything that is bothering you or that you wanted to say."

Maximus took a minute to evaluate his position in the team curving his eyes up as his thought process ran coming back with a quick – "not at all" Emily still giving him the questioning expression. As she said "in a way you're just like Angel over there except he's really innocent you're more the strong type and you keep yourself in an enduring state even of the simplest things Max you don't have to be strong all the time. You can let go we're your team – your friends you can trust us"

Maximus really lost here no map, no atlas, or any form of direction from any local could help him find his way either. Completely swallowed by confusion as he responded "but I don't have anything to complain about everything has been fine you're doing a great job!" Emily sighing she couldn't be getting nowhere any faster if they we're on treadmills, while they we're talking. Giving him the look like she threw in the towel with her eyes "I have been watching you like I have been watching the whole team but I won't push it anymore just going to put down as "work in progress" at least you're happy about it.

Emily then scribbled down onto her clip board as she walked back towards the group leaving Maximus to drown in his own pool of confusion. Emily was scanning around the floor, she then peeked her head over the crowd, standing on her tip toes as she searched for a certain someone. Stopping to stand in place as she shut her eyes and started hearing around like her ears had their very own sight, Duke then came up to Emily a bit concerned as he noticed her rigid search. Everyone gathering around as well "you 'lright Emily?" a few moments of silence later Emily opened her eyes discontinuing her own concentration as concern sprayed from her words "I can't sense him at all." Worry weighing down her words like anchors everyone began looking in their own separate directions because they knew exactly who this threat that terrified her. But weren't putting too much effort into their lazy search party where their necks we're owl turning around while their bodies stood absolutely still, Azuru doing nothing at all to help and of course he wore a mischievous grin like a fine suit. Emily caught this quicker than a starving man whiffing a scent of food as her eagle eyes dead locked on him, prey inside of an eagle's iron talons had a better chance of escaping.

"Where is he?!" Azuru's smile only grew wider as the urgency doubled by the passing moments. Azuru like a sadist taking enjoyment in causing this mayhem his pearly whites shining so bright as his smile only grew wider and wider finally letting out the information that Emily was about to strangle him for "three" was the only thing he said. Giving Emily the biggest left turn in a "right turn only" lane a completely taken back and disorientated Emily this was not even close to an answer that Emily so desperately needed snapping "What?! Where is he?" Azuru taking even more pleasure in dodging Emily's question this time even chuckling a bit "two." Emily screaming her head off at Azuru the rebel child "dammit AZURU!!!" Azuru's laughter like lightning in a bottle barely able to contain it as he pointed towards the ceiling and shouted like some sort of signal was in the mix "IT'S SHOWTIME!!"

The lights shutting off in the blink of an eye the whole entire room was consumed by darkness and shadows, confused gasps, murmurs, and questioning came from the others in the room Azuru then slid over to Emily whispering in her ear "I let Angelo out by the way." Emily almost reciprocating fire with her words verbalizing "I DIDN'T KNOW THAT THANK YOU! - AZURU WHY DID YOU LET HIM OUT HE WAS IN TIME OUT!" Azuru with an absolute jigsaw puzzled look on his face retorted "why did you let him be the lookout for me in the first place?"

Emily's hand coming to say hi to her forehead at hyper speed sliding it down her face violently in just defeat, Emily in a somber force of emotion "I really messed up on the Angelo thing didn't I? – All we need is for the newbie to say something and the whole team thinks I'm a failure"

Straight out the blue a voice was heard from overhead everyone like someone was screaming from the rooftops. But the spot light shining showed something otherwise a body was leveled on top of a cloud as casually as a surfer on a surfboard riding the waves, this body glistened like the morning sun climbing over the horizon, exploding the purity of a person's soul.

Radiating like the essence of potential of mankind wrapped into a single body so noble, so brave, so valiant, and valorous; his boots that glowed dazzling and robust silver, his footwear climbing all the way up to his knees a hard steel layer on the toes, top of the foot, shins and knees and a more wide sliced layer of iron on the sides of his calves and shins engraved in these boots, that probably seen hundreds of battles, was a vine that seemed to have a Spanish type of design as a representation of his homeland and pride – hmm Spanish? – II – I know a man from Spain who is very proud of his homeland but it can't be this guy! "Yo, talking voice with no body! The guy you are describing oh so nicely is Angelo!"

There's no way this guy is too badass I mean I haven't gotten a good look at him I've just seen what I told the audience but I know for a fact! That there is no connection between the two – not the same person no nope nuh huh no We're gonna keep going - he is ringing a bell though – on top of his mud brown poofy pants was a metallic skirt placed at his waist that trailed down his thighs. It.... Shimmered.... a ..... And.... Twinkled a blinding steel – okay more similarities are coming up folks but there is no way these guys are the same!! – I mean the skirt, the Spanish design that's pure coincidence – you know what?! I have to know now!! – Okay okay he wore a button up creamy white long sleeve polo that was looking to be a bit on the side like it was from Spaniard taste. Okaaaay he also wore steel plated forearm guards on each arm – alright – mysteriously only a single iron shoulder pad on his left shoulder... I know I have seen that before! – No! – No! There is no way that is him just absolutely, ultimately, improbably NO WAY!! He even wore a steel vest over his white polo shirt also having the same markings on his boots... sigh his... -h... his scorching green... eyes... like burning embers... - it's him I can't believe I gave him a compliment "I told you you're lucky you didn't bet money or else I would have already sold you for a cigarette!"

Shut up Azuru I will narrate you off a cliff! His hair a glazing and blazing neon – glowing blue, hair that flowed – to – I can't do this. I can't believe I complimented him of all people – oh by the way his long luxurious hair that Rapunzel would break a neck for, trailed all the way down his – big stupid head! All the way to his dumb weird shoulders! – and let me not forget his silver mask a blinding silver - just like all the rest of him to match his silverware. – HAS GET IT?! – SILVERWARE! HA! His mask was emotionless – kind of like I am now – all that was on the mask was the outlines on a face basically and it only went up to the forehead; only bad part was he had it turned around and wasn't wearing it to hide his dumb face! Oh he's gonna talk I'm outta here!

"Where there is light I am not far behind! Corruption runs in terror whenever I draw near! The guilty lurk in the shadows praying in fear, the malice and cruel wish for me to never arrive, here with my friends at my side. Weapons in hand there is nowhere evil can hide! Plead for it to stop, but I speak a language they do not understand, Justice! Until my shrine no longer glows, my Divinity runs out, and oblivion is at my face, I will never commit to evil if I know. Represent what true justice is about, and I –"oh look Azuru is going to save us all! Praise the heavens, snickering as he held a smoking ball of fire like it was a simple softball shouting before he pitched it as it was done in the big leagues "WE ALREADY HEARD YOUR ONE ANTHEM!" Lighting up the cloud up as if it we're paper it crumbled into dust right underneath Angelo as his face meteored down to the ground, and he got not one second of rest as the lights snapped back on as quick as they we're turned off. Emily picking his body up solely by the ear just so she could drag him lecturing him worse than teachers, parents, police, and over confident individuals all blended together. "WHEN YOU ARE IN TIMEOUT YOU STAY YOUR ASS IN TIMEOUT I DON'T CARE WHO LET YOU OUT! UNLESS I LET YOU OUT! – YOU KNOW WHAT YOUR PROBLEM IS?! – YOU DON'T LISTEN! YOU'RE WRECKLESS, YOU'RE ABRASIVE WHAT ABOUT OTHER PEOPLE! EVER-"

Fading away as Emily dragged Angelo to the back with rope in one hand Azuru watching the whole spectacle and actually feeling a bit bad... for a second he got over it though turning back to his group to a circle of inviting and encouraging smiles. The first one to greet Azuru was Zandra hands folded behind her back as she twiddled her shoulders, saying with joy and embrace just vibrating off her like an expensive perfume "so Azuru how does it feel to be our leader for a second year in a row?" Azuru smiling as he responded "well Zandra – oh hold on"

Azuru then screeched like some sort of animal giving its last cry before stepping into the other world. Zandra's face scrunched and folded up with confusion as she even dared to question him "what the hell was that?" oh sorry about that you might not have understood that because I don't speak very fluent hippo but don't worry I'll work on it!" Azuru's pearly white chaotic smile the biggest thing on Azuru's face, veins popping out and pulsing in Zandra's neck as she tried to bottle all of her rage and urge to absolutely tear Azuru apart and send limbs flying up into the air. Every exhale she took was like she was practically breathing fire keeping calm until all of her anger just boiled over worse than a tea past its time on the stove, finally pouncing at Azuru but Azuru simply stepped back so casually with his hands tucked inside his pockets and still smiling so big he squinted his eyes. Duke and Maximus caught her in mid – air by the arms pulling her away they we're practically security in a concert as she kicked, swiped her vicious claws, screeched, and breathed furious flames.

Ryker and Kenjin immediately coming up to Azuru afterwards, Ryker bumping fists with Azuru as he said "congrats man I'm proud of you – coming a long way from that punk that literally everyone on this team hated. But honestly no one deserves the leader title more than you" Kenjin bowing in his individual knowledge of respect, Azuru perfectly mirroring it back to him as Kenjin began to speak "I agree the wisdom you gathered along all our hard fought battles is very admirable and the way you fought it is no wonder you are the head of our family." Azuru smirking before he let out a scoff "yeah I remember you hated my guts haha I would piss you off on purpose Ryker aw man highlight of my day right there haha. Okay when you mean wisdom do you mean punches? Because if that's the case then yes Kenjin unfortunately I did pick up a lot of wisdom... an awful, traumatizing, will – shattering amount of wisdom... places wisdom shouldn't be... I don't want to talk about it!"

Azuru feeling the softest tap in his entire existence like a feather was punching his shoulder. He knew his whole team too well so he knew exactly who it was before he even turned "hey what's up Angel" Angel in a passive and shy stance glancing up at Azuru from time to time, but then going back to his usual direction of the ground. He spoke at a volume just above whispering to at least hold a conversation with Azuru.

"I –I am glad and rreally happy for you Azuru and h-h-honored that you're my leader." Azuru smile exploded all over his face spreading past cheek to cheek as he slammed his hand on top of Angel's shoulder. Almost giving the delicate boy a jump scare with the amount of embrace Azuru just pounded him with even the height of his voice earth quake Angel. "Thanks man! I really appreciate it! Hey you have been becoming more outgoing lately huh? – Yeah I could tell because normally you would have waited for me to walk in front of you instead of coming up to me that's great bro!"

A smile began quivering to a curve on Angel's face Azuru was pulling him out of his shell like the winning team in a tug of war whether he liked it or not. Angel lit up with excitement as his pace for conversation doubled "I –I have been trying harder to talk to people, not easy but I'll get there yeah what I really wanted to say was I want to thank –"

Azuru's attention was pulled away for a mere moment as he sensed a familiar energy. Pretty soon his sight was also stolen from Angel, peeking his head out the sides of Angel, and then over Angel as he began searching for this familiar aura then swiftly Azuru's eyes caught it like a child chasing down a majestic butterfly fluttering by in his front yard. His shrine suddenly flickered as his spiral pool got weak; he gulped and took a quick exhale patting Angel on the back as he dismissed himself.

Angel's glass heart like being dropped from a sky scrapper he even had the most disappointed tone in his voice as he spoke to himself. "I was sharing just like Emily told me to do... I should have just stayed in my corner" Azuru calling over his shoulder as he walked away "sorry Angel I gotta tend to something – but I promise we will finish this convo some other time maybe with a little less noise Kay?" Angel no longer was completely devastated like a budding green seed sticking out of the ground after a forest fire Angel's hopes raised up from the dead and his once saddened frown picked back up to an eager grin. He waived Azuru goodbye "some other time? Maybe I can get better at sharing within that time, challenge accepted! I know how seriously Azuru takes his promises too!"

Azuru like the longest nerve wrecking, confidence shattering, will power draining trek towards the back of the wall, his spiral pool being tied in knots as he got closer and closer to his target. Finally coming to an abrupt halt Azuru tucked his hands into his pockets poising up his right knee to balance his leg on his tip toes, typical Azuru stance his smile like a razor – edged blade, so sharp and deadly to the observing eyes Azuru trying to keep the anxiety and flustered feelings from leaking into his voice.

"Hey... s-so you um come here often Serenity?" Serenity with her arms crossed over her chest as she inspected Azuru with an interested and watchful pair. Her slight grin showed she wasn't going to shoo Azuru away, she might even let him stay for a minute or two, and she certainly wasn't going to push Azuru out of his probably only window of opportunity. She responded with an inflection dipped in sarcasm "well I do come here for mission briefings, assignments, team meetings, and all that sort of stuff which is about 90% of my life so umm-" Azuru completing her sentence with his brilliant mind reading powers. "So not very much right? – Sorry for asking such an irrelevant question" Azuru managing to dig out a giggle from Serenity, her hand covering her mouth as she fell for Azuru's desert dry humor. Azuru's smile widening as he turned his charm to overload Serenity bringing the conversation back "don't worry you broke the glacier that was separating us haha – so why did you Angel to come over here? He looked like he was telling you something important – oh and congratulations by the way I really am very proud of you for all your hard work. Sorry to be so generic about it though haha" Serenity mirroring Azuru's effect as he chuckled at her wits and presentation but immediately answering her

"I told him we could talk about it with less people around because it seemed serious and well what kind of guest would I be if I didn't individually thank my hosts for the party? If you really don't want to be so generic a hug would fix that – I haven't received a single one on my anniversary – so you would be my first. All I ask is that you be gentle" Serenity blushing and reddening up like a popped pimple quick to exclaim "AZURU DON'T SAY IT LIKE THAT! WHAT KIND OF GIRL DO YOU THINK I AM?!" Azuru with his arms opened up wide as he preparedly positioned himself for the impact of his hug. "A pretty cruel one if I don't receive that hug" Serenity's face only getting brighter and brighter more red spreading from cheek to cheek. Still had plenty of exclamation to shout from the heavens with "OF COURSE I WAS GONNA GIVE YOU A HUG! I JUST DIDN'T LIKE THE WAY YOU WORDED THINGS!!!" She finally began walking towards Azuru, and Azuru in his mind rejoicing like equal rights, over throwing of a government, the miraculous touchdown, "she said yes!" and of course "I just won the lottery" all clumped and molded into one single celebration. He howled and clamored to himself surprised this entire kingdom didn't hear it "**AFTER 20 YEARS!! WE HAVE FINALLY TAKEN OUR FIRST STEP INTO THIS THOUSAND MILE JOURNEY!!!! REJOICE MEN REJOICE!!**-... oh no he we freaking go!"

Just as Serenity also opened up her arms to lock bodies with Azuru, already shutting her eyes and tilting her head to the side so it could ever so softly pillow against Azuru's chest. It all happened in slow motion in Azuru's eyes; he heard furious stomping sounding like each step just demolished the floor with their iron toed boots. Azuru grinded his teeth for a second only letting out a "tsk" of frustration lifting up his index finger in front of Serenity as he ever so well mannered implied "excuse me one moment."

Azuru's neck began to bend backwards and his feet we're lifting off the ground as he seemed to bend physics like a plastic spoon, Azuru's right foot snapping forward so fiercely putting levers of catapults, that launch balls of fire as their job, to shame. As his leg whipped on top of a pair of wrists in an "X" shape blocking Azuru's steel mace –like foot; sending the body sliding back as he lowered his forearms from his face. The most notable piece from this very rude figure was the heavy – duty lively smile and excitement in voice.

"We're you distracted Azuru? You should have been able to break through my guard – maybe your skills are getting dull, or even more so maybe they we're never really as great as everyone says". Azuru landing back on his feet like he only took a small hop off the floor - replying with such confidence and arrogance "nah I just didn't wanna hurt you! Your stature does look pretty fragile after all! – That was just a little love tap Eminent. It is my duty to make sure my subordinates don't get hurt" Eminent growling as he was about to charge forward at Azuru, Maximus acting like the brick wall putting up his left hand out to Eminent's chest holding him back and in the other arm he had a kicking and screaming Zandra. Who was clawing the air trying to break away and get to Azuru, being completely useless against this mountain of muscle that was the absolute fortitude of defense. Azuru suddenly began looking around and said with a hint of wonder and disappointment at the exact same time "w-where did you go Serenity?" Looking over his shoulder to see Serenity leaning back on the wall she started from saying with spite spewing out like venom. "You would rather fight than touch me then go ahead and fight!"

Azuru at a loss for words as once again his opportunity as an eel passing right through his fingers. Trying to redeem himself was completely pitiful "no –no! I was protecting you – protecting us! – You can totally go back to giving me that hug now!"

Serenity didn't even give him the benefit of eye contact – not even looking in his direction Azuru's chances shattering like an expensive vase right before his very eyes. Only a sigh could express his entire anguish and heart ache, turning back to the action seeing as at least he has a punching bag to take his aggression out on. Maximus calling over his shoulder as he struggles to keep back the bull – like Eminent but still not using than his one arm "A-Azuru I never g-got tt-to tell you I am very ecstatic for you-your second year as leader –I coul-couldn't be happier for you!" Azuru's smile knowing no inappropriate times as it decided this was its time to shine Azuru wrapping his arm over Maximus's shoulder and stuck out his tongue in front of Eminent and Zandra who both turned blood red to Azuru's childish tactics of war. They reached for Azuru's face but he pulled it just out of their range in such a laid back and relaxed, somewhat oblivious voice "why you so formal Maximus?! Get loose feet bro you gotta kick off your Sunday shoes! Don't make me bring Kevin Bacon 'cause you know I am just looking for an excuse to bring him up here now!" Azuru riling them up even more, making it much more difficult for Maximus to handle them as he grunted with a bit of strain as Azuru fiddled with his tie "A-zuru stop agitating them!! Also for your information, I am wearing my wacky tie! For celebratory occasions!!! – So no need to kick off any Sunday shoes or anything!"

Azuru now noogying their skulls, twisting his fists into the top of their skulls as they began to tremble with volcanic rage still not acknowledging that he is even doing anything Azuru replied "really?! It looks just like the other ones and dude don't ever say my Sunday shoes aren't invited –I'll let you slide this time but this is your last warning – also what's so special about the tie? Hey have you seen Duke and Emily by any chance either? They still haven't congratulated me – how ungrateful and selfish of them to not think of their awesome, handsome, hard working, leader haha oh and Angelo too! I guess" "right here"

Azuru still not stopping his childish tactics as he creaked his head to the far left to see them coming from the far left. Duke tilting his flimsy straw hat upward to banish the shadows from his face, Emily with a stern and serious look on her face as she drug the incapacitated Angelo, looking like a baby caterpillar with all those ropes, wrapped around him and intertwined around his body. Even gagged so that his microphone voice could no longer be spread amongst the people Emily drug him as if he we're just a simple child pulling a little red wagon through the streets. Yeah she also had the look like she had just about enough of all the playful nonsense – at a party seriously?! Waaaaaay too soon to take a dump on this party party pooper! As soon as everyone saw that fire broiling in her eyes they knew like instinct they all had to fall in that included her own leader Azuru. As she demanded "everyone line up!" all forming a half circle with Angelo and Duke helping her fill in the gaps she then continued without hesitation "Azuru I need to speak to you about the team's status and progress later Duke you as well." Duke shooting out two fingers to Azuru and Azuru bobbed hid head up to him in acknowledgment "now we are still one spot short and I know this affects the team in a big way so we are going to go over-"just then there was a knock at the door that felt like a pen drop in a silent room a partygoer quickly running over to answer it as it completely cut in the middle of Emily's mission briefing. Emily was extremely irritated by this probably late guest who had the worst timing, as she shouted "WHO IS IT?!" The crowd of people stepping to the side to reveal a body that illuminated like ten thousand suns compacted into one single light bulb Emily even shielding her face as she said with surprise "oh! It's you ha I guess he is worthy to be on the team Azuru! He made it in the predicted time – well I guess now we can really start now that you're here"

Now That You're Here

Divine Intervention

Every single pair of eyes we're drawn to this young man, just the gigantic mammoth in the room. Everyone's attention was gravitated to him he might as well have been a celebrity; but his awkward and shy energy clearly spoke for him with bold letters as it screamed he was not the type to crave or even think of desiring the spotlight. The way he illuminated silver, gray, and white blasting off him with gold sprinkled on him simultaneously, with all this scintillate aura he could possibly lighten up the entire black void of space with dazzling radiance.

This walking light bulb this shining breathing star was trembling ever so delicately as he would glance around at the piercing eyes of the entire crowd that circled him so he kept his head to the ground. Emily with her almost magnetic spirituality and personality made him feel treasured and even valued even the manner of her voice simply brightened his soul. "No need to be scared now that you're a part of the team come on over here!"

The faint hearted young man looked around to see the masses, who once had blank and sort of unwelcoming expressions on their faces as they questioned this boy, who he was?, where he came from?, and what we're his credentials all with their crushing glares. Now began to shift and transform into smiles as they rose from the conflux even cheers, applause, woos and personal shout outs "welcome to the divine intervention!" "We can win this war with the young master!" he even could hear whispers and murmurs from the crowd meant to be underneath the breath.

"So this is the rookie that was talked about as a possible new recruit? – if he survived the training of course" he was being cloudburst with all of this as he continued to walk forward. The path of clustered people opening right up for this young man to walk by this blossoming youth still very shy began to swell up with joy and pure happiness inside. Not confident enough to show it of course but absolutely acknowledging the crowd with a heroic smirk and an agreeing nod here and there until he finally came to the nearly completed circle. The fledgling gulped before at least trying to mask his nervousness, Emily looking down at her clip board then said "okay now I think I remember your name but just to be sure let me check up on the notes I wrote down on the day of your first meeting just in case."

Flipping through pages like a cartoonist's completed flipbook but Azuru with his arms crossed over his chest, stature so intimidating, voice so rock solid he didn't even need sight as he spoke with his eyes shut "we don't need that! I remember his name!" The freshmen feeling so honored and touched that Azuru the one who trained him remembered his name, his sensei had respect for his disciple. The freshmen gave an affectionate and almost choked up smile as Azuru's eyes shot open he then declared with so much conviction in his voice his word was law and should be engraved into stone "HIS NAME IS OMAR!"

The youngling knew it was just too good to be true, his head drooping down as he let out a disappointing sigh and his lower lip pouted out. This was not his name Azuru out of the whole entire team spent the most time with him and not even he remembered his name, Ryker injecting his belief as well "No Azuru you're so insensitive, his name is Olimar how could you forget?!"

The newish yougin's eyes we're just stuck to the ground at this point with his head just dropping down further drooping closer to the ground another wrong guess "you are both wrong!"Azuru and Ryker turning their heads to the wise and "all knowing" Kenjin who had his arms tucked into his sleeves Azuru wailed this as false –well in his own way "BULL!" Ryker doubling onto his semi- statement "yeah Kenjin that's a bunch of bovine feces – what's his name if you're so smart alecky?!" Kenjin with a calm and cool demeanor not letting the rowdiest of the pack get to him with an expression of pure tranquil on his face "of course obviously his name is Octavio I know I have heard him be introduced as this before." The young buck's hands rubbing his temples as he began to build up a bit irritation "my name is not that long! And there is no "O" where are you guys getting these names from?!"

Maximus scratching the back of his head as he said "um sorry I have no idea – nothing comes to mind." The divine child a bit let down but it was a soft shove compared to these hooks of agony that these insensitive monsters we're throwing. The spotlight began to sparkle once again onto the harbinger of justice as he pointed his finger up towards the heavens... probably taking a few classes from Houdini on escaping traps as he just released himself from his entrapment. With responsibility, duty and heroic burden weighed into his brave words exclaiming

"I WILL DO IT! – I WILL RENAME HIM from this day fourth young upholding righteous lad you shall be known as JUSTICE JR. FOR I AM THE SENIOR OVER SHEER OF JUSTICE IT IS MY GOAL OF EXISTENCE TO PURSUE, INSTILL AND DISTRIBUTE JUSTICE FOR ALL! – WITH JJ BY MY SIDE WE SHALL NOT FAIL!!" A look of complete and utter devastation in the form of disappointment evolved to a blank sight pointed at Angelo as he spoke to himself "justice jr.?" That is not even creative" in the shadows of Angelo's blinding spot light, creped Azuru and Ryker so devious and mischievous as they snuck right

Azuru springing up in front of Angelo to take his invitation to fight for justice. Placing his hand on his shoulder as he said with admiration and pride sparkling in his eyes "I want to join you"

Angelo so moved as tears began to rim around the edges of his eyelids before he could rejoice by saying his leader's name Azuru's smile of respect cracked to reveal a truly wicked intended being conjured that poured out into his sentence. "IN HELL!!"

An act of absolute betrayal the crushing blow reflecting in Angelo's eyes as his heart disintegrated right before him. Azuru pushed with both hands against Angelo's chest the world was spinning and coming apart as he began to descend to the ground but while he fell like a star, he also felt a tripping pulling from behind his knee caps as he slipped backwards. He looked down with eyes wide with utter astonishment, seeing Ryker on hands and knees behind him also with a chaotic grin on his face. Angelo said with such pain and anguish strained in his voice "the injustice" but Angelo did not just fall onto the cold, hard, and unforgiving floor he fell into a black circular hole that swallowed half of his body only leaving his legs sticking out. Ryker got up off the ground to stand beside Azuru they both beheld the circular prison that Angelo was now trapped in –having "party trash can" labeled on with golden tape.

Not giving a moments' rest or any hesitation at all, they began furiously kicking it like two fearsome soccer players fighting over the ball. The youngster with complete shock and distress in his tone as he shouted "YOU GUYS ARE SAVAGES!! –WHAT ARE YOU DOING THAT IS YOUR FRIEND!!" Azuru looking up at him while still able to maintain his kicking pattern "whoa whoa whoa that is a big assumption there kid back it up!"

Ryker having a pondering visage asking Azuru "hey Azuru I'm thinking about that line you said 'I want to join you! – in hell' didn't really make sense" "yeah I get you but try and tell me that it didn't sound cool!" Ryker nodding his head in agreement "yeah not gonna lie it did" a muffled and stifled screaming came from inside the tortuous can "MY JUSTICE SHALL NEVER BE SILENCED!!" Azuru shouting in rage "quiet you!!!" as he intensified his punting to just blunt stomps. Angel in back of Azuru and Ryker finally going to speak up he had the answer to the question everyone was searching for "um –guys I know his name it's –"

Angel once again overshadowed by a confident speaker this time it happened to be Eminent as he shouted over. "Why don't we just call him "newbie" and be done with it?!" Before the young man could even have a reaction to that, Azuru shouted back "why don't we just call you "stupid" and be done with it?!" Eminent growling before charging to Azuru only to be interrupted by an Angelo – filled trash can that tackled right into him, ramming right into his chest.

The poor youngster is beginning to become traumatized as he watched all of this fighting and senseless violence he was almost frozen by shock. Honestly at this point starting to have second thoughts about this rash, abrasive, rude, crude, aggressive, headstrong team.

Angelo now standing up with cake splattered on top of his head and armor, right alongside Eminent who was barking his head off at Azuru; Azuru right across Eminent not at all phased by his shouts, yells, and exclamations or bursts of anger, hands dug in his pockets as he slouched back laughing at his and Angelo's anger Ryker right next to him on a golden portable playable device. His thumbs twiddling as he smashed the buttons on his child plaything, Kenjin walking in the middle of these four like he was the special referee going to make a game changing decision. Maximus rushing in afterwards standing in the way of Eminent's ticked off team, scratching the back of his head as he a bit hesitant to halt Eminent from going any further. Angel in the back of everyone peddling his foot back and forth as he kicked the invisible, air consisted can, pouting as he said with a dash of displeasure in his murmur "I knew his name."

A cough was heard from Serenity who was hanging back from all the rowdy action, it was merely a cough that just slipped out. But she soon regretted her natural bodily function as time seemed to stop just for her, all the arguing heads that seemed to be divulged into their battle where they we're ripping each other a part limb from limb. Suddenly took a treaty pause all to focus on what Serenity had to say, or to give her an opportunity to say something the floor was hers regardless. Azuru stopped mid –laugh, Ryker took his eyes off his gaming device that we're glued intensely a matter of moments ago, Eminent put a lid onto his anger, Kenjin took a brief moment from his peace - making to give Serenity his full attention. Angelo and Maximus's heads turning directly to her while Maximus stood in front of Angelo with his arms spread wide open (creed not included) Serenity's eyes swelling up with inept and just being flat out uncomfortable. From all the vision pinpointed towards her, she could feel the red hot lasers all targeting her. All these lethal guns we're ready to fire even the freshmen was amongst these gazing army. Serenity's eyes like a tennis ball in a professional game going back and forth inside of her sockets until she gripped her own hands and scrunched her body in a stiff stance. She said with a pinch of fear, a bit nervous and definitely ungracefully "I-I don't know his name – II was just coughing – I wouldn't want to call him something that isn't his name so sorry."

You know what I take back what I said about her being ungraceful because she handled that very swiftly. Everyone just nodding to acknowledge and take in this latest info, picking up where they left off arguing and tearing each other's heads off; Serenity just let out a sigh as she said "men are the worst"

The kind hearted young man a bit down casted as he said "disappointed that she did not know my name either but what she said actually did make me feel better." Duke in the back of the entire calamity tilting his hat upwards so he could get a full scale view of the mayhem steadily building more and more rampage by the moment, fire beginning to spark from Azuru his mischievous grin starting to twitch with excitement it was like loading the bullets into his shotgun and cocking it back. The urge to run rampid becoming uncontrollable, his hands slowly coming out of his pockets, Ryker paid the whole entire world no mind because the whole entire world was in his hands literally! That stupid contraption was the whole wide world to him; a silver aura began flowing off from the ground from beneath Kenjin who still softly had his eyes closed but we're tingling with each split second that flew by. Maximus was rolling up his sleeves as he saw that Eminent was reaching for his gun that was holstered fingers squirming on top of his belt of the pop - off holster, steam started to slowly resonate off of Angelo's hands as he clamored in fury.

The youngster suddenly started to feel the pressure in the room begin to crush him as it arose from all these combatants. He could barely find the strength to breath he became completely paralyzed, gripping his own throat as he shook and trembled he literally felt like a trash compacter was looming over him and crumpling him into a ball. How could this even be possible?! How could the pressure of someone's intimidation begin to smash someone into pieces? The youngster trying to dig deep down inside himself to find the strength to stay up on his feet and not faint in front of everyone especially on his first day not even able to last one minute with the elites. But how could he solidify his own footing as the world spun like a merry go round in his head, he so desperately wanted to just fall onto his knees, but he was finally rewarded for his persistence. A hand on his shoulder although it was just a pat on the back this simple stroke must've had healing abilities because just like that! The young man was able to stand up without feeling demolished, his vision was stilled, and the air once again became breathable and thinned out.

He then heard a voice from right next to him a frail elderly gentle voice lectured out to him "looks likes someone skipped the divine part of their training." The young man nervous and a bit hesitant to give a direct answer only able to stutter out a jumble but a playful laugh calmed him as she insisted "I'm just kidding kitten – these guys are all on another level when it comes to energy and could crush enemies with their presence alone so it will take some getting used to."

The youngster simply nodded his head being filled in on why he suddenly felt this way thanks to this elderly stranger who proceeded to stroke her cat. (Just curious to see where your mind went for a minute) he then began glancing over at his hand flipping it over side from side as he tried to see where this warmth was coming from what changes have occurred. Locking onto the glowing vibrancy coming off of his hand as he felt it flow feeling the power of the divine energy like a fire traveling through his veins, Duke somehow able to squall over them all as he shouted over to the youngster. "CAN'T WE JUST CALL YOU BOBBY?!"

Azuru reflecting everyone's thoughts and feelings as he scrunched the left side of his face, raising the eyebrow over his right eye as high as possible, everyone literally having the exact same look on their faces as they all in unison, finally ending the war between them to declare ware fare onto Duke with these very words, "WHY BOBBY?!" Duke the big country in this situation taking them all on. "Well I like the name "Bobby"....Bobby"

Azuru responding first with his typical witty assaultive attitude "well if that's the case then we should name him Azuru Jr. since Azuru is the best name ever created and he has to be second best of course! No doubt he will be 10x more handsome, powerful and memorable with that name". The juvenile couldn't help but image himself as a miniature Azuru, wild spiky blue bed hair, with eyes that just said "I really don't want to be here" with a matching attitude. The young man shaking the intrusive thought from his mind, rejecting the idea that strayed too far away from the person that he is; Azuru scoffing in outrage as he shouted over at the young man "how dare you reject your identity Azuru Jr. after all I've done for you! You ingrate.... You also smell bad didn't wanna tell you earlier but I overlooked it because I thought you we're my friend." The youngster quick to sniff his own body to make sure this was only a fib made from Azuru's scorn he then instantly flailed up his arms as he shouted his apologies, Azuru nodding his head in acknowledgment Kenjin deciding to cut in. "I think "Hoshi" is a very nice name and would suit him very well" Eminent scoffing up a storm as he threw out a name of his own "name him something manly at least! So I won't be ashamed to admit he is on the same team as me! – Something like "Chuck" or "Liam" yeah those are conquering names!"

Ryker sticking out his tongue as he only paid attention to the screen "you should name him "Flappy" in honor of this game!" Angelo pointing to the sky as he roared out "come with me JJ we shall purge all the evil on Earth!" "Cornelius is a very respectable name it has some prestige to it I believe" Maximus inserting, now names we're just flying out in random order from have fun finding out which person they're coming from. "Azuru's Eagle!" "Thomas!" "Jack!" "Thunder cat!" "JJ I TELL YOU IS HIS NAME!!" "Ryu can be quite fierce" "TOM TOM" "SAMUEL!" "Azuru Jr. Jr. Junior is now his middle name!" "Junior Junior Junior! Junior is all of his names!" "JJ! JJ! JJ!" "Bill is nice and common-""Haggusworth a nice weird name so he can fit in!" "You should name him Gerald like my cat" "get outta here Ms. Neko you have horrible cat names! Okay Super Azuru Jr. Not settling for any less!!" an intense shoot out type stare down between all of the gladiators in this fierce battle the new recruit being the prize. Completely lost, disoriented, confused, scared a little bit of everything rolled into a ball, all this crossing of swords left the newbie dizzy and with a head ache. Then like a miracle granted from all his prayers the rookie was secretly chanting in his mind;

shattered the entire extreme high spirited debate "HIS NAME IS AMAR YOU DUMBASSES!!!"

The rookie was in a state of shock and amazement it was like lightning struck him, he was inside an ocean of disbelief. He could not get over the fact that someone actually knew his name, excluding the foul language she was like an angel; the armature from my knowledge goes by the name Amar, also adding in I am apparently a dumbass for not knowing WELL SOOOORRRY! THE BOY HAS AS MUCH PERSONALITY AS A BRICK WITH A PARTY HAT ON!

Anyways Amar had a case of tunnel vision as she walked through the battlefield of names, completely surrounded by clouds, stunning Amar in enchantment losing himself in the sight of her. He then whispered to himself with disbelief as deep as the grand canyon, the sole purpose of his training and light at the of the tunnel actually that kept him going even when times were rough not only did she acknowledge him, she kept him in her mind "she remembered me" was all that Amar could put into words as the past rolling like a film reel. Amar was incredibly timid behind Emily like a new kid coming into class and being introduced to everyone "everyone this is the newest addition to the team Amar say hi and everyone...don't eat him alive okay?" Everyone in concordance "hi Amar" Amar even more apprehensive then he is now. Picking up his head to glance at each person individually and quickly putting his head back down. But once he laid eyes on "her"

His entire world at that moment came to an abrupt halt; his definition of beauty was redefined at that very moment. He was so stunned that he was practically gawking but this didn't bother "her" she found nothing wrong with this even smiling at the pure raw emotions of Amar; walking over to him and his fairly new shrine began blinking, his spiral pool twisting into knots, and he could not control his Divinity distribution leaking out from his forehead and underneath his arm pits.

She was so angelic not a single ulterior motive behind this as she said to Amar and her essence alone made him want to faint; he desperately fought it when was he going to get another chance to talk to her again?! "Is there some meaning behind your name Amar?" Amar's tongue so tied he could barely slip the words out but suddenly Amar was hearing an echo of thoughts as he was just reminiscing "it means eternal love in his homeland!"

Amar snapping out of his miniature flash back to real time events; and she was still here after all this time with hands on her hips as she punched holes into these bozos. Amar left in wholly astonishment as he murmured to himself "she even remembered that part?" Azuru trying to save his own skin standing next to Amar's angel mirroring her stance as he also growled "yeah you dumbasses! I told you his name was Amar!!" She shook her head and rolled her eyes as the rest of the group was flabbergasted Ryker even a bit disappointed screamed out "But Azuru if my ass did have a brain I am pretty sure it would be pretty smart don't you think so?!" "That may be true but where would you sit? Now that you have a smart ass?" "My gosh! You're right Azuru" "so for your benefit I will call you dumbass!" "Thank you Azuru" "no problem dumbass."

Emily finally coming up from behind while still not taken her eyes off her clipboard with a mountain of papers behind her; she confirmed "I found the notes and Zandra is right his name is Amar woo! It was buried deep in there but yeah that's his name moving on!" Azuru now giving Amar a crooked eye, a more piercing stare like he was gazing right through him he then demanded_"hey Omar! Come here I need to check something out!" Amar sighing with disappointment well at least the very important ones remembered him. He dragged himself forward to Azuru, who drew nearer, Azuru's hawk eye was analyzing his entire figure but there was something of about Amar that he just couldn't put his finger on. His left index finger underneath his chin as his thumb touched the side rim of his jaw as he kept wondering what about him has change in the past year. Because of the cloak, all that was visible was his stature. Amar was a medium built frame he wasn't the bulkiest, from what was available for the eyes to capture but there was of course room for improvement. Everything that wasn't his face and even parts of his face was shaded by the shadows of the hood that he wore. This cloth that dragged on the floor, like the tail to a king's robe, looked to be cut from a glistening star by the way it illuminated the entire room just a precious pearl shining brighter than all the others.

Resembling sprinkles of diamond dust speckled and sprayed onto the cape twinkling and sparkling, bits of silver and crystal engraved and intertwined. The cape - robe in a whole glowed more radiance than the ground they we're standing on that reminded them they we're no longer on Earth. Azuru yanking off his hood that shrouded his face throwing it off as if it we're some inferior rag to reveal Amar's space black hair, gently spiked but this looking to be the natural style of his hair. His face upon first glance; well for women it would be to hug and kiss him due to how pure he looked, clear face smooth texture, not a single feature out of place, and with the most perfect ratio of tan –it's no wonder "the knockout" Zandra would even give him a second of her precious and valuable time and for the guys... well probably dunking him in a trash can because of how innocent he looks.

He just has this harmless aura coming off him but he did not have a completely youthful and underdeveloped face, it was a bit chiseled, may be that is what Azuru was talking about when he says he seemed different. Azuru gripped him by his hair like a child in dire need of discipline as he twisted and turned Amar's face around like he was a doll or some sort of manikin. He began to realize his chin was not iron but certainly pretty strong jaw line and cheekbones, pretty masculine as well but he still had some growing to do. He was a young pup still a guppy just getting into the water, trying to jerk his head back or maybe pull away from Azuru's grasp he still had no idea of what was next to come. What Azuru was even checking for was way beyond him, tilting his head to the left and stared at him up and down scanning him entirely, then tilting his head to the right maybe a different angle would help him better find just exactly what he was searching for. Amar standing so stiff he didn't want to disturb Azuru's hunt for this invisible treasure no matter how many hairs he pulled on as he held Amar in place, now tugging his head to the left then to the right to maybe help him.

Zandra burning up as Azuru flopped around Amar's neck as she blurted out "geeze Azuru! Why don't you just take pictures?! You could take it with you to your private time!" This comment not stopping or dampening Azuru's investigation he simply, half effort answered her back while still inspecting "no... because then you'll just steal them anyway so you can have your private time! We won't see you for a couple days and you'll probably be in a wheelchair". Zandra really becoming a ripe tomato with that one as Azuru chuckled at his own joke, Ryker, Kenjin, Eminent, Angelo, and Duke at least got a chuckle out of it knowing exactly where Azuru was coming from. The pure ones like Angel, Maximus, and Amar it just flew right over their heads and as for Serenity and Emily; their hands we're just slammed against their foreheads as they groaned in disappointment, even adding in a shake.

Azuru not finding what he was looking for stepping back as he threw Amar's head back and let him have control again stepping back as he just shrugged and went back to crossing his arms over his chest. He then threw out possible theories "I don't know I know I felt it as soon as you walked in – maybe it's that you're not such a little girl like when we we're training, maybe you hit puberty, or maybe it's your energy. I don't know all I know is something is different about you could be something good could be something bad who knows? Who cares?"

Emily finally butting in and cutting the shenanigans off like an imperfect branch on a perfect tree "okay everyone this is Amar, Amar welcome back to our team we know you had a little "bad experience" last time on your first day but this time is different. Very different so make yourself comfortable on our team and this is a reintroduction to the Divine Intervention." Amar's shrine blinking as he realized all jokes and comedy aside this team was the absolute real deal; this militia sized army was the only thing standing against a planet full of darkness and they managed to stalemate the entire legions of evil. It hit him like a baseball bat to the face this team had the entire weight of the world on their shoulders, so with much gratitude and appreciation stuffed into these heart – filled words "thank you so much it truly means the world to me to be honored with a spot on the team".

Everyone taken back and a smidgen of surprise where did all of this gratefulness come from? Even Emily had an oddball look in her eyes she replied "you know we didn't let you join right? You we're handpicked you did all the work to get here all we did was give you what you deserve you should be thanking yourself."Amar's eyes widening with recognition as he finally became aware of the truth, this only made his shrine sparkle a bit brighter as he got weak in the knees.

With introductions finally over Emily got right down to it "alright everyone as you all know there has been A LOT of evil activity. The demons have been multiplying faster, becoming stronger; more areas are getting swallowed whole by demonic presence, curses and hatred are running amuck making Divinity harder to create while on Earth. The innocence are slowly becoming corrupted, the fallen angels have been striking key points and leaving just before we get there. The false light still has not shown their faces and you know what that means if we have not taken down the true source of the darkness then all this progress will be for nothing! –No head honchos of the dark side have been taken down, we cannot allow them to roam free if we are going to retake Earth, they will just restart the war all over again destroying all of our progress in the process. Negativity is slowly beginning to shift into the rule of Earth, all of the factions are taking big steps forward and if we don't take ours we will without a doubt lose this entire battle that has been waging for thousands of years. Lastly Lucifer is going to surface on Earth I am sure of it if what you said is correct Azuru we cannot lose a single inch or we might lose the entire world to darkness.

We have done our part to light up the world enough to keep him and the rest of his brothers down there, but for how much longer? I feel like he wouldn't have told you what he did Azuru without reason –"

Azuru's eyes so dull as he thought back to that time standing on red hot bedrock, walls of fire surrounding all around Azuru. Bodies of varied sized demons with torn limbs, punctured holes, blue flame blanketing, and crushed bodies scattered all over the floor like a game of 52 pickup. Some mountain sized demonic entities, some demons that we're slightly taller than Azuru as they we're sprawled on the ground, everything in between of every category decorated the entire world of burning embers, bodies' pile driven inside of the roof of this cavern others, half – hanging off of the edge burning in the flames they we're born into. Above Azuru a light shined through this literal inferno in a crater sized hole like the moon glistening moonlight onto the shadows of the night, Azuru backed towards this hole roughly panting with a man thrown over his shoulder but a new army was approaching. Demons looked like humans with blood red skin, blood trailing down their sockets like tears but fire shot out from their eyes and mouth others, we're pure primal beasts bigger than Azuru, some the size of a mammoth all ready to rampage onto Azuru.

The demons so cruel and animalistic to eat the remains of their fallen brothers that we're on the floor; suddenly a stern voice stopped each and every one of them with the mere words they completely froze "Enough! He has shown to be a formidable leave him be!" Like obedient dogs they did as they we're told, Azuru tried to look past the crowd of beasts to see exactly who it was calling the shots, commanding all of these brainless creatures with such authority. The flames stood in the way of Azuru's vision blocking any possible sight he could have gotten, all he could see was a silhouette sitting on a throne so arrogantly not at all worried or concerned; the only noticeable detail that Azuru really was able to pick up on we're the chains that chinked around as he moved his limbs they went all the way to the roof and reached down to what seemed to be the person's wrists. The havoc Azuru was reeking in his home meant absolutely nothing to him he only further proved this as he continued "don't worry your little pretty head boy! We will meet each other on the battlefield I will hang your head on my mantle then! Just give me a couple years" Azuru even exhausted as he was his motor mouth was still running "*pant *pant w-when I see you -o- on the battlefield that –that ass is mine! So you better start polishing and waxing it now!" a chuckle was heard from the ominous silhouette, Azuru turned his back on this hell hole and began moving to light.

Like a bite from the door on the way out, the last word was said "oh and do tell Father I said hi! I do miss him" but Azuru being Azuru he had to have the last word stopping mid – way as he trekked up towards the light. "He is my creator not yours! Keep his name out of your mouth before I rip off your tongue and make you taste your own ass!"

Azuru chuckling at his own comment in present time as he said out loud "I'm funny" Emily continuing her mission information speech; "that was just last year so time is running out for us. We need progress and a lot of it!" Everyone in the room heard the whole status report and Emily metaphorically took a dump on this party. Music stopped, people's optimistic moods we're crumpled up and tossed out the window, heaviness began to weigh onto each individual; Amar's head was just spinning he didn't even know what 99% of the terms Emily used were but as he looked at the faces of everyone there and it was clear as a cloudless day. The stress, anxiety, and even fear was starting to swell up inside all of them, the energy in the room completely shifted and it wasn't just the people in the crowd even Amar's teammates like impending doom was right on their door step. Apprehensive, nervous, hesitant and a bit overwhelmed Amar could read them all like first grade books with pictures.

The only ones who didn't look affected was the serious bearer of bad news Emily, probably because she dealt with it by herself on her own time when she was briefed with this tremendous information.

Azuru was the other who looked bored as ever with his eyes pointed up towards the roof with a belittling tone spoken "that's it? – thought we we're gonna be off much worse". Eyes began moving towards Azuru like he was lassoing each and every one of them, his energy like a vacuum and all the people we're the scraps of a broken will. Azuru was pulling them towards him, Emily with a disciplinary tone and anger mixed in there as well. "This isn't a game Azuru this is serious! This is life or death of trillions of lives". Azuru scoffing up a storm "I know that! They know that! You know that! So it's not something you have to keep repeating! Every punch we throw the fates of each and every person on Earth is at the back of our minds, every time we go out on a mission, every time we return to recharge and meditate, every time we laugh, every time we cry, every time we think of giving up, every time we get up from life knocking us down the thought of them all are at the back of our minds. They don't leave us and there isn't a single person here who doesn't think of that at least one time a day!" It was so silent you could hear light shine from every single shrine in the room; right now Azuru had the attention of every single person in this room. He was like the television screen and they we're the toddlers silently watching;

he has the hopes, dreams, and wills of every single person in his hands right now at this very moment.

Continuing right where he left off "without a doubt there are three times as much - maybe even four times as many demons then there are you guys, yes the fallen angels are extremely crafty and formidable - and yeah we haven't seen the false light yet – whatever! Let me tell each and every one of you right now right now – I would not take those cookie cutters, cheap paper - consisted demons over you guys because I would choose quality over quantity every single time! Just one of you is worth an entire army of them! The false light all they are is a bunch of painted on gold demons wearing white human faces. Their faker than a magician using a toy cell phone to call their gold digging spouse that is wearing the rhinestone ring they got them! They don't know real power! – Real love! The real God!! And the fallen angels, a bunch of cowards that hide in the darkness and have selfish agendas they are trying to complete... I mean I shouldn't have to say anymore about them do you think they could stand toe to toe against a child of God? A warrior of the light? Of course not so they run – look I shouldn't have to tell you just how incredible you all are you all worked to get here! Pulling yourselves out of that vicious hamster wheel of darkness that sends everyone crying to the fake light!

You all asked if there was something more, you all walked different paths, come from different times, and come from different lands, but one thing that connects us together, bonds us like family is we all have the same creator and we all know this. We all have a creator who is desperately been trying to get to his children - we heard him each and every one of us heard him speak to us, as we cried out for help and he brought us all here! Then gave us a new life and everything we need to change the entire world for the better! We have the light beating inside of us – WE HAVE FOUND THE REAL CREATOR SPIRIT; we have with us a love that makes us stronger than any weapon they could conjure in any three of those factions! A fire they can't dose! A bond they can't break! An iron they cannot bend!! A LOVE THEY WILL NEVER STEAL FROM US – that's it I was gonna keep this to myself but here it is! This year... WE WILL DESTROY THE FALLEN ANGELS! I WILL TAKE DOWN BAPHOMET THE GOD OF DEMONS!! WE WILL SHAKE THE FOUNDATION OF THE RHINESTONE HEAVEN! THIS YEAR THE REBOURNE ESSENCES MAKE THEIR GIANT LEAP FORWARD!! I felt like all these things needed to be taken care of and my first year of leader was just to feel everything out. Now that I have, get ready because anyone who slacks it will get left behind!"

Everyone's jaws we're open so wide a baseball could fit into their gaped opening, their eyes wide enough their eyes looked like they could roll right out of their sockets. Each and every pair of sight seers we're locked onto Azuru even his own teammates looked like they had been struck by lightning; they we're absolutely, utterly, completely, definitely speechless. Not even a thought was able to muster up in anyone's brain Amar had a regretful look on his face as he wondered what he had gotten himself into,_Azuru without doubt, regret, and of course fear, crossed his arms over his chest as he stood statue still. Looking around to see the faces of those who we're still trying to wrap their minds around the thought of this humongous obstacle of a goal that they we're going to begin to climb over. Azuru backing up in his declaration for change "if you don't believe in me that's fine – but believe in yourselves because that's what I believe in it's the reason I am able to act so mighty. Because I know the power of our team, I know our limitless potential, our unbound able love, and uncontainable light. You might not think much of yourselves but I do! You guys are the pillars holding up the roof of our temple and I am proud to be your leader!"

The blank, overwhelmed, and surprised faces slowly twitched to ear to ear smiles; applause began breaking through the gigantic mountain of silence, woos, cheers, hoorays and huzzas showered upon Azuru like raining diamonds. Putting a confident and smug smirk on his face as he murmured to himself "I finally reached them" the biggest smiles coming from his team his close knit personal family even managing to flip Emily, the biggest skeptic, frown upside down. Azuru began waving at the crowd as he bid everyone his farewell calling out as he took his leave "I wanna thank everyone who planned this for me and everyone who took the time to come and listen to my insane – ass rant on about goals and what not I need more preparations. Also need to speak to the higher council, once again thank you everyone be safe!" Azuru saw Minerva way in the back and a light bulb went off in his mind as he just remembered reaching into his back pocket to pull out his tiny jar. Pitching it over the crowd and right to her that she instinctively caught a mysterious wonderment look came over her as she read the engravement for some sort of clarification. As soon as she read "pet goat" she quickly looked back up at Azuru to make epiphany filled expression she then made an "ok" with her fingers.

Azuru just nodded his head in acknowledgment and looked back at his team; with his hands in his pockets at first just a blank expression occupied his face. But as the Divine Intervention gathered around to form a circle in front of Azuru, his facial appearance gracefully broke into a smile so big he was squinting. He pulled up his left hand to put up only his index and middle finger as he said "later guys" but before he could even turn his back the team themselves called over "so after that speech that's how you're just gonna leave us?" Azuru stopped in his tracks like an emergency brake on a train turning half ways to see his team take a few steps forward toward him with smiles of admiration, respect, and love. Azuru reflecting their smirks and their feelings right back to them as he came back to them Ryker, being the first one to greet him as he smacked Azuru's hand, like a defiant child who refused to eat dinner, the clap thundered throughout the entire room and turned everyone's heads. Immediately after the slap they hooked each other's arms around and pulled each other for a shoulder shove both chuckling as he said "take care Ryker I'll see you on our next mission don't worry behave though! – Emily's watching you! –I'm not 'cause I really don't care." Ryker snickering as he responded back "I'm the most innocent one here it's that trouble – making Angel that you should be worried about!"

Angel had a half shocked and a half already prepared apologetic face as he questioned a "what?!" but Azuru already there to settle down the distraught golden child. Azuru wasn't able to hold all of his laughter snickers, chuckles, and scoffs leaked out as he patted Angel on his shoulders. "Don't worry Angel you're fine Ryker is just jealous because he's a miniature devil" Angel a little bit relieved as he said with generosity coated words "well if he wants I could teach him to be nice." Azuru laughing at how pure, how innocent, just how honest and kind – hearted was unique to him and him alone, Azuru realizing this within several thoughts is what made him burst out laughing more of amazement than actual humor. Angel lost and distraught as he asked with such self consciousness "what did I say?" Azuru shaking his head as he still giggled and sighed out to push it all out of his system; opening his arms out wide inviting Angel in like a shelter and he was the homeless. Azuru then said with excitement "bring it in man I gotta get going!" A nervous smile creaked across Angel's face scratching his head as he came in to wrap his arms around Azuru and Azuru did the same not holding back an ounce of emotion his tough, macho, ruggedness, was defiantly taking a seat right now. Honestly Azuru didn't care what others thought of him either he made this very clear in this moment but a tsunami of heart wrenching "awwhs" was heard from all around before they released each other and patted him on the back.

A piercing gaze caught Azuru's eye like a new toy poster, him being the child that he is he was gravitated to this. He also didn't break this lock of vision his shoulders stiffened, his muscles tensed, his smile disappeared like a neglective father; biting his lip in anxious excitement, his shoulders swaying forward and the rest of his body following his vision tunneled as he only saw this. Maximus walking into the middle of this mirrored scene on the opposite side was a pair of dominant shoulders oozing intimidation; a drilling stare as well as he didn't see anything that wasn't Azuru either. Just as they got within speaking distance, Maximus truly stepped into the middle of this storm of daunting presences being the wall between them. Azuru smirking as he finally came close enough "don't worry Maximus I think he's cooled down right Eminent?" a short smirk the size of a pinky finger, the closest thing that will ever be a smile on his face, cracked up upon him; a fist launched forward like a torpedo, Azuru's right fist also being shot forward like a cannon ball straight outta the cannon. Maximus exclaiming "I thought you said he was cooled!!" Both fists reached their destination each other's shoulders, landing like pirates on an island Eminent even with a chilled texture in his voice "I am cool... this is just how men say farewell" smoke resonating off each other's shoulders it would be no surprise if both of their bones we're shattered, but not even a flinch of pain was expressed.

They seemed more excited than anything Azuru's grin burning with enthusiasm as he said "so I am more than happy to oblige." Maximus sighing as he shook his head like they spoke a completely different language they began pulling each other's fists from out each other's arms engraving of their knuckles we're carved their arms. The pressure of the impact practically painted a masterpiece, but nothing other than excited smiles we're shown looking like a pair of sadists enjoying the pain they inflicted amongst each other. No other words needed Maximus speaking in a superior tone "you guys could have done a friendly hand shake it doesn't need to be so excessive!" Azuru's attention then switching to Maximus as he just used his punching hand to stick out for a shake still wearing the same aflame smile; you could hear the eagerness in his voice "put 'err there Max!" Maximus taking a second to glance upon his hand simply for cautious reasons and because of his knowledge of Azuru, but of course he didn't want to be rude and reject Azuru's offer. So he met him halfway with his right hand clamping right together and squeezing down upon contact, of course Maximus knew the golden rule of the handshake: the tighter the squeeze the more respect there is and Maximus wanted to show Azuru how much he respected him so of course he added a tin can crushing amount of pressure. Azuru doubled that with a hard iron crushing amount of pressure, Maximus's eyes widening in surprise as he looked down at the clutching lock, then looking up at Azuru's devious smile.

Knowing exactly how to get Maximus's motor going, he was not about to be disrespected by the lack of respect he fell short with, his eyes came alive as he matched Azuru's grip lock the sound of skin tightening like a thunderstorm over head. As the muscles in Maximus's arm began bulging, and the threads on his sleeve on his white polo tearing like a human paper shredder; Azuru's arm getting more and tenser as the muscles pumped the power and energy he needed to win this respectful war. Pretty soon the magnitude of pressure they we're applying could compress steel genders into flimsy wire hangers in a single clasp, the ground beneath them was beginning to shake as now they really began to get into it. Teeth grinding so hard together sparks we're bound to fly and cause a fire in this very room, but like Mother Nature's sudden impulse the eye of the storm passed over with Maximus pulling his hand back. Saying in an embarrassed tone "I see what you mean" Azuru's smirk just growing wider as he explained "it's just the quality of a man it's unavoidable" Azuru throwing up his peace sign as he walked away from Maximus. Kenjin coming into his path Azuru with his casual stance, hands in pockets, slouching back, and boredom eyes he suddenly at a drop of a hat transformed his stance; back erect like a tall tower, palms slapped together and held in front of his chest and his eyes now looking alive.

Kenjin was already in this stance his back not as sturdy as it used to be, but doing the best he can, his palms ever so fragile being held together. His fingers not as ripe and straight as Azuru but nothing else he could do but he stood with such grace and elegance. From Azuru's point of view he was definitely still learning as they both bowed saying in an echoing duet unison "remain safe on your prosperous journey" Azuru picking up his head in playful mischief. Tongue stuck out at Kenjin, Kenjin with his face still towards the ground even eyes closed could still see Azuru as he said with a disciplinary voice "Azuru no peeking and where I grew up they would cut off our tongues if we stuck them out at the elderly." Azuru chuckled before putting his head down for some solid moments of silence before picking their heads up at the same exact time. Kenjin merely stepped to the side out of Azuru's path as Azuru placed his hands back in his pockets as he continued on his way once again for the third or fourth time today.

The lights completely dimmed shadows swallowing everyone, darkness running free sending everyone in a frenzy of... mild discomfort for the inconvenience and confusion, not bothering Azuru at all though, he probably had nocturnal vision. He just kept walking forward unthawed, indifferent to whether or not he could see, he knew what was coming anyway. Picking his head up from the spotlight beaming down a glistening ray of light that looked like it shined straight from the sun itself, no one other than Angelo was able to stand in this position already in his "point to the heavens" pose but he slowly lowered his arm bringing it like the wooden arm in a toll booth. Pointing directly at the already journeying Azuru, a spot light flashed onto him as well this not stopping him either as he trekked forward while Angelo began his words of admiration "you my leader, a head above the rest, climbed from the same mountain as we, you share battles as we, fought your demons as we fought ours, never present or think of yourself higher than others but others higher than you, golden - hearted sleeves, strong iron nerves, unbreakable knuckles and unshatterable resolve, I truly salute you my leader!-" Angelo's feet snapping together as he placed his right hand horizontally over his chest. Looking dead ahead at Azuru who was sharing the same sight, not taking his eyes away as Angelo poured his heart out to him. "I believe every word you say because there can be no justice without trust! – I will follow you to the end of this journey even if it leads us to hell! I have faith that the impossible will become possible, the unreachable will be within our grasp, the indestructible will be shown how weak they truly are. For with you my leader miracles are a given! I am happy to report in that I am excitedly waiting my first mission to turn the tide."

Azuru now standing in front of Angelo the two spotlights becoming an eight, Azuru clacking his heels together like two magnets that we're drawn together; as he slammed his right hand horizontally over his heart like the commanding officer that he was. Looking Angelo dead in the eyes as he said "I will not let you down Lieutenant! Emily will inform you of your next mission no need to worry and also –"Azuru loosened his tight stance back to his more natural relaxed state. His smile glimmering brighter than the light that was above them "thank you... enough with the damn dramatics Shakespeare!" Angelo becoming a tiny bit watery eyed as soon as he heard the words "thank you" but as soon as the rest of the sentence passed through his eardrums he quickly began rubbing the golden stream away with his armor "clinking" against his face. The lights then flickered on to show Azuru already back on his path and standing dead center in the middle like left over road kill was Zandra. Hands on her hips as her legs we're deeply dug into the ground, you had a better chance hand pushing a sky scraper than get her to move one single inch.

Her eyes more furious and fiery than a hawk seeing something messing with her eggs, getting her talons ready to pick their eyes out. Her frown just spelled out there was nothing good about to happen either, Azuru was absolutely oblivious to these warnings of a storm, or he somehow knew how to put a lid onto this volcano. His smirk glistening like a mischievous blade as he didn't flinch, didn't hesitate, stop or walk in another direction, he walked straight regardless heading toward her so walking to his doom basically; stopping in front of her to look down to her, literally not so sure figuratively as she stared eyes blazing up at him. Azuru just scoffed as he put his hand on her head laughing "don't be so pissed! Big brothers are supposed to make their siblings lives a living hell I'm doing the best I can!" Zandra slapping Azuru's hand off her head as if it we're a fly screaming in defiance "I'm not little! I can take care of myself! I have purified my fair share of areas, brought my fair share of souls here to be a part of this army, and slain more than enough of my fair share of demons! I have proven that... I – am .... Not... –you – your "twin rivers of golden streams that glimmered a sparkling silver and crystal began flowing down her cheeks. Her voice becoming flustered with all the emotions that was trying to force its way out "your little sister! Bbecause then th-that means I'm a burden to you!" She rushed to Azuru quicker than the blink of an eye, she tightly wrapped her arms around his body digging her head into his chest her golden tear drops we're already falling from her face "I am not the one who needs to be rescued! YOU'RE MY BROTHER AND I WILL PROTECT YOU TOO!"

Azuru' s smile going ear to ear as he had one arm wrapped around the back of her neck the other was patting her on the head; calming her as he even spoke with an actual tone of maturity – probably had to dig down deep for that one! "Ah sis I get it! You're the symbol of love; you love everyone else and everything so much more than yourself it hurts. That's why you're so hot headed because you're passionate but you're no burden to me, your love gives me strength that is absolutely immeasurable and you already rescued me from being so cold – also gonna throw this out there how is it you're almost as hot headed as me but yet you can be so calculative and so filled with thought process you're weird!" Zandra releasing Azuru as he gently tapped he chin so he could look up at him. "That is why I will never let you get swallowed by darkness again" Zandra brushing off her tears onto her forearm with a smile as he gave her one last pat on the head when she cleared all the glowing illuminative dust around her blurry vision.

Azuru' back was all she saw, Azuru stopped for some reason as he pondered a thought in his head for a second "hmm so I seen and talked to everyone except Serenity, Omar Azuru Jr., Duke and Emily are gonna talk to me about something later so they don't count wonder where Serenity I-"suddenly a pair of so delicately, crafted like master pieces, arms the most beautiful pair that Azuru instinctively knew they belonged to a female. His shrine flickered like Angelo and the crowd fighting over the lights, they we're just so tantalizing as they waved around his neck like an elegant cobra; so smooth, so magnificent, so lip biting, Azuru about to puncture his right now. They finally crossed over each other as they laid on top of his chest Azuru leaking Divinity, as he couldn't control himself, his spiral pool spinning then twisting itself in knots he knew as soon as he seen those fine sculpted appendages but it is just a matter of believing he couldn't even get a single word out from his motor mouth. His face glowing brighter and brighter as the passing seconds flew by; and the arms remained on top of him like the whip crème and cherry topping on his favorite Sunday it only got better with these words "here is the hug you asked for earlier, I also liked what you had to say about us it just made me respect you a bit more."

These words like the words of acceptance from a student's college that he practically killed themselves to get into, like an actor pouring their soul onto their film only to be rewarded with the exact reward they we're striving for. Confirmation the greatest gift Azuru could ever have right now he could feel the side of her face on his back, in his mind right now Azuru was celebrating with his own pack of Azurus each one a precenter that helped make up Azuru to the current wonderful Azuru, that causes the mischief that we love today – don't lie he is probably the only reason why you are still reading this book wanna see what he's gonna do next huh?! Anyways fireworks blowing up in his mind lighting up the midnight sky "18 years" being spelled out with explosions. All the Azurus began to tear apart the dance floor with all their devastating and deadly moves screaming in unison "**woohoo!!!**" that is what is going on the inside but on the outside he was a frozen stuttering mess. "Ss-s-sss- Serenity I-III- how are we doing today – I-I-I-I- uh umm heard the stock market is down darn shame... I – I mean yo – you- y-you l-look – look so beautiful in the moonlight.... NOT THAT A MOON HAS TO BE THERE FOR YOU TO BE BEAUTIFUL! – AND WHEN I SAY BAUTIFUL! I MEAN YOU AS A WHOLE P-P-PERSONALITY AND ALL!! I KNOW HOW YOU HATE IT WHEN PEOPLE ONLY LOOK AT YOUR APPEARANCE I KN-"

Azuru going off into his machine gun mouthed rant with no brakes built in or even thought of Serenity answering each of Azuru's awkward and flustered statements with a "mhmm" "mhmm" "mmhm?" Azuru couldn't see her eyes we're closed and he certainly couldn't hear her trance of hums. Far too busy about what he was doing wrong he didn't take a journey into Serenity's mind like we are about to; it was actually pretty similar to Azuru's, all the different Serenities that made up the enchanting, majestic, beautiful presence that was Serenity. Who was in the form of a concert all screaming with glee as they danced in victory all of their collective styles sent the dance floor to its grave; it had an overdose of "sick" and she had her own frilly and astounding fireworks that lit up the shadows of her mind like the rising sun and with dazzling flames "18 years" was spelled out. They all rejoiced with a final scream a world completely different from the outside, Azuru was still going on about who knows what let's see, a very frantic and rapid "I'M NOT SAYING YOU SHOULDN'T ENTER MS.UNIVERSE CONTEST BUT I'M JUST SAYING THEY WOULDN'T STOP STARING AND I KNOW YOU HATE THAT! – NOT BECAUSE YOU WOULDN'T WIN OR ANYTHING!! – PLUS YOU WOULDN'T SOUND LIKE A COMPLETE MORON WHEN YOU ARE ASKED THOSE MISPLACED QUESTIONS –"so just like when we left him Serenity giving a tranquil and harmonious sigh as she loved the position she was in. But only then did it begin to dawn on her like an alarm going off in her dream, making her realize where she was at; waking up to the blaring alarm being the form of the still rambling Azuru.

Serenity jumped off in distress, embarrassment all over her face in the form of a golden blush, ashamed that she didn't have her emotions properly in check. Azuru even jumping a little bounce in the realization of what just happened cutting his rant in half as he finally bolted his mouth shut. Absolutely no eye contact between them Azuru's face aimed towards the ground as he scratched the back of his head, a glossy gold line lighting up like a light bulb right across his face; Serenity directing her attention to something over her shoulder, even shivering a bit as her entire face low glowed. Both of them stuttered and choked on their own quickened words "I-I'm h-hhappy for you Azuru – ggo-od j-ob" Azuru not taking his eyes up from the ground and Serenity not moving a single inch out of place not wanting to face Azuru as he answered her back "t-tthank you I am happy that you're happy." The tension and awkwardness in the air was so thick it could be cut with a plastic spoon; a tap on Azuru's shoulder wiped away the blush on Azuru's face like marker lines on a white board as he turned around to be facing Amar.

Surprisingly seeing this as an opportunity to jump out of this bear trap that he was about to gnaw his leg off to get out of this; as he even moved Amar a couple steps back grabbing him by the shoulders as he exclaimed "OMAR AZURU JR.! WHAT CAN I DO FOR MY PRECIOUS DISCIPLE?!"

Not even waiting for a response from him just nervously looking back to see if Serenity was angry, as Amar began his statement Azuru sighed in relief. He saw not a single ounce of resentment "it is Amar – the Azuru Jr. part is not included... just Amar please" Azuru with inattentive and uncaring stance as he picked his ear with his pinky nail digging in as Amar spoke, pulling out a crumb of divine light that was crumpled in a ball. He tried to fling it off his nail as Amar continued his concerns but seeing no other way out he began reaching for Amar's sparkling robe; Amar smacking his hand away like he was blocking a deadly attack outraged Amar shouted "Mr. Azuru can you please pay attention?! I have been training for an entire year and although I am grateful for my new found strength, you never even spent any time actually teaching me! – You would just show up beat me to a golden glowing pulp, instruct me on how I can defend myself next assault – that would be completely random by the way – and I would do only slightly better!! – There is so much I do not know! Everything Ms. Emily said! And what you said!! I need more training to get on the same ground as you guys, but hands on this time!!!" Amar's voice getting more and more flustered with each word that roared out Azuru with his arms crossed over his chest and a blank stare as he let Amar say what was on his chest.

Now it was his response "hey! Who came crawling to me begging for me to train his sorry pathetic ass a year ago?! A pup, a guppy, basically a baby! But you we're jaw dropped by what you saw what took place that day! An ocean of demons that we're released by... him... all rushing to you and Zandra and they we're gone as soon as you blunk, but you closed them in the first place because you knew your doom was Eminent! – *sigh* can't believe I used his name – you said you wanted to become stronger! I just got out of my training session I did the same amount of time as you! – My entire world had crashed around me as soon as I stepped back into it and before I could start putting two and two together, I have this little brat basically tugging on my leg. Desperately craving power –"Amar not wanting to hear a single word of this, but for some reason the little time he did spend with Azuru told him that this was his mentoring instincts; giving him the rawest and unadulterated, unaltered source. So he could have a different bar than everyone else a different height for himself than others, and a much lower rock bottom it just gives a new level of strength. Of course this was just Azuru's teaching and his way as a person, so not wanting to waste his master's affection he did not look away, he did not interrupt either this was a lesson in of itself.

Amar remembers that day exactly, even down to the clothing he arrived in, introduction after the incident that left him with a torn and ripped shirt, completely nonexistent one leg of his pants turning it into shorts. The other torn so bad you could see his shins through the holes and rips all the way up to the knee; Divinity water - falling from his left eyebrow completely drowning his left eye trailing down to his jaw line dripping off like a broken faucet. The other eye looking dull and like Amar was phasing in and out of consciousness. He was panting more than he was actually breathing, hunchbacked as his face was aimed to the floor not having enough strength to pick it up. He just managed to catch the fresh out of battle Azuru who had the putrid; sewage toned black blood from his slain demons all over his hands, feet, elbows, and knees even a small amount was splattered on his face like war paint. Tugging on the leg of his pants - with that being the only thing he was able to focus his entire effort onto Azuru. Who slowly creaked his head not even giving him the full turn of his face only giving him the benefit of half.

He glanced over he nearly instantly noticed his right arm completely missing just a massive amount of Divinity was spewing and dripping from the torn out gash. Soaking his right side of his pants, but Azuru still full of rage even though he was concerned he couldn't shake the wrath out of his voice "WHAT?! – leave me alone! I have a lot of work to do!" As Azuru attempted to keep walking Amar gripped tighter to him to keep him stationary and more importantly, from leaving Azuru now turning with more of his face focused on Amar, this time teeth showing along with irritation "what do you want?! – Go get medical attention or you will die dumbass!!" Amar's panting frustrated Azuru as he believed he was wasting his time, he had so many circumstantial things to attend to, absolutely no time to dawdle. Just as Azuru was about to smack his weak hand away Amar with a faint whisper "stronger" but loud enough for Azuru to hear as he viciously asked again "what?! – WHAT DO YOU WANT?!" Amar speaking in conversational tone with enough volume for Azuru to hear his drive and thirst "I ne –need you – to make –m...mme stronger!" Azuru scoffing as he said with a dismissal texture "shut up! You need to lie down before you die!" Amar fully yanking Azuru a few steps towards him Azuru even taken by surprise as he murmured to himself "what the hell?!" He couldn't stop a mischievous smirk from forming onto his face even in this dire situation because right then and there he knew his potential, Amar speaking clearly and fluently "I need to protect! My family! My friends! Her! Everyone!! WHAT GOOD AM I IF I CANNOT DO THAT?!"

Azuru's smile nice and large as he said with such a fiery anxious consisted phrase "I promise you this! If you do not die then without I will make you my student!! Deal?!" Amar giving a flash of a smile before going limp, starting to fall forward but not hitting the ground face first but straight into Azuru's arms, catching him before setting him down – the last part was a blur of darkness. But he still remembers all of it

Azuru was still on his rampage of Amar's morality and feelings "SO I WAS GOOD ON MY PROMISE! Throwing your ass in the chamber to train and no matter how difficult and hellacious you believe your experience to be I want you to know I only gave you a quarter of what I went through! –"Amar's mind just utterly destroyed ONLY A QUARTER?! JUST WHAT KIND OF MONSTER WAS HIS MASTER?! Azuru creaking his neck to pull his face closer into Amar's "but you're right I really didn't train you – that's because I don't train rookies! –Don't have the patience – that being said go find someone else because I'm not going to! You wanted to become stronger and I made you just that – you're welcome! – Oh! And that thing I was thinking about, it was in the back of my mind, but it was still there I figured out what it is! Why I felt something different about you –"Azuru then put his finger right in Amar's face inches from poking his eye out "you found it didn't you?! The last step that I told you, you probably wouldn't complete, you did it didn't you?!"

Amar with head down in shame and the embarrassment was so strong he couldn't lift up his head to look Azuru in the eye as he tried to excuse this achievement that was great in of itself as a lucky fluke "yeah but it only worked that one time... it will not even open anymore when I try to command it" Azuru scoffing a "pfft" cloud up into the air "it has to come from within you just like you did the first time, until you get the same feeling you did when you summoned it in the first place. – Yeah there certainly is something... special about you – there is no level you need to jump up to! You just need the blanks filled in – I can tell you don't fully understand it yet what you have – but you will and when you do – who knows you might make me jealous."

Amar's eyes star struck his body stiff with paralysis although this is the closest he will probably ever get to a compliment from Azuru, he took it none the less; he fully understood Azuru when he said he didn't understand what he had, he put his hand over his chest on top of his shrine. But he was more than willing to day by day take steps to further understand it better, Azuru then patted him on the shoulder as he began to take his leave; although there we're many harsh words that rocked Amar's gentle core, it wasn't meant to hurt him but more to strengthen his resolve. Believe in himself that is exactly what Amar took out of this miniature lesson and proudly watched his master tread off.

Azuru was counting on his fingers while throwing out names simultaneously "okay so Ryker, Angel, Eminent, Maximus, Kenjin, Angelo, Zandra, Serenity, and Amar miss anyone?" Azuru looking ahead to spot Emily and Duke patiently waiting by the exit door; Azuru then answered his own question "nope!" throwing up his two fingers as, he took his leave an uproar of applause and cheers following him out before he crossed into the exit. Emily and Duke falling in into this space – black hole pitch darkness

Duke calling after Azuru "don't leave them wanting so much more Azuru you might cause a riot" Azuru so glacier tip cold and cruel as he responded "eh you're guys problem not mine!" Emily_intercepting with a strict and responsible tone "no! It is caused by you therefore it is your problem!" Azuru merely shrugging in a kind of "eh you win some you lose some" type of fashion. Enraged Emily snapped "you just can't shrug away all the trouble you could possibly cause! What if you hypothetically hurt some kittens in the possible process awwh! Poor imaginary kittens" Azuru scoffing – a spit in the sun type of scoff as he said "then they shouldn't have hypothetically looked at me wrong, they know that I am crazier than a guy who might possibly hypothetically do something – per chance". Emily pouting as she clamored "Why do you have to be so dark?!" Azuru replying quicker than the thought that popped in his mind "because you're too bright, you blind yourself"

Speaking of light and darkness the hall the trio was traveling in was the universe – like literally THE UNIVERSE! A hallway with no walls, a rug of galaxies and quasars that flowed like a river underneath their feet; illuminating the entire pendulum of colors mixing in so majestically as if it was able to light up the blacker than darkest black that was space. An endless ocean of stars glittered on the left, right, above every single direction except the floor. Comets shooting overhead the size of fireflies, planets we're seen minding their own business spinning on their own planetary axis, moons orbiting them the size of bouncing balls as these three stepping over it making a "droop – droop" with every step they took down this magical road. Making a small ripple in this galaxy underneath them but completely harmless having no effect in the actual galactic world; Azuru directing this conversation to Duke now as he curiously asked "Duke you have anything to add in this?" Duke just laughing as he grabbed on his belt with one hand to pull up his pants, a genuine and earnest smile glistened as bright as the stars behind him as Duke said "nope I just love watchin' the wild direction that mind of yers leads ya I also like the situation it gets ya into let me know if ya need bailing out by the way!" Azuru nodding his head in acknowledgement as he said "why thank you Duke that is very kind of you" Duke tilting his head in respect as he replied "it's what I do"

Emily breaking up this warm bonding moment with her iron fist and heart of ice, she exclaimed "Azuru trust me! I would love nothing more than to hear you get along with every single member of the team all day, but I have a very important status report on the team you told me to gather on them since you put me as supervisor. I have yet another annual report in "Azuru looking straight forward as he spoke with such ease "okay shoot!" Emily knowing Azuru's ability to wander, having the attention span of a crack addicted squirrel "so what I gathered so far is current strengths and weaknesses of the entire team and where they need to improve to bring out their full potential. Team squabbles that I have noticed in my years amongst them, also stepping back to get a different perspective let's start with Ryker: now due to his background he is very valorous I mean he has it in his name! Ryker Valor but that is when his downfall begins, he is too headstrong-"Azuru injecting himself to ask a very important matter "But!... is he headstrong to take on anyone?!" "Azuru what are you talking about?!" "I know that you are wrong, but is he headstrong?... headstrong?... sorry continue" "aaaaanyways as I was saying and when he rushes in 90% of the time it is without a plan and I will give it to him he thinks on the tips of his toes but most of the time it merely complicates his situation. If he didn't have the amazing luck that he does or us to bail him out he would have unfortunately met his end a while back, without a doubt he is the fastest on the team fast enough to rival you Azuru, this is with your training included as well. He has a variety of ways to attack and battle, with his soul being an expandable element only problem with that is that he needs to work on endurance and energy consumption if he chooses the wrong variation to do battle with he will completely drain himself and leave himself defenseless." Azuru nodding and easily giving a plain "okay"

Emily noticing this but decided to keep going "next is Serenity: now Serenity is well rounded elite; she has intelligent insight, impeccable unique fighting style, a quite devastating source of energy, that only steadily drains her, keeps a cool head in battle, and is one of the team members of certain success. You send her on a mission there is a high chance of completion, basically a low causality or destruction rate, she is compatible with just about everyone seems like the perfect warrior. But I did pick up on one thing both you and I know what it is Azuru-"Azuru's eye gently leaning over to Emily's side as she caught his attention like an outfielder jumping over the fence to catch the pop flier. Knowing that she had Azuru right where she needed him she continued on "when I was on a mission with her long ago we we're just about to close it up when... it happened, out of respect for how you feel for her I won't say anymore but I know you have been there when it's happened and you seen what happens to her. I just need you to understand how dangerous this is for her, other than that she is nearly perfect her ability does well for coverage in battle, not mattering if one on one battles or groups even able to go toe to toe with the big demon names fighting up close and personal, from a far, or even a balance of the two. It is just that little imperfection that is stopping her from being the absolute best that she can be." Once again Azuru so casually replying to the entire speech just gave Emily a simple "interesting" two strikes three strikes you're out, Emily once again taking a foot note of Azuru's kick back stature but forging on.

"Kenjin Tetsujin now Kenjin has been around since the feudal era or the time where clans and assassins run rampid across the land of his birth. Kenjin is the oldest one of the entire team, now there is a good and a bad side to that, the good side is when Father brought him to his realm he remained vigilant on Safe Haven as he kept watch over the earth for centuries picking up wisdom like a common cold. As the years passed him by he learned so much and his wisdom has become almost infinite by the amount of growth he has achieved as a being. How that is exactly is the problem, begins this is a completely different state then all the previous year's an apocalyptic chapter is coming and there is no previous path trekked upon that forged this path before us or trail blazed the way, no we are in foreign lands he needs to get with these times. It is like he has a whole arsenal of guns but doesn't have any of them locked and loaded, although his abilities is the most convenient and the most useful, he is being able to mold it basically whatever he needs at that exact moment running on endless supply of spirit energy and the energy of the universe. His powers definitely the most efficient and dependable" Emily just intently watching Azuru ever so closely to hear just what he had to say "alright" just a lone "alright" while he nodded his head. Emily starting to get irritated as she started to built with up anger but let it go in the form of a sigh as she reclaimed her professionalism.

"Moving on to Eminent, noooow this case... okay Eminent is a very excellent soldier his skills are perfect, his movements along with plan of attack and tactics of destruction. Flawless his dynamics going hand in hand in the form of a partnership almost as good as you and Telilian Grace, the mission is the only thing that is in his mind once it gets put there, he is reliable, formidable, offensive striker, and an unbreakable fortress of defense as well. Long range, short range, and middle all dominated in his field... nooooow here is where we get down to it, his ratio of outside interaction of people is extremely low he doesn't try and help out nearby situations that could greatly impact others by destiny. His intervention – I mean are called Divine Intervention for a reason! – He is almost like a machine that is objective orientated and that is his downfall. How does he expect to grow if he shuts himself off from the rest of the world that needs his help?" Emily's eyes as quick as lightening shooting to Azuru as soon as she was done with Eminent's report; Azuru still not even giving half of the effort "mhmm" the frustration beginning to leak out "mhmm?! Mhmm what?! Don't you have anything else to offer to this?!" Azuru shaking his head for an answer as Emily released a growling sigh "of course you don't why would you it's not like you do the resear - Now onto Angel now given his calm demeanor I was extremely jaw dropped when I first witnessed his strength.

He seems to be just an entire Miraclelyte version of passiveness, and I understand that due to his massive amount of his untouched innocence that he holds in a lot of his true feelings, desires, thoughts, and pain but because he does not properly share it that it is stuffed into a bottle until the bottle is too crowded and breaks! I do give him credit for him knowing when to unleash his hidden nature and is 99% of the time being put against the enemy. The remaining 1% only being a possibility with his humongous amount of strength and path of destruction that follows him, as he is lost in his wild emotions. The percentage of the possibility grows in number and becomes more than just a theory as he has proven to go into a berserk rage, something as small as sharing, healthy dealing with his emotions and how he is feeling or talking about his past maybe something traumatic happened, will do a humongous effect on him, to help him put a leash on this beast that is his power his destructive capability will be on par with yours." Azuru stroking his chin to the statement seeming like he was deep in thought with this one, sparkles blazing from Emily's eyes as she grinned so wide with glee, he might finally give an actual opinion with this one. She had to step out of her professional box for a little bit but it was worth it, if she can make even the littlest bit of progress. Azuru spat out "you're right" Emily's hopes for him crushed and stomped upon, Duke even backing up a couple of steps as they continued walking.

All of Emily's hopes and anticipation was replaced with anger and blind fury finally having it "WHY DON'T YOU CONTRIBUTE A THOUGHT, YOUR OPINION, MORE INFORMATION SOMETHING!!!" Azuru so calm dodging her bullets like she was wildly flailing her gun "because I am just listening right now, there is going to be a time for me to talk I am just hearing the reports for now, and continue." Emily clamping the bridge of her nose with her left index and thumb fingers, vigorously growling out a sigh as she had to suck it up not wanting to break her qualified mask that she wore; "Angelo now this is a tricky one due to his massive resolve and dedication to justice he is even more reckless than Ryker, dashing in without the skills that Ryker has and sustaining heavy damage. Absolutely the worst idea every single time, but when it comes to crowd control he is one of the best, still needs work on his one –on - ones – I gotta say he is one who needs the most improvement but I do take my hat off to him. Because of his steel determination, yes he might start off horribly wrong but the end result is given somehow some way he will find a way to come out on top putting his body, mind, and soul way past their limits that are ever changing ha kind of like you Azuru."

Azuru quickly inserting a comment "justice can also be an exploit if angled right" Azuru was actually just thinking out loud, he looked over to see an overjoyed and happy expression on the face of Emily; Azuru even questioning her as he asked "something wrong?" As quick to respond as Azuru's under the breath comment "just happy to get some feedback from you I don't really care what it is about – Maximus is up next! He is almost as professional as me except when he steps onto that warzone. That blood gets pumping into his veins he gets engulfed into the battle, now that isn't necessarily a bad thing. By being so self aware of every action that is going on around him, but when it all comes down to teamwork he forces himself to be alone, and forces the rest of the team out; he wants to be the singular pillar to hold up the roof when it doesn't work like that. There is much more than one pillar to share the burden he brings it all upon himself when you have teammates to help share the load and I know it isn't an attitude type thing it is more of an instinctive action, which happens before he can even control or fully realize it. So again we are running into the subconscious – I can't believe how many ticks this team has that weren't nipped on the butt once upon first realizing it – but all in all he has enough strength to keep up with you. Have you guys had a contest to see who is stronger between you two?" Azuru staying quiet for a couple of moments only to address one of those concerns "that is because Benedict was a horrible person when it came to feelings." Emily giggling as she knew full well that Azuru would avoid the last question

Duke suddenly raising his hand to insert himself within the one - sided conference that seemed to make him feel like a third wheel "can my status be next?" Emily with slight confusion inquired "why do you want to be next?" Duke taking out a page from Azuru's book of simplicity "just curious" Emily rolling her eyes but obliging to Duke's harmless request. "Okay then Duke what I have taken in note – wise about you is that like Serenity, you are well rounded, cool headed because of your unique special ability you can take down large masses of enemies, one on ones are extremely easy for you, and when backed in a corner you can easily defend yourself and come out successful if faced both. Long range, middle, and short range are all within your grasp; you can defend allies as well as attack on the front lines. One of the few that can do this simultaneously due to your unique ability once again, you are unpredictable and directionless when it comes to attacking being that your attacks can come from anywhere and everywhere with a fighting variety to keep the enemies guessing. Unlike Azuru you do analysis and keep your head cool at all times not letting the heat of battle take over your considering mind, and more importantly you never let your heart be corrupted by darkness no matter how much of it you see – very admirable." Duke tilting his straw hat up so Emily could see his blinding golden capital D shaped smile with a bit of anticipation on his tongue "so far so good, where do I trip and fall from grace?"

Emily sighing before continuing "but what I think you need to work on is your motivation you can sometimes be too laid back – too nonchalant and relaxed about matters that require more discipline and much more affirmative action. You are in an important ranking position you should treat it with respect! You need to be more involved with the surroundings around you – also stop trusting everyone! You give them the shirt off your back to wear and as soon as you turn around they are already selling it – be careful of who you give your trust to at least, be weary of who you help out too because they might just be taking advantage of your kindness - you have plenty of it to go around." Duke's head staying still not a single thing had changed or put an scratch on the half the moon smile he had before the lecture came up was still in full effect a chuckle carried through his reply " I'll start workin' on it."

Emily just taking a brief exhale as she felt that it was basically just a happier version of Azuru she was dealing with, another trait of Duke's kindness is his willingness to forgive and forget is very high so she wasn't very sure if he really would "work on it" this not being the first time that she has given Duke these stern warnings due to the flaws in his character. Azuru only dousing this fire with gasoline as he slapped Duke on the back pushing him over a couple of steps "yeah, Stop being a piece of shit second – in –command I need your straw – pickin' ass partner!"

Oh the immorality but only slapping a bigger and brighter smile on Duke's face as he literally LOL "Azuru that wasn't nice" Azuru taken back as he responded "whoever said I was nice or anything of that sort?! Let me know so I can kick their asses for speaking nicely about me... I bet it was Ms. Neko wasn't it she's always starting problems!" Emily once again wrecking a perfect bro moment as she literally came in between them and hollered "okay Azuru! We still have team members we need to go over we aren't done yet!" Azuru raising a brow to her "what are you talking about all the members who matter have already been read out and talked about."

Emily forcing to pick up the ball as it was thrown into her court "what are you talking about there is still Zandra! All the members of our team are important!" "I guess but go ahead" "she is an interesting case this one we have, now as all three of us remember the "incident" that happened years back when we we're still pretty green to the team –"Azuru closing his eyes as the thought of that day flashed like his life before him, not something he liked to think about or dwell on so they went by like lightening. The carnivorous, blood thirsty, ravenous, monstrosity that had the appropriate label of a demon, in size it munchkined Azuru, it's long slender but bulky edged limbs we're drawing nearer and nearer towards Azuru; it's shadow toned skin that was so alligator rough, with cracks, stubble, and crust but what irked Azuru the most about this putrid creature, besides the horrid trail of destruction of the city behind it, was the blood red eyes that we're piercing right through Azuru.

His skin tightening so hard it could be heard out loud as his smile began to replace his purer rage he had moments ago fusing them together to become one. A new level of anger and wrath reached, a very cold and unfeeling voice called out to Azuru like no heart ever existed in the body "Azuru come on we got to go! Leave her!" Azuru laughing a chatter of complete madness fueled completely by the reaction to such a ridiculous and plain idiotic statement as he shouted back over to him "SHUT UP DON'T TELL ME WHAT TO DO! – YOU MIGHT BE ABOVE ME THAT DOES NOT MAKE YOU MY LEADER! – YOU'RE A STUPID BOSS MORE THAN ANYTHING!!" Azuru began walking defiant and dominantly over to the roaring, snarling and howling demon that looked like it was begging to battle with Azuru. Azuru's face so blank as he clenched his fists that we're tightened at his side, Azuru shooting his eyes open as he quickly tried to discard the train of thoughts; it was like a repressed memory he was aware of maybe more like an intrusive thought. Emily continuing as soon as she seen Azuru snap out of his trans "now she has the most brilliant mind that is always thinking, planning, and analyzing the field around her within the first seconds of contact. She can predict the enemy's next move before they can make it and is already coming up with a counter she is swift, cunning, and considerate to top it off she is a very loving and generous person.

She will gladly fold herself in half to help those in need her abilities and battle line skills goes perfectly with her like a ball and a chain, she knows her limits and strengths with her power that is Taylor -made for her and is like Kenjin in the regard of it being infinite. The only way she would run out is if the sun completely lit up the entire world which is very unlikely, the more crucial thing with her is when her emotions begin to mix in that is when troubles starts with her. It is like playing Russian roulette with her if she lands on a good emotion based on whatever she remembers, that could be triggered by anything it will without a doubt benefit us to the point of complete victory. But if she remembers something bad then all hell storms through the gate and she causes more destruction than the demons themselves – she is truly a wheel of fortune go big or go home!" Azuru eerily quiet like he was lost in thought part of Emily desperately wanted to hear some of his thoughts, but part of her is just happy that he is probably thinking this over he just hastily said "and the last one" quick to go on to the next subject Emily a bit distressed in her demeanor with this one as she let out an exhale of bottled in thoughts and worries. "Little is actually known about your student other than what you already know, he seems to have a incredible amount of potential just from what I have seen of him today, with him completing the training that none of us thought he would and all, but the fact that he doesn't know anything is really going to hinder his growth and only cause him to struggle further instead of being able to ride on through with all he has learned.

You should have taught him something while you we're training him you are his master after all!" "Master yes! Babysitter and ass –wiper no! He can learn the basics on his own he isn't dumb!" "Be that as it may he is still unaware of certain things and still in the learning process. But still he must hold immense potential if he was just added straight onto our team I'm surprised that they didn't pick someone from the lower teams to fill the spot which keeps me curious about him but still he needs to learn so much. Well that seems to be about it" Azuru Duke and Emily coming to what seemed to be the end of the river of galaxy, it being an illuminating tower of light in the middle of the universe like the red dot in a bull's eye circle. This tower of burning light glistening and glimmering every single color known to these galaxies inside as it shined the most blinding light to ever exist; suns like dying light bulbs in comparison Azuru with his back to all this enchanting majesty and a smirk on his face "what about you?" Emily even pointing to herself to make sure Azuru meant her she was taken back a step or two "me? What do you mean?! You have notes on me?"

Azuru so smug and confident his smile saying it all "a few that I noticed about you as well" "well go ahead and share them and I'll tell you which ones are wrong!" Azuru chuckling with conceit or was it proof? "You are hands down the most professional, the most punctual and mature member on the team, which is why I made you the supervisor in the first place. But when you put professionalism before everything in your life it begins to break you down inside tugging on your soul because you aren't allowed to behave properly. Taking the road of legitimacy is a high one! You won't even allow yourself the satisfaction of anger or sadness emotion Father blessed us with –""but how is that a downfall?! How is that a bad thing?! I am the glue that is keeping us all together; I have a lot of work that always needs to be done! – If I don't do it, it won't get done!""Maybe but is it still not a thing when you come back half dead every single mission you are given because you go above and beyond once completing the mission, and I know for damn sure it wasn't because the demons we're tough you we're helping others and I get it! You love to help people, which is what you love to do! – Not for the reward, recognition, or fame but because they need help and you don't want them to suffer! – You need to think of yourself and stop spreading yourself so thin!" Emily looking Azuru dead in the eyes not giving any retorts or responds because she wanted to hear him out, he had her hooked lined and sinker with his words "You're my sister so I am gonna tell you this from my heart on top of my duty of being your leader – you don't think you deserve to share how you feel? All this professionalism is highly respectable and dignified but it robs you of this! –"Azuru pointing to the shrine in the middle of her chest as he picked it back up "then I don't want this for you! – Okay I want you to work on that okay?"

Emily nodding as she put her hand over her eyes quivering a bit Azuru wrapping his arms around her as he held her close. He then told her at the same volume as everything else, "I love you big sis take care of yourself okay – I will see you when you get back" Emily now returning the affection as she heard Azuru taking his leave tossing her arms around Azuru's neck even returning his compassion "I love you too little brother – be good okay don't give Father a hard time." Azuru laughing as he slowly backed away taking his leave "hey he knows what kind of son he has!" Azuru then going up to Duke for a horizontal hand slap, at first then a clash of back slaps, grabbing each other's shoulders as they yanked each other for a half hugging muy macho form. Azuru patting Duke on the back as he did Duke did the same to Azuru, the grip's on each other's shoulders slipped all the way down to the tips of each other's finger tips both of them balancing on the balls of their heels, almost nearly falling but both of them we're hanging on by the trust of each other. Neither one giving more neither one giving less the tips of their fingers turned into their full hands, as they both switched their grips and simultaneously pulled themselves up from the brink of descending to end this handshake; they both whipped their arms to form a firm manshake, or manly handshake before Azuru also giving him his farewell "take care partner in crime" Duke smacking Azuru on the shoulder as he said "ya too Mr. Badass!"

Azuru dismissing himself as he walked into the tower of light, the more he divulged himself in the deeper he went like it was a flight of stairs. At his waist point Emily just remembered yelling over to Azuru "WAIT AZURU! I forgot to tell you about the team's squabbles!!" Azuru yelling back over "believe me! I know all about the team squabbles! – we're fine!" The last thing that was seen from Azuru as he vanished like he was taking a dip in the pool was his arm holding up the index finger along with the middle finger on his left arm. That was pointed towards the sky

(Meanwhile) "Um Mr. Ryker you said you we're going to show me where I could find my residence... really want to see my Mom you know –"Amar looking around nervously as they passed all the neighborhoods behind them becoming squinting figures as they continued to walk forward a huge dome – like structure. A group of guards statue still and completely concentrated as they stood outside the building, Ryker replying as he forged ahead so casually without even 1% of worry and anxiety that Amar had. "Yeah yeah we are Rook don't worry! Geeze you're worse than my mom – God rest her soul – I just need to check up on something see–"Ryker trailing off as he looked at the guards their entire collective eyes glowed and glossed. To check their data banks of information with their minds, pulling up Ryker's file and all the Intel on him matching him to the man standing in front of him just to make sure it was him; they nodded their heads for the "okay" allowing Ryker to pass into the building Ryker giving a kiddish smile as he waited on the other side for Amar. Who was going through the same process, even though his file was small it was still present and they also let him go ahead, joining back up with Ryker he picked up where he left off as they entered this advanced technology secure establishment "I overheard Azuru chewing you out like bubblegum earlier, when he told you to go find someone else because he wasn't going to train you and well I wanted to give you a tiny bit of things I picked up over all the years."

Amar's eyes wandering all over this laboratory – like foundation there we're intelligent minds that looked to be fully capable of running this entire system with half a brain. Holographic screens - no sets, monitor, or box around it just the paper thin golden edged screen that glowed intensely inches from each hard working staff member there. The picture display looking to be involved in some sort of new three dimension development a river of silver, gray, gold, and black wind, the ratio of wind flowing from the informational picture straight to their shrine; the person stroking the wind like it was long, big, thick .... Bundle of luscious hair I hope your mind didn't go anywhere for a second, okaaaay I'll trust you this time – and at some instances they would nitpick and pinch at the wind to remove certain clouds, that others would catch in a miniature ball of cloud or would just disappear into thin air. To those that caught the golden puff used other senses than just their eyes, on the screen in front of them with splotches and blurring wind marks splashing all over from the information that their noses and tongues we're able to rake in like the gardeners; using their hands to further feel out the texture, the information flooding into the pores of their bodies. The river of intangible gold streaming to their ears as well like a disc jockey with his ear muffs that just blast out music, appearing similar to sonar for a bat on screen to show everything in the area.

A man above them in a higher podium like level shouted "semblance! Status report on each individual area" all in a row calling out as they simultaneously responded in a role call discipline "area N57 W70 part 1 is clear in parameter! Silent actions! And secure!" "Area S12 E84 part 2 is yellow in parameter! Dormant in actions! Nearby squadron moving in to secure" "Area 00 W 102 part 2 is orange flashing scarlet in parameter! Actions still being taken to avoid disasters since yesterday! Victory in bound" As the rest of them kept going on and on Amar turned to Ryker who was just steadily listening to the reports coming in but had no clue what was going on.

90% of what was going on was a complete ocean of confusion that Amar was sinking to the bottom of "Mr. Ryker what are they saying? And how are they doing that with their screen?! What are all these codes they are saying?! – I have so many questions!" Ryker looking over to Amar to give him a casual shrug and carefree "too many questions you'll learn it some other time – right now I am trying to find something "appropriate" to show you, some things here and there" Amar echoing his temporary sensei as he flooded his words with confusion "here and there?" Ryker pointed forward as he leaned against the wall one foot yanked up pointing over to a group further down the circle of information maniacs, a completely different section. Their hologram was not in the form of a screen but in the shape of a digitalized world that each person had their hands dug into this beach ball sized digital glistening world. Each person had their hands drilled into this glowing haywire ball, digital glistening information into their eyes, golden rays of light like searchlights as they stared deeper and deeper into this miniature planet it almost seemed like they we're actually sticking their hands into electrical sockets. But to them this was just a simple laptop that they could get all the information they could possibly ever need; receiving regular information calling out over to the commander who was hovering over them "Captain *Empath* is leading the Beta team to the defenses of the enemy they are going to begin purifying the area – looking at amount of demons – most primal, hell hounds, scatters of damned souls and a few Pee Wees they should be able to purify within 15 minutes or so that is estimated with difficulty!"

"Commander Alpha team is having trouble recovering the last soul – it was first assigned to Forrest and Ex but Kayoh has been called in for back up, it seems the demons are using the getaway tactic to get further from them. They might need support if we want to recover that last soul in the area" the commander instantly demanding "get a valiant squad down there! – keep going down the line!" Picking right up, as a light was shot from the finger of the informer who requested back up for the struggling Alpha team, as the convoy line of informers still kept going "valiant squadron captain: *Wan Shotto* have succeeded in defending area part two S40 E40 – the wave of demons would have caused an earthquake even a few hybrids amongst the mix! – Small casualties we're sustained – returning to Safe Haven momentarily" "good! – Another pack of hybrids more and more of them keep coming, since pass year got to say they are the biggest pain in my ass!" The spark of light like a bullet being shot to what appeared to be a golden pipeline but electricity sizzled out off it. Like a broken electrical cord, Amar was just looking at it travel like a shooting star and just as he looked over his shoulder to ask Ryker about it, he only saw a white and black trail of sparks in the shape of a lightning bolt. He frantically began turning his head left to right, to try to find his mentor like a scared child trying to find their mother in a supermarket; it was only when he looked at the least expected place he found him – up in the air, grabbing the ball of light like he was the best defensive end in the league.

Amar's eyes shot out of his sockets, wide with surprise as he spoke to himself "h-how-did he get u-p up there?! He was here a minute ago!! What is with that white lightning by the way?" Amar noticing the slightly visible amount of lightning turned glowing neon white surrounding Ryker barely visible enough to be able to squint a focus, Ryker swiftly landing next to the commander. The lightning vanishing as quickly as it realistically does, as he slowly rose from the ground, the Commander not noticing Ryker when he came in but he for sure noticed him now! Even turning Informer's heads - and their job is to focus is mind you! Focus on the influx of information coming in, only able to give Ryker a glance before hastily going back to their leak of information.

The Commander bowing as he saluted Ryker even he was a tiny bit disorientated with the surprise arrival of Ryker "c-captain – Ryker sir please sir excuse my-"Ryker stopping him midway with his hand pushing the air as with complete calm and relaxation "at ease Commander – sorry to disturb your daily grind of information –"The Commander now interrupting Ryker, NOW trying to put him at ease "oh no! Sir it is an honor to have you" "thank you very much – yeah I was just planning to show Guppy over here what we sort of do, on missions and the whole deal of our community – I heard the whole situation going on with Alpha having a bit of trouble so I thought perfect chance to have Guppy get his battle legs orrr whatever Guppies get" Ryker pointing over to Amar with his thumb over his shoulder. Amar looking completely clueless as he was just trying to get a grip on what was going on, Ryker just swiftly in the driver's seat as he took control of just continuing "you could give the valiant squad a break – let them keep meditating me and Guppy will take care of this."

The Commander full of panic insisting like a host hectically trying to stop their guest from having to serve themselves "C-Captain that isn't necessary! That is too low a mission for you it would be like a chore and besides – "the Commander coming in close to secret and discreetly fold his hand over his face (instantly making the conversation private) "you do know that Forrest Evergreen is going to be there don't you? – He specifically asked for a mission so he could not be present during Azuru's ceremony – he was heard screaming "damn Queen of attention! Soaking up everyone's time like the attention whore she is!!! –"

Ryker just laughing out loud bursting as he bowled over to slap his knee trying to get some words out "H-HE HE –IS I-IIIS STILL PISSED ISN'T HE?! ALL THIS TIME AND HE'S STILL PISSED THAT'S FANTASTIC!! – I GOTTA TELL AZURU-!" Ryker suddenly cutting his off so he could concentrate, snipping it off so easily as if it we're a stray hair on the top of his head forming a circle with both hands over his shrine and the middle of his chest flushed a splendor vividness that shined through his skin like he swallowed a searchlight. It beamed through his hands; he slowly began to pull his hands gently away from his chest to as far as his arms would extend, delicately taking his hands away from the circular light like taking off the cookie cutters from the dough. The ball was now formed; the light kindled a brilliant and vibrant gold, hovering still in the air like a baby cloud.

The big puffball of gold started to static a blue flash, a blue blob but momentarily grew to a tan toned face, the definition fixating better than the highest resolution of a television could ever achieve. Now showing Azuru like a person had a camera inches from his face already having an annoyed expression on his face as he said "what's up Ryker?" Ryker already giggling, he tried to spit out the hilarious news "pfft, A-Azuru h-h-he's still pissed!"

Azuru responding with a ponderous and thoughtful expression as he tried to configure just what Ryker was referring to... it only took him a matter of moments before Azuru was wildly guffawing not even able to catch his breath as he was consumed by humor, Ryker going back to his hysterical howling laughing right alongside Azuru as Ryker's arm swung down to smack his knee, the same whack sounded off over at Azuru's side. Amar and the rest of the Informers including the Commander all stared in an awkward wonderment, just amazed at the connection and how strong the bond was between them that with one simple phrase the same thought were reached and the same feelings we're felt. Ryker cut into his laughing to squeeze out "hahaha – la-ter –hahaha Azuru!"

Snapping the bubble of light away that disappeared like the vision on the old tube the entire screen condescending into a single line then a dot then just completely had gone; all happening in the matter of seconds. The last of his giggles slipped out but sighing the rest of them out as he regained himself speaking to the Commander "yeah we'll be fine plus he needs to understand that he is not more important than the mission, if the mission becomes even slightly in jeopardy it is the job of the valiant force or you the commanding officer to send aid so the mission is a success – Forrest is just too thick skulled to understand that! – He refuses help and sees it as a sign of weakness – so in a way I am just helping him learn."

The Commander fully respecting and admiring Ryker's decision as he responded "very good sir – follow me and I will direct you to the pin point room" with his hands folded behind his back he walked in front of Ryker. Ryker mimicking him as he also folded his hands behind his back, even pulling up his chin to further disguise himself into the Commander, he then signaled with his index finger to come along directed at Amar. Amar quickly catching this as he began to jog around the other side, to catch up with them as they jumped off the edge and onto the ground floor

The Commander leading them to a room in the back of this already humongous building, Amar stunned to see that there was still more. As soon as they stepped into the hallway, doors decorated the entire hallway like wall hung photos two to three full sized doors stacked up on another all gleaming gold, silver, gray and black. Amar's head almost spinning if it weren't for his spine, as he looked at all the doors this entire hallway was made of; even the roof had pairs of doors alongside each other going down the whole lane. A dinging beep was also gently rung as if on the other side of each door was a person waiting as they rung the door bell, Ryker also looking around but not with astonishment or amazement like Amar no more like inspecting chuckling before saying "haven't seen these doors so quiet in ages usually they're flapping open and closed like if they we're made of paper!" "Yes a lot of people attended Azuru's ceremony – I really am happy for him the moral of my soldiers have completely changed since he became leader. They went from feeling like people with an absolute duty that no matter what must be complete, to an actual band of soldiers that know that no one is perfect and I believe Azuru has shown them this way I mean we all in a way watched him climb from the bottom. He earned this leadership and this ceremony he is going to do very ground breaking things for us I just know it, now I just have to wait for it all"

Ryker injecting his thoughts "he would want you to realize your own potential before you realize his, knowing him – he is something special isn't he?" Amar even thinking of his master who just seemed to be a whole different type of unique that was impossible for anyone else to replicate - speaking of, Amar just remembered to ask his half assed sensei about everything he did "Mr. Ryker so how did you get up there so fast? What was that thing you did with all the glowing? Also why does Forrest hate Sensei so much? Umm still a lot of questions" Ryker just sighing without looking back at Amar he could dodge one bullet miraculously, but all three he was bound to get hit once and Ryker fully knew this "my speed?... you fully understand that in a couple of minutes –" murmuring almost whispering underneath his breath "hopefully there are demons worth fighting" "and maybe another time I will show you or at least tell you there is a more simple explanation, it is a huge tree with prickly branches annnnd well I can explain all that in a bit – if I have time – maybe... probably? Uh most likely not though." Amar feeling somewhat satisfied that answers we're on their way, at least some we're in sight last time, they we're brushed off like a child asking their neglective parent to play ball; the Commander stopping at a light blue shining door as he opened it up for Ryker and Amar "this is the door for trainees and beginners, so Cadet Guppy should be fine using this one – I take it you wanted him to beam you two there for practice." Ryker smiling with joy dripping from his grin "Commander you just have a habit of reading my mind! – Don't go too far though you might get dirt all over you!"

The Commander going on thinking nothing of this comment he had grown too used to Ryker to be weirded out, the joke going right over Amar's head "affirmative will do – this room is specially designed to gather Divinity and paint pictures so they can properly exercise on the ways to beam down and pinpoint the location, also it helps steady their aim so if you're aiming to go to N41 W74 he doesn't send you to N17 E91 am I right?!" Ryker and the Commander both bursting out laughing, bowling over and trying to put the lid on their mouths but Amar was just as lost and left out as the reader who couldn't follow them even if the instructions we're written on the floor in a trail behind them. Ryker wooing off the laughter as he wiped out an emerging golden tear on the rim of his eye, the Commander holding his gut as Ryker barely able to put himself together "y-you might need to send an evac to - to part two S11 W72!!" starting them up all over again Amar just watching them, made him feel like a child. In the sense of humor was not yet developed and they had a special inside joke of comedic genius, the Commander yelping over his laughter "stop! Stop! I'm gonna spew Divinity!! My spiral pool is in a knot!! Here! –"The Commander's hand glowing an illuminating gold as he tightly grasped Ryker's hand like passing on the light to him as Ryker's hand now sparkled a bright gold and the Commander's hand was his regular dull skin tone.

Ryker still cracking up as he said "g-got it th-thank you!" Patting Ryker on the back as he entered the room, Amar like his tail very close behind; the Commander giving him a pat on the back of encouragement saying with still full of heckles and giggles "good luck Cadet Guppy" Amar pouting not too happy with his nick name or ranking only giving a mediocre and forced "thanks" closing the door behind him, the Commander went back into his perfect posture with hands neatly folded behind his back. Ready to jump into a pool of professionalism but then a giggle slipped out as he repeated "part twoS11 W72!!" Then shamelessly laughing his head off as he went back to his subordinates

Ryker and Amar in an all neon white glowing room completely blank like a new sheet of paper, the two like the imperfect dots on that brand spanking flawless page. Amar not even knowing what to think as he walked aimlessly in this endless and infinite space of nothing and forever but as his head and body we're rotating around as he tried to see how far this place went on he heard a "clank" like he was stepping on loose metal instantly looking down to see a circular pad the size of a baseball batter's diamond. He lifted his foot up to inspect it more thoroughly, Ryker finally acting like a true mentor as he guided the lost Amar "don't bother to try and see how long this room is it goes on for-it's a paradox and will only send you back to where you started if you go too far." Amar looking up at Ryker to see the seriousness in his eyes and strict tone in his voice, Ryker himself looking onto the horizon of nothing; gazing at the complexity of absolutely nothing.

He then looked down at Amar and completely changed his outlook with a more encouraging and inviting texture in his eyes as he said "go ahead stand on it, I'm right here I'll let you know if you're doing something wrong – you're fine." Amar hesitant but still nodding a partially unsure and fearful nod putting both feet onto this metallic and loud pad of iron once again "CLANK" off as soon as Amar stepped on it Ryker then pointed in the middle of the circular pad module to a smaller circle the size of a person's personal space instructing, "step in there that is where you can start pin pointing. The outside rim is where teachers stand to help you out" Amar looking at the smaller sized circle and noticed it wasn't one big circle, but a small circle with an even bigger circle surrounding it. Even began noticing the divine silver and gray engravings on it such a beautiful trace of designing but Amar couldn't focus on those pretty lines right now, he had to do as he was told stepping into the inner rim of this panel but once dripping the toe of his shoe into the circle he felt a puddle, and even saw a metallic pool of water began to ripple. Amar quickly pulling his foot back like there was piranhas inside the silver colored water – Ryker inserting his knowledge "easy easy! It's not gonna hurt you it's supposed to help you! It senses your energy and helps you gather it so you can focus on pin pointing. Geeze – I know! This is a whole entire new world for you! – You're alone, don't have all the training you might need, you don't exactly have the best trainer, and after hearing those heart-felt speeches. How could you not feel the pressure?! But listen I know where you're coming from! Exactly where you're coming from so I can assure you, you have nothing to worry about. You are no longer alone, as long as this team is by your side we're you're family man – all we wanna do is help you and watch you grow, and training or not I can tell you're a quick learner and even if you're not – I got two kids that are adults now, I know a little thing about patience so don't think you're getting on my nerves or anything.

The best thing to do is not feel like all that pressure as an obstacle, but more like a goal, like each day each mission is a step closer and you gotta take it slow believe me when you get there it will be perfect timing. The web of destiny will not steer you wrong... now try again" Ryker welcoming Amar to try retry with an open palmed pointed towards the silver kiddy pool

Amar's doubts and fears beginning to leave like unwanted guests finally getting the hint, a new belief in his self and a anxious excitement to grow and experience all of the adventure, but it all started with this difficult, final, and grand first step. He looked down in the crystal pool, now that once again settled from all the ripples gulping as he once again ever so carefully dipped his foot into the pool; his entire shoe up to the top of his ankle sank in and it was strange it had no connotations of wet or liquid, it wasn't a temperature of any kind. It felt like he had stuck his foot inside of a cloud completely weightless hearing a deep "clank" behind him, glancing over his shoulder to see Ryker just stepping on the outer rim of the circle. Beckoning Amar to take further steps to completely divulge himself into this, no half – assed work here, Amar taking a deep breath as he tugged his other foot to join in, the second it came into the feeling less water; a tower of light erupted from the miniature lake Amar was standing in. This room that had not a single thing in it other than this contraption suddenly sprang a golden intangible self map of the entire world right before them.

Ryker and Amar standing inside what would be the core of the planet, Amar blown away how did all this happen?! What was going on?! Just a couple of questions sprinting through Amar's mind this current moment; he took steps back and really started to freak out, Ryker calmly reminded him "remember what I told you take it easy... it is only amplifying the energy in your body or Divinity. This is the map of the world it is under your control what you want to see or where you want to go is up to you, go on touch it you can't go anywhere yet so don't worry" Amar turning his attention from Ryker back to this humongous like sun ball. That was slowly rotating with them inside Amar trying to do as instructed and touch the shining orb, putting his hand onto it; stopping in its turtle – like tracks it slightly rippled where his hand was put Ryker continuing his guidance "now use your finger like a pencil to guide it, spin it you know! –"

Amar following every instruction like a game of Simon says as he picked up the rest of his fingers to leave his index finger by itself, he still held the whole world down with one finger then gently swiped it to the right. It began rotating clockwise at a speed a bit faster than when it started, after a few moments of watching the Earth doing some laps Amar stopped it once again with his index finger. This time he swiped it to the left to spin it counter clockwise at the same speed, Amar absolute star stricken as he watched the lands of Earth glisten a gracious gold, a smooth silver, a giving gray.

It was like when the first television was given out and Amar was the first child to watch it, his concentration locked onto the world in front of him right now. His inner child began to come out from within as he smiled so naughty like a scheme was going to hatch as he swiped the world with his entire right hand like a bear striking its enemy with its mighty crushing claw. The world going from rivaling a turtle to the rival of a racecar, just a blur as it spun on its axis like a ballerina on her toes, the lands going from up to down as the world spun all the way around. One second North America was on the top, next it was on the bottom and Antarctica was the top dog; before even letting it slow down in momentum Amar slapped the world with the other hand to send it in the other direction spiraling it like a 360 dimensional wheel that had rocket fuel for gas. Spinning at a diagonal angle where the top would once again become the bottom Amar's smirk sparkling with excitement as this world was completely at his fingertips, then with both of his hands he condensed the world to the size of a basket ball by slamming both of his hands almost together. The world like a stray puppy following Amar's movements, more like he was its master Amar just staring at the world in his hands; trying to contain all of his enthusiasm Ryker actually impressed by the spectacle that took place right in front of him.

A rookie none the less "well – I was right you do catch on fast! All I told you was use your finger like a pencil – I didn't even have to explain the other stuff – but I do have to explain this part so back up a bit –"Amar nodding his head obediently. Ryker began to stretch the world by pulling his arms apart until it was the size of a good Chester darer The Earth was now almost bigger than him and it just simply floated in front of him as Amar again astonished and breath taken by how easily it would grow and shrink. Ryker then did a pushing sign with his hands and Amar treading carefully as he did, his temporary sensei's eyes we're deeply fixated onto his every movement and would also turn his head to watch the effect on the world, but Amar succeeded in gently shoving the world away from him now a bit more in front of him. A person's length away, Ryker now standing right next to Amar but outside of the puddle "epicenter enter" just then the Earth twirled on its own without the touch of Amar's fingertips. Continuing to spin until most of the main continents we're within view it was like Amar was looking at the most high definition of the greatest atlas ever made, that was just dumped upon with glitter and gold. North America, South America and

Antarctica in plain sight, but part two Australia, Europe and Asia we're on the other side, Africa being the epicenter of the point; the target being pin pointed and aimed at the mother land. Amar said out loud but more to himself "this is the world?... somehow it is just so different from any map or globe I have ever seen."

Ryker replying "that's because it is, this is the gateway to the world the start of a movement it isn't just directional." They both took a few moments to admire this breath – taking and just improbable phenomenon that is the pinpoint technique: Ryker pointing at the world and jumping back into his teaching boots "you remember when you asked me what we're the codes those guys were spitting out back there in the lab?" Amar nodding his head to answer Ryker's question Ryker then pointed at the dot on Africa and said "see that? – that is the epicenter or origin point of start, that is the middle of the world from part 1. We will have to go over part two some other time but right now let's focus on that origin point – zero point" Amar nodding with acknowledgment soaking in all of this information like a sponge mopping up a soaked floor Ryker saying out loud like he was in a fast food joint and the world was his cashier "N and S lines" suddenly a red line cutting into the golden globe straight edge in the middle, sticking out like polka dots on a blank paper. Ryker now explaining all this new information that came up

"okay – now those are north and a south line, if it goes up it is north if it goes down it is south – basic stuff, however far it goes into each area is measured by a number. The greater the number the deeper divulged the point is crossed over – E and W lines" once again the obedient employee of the month at Safe Haven gave him just what he was asking for with another red line crossed the middle of the origin point going in a perfect line from the top of the world that was the ocean, trailing all the way down to Antarctica, slicing right through Africa and making a cross with the N and S lines.

Ryker then asked "can you guess what this line does?" Amar almost instantly had an idea of the line's function "it provides the territory for east and west basically the same as the N and S lines". Ryker smiling so proud of his student "that's right! It separates which side is east and which side is west, it usually goes after north and south" Amar very childish but also very curious and slightly nervous raising his hand and Ryker not hesitating to call on his best student of the class room of one. "But is that not just latitude and longitude? I mean it is basic stuff like you said" Ryker nodding with a smile on his face incredibly impressed by how much this rookie was picking things apart. "Yes it does start off like that but let's try so you can see the difference- try and find Forrest's location here I have it right here" Ryker's right hand flared a bright gold as he put that hand onto Amar's shoulder, his eyes then flushed gold for a mere moment as he repeated "N175 and W55" he then pointed at that spot he landed upon. North America and began reverse pinching almost like instead picking at the point with his index and thumb, he pushed outward with those fingers until the entire sight of the world was taken up by that area of desire. Amar mouth wide open but jaw still intact and nowhere near the floor, as he said in astonishment "I... I landed on America – I always dreamed of going to America... the land of the free home of the brave" Ryker scoffing as he said "they are very far from free Rook! Them and the rest of the world – what they are is a prisoner with a ball and a chain hopped up on so many damn chemicals that they believe that they are free, the rest of the world is in the same damn boat as 'Merica!"

Amar gripping his fist tightly, with silence building anger Ryker seeing this and rested his hand on his shoulder as he empathized with him "if Emily were here she would probably say "let go of that anger it is not good for you!" Ryker stopped pinching his nostrils together to create his nasally Emily. Picking up the lecturous ball as he dunked it into Amar's court "but honestly I think it is good we let it build up so when we finally get to the heartless monsters who made the world this way you have something to give 'em – sometimes it could even be used as fuel when you have nothing else left!"

Amar releasing the tight grip that clenched his teeth together also relaxed his fist readjusting their focus back to the image of America's left arm (depending on where you're standing.) The slim slither of packed land that America first started with Amar then said "Washington D.C. huh the nation's capitol?" "Yup! Okay now where is Forrest? You got the coordinates correct so where is he?" Amar scratching his head as he stuttered a stunned "uhhh – umm mmm" Ryker laughing as he now explained properly "what did I tell you? It only starts off like that, the basis is pretty mathematic but only a starter the rest is all soul" Amar looking confused as he asked "and how do I do that?" "You have the coordinates don't you? – I can't force you or even teach you to find it; it's just something that happens naturally, like it's supposed to be - hearing music is an example, when it hits your ear drums or colors hitting your iris. Unless you're tone deaf or color blind you should be fine you know, there is a thing like that though but it's for the soul – it's called soul constriction it's when the cord of connection from the soul is complicated and becomes inaccessible. It's exactly like when you squeeze a knot in the water hose, you can't control your Divinity and your powers become dry and wither away – oh but anyways you should be fine – just try to feel it out with your soul – you'll know it when you see it and just follow it with your finger."

Amar gulping so full of paranoia and anxiety way to motivate a newbie by telling him the biggest symptoms for failure, he is so nervous he might even cause the disease himself just by pure imagination alone.

Amar closing his eyes as he thought so fearfully "I do not see anything! – Am I supposed to see something?! – He said I will know it when I see it! – But what is it?! He never told me! I forgot to ask him!! Is it a pitch black object?! – Then it would blend in with everything else!! – I will be stuck here in this very room because I could not get past the first step the easiest step!!! – THEN I WLL BE OFF THE TEAM!!... or worse... BECOME THE JANITOR!!! AAAAAAAAAAAAAAAAHHHHHHHHHHH!!!!!!!!" Ryker noticing a bit of Divinity dripping down from Amar's forehead, nibbling on his quivering lip, his facial structure moving around a lot with troubling concentration. Ryker shaking his head in disagreement as he thought to himself "he is trying too hard to find it – I wonder why he is so nervous... eh he's just a nervous guy! ...Oh my Father! I – I didn't... save my last level! – I know I am being a worry wart but I have to check because it took me forever to beat that douche of a boss! Straight up cheating with his B.S. game glitches!" meanwhile in the head of our poor trainee "NO MATTER HOW MANY TIMES I TELL THEM NOT TO CALL ME SWEEPY, THEY WILL – they are kids, they do not care!! They do not care about anything, especially janitor's feelings!! – Then their parents and or guardian will come by and will say something mean and snobby like 'oh see son and or daughter! This will happen if you make bad choices in your life and cannot pinpoint yourself to Earth!' Then all the other parents and guardians will gather around and all together will point and laugh!! – I DO NOT WANT TO BE POINTED AND LAUGHED AT, AT THE SAME TIME!! – and hey what is that?"

Amar's motor mouth fueled by an endless supply of fear and insecurities was finally put to an abrupt stop, like a brick wall suddenly appearing in front of it and he saw a mysterious white squiggly line that shined out of nowhere in the shadows of his mind. He reached for it, but it pulled away and got bigger becoming as long as a string, on the outside of Amar's mind Ryker looked up from his gaming screen to see Amar's arm flail up like he was reaching for something. Ryker gave a slight rejoice in his mind "yes! ... I did save it, I knew it! Oh and I think he's finally getting it, whatever you do don't stop Rook this separates the ones who are meant for war and who aren't!" The white baby eel once again eluding Amar's grip; Amar boiling over with frustration as he kept throwing his arm forward to try to catch it and every time it would grow in size. To a wavy white baseball bat, then a slithering ivory yard stick, then a small single tree branch with all white bark and even growing past that. Each time Amar was taken back a bit as he realized how big this thing he was reaching for, but that didn't stop him from trying. Now a very furry and stringy pom of white fur was as big as Amar's head, he hopped forward to try to catch it in the interval of Amar's chase; every time he would flail his arm he would be stroking the world to go forward with each miss, sending it more and more upon Washington D.C. until they we're straight out of the area and onto Pennsylvania, passing Maryland and onto New York. Amar barely beginning to notice that, white outlines of clouds started to appear at each failed attempt to grab the tip of the tail of whatever he was hunting down.

Suddenly it dived down, like a kid trying to see how long he could hold his breath underwater, Amar seen this thing begin to spin as it nosedived like a dying airplane. For some reason Amar had a strong urge to follow it, he wasn't going to let it get away after all the effort he had put into trying to catch it. He also dove down, hands at his waist as his head was aimed toward the ground so he could keep a watchful eye on that creature that kept evading him; he started to see outlines of a city in silver, gray, and white come to life like they we're being draw right before them. He could see the outlines of tall sky scrapper – like buildings, the railroads that we're bridged over short stubby buildings, the rooftops, the bumper to bumper cars, people looking like ants as they all waked in one bunch across what seems to be a road. The people became more and more visible as Amar came closer and closer to the ground at a rapid speed, he noticed that along with a simple outline of the varied people themselves. Inside of the single boundary that created an image for them was a flame now within each person, the colors were different, the size of the flames we're also varied and the amount that the flame took up was definitely not the same, some only had a match – sized fire in the middle of their chests, others had a baseball breathing hot air. There we're even some who we're an entire embodiment of fire looking like a regular human torch, but another thing that Amar noticed as he was just within building range was that not a single body was moving, it was like they we're all manikins standing completely still.

Stuck in a pose they looked like they we're positioned in, Amar then heard in a voice of echo like God was speaking straight to him "pull up you're gonna hit the ground" Amar looking around as he came within the second storied building range saying out loud "is that you Father?" Ryker pouring a waterfall onto his parade as he shouted over "no its Ryker, I can see everything you are doing right now on the screen now pull up!"

Amar still not completely getting it until he seen that he was about to crash and splat right into the street. Even the white fiend in front of him had did as Ryker instructed snake – waying its way through all the cars as it barely hovered above the street, Amar not knowing exactly how to do this "pull up" he didn't even know where he was. But he just remembered what it was like to chase the white culprit in the first place, he then corkscrewed a harmless spiral that twisted all of his furious speed into a boost as he drilled through the air and around the white ... dragon?! What started off as a tiny white string is a full grown ferocious white eastern style dragon? A long slender body full of scales, claws that could turn the cars it was flying over, into a crushed tin can. Just a quarter of its tail was already bigger than Amar it's eye alone was as big as Amar's face, it puffed out air from its nose in Amar's face distracting him; as he wiped the snot from his face, when he cleared it all away it was ahead of him once again. He got back onto his hot pursuit after his prize that ceased to stay still, chasing it down Amar happened to notice a cross sign that said "70th street" and above it was another sign that said "Lexington ave."

Not a single clue came to help Amar out in his confused time but all that mattered to him and was truly important was subduing the beast that was currently ahead of him and zig – zaging away. Block by block, street by street they we're flying by each section of buildings, it wasn't until the dragon took a wicked left turn and continued to go straight that he noticed a thunderous boom, rumbling and shaking. The ground and from the distance he could see a humongous, colossal whale – sized red and jet black outline of what looked like a vicious mountain with teeth; spitting out venomous drops of blood at someone or something, clouds of dust began erupting from the upcoming forest area as they came up upon it. Amar was so struck with amazement even the dragon had to remind him to chase him huffing out a puff of irritated air. Amar snapping out of it as he said "oh right sorry!" their pace only gotten faster as they drew near and it stopped being a deadly game of if Amar can catch it or not, to proper guidance the dragon showing him the way of the battlefield making a hard turn right. Pretty soon they we're in the park, inside demons we're crawling around like bed bugs jumping from trees, running on all fours, or trying to touch and grab the humans; but for some reason every had a light coating of evergreen on them. Acting as an aura that burned the limbs of the demons, Amar and the dragon we're just passing the institute for study of the ancient world, when they saw exactly who these demons we're fighting against

Cutting through the trees and hovering over the action alongside the dragon to see the three warriors standing against the impending army of demons. For some reason Amar could see them perfectly, like if he we're in reality seeing them right in front of his face no single dash line and flame for them, but Amar could also make out their burning auras and could measure just how strong they were. It was two males and a female all kicking the snot out of the demons, left and right sending them flying like they we're the wind and the demons the paper; one of the men was dressed completely head to toe in black. Every single article of his body was black, from his light footed design body of footwear looked to be very popular among ninjas, space black slip on, lace - less but iron toe shoes, black skin tight black lower waist wear, over that was a pair of iron knee pads and shin guards that even guarded the back of his calves. A gap the size of a hand between the knee pad was the thigh guard seeming to be shredded iron now this is where the samurai ninja feel ended, and took on a more – let you be the judge of that, the chest plate only the size of a book it was made of steel but truly not a big enough layer, surrounded by metal chain link mesh, underneath this was a black silky long sleeve, the chest plate came with two straps that connected to upper arm guards that connected to elbow pads then finally conjuctioning to forearm and wrist guards, there absolutely no guard for his back. Finally the topper and finale he had a normal shaped head, after that there is no notable facial feature other than a red line across where his eye should be, about the size of his eyes as well - that's it a red line that is it!

The way he was waving around his blood red bladed sword it had frontal advancing slice type design, a middle eastern feel but instead of going full force with it towards the end or the tip of the blade it came over like a huge candy cane. So it was a mix of the scimitar and the hook blade. The hilt of the sword looked like it stole the handle from a shotgun, this was some sort of Franken – sword; on his utility belt it looked like it was connected by a use of Divinity acting as a chain, a golden string looking feeble and about to tear any second but it was strong enough to carry a cruise ship just by being tied to it. This all darkness man held the hilt as he swung his blade, the hilt stayed in his hand and the blade itself went off to hook itself into a gorilla sized bulky demon that was in the trees; the blade had the golden tie coming from the bottom of the blade like a thread going into the needle. As the blade hooked into the shoulder blade of this monstrosity that howled in agony, he grabbed on with both hands onto the hilt and began swinging fiercely to the right as the demon swayed furiously to the right; the line got extremely shorter and by the time he came within shouting distance this man of darkness already had wheeled him to the 2'o clock position taking out three leaping animalistic demons that looked similar to oversized panthers just horrid, ungraceful, and a hundred times more beastly, but the oversized stocky demon slammed right through them like they we're a wall and he was the wrecking ball. This shadow man kept swinging full circle taking every demon within the vicinity and taking them for a second go as he heard "hey Ex! Bring him back this way I got something for him!"

The girl in the group then crouched down into a fearsome stance sliding her dominant right leg back, clenching her fists and nibbling on her lip as she waited for this horrible gorilla to bring its ugly mug. As soon as it came in front of her personal space, not even inside she quickly sprinted forward and thrusted her leg full force, driving her foot deep inside its face cracking every bone quicker than a rock going through a mirror. Wind blustering into a hurricane before she sent him whipping back, the one known as Ex used the ground as a trampoline for his personal pocket monster as he flowed with the momentum to fling it forward like a catapult launching a fireball at a fortress just replace the fortress with the big humongous titan – sized thing that dare not call itself a planet. As soon as it hung over the straight above or noon position Ex pushed a button on his hilt, suddenly a "chink" was heard, his hook blade then turned into a straight broadsword type of blade releasing that putrid demon of what seemed like eternal agony as he was projectile with perfect precision at the monster's pupil and it was not lucky enough to blink before the demon hit it. The fortitude of evil began roaring in pain as it put its claws over its wound to protect it, the girl then said "wow nice job Ex!" But then an exclamation was heard as she took her eyes off the battle "Kayoh!" She instinctively ducked as soon as she heard that falling onto her back so the demon was over her, in an upside down view from the woman called "Kayoh" position cocking back her arm for a punch like a cannon ball rolling into the cannon or a bullet being put into a tank – to put more modern perspective. The buildup of her words like a earthquake that first began by trembling "K...-aaaaaa....Y" the demon's drool like a spider slowly climbing down from its web hanging about a foot above Kayoh's face, as her eyes narrowed to it in the middle of her face it just all the more made her want to knock this thing into space.

She finished the rest of her charge up mantra "OHHHHH!!!" Her arm like the bullet from a magnum revolver shooting dead straight, a snap echoed throughout the entire park as Kayoh without a doubt felt a snap breaking the jaw of the demon in half as if it we're a simple block of wood, launching it off the floor in less than a second like a jet breaking the sound barrier. Putting her hands in the back of her shoulders as she sprang up to her feet, dusting herself off then shivering with disgust as she said "oh my Father that thing was repulsive!" She then snapped her fingers and an explosive shaped like a ring lit up the sky at cloud height the dangerous, deadly, and destroying woman who took the name "Kayoh" was actually a beautiful and alluring as her fighting skills, so in short she was drop dead gorgeous, from her impeccable, clear, and smooth peach toned skin and flawless face, to her unique colored silver hair that turned to onyx half way that trailed all the way down to her waist. The tips of her hair spiked instead of split ends in a group of seven spikes total, other than that she had normal looking luscious, healthy hair that even had its own sleek and shine, a petite body but fights like a heavyweight, her hips and waist shaped like a pair of grater and less than signs pointing at each other. Very nice and curvy the most strong built looking things was definitely her fists, that we're covered with black sewage blood Kayoh then groaned "he got my gi dirty! I can't believe this! – I wasn't even dressed for this but you two idiots had to "stumble" upon this area and didn't know it was linked to two other demonic rings causing a trinity effect when you tried to free all the souls and purify the area!!"

The gi Kayoh was referring to was the black hooded jacket that she was currently wearing, a zip up that she had open sporting a plain white shirt underneath. On the back of the jacket written in a circle and in white was the words "Turtle Hermit" the rest of her outfit wasn't as flashy as he jacket; navy blue skinny jeans and black low top shoes she still was going off on her commanding officer "oh no! But oh great Forrest my beloved leader had to drag poor innocent me into this! "We have to purify the area once all the demons are gone you can go! – Please there is a lot of them – ow one just bit me!" So I am thinking how could I say no?! – yup did not in the least expect a mountain of lard over there!" The grin of their leader in the face of danger was a bit admirable to say the least, laughing it off as he hammered his fist into the face of a demon slamming its body against the ground with tremendous impact that trembled the floor, stomping onto his fallen prey with his foot speared onto its chest. Digging its body into a grave in the hole he made himself a miniature crater he then clamored with laughter present in his voice "I did not say all that! Kayoh chuckling "you might as well have" a whole line of demons began charging forward, but it was like they stepped on a land mine that also contained evergreen paint. Burning them all to a crisp, now this courageous and audacious man who just oozed intensity and masculinity was their commander – in – chief, their captain, the leader of alpha team. Not standing at the most intimidating stature five feet six inches pretty average if you ask me, he was a very pasty pale skin tone, his muscles were toned just not that big – he could still use improvement, his shirt conveniently pulled down for battling purposes but it happened to be tied around his waist. As his sleeves flailed around, plain jet black skinny jeans with rips and tears at the knees, same toned black high-tops.

The thing that really stuck out about this guy, besides his burning embers that he was firing at the demons as we speak, was his hair a bright light green, spiked leaning forward over the plain green bandana that he had tied around his forehead. Even his eyes we're a pretty soft green, the flames sparking fiercely off his shoulders as he pitched evergreen consisted fireballs at the demons, combusting them upon impact. Kayoh swung over to her captain "hey Forrest! So no reinforcements!!?!" Forrest yelling back over as he chucked fireballs like they we're rocks at an old lady's house "not unless the commander wants me to break his neck!"

Kayoh smiling as she charged forward to a clump of demons knocking them all down with one punch it was as if she was the bowling ball and they we're the pins. Ex going back to whipping his sword around slicing and hooking it onto other demons, the colossal demon finally getting back up and pulled it's fists up and brought them down like a meteor was hitting earth. Amar and the dragon looking awkwardly at each other as they both heard Forrest say "no reinforcements!"

suddenly Amar's dragon was engulfed in a white cloud as it exploded into a poof and a tiny creature fit perfectly into his arms, as it leaped out at him Amar holding it up by the armpits as he analyzed and recognized it was the same ferocious dragon now insta - baby, Amar couldn't help but let out an "awwh"; just by looking at it, its claws disappearing turning into short stubbles coming out of short puffy marshmallow like paws. Its iron abdominal was squished down to a soft pink tummy that just urged you to raspberry it, the fur it had as an adult a long luxurious pelt was now just a big poof of cotton candy, the horns we're now short stubs on its forehead it was more like horns in training. It's mighty tail that was long now is slender and barely even a pollywog, something more that a puppy would be proud of, it's arms not even close to the monstrous crushing machines it was minutes ago now short pudgy little flabs of beginning muscles and lastly it's face now a smashed version of the muzzle that would have been able to chew on iron girders like chewing gum, only two teeth we're present two big blocks in the back closest to the throat taking up a quarter of the mouth space.

I am gonna be honest it looked drop dead adorable! Amar now holding him in his arms as he cradled him, letting him nibble on his finger as he told him "hmm you have to have a name – I do not want to call you dragon all the time that would be pretty insensitive I shall call you... CAMARADA – you like that?!" but little Camarada couldn't even answer he was fast asleep Amar petting him as if he was some kind of simple puppy. Ryker's voice echoing overhead like an announcement from the school principal but still very low toned careful not to wake the sleeping little angel "looks like you found your spirit animal –"

Amar nodding with satisfaction Ryker smiling to himself as he watched Amar on screen "put him close to your shrine so he can rest there, trust me he will be safe there and he will get the nourishment to grow whenever you need him all you have to do is call him, from now on he will be the guider for each and every mission you go on – he is a part of you." Amar doing as instructed putting Camarada close to the middle of his chest and like a vacuum sucking a year's worth of dust bunnies Camarada went in no problem. Amar feeling a bit strange that of all things would be where his heart would be, but what isn't strange around this place? Ryker speaking in normal tone as he instructed "okay now close your mind I have the coordinates" Amar so confused how does he close his mind? It took opening his mind for him to get here so maybe if he remembers that this is all a state of mind he will be able to wake up repeating the mantra "remember your eyes are closed, remember your eyes are closed, remember your eyes are closed, remember you –"

but by the half of his saying his eyes shot open and Ryker was standing in front of the digital like golden globe with Forrest's team battle on camera dust rising like geyser spray, Ryker then looking back at Amar as he realized he was awake from his trans.

Then pointing at the screen saying with an impressed tone "look what you and Camarada did – you're doin' great – you finally ready to go down there?" Amar's mind being blown one by one thing after another, first the experience as a whole, then the ferocious beasts and now he is going to have to fight that mountain with teeth?! Now Amar is rethinking exactly what he signed up for maybe he needed more training or at least some help so he isn't eaten like a tic tac "g-go down there? – How and with those things? Y-you seen that big one did you not?!" Ryker then smirked as he twisted his foot on the rim that he was standing on; the liquid began to drain like a plug pulled out from a tub revealing a sky view from underneath Amar's feet. Like he was a satellite hovering over Earth going to fire a laser upon it – well he was sort of doing it that but the laser was himself – so no harm done, he then saw from his position high above Earth a dot that glistened like a star as Amar recognized the land shape. He could tell it was North America as he squinted and focused harder it zoomed in to North America area only, only then only the east side, then the north east side, then zooming to New York as he tried to focus closer onto the city hovering directly over central park it began to pick up static on screen. In Amar's sight it was trying to lift 200 pounds with just his eyeballs his first try – in lifting weights ever!! It was becoming extremely strenuous, everyone has their own limits and restrictions Ryker saying over in a calm and collected tone "Just do what you can"

Amar panting as he tried with all his might to just focus his energy, Ryker continuing to guide Amar through his difficult path "now envision the ground in your mind, envision the street or sidewalk of where the battle is taking place and that is where you will appear." Amar remembered the ground floor that Forrest's team fierce war was going on as he pictured the sidewalk on top of plush, healthy, green grass the leaves from the trees above it speckled and sprinkled on top of the sidewalk. Amar perfectly captured this small almost insignificant detail but no matter how hard he tried to repaint the battlefield of team Forrest, a static second vision of the black top streets of the concrete jungle kept butting in trying to take the main frame. Amar struggling as the two images fought inside his head but ultimately the sidewalk in central park would be the victor, with the static loser forced to celebrate his victory; Ryker now leading Amar forward for his gigantic leap in progress "okay now get ready to go let all the energy flow through your body simultaneously and DO NOT BEND when you are beaming down it will break concentration and influx of energy you have going on – in short you will be a flying space monkey... that would be pretty cool actually – change of plans no pressure if you bend it has become a win win situation with me!" Ryker's teeth showing smile throwing off Amar because maybe not be bad fort Ryker but Amar doesn't want to be a monkey.

Amar took a deep inhale and tried to focus onto the energy, seeing it as a fire inside him that made him burn brighter each and every second his body glowed like a human florescent light bulb. Amar could feel his body getting warmer but he didn't want to take the chance of breaking his own concentration.

A silver and crystal aura began softly blowing off of Amar, gathering as he brought together his energy; Ryker raising his eyebrow as he put his hand on Amar's shoulder. Suddenly like the hole that viewed Earth had become the gun of monstrous proportions, it fired Amar and Ryker like they we're golden bullets Amar had transformed and was put into the shoes of a shining beam of light. The freezing vacuum of space punching Amar in the face as he traveled at the speed of light, all he could see was he was getting closer and closer to his destination he shook and trembled so violently he thought the entire world was quaking around him.

Ryker glimmering completely gold like his skin was made of melted gold his hair, eyes, and mouth as well only waist up was present his legs still taking the form of a trail blazing stream of glistening light, grabbing Amar by the face as he shouted his repeated instructions "DO NOT BEND!!" Amar heeding Ryker's words or at least trying to as he returned to being a single beam bullet of piercing light, Amar trying to straighten out his curving trajectory but it was like trying to straighten out a freshly broken arm, with the elbow being completely shattered. Amar grinded and clenched his grills or golden teeth as he strained as much as he could to push his trail – like body into a straight edge heading over New York they we're out of time Ryker shouting "Whooooooo! –" as the light crashed onto the floor but instead of exploding the ground beneath them like TNT it just dissipated like the light was simply switched off or the light bulb exploded. Just spitting out its riders, Amar was now on all fours on the floor with mouth gaping wide open, wrenching already and violently gagging.

Ryker jumping up and down waving his arms sporadically in the air screaming "you did it! You did it sort of!!" Black trail of lifeless Divinity dripping from Amar's mouth as he spit it onto the floor with a sickened and aching tone lingering in his voice "sort of?"

Amar just noticed that he was on top of black asphalt he looked around to see cars inches apart from each other as they kissed each other's bumpers, but none of them moving a single centimeter just parked completely still like cars on a dealership parking lot. Seeing people in bunches as they walked through the cross walk spreads of them scattered on the side walk but not a single one of them we're taking a single step it was like each and every one of them we're paralyzed in time stuck in their current facial expression. It was just as Amar seen it in his mind with Camarada, he looked to see on the inside of the cars the people we're stunned motionless in time paralyzed in a single expression – some we're blankly driving, others we're jamming to their driving tunes, and some we're stuck in their fit of rage and their hand just about to press on the horn. Even the birds we're stuck overhead in the air, before Amar could even ask what was going on he sniffed the air and went back to the floor gagging hid spiral pool as it tied itself in a knot wrenching out his discharge. "What is that smell?!"

Going back to his squirting and squishing from the mouth, Ryker sniffing the air and stuck his tongue out in repulse "yup that's demonic activity for you –dead carcass and strong sulfur, I'll give you a minute you look like you could really use one"

Ryker walking down the side walk, looking at stores as he passed by them until he seen a video rental store and smirked exclaiming "oooh! Can't wait to see the latest in devilish manipulation entertainment!" Rushing inside as he began looking at the titles, picking up the boxes and flipping through them from front to back – reading this particular one out loud as he seen all the images "hmmm Lucy? – Yeah because that's not a play on the name Lucifer at all – here take this enhancer and you will become stronger... once accepting our dark lord hahaha oh Hollywood you and your hidden subliminal messages"

he began to flip through the rows of movies throwing around boxes like a child looking for a certain toy "sequel, sequel, prequel, bad sequel, unnecessary money – hungry sequel, stupid trilogy, bankrupt avoiding sequel, remake, remake, remake, remake, remake, remake, remake, geez I get it the 80s was a golden era for movies but you can't remake the whole damn era! Just because it's present doesn't make it good! Comic, comic, comic, comic, comic, comic, comic, comic – damn! You guys aren't even trying anymore are you?! Well why try the whole world is under your thumb you don't have to dance around and entertain them to distract them from the bloodshed, corruption, and evil with good movies anymore huh?! Beavers in zombie form, sharks inside of tornados, some stupid cyber ghost, a glorified pornography, and ANOTHER STUPID MALL COP?! Okay so when you guys we're making the first one... at what point did you guys realize this was shit? Or are you guys' evil enough to know and supplied us with a second one?! Movie industry sucks right now well at least vampires are over and done with –"

Just then an explosion caught Ryker's ears as he thought in his head "I take my eyes off you for one second –"rushing out of the store to see what used to be Amar in a pile of fire that engulfed him. Ryker's eyes widened clenching his teeth, not really sure what he should do at this very moment "AND THIS HAPPENS!!!" Looking overhead to see a demon hanging its body from the fourth storied window Ryker grinding his teeth looking over at the chubby, stumpy little monkey, round gray gut, the rest of him was a dark black with long slender elastic – like arms and legs perfect for climbing. Reaching his claws even came in shape of drills; he definitely wasn't the most intimidating of the bunch; no horns or decorative evil added on for intimidation, besides his jet black eyes but blood red pupils. The defining feature about him was his mouth, it was abnormally large shaped in one big "O" with fire leaking around the rims from his fresh shot, Ryker with a frustrated "damn by an O of all things, crafty bastard! I better try to get him out of the flames fast or –"suddenly all of the flames we're blown away like a birthday candle only to make a scorched circle in the street. Ryker's eyes so big and taken by complete surprise he could've sworn his shrine blinked, his face of pure astonishment but it was suddenly replaced by an anxious smirk as he said with enthusiasm, excitement, and anticipation building, ready to break out of his voice "oh – that is good, very very good – I am really surprised – but none the less proud to be your master .... Now we can really start"

We Can Really Start

Amar & Ryker

Amar standing in the middle of the burning halo like a man standing in the middle of the sun, except – he gleamed brighter than every sun combined. Added with all the stars, nebulas and comets

Ryker covering his face as the heavenly divine light stung his eyes within seconds, making the demon overhead hiss in contempt and disgust falling from the building frantically trying to shield its eyes, it wasn't until Ryker seen the shadows return that he gently put his hand down to see the glowing glimmer.

The true definition of light that was now Amar, a neon white aura pulsing off him Ryker almost couldn't believe that this was the same trainee that he had, well this must've been the reason that he was put straight into their team and not start off at a lower ranked team to climb up from the bottom the next thought that immediately emerged in his head was "dear lord Azuru -... just what did you put this kid through?" Ryker now examining Amar's iron clad, indestructible, unbreakable, invincible, just absolutely intimidating suit of armor. The boots, shins to kneepad, a thigh guard belt instead of the man - skirt fold, an abdominal board that wouldn't surprise me if they we're Amar's actual abs pressed up against the metal and not an engraved design, this abdominal plate slid under, a double layered thick enforced chest plate that had an arrow shape as it collared around Amar's neck. A shoulder pad that rippled two plates down to protect the entirety of his upper arm, protecting and covering all the way to the forearms, his gauntlets taking over at that point; his cape waving like a proud flag in the wind not even a single burn, tear, hole or snatch singed in it.

Shining as bright as the armor he wore, his boots looked to double the size of his feet - damn lead foot! The boot, shin guard, and kneepad we're one in the same, all creased and curved so smoothly together. Indents and cracks to indicate where one part started and another one ended but they we're all connected, his thigh guards like bubbles on the sides of his legs ovaling over his thighs, that we're held up by a metal belt that safely secured the crotch (hehehe crotch, okay grow up Christian) and set up a defensive fortitude over, that is where the abdominal plate came in conjunction into it and the rest of the interlocking parts. Co existing and cogging together like a human's body, underneath all of his armor where spots of skin would be actually weren't, articles of white clothing covered Amar's body. Glowing like a tow truck filled with glitter was dumped onto his pants and long sleeve shirt, his pants appeared to be fitted or loose roomy pants shown at the gap of the knee and thigh and the spots where the thigh guards weren't, his long sleeve parts we're able to be seen at the edge of the bicep to the forearm area; just in a whole Amar's armor had the greatest radiance, flashing, glaring and glazing an amazing brilliant glint. His boots a gentle crème of white, the thigh guards a fierce shade of silver, his abdominal plate appropriately a sleek golden (cause you know he has abs made of golden – not that I was looking at them or anything! Keep reading what are you doing?!) His chest plate clashing with this as the strong silver collided with it, his upper arm guards following the same pattern of silver but his gauntlets we're a burning passionate gray, his cape still remaining a vigilant snow white.

The look in Amar's eyes was completely different as the O demon just pushed itself up against the wall in utter fear;

shivering and shaking as the bright burning light that once was Amar's blinding companion is now his aura, resonating off him quickly like steam from a glowing fire.

Amar pointing his eyes to the O demon, who was making frightened whistles through that big gaping hole that he called his mouth, before he could even begin to process to think about a plan to escape, a fist was smashed right into the dead center of his face the gauntlet completely caving in the "O"; eyes beginning to bug out as his face cracked like a nut in the mouth of a nut cracker. Until Amar felt no more struggle, the body went completely limp and Amar seemed to turn it straight to ash without any fire or maybe the light was plenty enough to burn it, suddenly Amar's gauntlet that he asteroided into the demon's face, like the same space rock that wiped out the dinosaurs, began sucking up the charcoal remains of the demon into it like a vacuum, it all twisted and floated into the pinky of Amar's gauntlet.

Amar pulling his body back completely lost to what was going on or what just happened, just holding his hands out in disbelief as they gently trembled, now staring at the new dot of darkness that was on his battle glove. Amar now examining his hand there we're no other black dots other than the one that was on his pinky, Ryker kept getting hit with surprise after surprise like a man with instant amnesia in a surprise birthday party. Semi stunned mixed in with impressed "he's so fast! – I could barely keep up with him! How did he get that speed?! One second he was there the next he is sucking the demon into his hand" shaking his blinding admiration away, Ryker needed to remain disciplined and remember that he is supposed to be the mentor here. Walking over to Amar who seemed shaken up, still shivering and trembling, finally putting down his hand though, his gloves being squeezed so tight and rolled into a rock hard ball with his face shaking as it pointed towards the floor.

Ryker now concerned what could be troubling Amar so much? Did he sustain some damage? Ryker looking and peeking around Amar to see if any burns or any sort of bruising – but it's impossible there wasn't even burn marks on his steel clad armor so how could his skin – that is designed to be harder than rock take some damage? Ryker tired of beating around the bush, as he put his hand on Amar's shoulder pad and finally inserted the question to which he hoped he could find the answer to but even before he could ask he seen it.

The golden streams on the edge of the rims of his eyes about to pour over like a tea pot on the stove on for too long "Rook? What's wrong? Are you hurt anywhere?" A sort of relief overcame Ryker as Amar shook his head, choking up and sniveling as he tried to fight back the tears made of gold, but this still confused Ryker exactly why what was he so shaken up about? The sudden action shouldn't have traumatized him this much, if anything Azuru should have done that especially after a year but maybe Ryker could cheer Amar up, this was probably just all the new experiences all hitting him at once "your armor! It is amazing I had no idea you had this underneath your robe – so is this your power or a part of it or something?!" Amar shrugging as he chinking his forearm protector against his face as he wiped his tears onto his armor using it as a tissue, Ryker thought he had some sort of idea what was bothering him but now it was safe to say he was completely lost.

"I do not care about my power or whatever I just killed something! – It happened so fast I did not know what it was I just reacted – I-I if I would have – what was it doing there anyway?! - I mean look at the dent I put into this building to kill it!" Amar pointing at the crater he pressed into the wall of the building that it slid up against in complete desperation like it was a tool he used to commit the crime, as he continued to plead guilty to the crime no one was even accusing him of doing "I mean! I butchered that thing! It did not deserve that!! I showed no mercy... no ounce of decency at all..." Ryker could not take his eyes away from the mess that was getting messier, with thoughts racing through his mind like a drag race track "he just reacted? So fast he couldn't even stop himself huh? – But he seems to care for it like it is some sort of animal I can understand if it we're an animal – you know something God created but this is something completely different – what Rook just did was rid the world of malevolence incarnated and he feels bad for this? ... Please tell me that Azuru at least told him why demons are our enemy... by the look of those baseball sized tears I am guessing not! Okay then this should be fun! – But this kid is something else he is very... innocent no – he is pure yeah that's the word." Ryker now looking up towards the edge of the rooftop to see three heads popping up all with big Os for mouths that took up 70% of their faces, the rims of their lips we're glowing with fire about to ignite Ryker then said to the hysterical Amar "wait here I am going to play teacher with an up close and personal example!"

Just then only a trail of white lightning that sparkled black was all that was left behind before Amar could even question his teacher, and within the blink of an eye Ryker was now in front of the pack of Os appearing like a static ghost before them startling them all to a jump. Before the entire O could ignite like a loading ring on the internet, Ryker simply pointed at one and a bolt of lightning speared right through the O's body sending it flying right off the building and onto the other side of the building to crash upon the cold hard concrete. The other was only half way with his charge up and looked oh so frantic as Ryker was floating upon bleached lightning, only smirking as yet another bolt miraculously struck and not a single cloud even overhead, like a shower of electricity thunder – clapping as it fell down upon him he only fell back over as his now charcoal body was cooking to a crisp. This only leaving the middle child of the three who was ever so desperately trying to charge faster, charge his meaningless one shot worthless excuse of an attack but hey whatever makes him feel good you know; Ryker stepping down onto the roof in front of him, the deformed dwarf of a demon backing up it was at 3/4ths complete only a quarter away from blowing hot air at Ryker. Ryker not planning on waiting as he swung his right arm from an under hook climbing uppercut to hit the demon that clashed with the short stubby demon's chin, and what the demon expected, you the reader, even me and I am seeing this damn thing happen right in front of me. To all of our surprises, he did not become the new rocket experiment for NASA to send to mars, no he wasn't even lifted off the ground but Ryker only gave a soft whisper after his fist made contact with the demon's flabby chin "impact: countdown" but what he did successfully do without a doubt he made this thing flinch, as he took advantage of this monstrosity grabbing it by its cranium as it kicked and screeched and fired its last and only resort.

Fire showered Ryker as the ball of fire launched from the O's mouth popped up like a bouncing land mine, spraying like a water hose in Ryker's face but Ryker's hand simply fanned it away like he was swiping away a stress candle. He then said with a bit of irritation "oh please! That won't even burn the threads of Divinity that sewn my clothes together! Now stop struggling let's go!!"

Before the O demon could even blink, the rooftop gravel was gone and it was staring down at the sidewalk where Amar's boots we're firmly planted on the ground; Amar jerking back with shock on the frightened creature immediately exclaiming as Ryker held it like it was some sort of ugly puppy experiment designed to go wrong. "Mr. Ryker what are you doing?! – What is that?! – Put it down before you hurt it!"

But Ryker kept his grip clamped onto the demon and stared straight at Amar with as much seriousness his eyes could shelter, "Rook do you know that this is what you slain? This is a demon, it attacked you first! Do you know what they do and why we hunt them? Do you know why you should not feel bad about killing one of these things?" "I do not care! They are living and breathing just like me! What right do I have to take their life from them?! I am not some butcher! – I mean the only one who has that kind of power is God only he should decide who is guilty or not."

Ryker sighing as he seen that his suspicion of Amar not knowing the reason they do what they do, and he had to explain the entire reason of existence. He then slipped his grip on the demon's cranium to only pinching the skull with his fingertips and from there a red glow began emitting from his tips, the demon's body began seriously kicking now struggling in absolute desperation. Just before it went completely limp by that time Ryker's entire hand now was a low vibrating red, he then looked over to Amar and with his available hand pinched the glow of ominous red aura from his hand saying as he flicked it into a tornado into Amar's eyes "here don't blink this is what went through the mind of this O demon, everything he did up until now you will be able to see... hopefully then you will be able to understand why we do what we do."

As the magic malevolent dust was sprayed into Amar's eyes that he violently began rubbing to try to scratch out of his eyes groaning in frustration, Amar's eyes creaked open to pure blackness but out from the darkness we're two claws that appeared from what looked like where he was standing from was this his point of view? Amar even a tad bit confused "what is this? – Is this that demon? – I mean Mr. Ryker did say I would be able to see that demon did is this what he meant?" So now curious to see if this was the case Amar patiently waited, the darkness began to clear as he seen the pair of claws creeping up hunched and cringing as it slowly took each step down a narrow alley way in the dead of night, tip toeing with the edge of the claws on its feet.

Where was it going? What was it doing? Why was it trying to conceal itself? – All questions Amar desperately needed answered but he had no choice but to let his spiral pool spin like a merry go round as he watched on. In the middle of the alley way was a little boy throwing his plushy dinosaur up into the air, so innocent, so full of life, so unprepared; he laughed so easily as he looked like he barely learned how to walk babble still being his only proficient language.

Amar's trembles returning as his body all stiffened and cringed what was that boy doing there alone – Amar was slowly putting the pieces together but he still had no idea what the outcome would be of this situation. The boy throwing the dinosaur up in the air and catching it himself not needing a partner to toss it to, he was all he needed and this was a barrel of laughs to him, but behind him like his shadow was the O demon that was double the size of this unsuspecting child; out from the rim of the circle that was his mouth was razor – sharp teeth that all slid out like box cutter blades. As he slowly got closer and closer – now to any normal person they would have already predicted the ending and looked away because they would not want to see what was about to happen next, but in Amar's case due to his pure personality he had never seen something like this take place before he was all new to this and didn't even know that this type of world existed so he could not take his eyes away.

Now was the time of pouncing as the demon was in position leaping onto the boy digging his claws into his delicate, still developing body as his scream shrieked throughout the night, Amar closing his eyes shut as he turned away.

Hearing the chewing, gargling, gnawing and screams of both pain and terror Amar couldn't just leave at that, creaking his eyes only to see the very active shadow moving up on the wall. Amar putting his gauntlet over his mouth trying to hold the Divinity from spewing out; he could not stop shaking his head trying to get rid of this vicious nightmare but it would not go away and it was all that he could see,

Fortunately for him a new image was now being forced down his eyeballs. He was looking up at a tall slender demon, wings like he tore them from a giant bat, skin a crusty, raunchy, rough, tough, and full of scales, dark purple. Having a rippled and define physique chiseled out like a statue in Italy, blood red eyes burned through Amar as they stared at him, or the O demon as he was currently walking inside of his shoes the shadows still concealing the rest of his devilish features; his face, head, upper torso, and the rest was still in the dark quite literally. He spoke in a twist and growls of tongues before pointing for the O demon to go forward with his jagged index claw to which the bumbling fool skipped over itself to scurry away, Amar curious to see what it was up to next but at the same time he didn't want to know. The demon was on the prowl galloping on all fours as it leaped from rooftop to rooftop of the low income apartment buildings until he finally stuck himself to the wall of one apartment in particular, digging his claws into the brick as it looked down.

From below it saw a man giving him the thumbs up, glancing around very discreet looking around to make sure no one saw him. A body was sitting up next to him it was limping over to the side, stripped down to the bare boxers and this man was beginning to tuck his shirt into his pants fidgeting and fiddling with his newly acquired police uniform; after seeing this signal the demon began to climb up

Peeping his head into each window as he passed by each and every one searching for something - or more like someone, as it passed by it saw the casual portly man who was alone sitting on his recliner watching television eating chips, moving along he saw a woman tightly pulling her child by his arm as she forced him to kneel down next to her in front of the bed opening a book and telling him to read it. Moving even further is that made this demon stop and stare, he saw an ecstatic man in a business suit, a very young energetic man he held up a paper and read out loud in front of his family of two his wife who wore a big grin and his daughter who with hands under her chin as she watched her father like he was the next president giving out his speech. They both clapping joyfully as he bowed in respect for his audience, even though this home was missing furniture, the room had wear and tear, dirt and grime this filth could not put dust onto their hopes and their vibrant energy that even Amar could see radiating off them like human light bulbs. As they all left the room to go inside of the kitchen the demon climbed his way inside of the apartment complex sniveling his way in like the cockroach that he was, as soon as he was inside he began spouting flames like a demented sprinkler turning each and every possession that they worked tooth and nail for was burning and slowly turning to ashes. Hearing the sudden roars and howls of the flames the entire family came out to the room being torched halfway and the flames slowly rising and picking up ground, as what seemed to be the father of this family put his family behind him as he shielded them from this beast that they we're amazingly able to see.

But there was nothing the man could do as a ball of fire hit him chest - on spreading onto him like his skin was paper, but he did not fall over he wanted above else to make sure the loves of his life we're unharmed. He made his way to the door to fling it open with all of his strength to shove them out the door and into the hallway, the last thing his woman and child saw was him being dragged away into the flames by his leg from this mysterious beast as the father slammed the door on himself to trap this thing in here with him. Amar was shivering and shaking with streams of gold racing down his face as he whispered to himself "why? ... Why? What did they do to deserve that? They we're just trying to live and you took that from them"

It wasn't done showing moments later the O mouthed demon was crawling back to his skinny master with a white smoky ball curled in between his claws like a child going up to their parent with a present for Christmas. To which the slender demon merely reached down and picked up the pure white ball and put it into its claws simply patting the creature on top of the head, but pointing forward with its crusty claw like there was still work to be done and this thing better go do it. Hopping right to it the O demon was trailing down the dark hall on all fours; Amar just could not take what just happened, this thing killed an innocent man and handed off his spirit in the form of a ball, somehow Amar has no idea how but he could tell that it was the same man, he could sense the energetic spirit that made up this man there was no doubt about it this was him but what Amar was questioning was how did that thing do this? An even bigger question was what was this demon going to do next?

Now Amar was seeing a one – sided, one man army absolutely devastating all these demonic forces in the middle of the street at the dead of night. Amar had the perfect overview like a hawk looking at its prey scurrying around, this golden aura man was flipping back and forth slamming roundhouses into the faces of demons that we're the sizes of gorillas, backs hunched over and jaws as big as that of a lion and muscle tone of a body builder from a strong man competition as it leaped to the one – armed golden armored soldier with golden, silver, crystal, and black blood leaking from his arm that was no longer there, but he viciously panted as he slammed his heel onto the top of the skull of a demon creating a crater with his face in the street. Using his body as a trampoline to flip off of into the air but was chased by three fireballs shot by three of O demon's kind, but luckily they all missed him by hairs length as he landed, panting he turned around and said to himself "I just need to hold them off a bit longer so my team can get away haha I guess it's just bad luck that we had to run into them after our mission -" ducking to the side to dodge a massive claw swipe and pulling his face back again and again as the pursing demon lunged forward, hearing a snarling behind him the soldier did not stop speaking to himself out loud as he was the only one who could understand what could possibly be his last words. "If I wasn't so fatigued and could use my Divinity you guys would be lingering dust –" using his available and only arm to wrap around the back of the neck of the demon to flip him on top of the chomping demon in front of him, stomping on both of their backs that made them howl and screech in pain but the soldier only added in his other foot in as well, once again moving forward he had to keep moving forward if he got stuck he was done for and he knew this.

Turning tail to jog away for a bit only to spin around and whip kick his three pursuers. Lingering in the air for a matter of mere moments he continued the thought "if only I had just taken us home from instead of trying to keep going to complete the mission –"the soldier then tuck and rolled under the three in coming fireballs that we're raining down above him, he looked up to see three of the O demons hanging by the tips of their claws that we're drilled into the wall of the building next to the soldier. Scanning around even more he found that more demonic Os we're popping up more and more ugly heads we're peaking up the soldier then heard roaring from behind him as more demonic beasts charged from the forest up ahead, the soldier's face becoming more grim because he didn't expect any of this in the least but it is not like he was surprised. This is something that these crafty devils would do – use all the forces at their disposal to try and end at least one of the lives of a Miraclelyte

Smiling at his coming fate because now all he could do is go down like the warrior's code would allow him to as he fell onto one knee he then pointed at the wall as his index finger glowed gold and he shot a bit of light at the wall like his hand was a gun. He gave one final smirk before he said "I hope you can forgive me little brother for all the times I must've hurt your feelings... I just hope you get that note and... you can find it in your heart to forgive me!"

He then charged forward like he had nothing to lose with one arm cocked back he rode towards the horde of malicious, diabolic, and treacherous demons who all rode on all fours to him; fireballs burning at his back did not bring him down, two shots from two O demons, made him skip a step did not bring him down, four shots, made him stumble did not bring him down, six shots, he began to trip forward but this still did not bring him down. As he drove his fist right through the face of a demon like his skull was made of wet tissue, managing to stick his arm so deep, he stuck his arm through the skulls of three demons behind him as well. The thunderous blow of epic proportions blew the demons to the side of the impact point away as if they weighed nothing, the soldier trying to swing the now dead weight – literally – off but it was taking too long too late as he turned around to use his momentum to do all of his work, but he was hit with a triple triangle of flames at the chest that made him take a step back.

The demons around we're using this as a window of opportunity that they weren't going to let close on them, chomping down and sinking their teeth into the soldier's arms, legs, chest and back. Trying to hold in his clamors of pains as he was able to lift up his arm to bring down onto the bodies that had stabbed their dagger like teeth into him, the combined weight from the bodies we're able to make his fist weigh like a bat. To which the soldier was able to knock each and every one of them to the ground and keep them there, with the first victims sliding off he began to feel it the exhaustion entering his body; also the flames whipping at his back and made him cringed his teeth tightly together, forced to take a few steps forward and when he focused his blurry sight forward all he could really see was a blurry dark blob pouncing forward to him before he could truly realize what this was he felt the most unbearable squeezing with jagged edges on both sides of his ribcage squeezing and crushing. Now he wasn't able to hold back this scream of agony with that demon that clamped down onto the soldier with its massive and powerful jaws, even more we're to follow gorilla sized demons that dug their fangs onto the soldier's legs, arm, shoulders, back, thighs, every square inch of him that might be able to move possibly.

He only stood there as now the O demons began leaping off from the roof to latch their teeth onto their now stilled target. Each one latching onto available skin, even the O demon whose life Amar was living vicariously through. He being the last thing he saw as leapt onto the face of the soldier

As soon as Amar seen that he flinched and blinked to see Ryker holding the demon by the scalp and the O demon had now become very limp and still. Amar just could not believe what he had seen, that such a primal creature was capable of such malevolence, harm and dismay – and he knew the hearts of each of those people, pure, innocent, good – loving people but this – this thing! Struck with no mercy or without a second thought and killed them all in cold blood, as he looked at it he picked up his hand and drew it closer and closer to the demon's face wanting to just clutch it and break it like it was the frail side of a wishbone. But Ryker pulled it away and struck Amar with wonder, "why are you taking it away from me it killed so many people!?" Ryker shaking his head with a growing smirk as he explained "no young grasshopper I understand your pain and yearning for justice but you must understand that we are not warriors of vengeance and darkness! When we become that... when our hearts or our souls become corrupted by ambition, revenge, hatred, anger, or depression then we lose our resolve, our power, and more importantly our way – we lose everything that is near and dear to us and we become no better than them the darkness – plus there is something inside of you that I just cannot bring myself to stand by and let you corrupt. Your soul is too golden and full of light for me to let you throw away by fits of rage; although justified you must understand when you slay it is not for self pleasure like rage vengeance or seeking of your own self justice, no it is for protection, protection to eliminate the darkness in any way possible to help cleanse the world. When we begin to enjoy the torment that we inflict on our enemies how much better do we become from those that we fight so desperately against?"

Amar dropping his hand in such confusion and such loss of direction "so then what – how do I do this – if I cannot kill for the evil things that they do – I just do not quite get it! We cannot let them get away with these kinds of things!!"

Ryker nodding his head as he agreed he then squished the head of the O demon to the point where he popped like squeezing a balloon its body simply plopped against the floor next to him as he walked over to Amar. Putting his hand onto Amar's shoulder pad as he looked into his lost pupils with fire in his own eyes, "I understand it is a difficult concept to get because to go to war you have to have some sort of hatred for your enemy, some sort of disdain or anger towards them but that's the thing with us Miraclelytes if we carry all that anger and all that hate believe me we will not be able to function properly. Don't get me wrong I have lost friends, family, and had to suffer watching my children growing up almost without a visible father, but this path that we take is not even close to be an easy one. Most people not only will probably never get the concept of our lives that we live and the virtues that we are built upon, and this is one of the difficult lessons that we need to learn on this jagged path that we crawl upon – all I can say is that you we're chosen for a reason so I know you can handle it, *you* just need to know you can handle it!"

Amar looking at his own hands then peering over to the slain demonic carcass on the floor behind Ryker, but suddenly like its fuse had just run short to spark its gun powered hive, The O without being touched what's so ever rocket shot up into the atmosphere above the clouds within a matter of blinks. Now trying its absolute best to be the best selling illegal firework blowing up to pieces of lingering ash in the sky, Amar with his eyes stuck up in the sky tracking the specks of burning soot with his pupils; not taking his sight away from the black puffball asking how to walk the path of the warrior "so then could you tell me how to not feel hatred or any ill will towards my enemies when I am fighting them?" Ryker curving his arm around Amar as he responded "of course! Walk with me talk with me! First off you set us on the wrong street by the way. We're supposed to be at Central park, we're at 70th and Lexington ave."

Amar getting a bit down with disappointment "I know - when we we're shot down – it – it was just so overwhelming – I really didn't expect that much pressure! So I started off sort of bended and the whole time I was trying to straighten myself out – I completely forgot our location – I tried to get as close as I could but it was already too late."

Ryker patting the gentle soul on the back in encouragement as he said with so much admiration in his voice "don't worry about it kid! We're only a couple blocks off not too far! – You know Azuru used to send us like countries off before he was leader, we would have to go to Italy he would send us to Africa, we need to go to Brazil he would land us at Detroit - you know that kind of stuff". Amar wide eyed and amazed "really?" Was all he could really say, he asked as they walked down the road on the way to Central Park, Ryker replied "haha yeah turns out he just wanted to bond with us by taking road trips" "would you guys have to beam back or what would you do?" "Well – and this is for another day to talk about cause we already have the lesson plan for today but, we can make vehicles appear we create them with Divinity – let me tell you it wastes a hell of a lot less energy than teleporting, readjust the pinpoint, then being beamed down again! That just eats a huge chunk of power so yeah."

Amar just "oooh" ing in acknowledgment to Ryker now bringing in his serious tone "before I get into our topic for today, I want to bring up your power – now I know you probably weren't in the best state of mind to talk about it then. This is fine, but now that we had a little time for explanations I am going to bring it up again you said before that it happened so fast you didn't know what happened you just reacted correct?"

Amar nodding his head to his questioning sensei as he continued "and how long have you had that armor? Is that a result of your training?" Amar taking a quick second to look at his armor that had basically become as natural to him as a backpack that a child carried to school, once taking a second to look at it Amar responded "umm Mr. Azuru told me not to tell anyone besides him what I received after my final step but this is part of it, but yes" now Ryker was truly curious why was Azuru keeping this kid a secret? His possible potential and possible power that he would be capable to unleash – is he protecting him? Or saving him as trump card? "Did Azuru tell you why you can't share it with anyone or did he just say? "Or I'll beat your ass an inch from death!" Amar nodding his head and lifted up two fingers from his right hand, to which Ryker just shrugged it off and continued onto his actually intended lecture "well he must have a reason for it – and I'm gonna watch you carefully so I can gather further info on your powers of what I might think they might be. Anyways today, or this time I will be speaking about our enemies – what we as Miraclelyte fight against."

Amar nodding as acceptance of this lesson and just barely realizing that he didn't even really know what Miraclelytes we're to begin with; yes he knew that is what he is now but what exactly is he now? One of Amar's trademarks politely raising his hand, even though they we're far from a classroom "umm Mr. Ryker what is a Miraclelyte?" Ryker repeating what he has been saying this entire time "that is gonna be for another damn day you brat! – Shit you wanna take the whole universe inside your damn brain?!" Amar instantly apologizing, even though curiosity was something that is supposed to be perfectly fine; Ryker was just lazy, but picking his teaching stick back up "demons are the topic young Rooksworth! – Well enemies in general –"Amar listening very attentively but had no idea why Ryker was now speaking like an older type fast speaking Englishmen (yes the pip pip cheerio type) Ryker continued "but we shall start with the demons, now demons have several classifications- or well at least the commoners in this area there are many classifications but let's stick to the ones who show up here. Like the one you just mercilessly destroyed without a second thought is a low ranked primal demon ... you cruel bastard –" Amar frantically waving his arms in apologetic distraught "I- m –I am sorry! – He came for me! – It was self defense!! – can I have my one phone call?!?!" Ryker chuckling an odd region of humor chuckle "now dear boy nothing to worry about – it had no friends – no family – no one to love it – forever to wander the world alone without a single ounce of emotion invested in it. –""aaaaaaaaaahhhh – you are making me feel worse!! I am worrying about it when you just instructed me not to!!!"

While Amar was tripping over his own self created hole of guilt Ryker went on to explain "those demons are the lowest of the low and I don't mean that morally I mean that fundamentally and physically. They aren't too advanced or even strong – they have one mission and one mission only, gather souls so their body does not decompose and to make their creators happy, because they need to earn their keep or they get sent back to hell to become nutrients for other stronger demons. Demons that are beyond this form can usually become more advanced by however much souls they devour or malevolent energy they bask in and you wanna know something really messed up? A great way for them to boost up faster in the evolution cycle is by eating their own kin – yeah they can gain some energy and boost from eating demons but if they eat from the same family tree they get a bigger boost. The closer the bond the more stronger they will become – it really is messed up a son eating a mom or a mom eating a son just for strength, but uh we call these demons that are beyond the O form primal: because that's basically what they are. They have little to no thoughts if they do have some sort of thought process it is on the same level of an aspiring cub or baby, also hence their body work is made after really bulky, animalistic, and just beastly type designs. This also means their move sets are limited only resorting to the attacks they instinctively know

– nothing really special or flashy, see now the reason why they have a build like animals same bone structure, muscles, and even some of the same organs as animals is because when they are made in hell they have not a single clue what they are doing – they only know how to destroy.

They have not even the slightest idea on how to create, they do give it the hatred and negative energy that it needs to exist, that they do but other than that they do not even begin know where to begin. So they just get a template from Spirit because we are truly a design of a divine masterpiece that on one can copy or plagiarize. Taking his creations of animals, they made their pawn soldiers now after the disposable animals come the pet goat: these are only slightly above in strength they can control the humans with telekinesis and force attacks, but they're picking on people who have their eyes shut, mind closed, and spirit is borderline nothing. So not really anything impressive, just a bunch of bullies if you ask me! Now they are self – aware, somewhat intelligent, and somewhat tactical – they **do** know how to speak – they speak their own language of origin – but it's speaking none the less. For body types they are basically a pile of bones well stacked up – I mean assembled in the shape of a creepy, ugly, goat – man monster; all of the pet goats resemble a goat in some way the horns, body posture, the baaaaaah, the legs, the tail, or more baaaaah! They aren't all the same some have variations and what not just letting you know so you can be prepared – there is also human versions of these pet goats, they either posses them or they take their form in disguise. There is always the option of killing the person taking their soul, trapping it within them and impersonating them... but that's just them.

Their job as humans is slowly to make a downward incline, of civilization, society, and humans in all. There are some pet goats in politics of course... some in the music industry; sometimes they are just straight up serial killers – like they could look like a normal white skinned boy, who goes into a peaceful church of praising, and mercilessly murders people - even admitting to it but just simply classified as mentally ill – see there is a lower ranked goat getting what we call a "bailout" by bigger goats in higher places, and last but not least on the first three steps. The three popular names amongst us that we have for them are "cyclopean, gargantuan, and Pee – wees"

Amar caught off guard by the last one - you know the old saying one of these things is not like the other as he turned his head to give Ryker an awkward eye, Ryker only had to utter one word to clear up any confusion like the perfect pimple crème on a face full of acne "Azuru" an epiphany hitting Amar like a truck, he then said with a confirming "oh" full of belief. Ryker trekked on his journey to explain the whole damn history of the demons, pointing at the upcoming battlefield where the monumental stack of demonic being was slamming his fists down like a pro wrestler

The ground seeming to be his rival in this match to the death as he pounded viciously. A cloud of dust detonated from the ground up into the sky within first contact, Ryker with a bit of urgency jolting him forward panic in his voice building up as he said over to Amar "oop! We better start running over there! – I'll explain on the way! – When they look like they are really in trouble then I'll zip over there okay?! – But for now they seem to be fine! They are alpha team after all!" Ryker then dashing into a furious sprint, arms wrenched tight at his biceps as he seemed to have broken the wind (no cheeks needed) air being pushed out of his way – trailing alongside him as he bulleted down the street.

Amar stunned that someone could be that fast, but snapping out of it as soon as he looked past Ryker to see the goliath in the distance he could see his building sized fist trying to pile down onto Kayoh, Forrest, and Ex. Kayoh taking one for the team as she lied on her back..... hey hey where is your mind going?! Just because I worded it that way doesn't mean anything –Kayoh is a kind, classy, lady I'll have you know! - She wasn't doing anything of that sort she was actually keeping the entire hammer area of the fist off her entire crew by jacking up his fist like a car in an auto body shop. Just solely with her legs they trembled a tiny bit but she wasn't struggling, behind her Forrest had his arms spread out like security guards holding back the entire crowd of fans from tearing apart their favorite singer – like that guy ummm what's his face? – Yeah there we go good old who cares! But unlike most security guards Forrest gripped the faces of the ferocious demons, tightly squeezing like he was trying to squish grapefruits with his bare hands but the faces of the demons we're viciously trying to pull away. But the vice grip of his just wouldn't budge it was because beneath his falcon talon - like hands was embers burning their faces the longer he held them, until fires literally broke out onto their faces, wildly resisting by flailing and tugging just before these prime ape bodies grew limp like ragdolls in his hands. Forrest then said over to his comrade in front of him "you okay Kayoh?" Kayoh letting out a slight grunt of discomfort "never skip leg day ya know!"

Forrest turning his head over into Ex's direction who was in an 80% laying down position postured like a determined injured victim tenacious to push through injuries right before he is hushed by the doctor or nurse to rest their hand halting their chest, he was holding the hilt against his abdomen pressed up like a butt of a gun against a solder's shoulder.

Ex shaking due to this unusual position but lifting up his sword that was as long as 4 yard sticks he shish kabobbed 7 demons onto the blade, the cold steel drilling right into the middle of their intestines. The stupid animals all tugging on the blade, trying to pull themselves off, some even trying to bite it Forrest finally popping the question "Ex what about you? You alright" Ex slowly bobbing his head up and down Forrest then said "okay thanks for the save Kayoh! I'm gonna take this one now" Kayoh smirking with mischief as she responded "yes sir!!" She then said like she was charging up her words "ss-s- shotgun! – Blast!!"

A pump was heard as she touched knees to shoulders really scrunching everyone in as the ginormous fist umbrella over them. They simply crumpled their bodies and just dealt with it, knowing it would be worth it in the long run, pushing with the force of a bull ramming through a person's body, she shot her legs forward shooting the giant's fist up like it got the call to all of sudden raise the roof. Golden and red flames blazing and torching the bottom of the fist, as shards of black, red, gold, silver, and crystal Divinity all darted at his gut; now seeing their way out, Forrest spun like a perorating ballerina so he could chuck the two beasts he had in his hands at the Pee – Wee at bullet speed they jet through the sky right into this giant's gut instead of bouncing off they drove straight in like a car through a wall – half of their bodies hanging out from his stomach. Roaring with agony the mountainous demons waved his arms in the air with fire coursing through his mouth like overflowing saliva and just as he was about to open his mouth up wide to cannon this blast of hellfire, Ex slid in front of the group with his sword at his right thigh.

With both hands he swung with all of his weight behind it, full force swaying a full chain gang of screeching demons. Slicing his sword diagonally up left like he was lashing his baseball bat at an unhittable insane curve ball, but Ex wasn't giving up even if he was on his second strike he was still going for the homerun. The blade came up along the chin of the monstrous Pee –Wee he pressed a button on the hilt, and the swaying blade converted to a straight edge, the ape demons slipped off one by one with the force of the speed they we're traveling the first demon being shot out at the Pee – Wee's jaw as the second one, the third one both chipping the lower left tooth. The forth busting the upper lip, the fifth literally nailing him right on the nose instinctively brought down the monster's face, but before he could even fully face downwards the sixth prime ape, shot right into his right eye perfectly sliding in between the two flaps of the eyelids bouncing back his right eyeball with tremendous force enough to knock his tiny comrade unconscious. Just floating in the gelatin of the eyeball right in the middle of the pupil, this really set his blood a boil roaring with furious anger and just as he was about to unleash his wrath onto his persistent ant – like foes, one more comrade came to his aid but definitely not in the way he wanted or ever would want. Drilling a crater into his skull as he torpedoed into him, the whole world spun before the gargantuan just as it felt like it was hit with the world's most humongous baseball bat.

Taking a step back filled with haze it tried to regain its head before anything, Forrest taking advantage of this particular time as he glowed a fiery pillar of light; his eyes shining like flashlights as a circle of evergreen embers ignited around Forrest. The circle of evergreen slowly trailed up his body until the green embers covered his entire structure – toes to the tip of his hairs like a suit of armor, he shined like the most beautiful jade emeralds he then said "Evergreen!... come out and play!!"

He then laughed as he disappeared right before them, the Pee – Wee still trying to shake away the haziness of all the concoctions blows but then it felt like he was making it worse as it felt the ground beginning to leave him, its foot picking up right off the floor and it wasn't doing this! Did it have some sort of flying ability that it wasn't aware of? Oh we it was gonna fly alright, it just isn't aware of it, Kayoh and Ex turning around to face a horde of demons the size of a militia coming at them worse than black Friday charge at the doors at the break of dawn. (I mean seriously the day before you guys we're just giving thanks now you're going to break an old lady's skull with her own oxygen tank for a HD TV that is only 5 dollars off than it usually is, whatever) getting themselves ready; Kayoh cracking her neck in anticipation, Ex dusting off his blade as the savages charged to them without hesitation, but a black cloud began falling over them; Ex and Kayoh though we're as clear as day. They examined themselves and the ground but and they looked back over at the side of darkness they curiously looked up, Kayoh let out a giggle and a grin, Ex would have also if could but he just played the waiting game alongside Kayoh.

So patient as the demons roared and howled at them tearing up the ground as they charged and scurried to Forrest's team; the cloud getting darker and darker as they got closer and closer and not one of them had the common sense of a decent mind to look up, when they arrived within yards of Ex and the ever so relaxed Kayoh. Just as the lead demon was about to lunge and pounce forward it was like the titanic ran out of jet fuel and decided to safely crash here, dirt rising up like a wall of flame but not a single speck of it landed on Forrest's team. The vicious force of air buffeted their faces and blew Kayoh's hair a frizz but other than that they we're completely fine; the arm of the lunging demon was the only survivor amongst the dark army that had been crushed by their big comrade's backside. Forrest pulling up behind them as he said with his blood pumping and all charged up "ready for the return attack team?!" Both Kayoh and Ex nodding their heads as they got back into their fighting stances and another army began sprinting from the trees to the left of them, quickly shifting their attention to that active side deep within the trees Forrest seen a human – like figure in the back of the whole entire rushing crew. Bouncing what seemed to be an illuminating gleaming ball of neon white within its jagged claws, Forrest's balls of fire that used to be his eyes flared up as soon as he seen this silhouette declaring "there he is!"

Just about to charge Amar was desperately trying to squint harder, tearing up the blocks as he sped through like a Ferrari despite all of the traffic; jumping onto the hood of cars running through them like he was riding the tide of a tsunami. Not wanting to take his eyes away but then he heard a calling over to the left side of him "Amar what are you doing?! Get a move on!! – Better yet come up here and you can learn to run at my pace!!"

Amar's eyes almost popping right out of his skull when he was seeing the stunningly remarkable Ryker just running along the side of a building like it was a regular track meet. Sprinting like he stole something every step he took he shattered the windows from every apartment building he touched, even engraving his foot into the wall, jumping over ladders whenever they came up. Amar screaming out in star struck "Mr. Ryker!! How do I do that?!" Ryker concentrated on the obstacles in the road in front of him but still directed his words over to Amar on the ground floor "you got the speed – all you need to do is believe you can get up here! Let go of your old human limitations its part of rebirthing yourself as a Miraclelyte!! You're one of us now time to act like it!"

Amar not having time to think he had to just put his teachings into play repeating the instructed words back to himself once he truly got it he gave a solid hard "yes sir!" Obedient and proud enough to make a drill sergeant cry with tears of joy, jumping from the hood he was currently stepping on to projectile him into the air bending the car so hard he shot the hood straight open once he launched himself. Definitely leaping farther than Ryker but he was over the sidewalk and still had to get over to the wall that he was on.

He slowly started to descend as gravity began grabbing him in its evil clutches, but coming up on the rear was Ryker traveling faster than Amar was falling and snatched him up by the hand. Yanking Amar with a tremendous amount of speed that Ryker was catching him up to, Ryker then said as he dangled him over the concrete that seemed to blur by "you're gonna have to hit the ground running okay!" Amar just giving a confirming nod before Ryker gripped the other hand and slammed him over to his left side but Amar did as instructed, stumbling at first but then bursting it into a rush to match Ryker.

Ryker getting right back into it without a delay "very nice you're learning quick – now back to the lesson now that we have time! – Okay so Mr. Tub of lard over there! He is something that usually starts off from a demon that has consumed a lot of souls or has been promoted by the dark forces! – He then slumbers, is able to produce negative energy as well take it in when his sleeping nest becomes a home base for other demons to come and circulate their energy – he grows by however much energy is gathered and wakes up once his negative field has been disturbed for whatever reason! – Now that one that they're fighting is known as a "norm" or a "Jane" because he has no veniality running through them! Now the end of the norms and onto the – shit! I forgot one more shit! shit! shit! Okay last one the damned souls! These guys are people from hell or captured souls converted into evil beings due to the amount of evil or corruption. This is usually their main goal to capture people and take their souls because from there so many variations of powerful soldiers are possible; the soul gives them their own identity and all the evil and hatred they are fueled with gives them the body, the longer they are here on earth the more powerful they can become for standards though, it takes about a week for them to get out of their baby zombish stage and to further progress as they pick up souls and negative energy and cause further mischief – okay now I can get onto the categories!! Hope I'm not frying that brain of yours.

Anyways!! This Earth is such a wonderful place more wonderful than all the rest of the other versions of Earth! That's why I believe our Earth is so wonderful there needs to be a huge force of evil to counter our wonderful world's wonderfulness – so what does the evil side come up with?! Instead of having one devil, we have seven! Yes! Seven!! –"Amar's soul about to jump out of his God given body, his shrine flickered on and off like a low budget spooky house, and definitely a new pair of under ware was needed. He was a bit more different than Ryker's excitement who was more hyped up than how fearful Amar was "wha- what the actual hell man?! Where did they all come from?!?! I mean sure the devil had a lot of names like Lucifer and Satan and such, but seven?!!?" "Oh yes my poor student and those are just two of the several, they are very much separate beings in all there is Mammon the desiring, Belphegor the sluggish, Leviathan the green eyed, Beezlebub the hungry, Asmodeus the lonesome, Satan the wrathful, and little Lucy the light bearer. All these are the generals or commanders of hell, demons work their entire existence to be recognized by them to be directly under their squadron and once they get past the third stage they do. Depending on what kind of negativity or hatred they picked up determines which category they fall under, trust me it goes even deeper than that but I'm gonna have you under my wing so another thing we can go over later, sooooo.... What do you think of just **one** faction of all your enemies?"

Amar's body was pacing forward like he was fine but on the inside he was floored, stunned, dumbstruck, paralyzed, frozen with astonishment, he didn't even know what to say, he didn't even know what to think. It was like he was on a small island and trying to balance on it while a ring of frenzying sharks swam around with Amar dripping blood, further onto safe shores that we're only a leap away was a flower field of landmines. He just felt absolutely overwhelmed, just how did Azuru expect to take down a demon of such high stature when even these "small fries" seemed to be a well match; Amar now beginning to drown in an ocean of thoughts until Ryker smacked them away with a thunderous stinging slap that would've really left a mark if he wasn't wearing armor but the sudden snap did have Amar in a panic. Ryker as serious as he possibly could be as he said "sorry you we're zoning out and I need you here right now! Also one more thing before we shut this tutorial down –"Amar's still very shaky and Ryker almost see the worry and pressure zig zagging in his pupils like race car drivers, but he tried his hardest to focus onto Ryker and Ryker accepted that; as he continued his ponderous thought "I need to know do you have it in you to slay a demon? I hate to be the one to say this to you but if you cannot find your resolve on how to slay them without anger or hate to fuel their ever burning fire then I am sorry I do not care how special you might be I am going to have to recommend to have you taken off the team – you don't have to tell me now but when we get onto that battlefield if you can't bring yourself to do it I will have my answer."

This was the longest eye contact that Amar had ever held with someone in his entire life it made his shrine sink into his spiral pool he could feel it swirling around like a child caught in a whirlpool, Ryker pointed to the ground and just signaled with a look deep imbedded in his pupils "follow my every move!" Speaking without words Amar nervously bobbing his head in acknowledgment

Ryker then sprang from the side of the wall, tucking into a ball as soon as he was in the air and gravity trying desperately to figure out where to put him. Flipping as he went from horizontal to the vertical plane just by simply drooping down third storied height in the sky releasing his legs as he hit the ground running, Amar sighing as he said to himself "I – I can do this I know I can I just cannot let them get away with killing innocents and my comrades... I know I barely started but I – I like these guys and I do not want to have to leave them because I am not able to pull the trigger!" before Amar leaped an exceptional height over the sidewalk tucking himself into a ball but there was almost no need, he was already over the street in the horizontal plane. Releasing his legs as he rolled like a wheel of a car on a freeway and he himself dropped down into the vertical plane onto the street, stumbling a bit as he began to run alongside Ryker. Who smirked at him and scoffed and said with a confident tone "well you passed one test! When I talked to you about your resolve that was the perfect time for you to turn back if you didn't believe you could do this, you're still here so you must have some hope for yourself - we'll find out right now."

Amar was now past the point of paradise and onto expectancy as they came up onto the battlefield closing in, Ryker and Amar began trekking up to the final street that lead up into central park just then Ryker had an expression of question that Amar almost immediately picked up on "Mr. Ryker something the matter?" Ryker still thinking and processing something as he replied to Amar "I – I could have sworn I heard them say something about a trinity in your vision of them fighting" "they did – I don't know what that quite is but they said that!"

Ryker and Amar upon the turn at the central park steering a hard right as they followed the trail "that doesn't make sense then because yeah that Pee – Wee is pretty big but he isn't big enough to be the entire trinity. There has to –"Just then the Earth began to quiver and shake rumble and tremor, stopping Ryker and Amar in their tracks Ryker shaking his head as he said out loud "I knew it – kinda hate it when I'm right!" He then began looking around to see not a single person in central park was closed today and they we're enforcing that with the law. The ground on each side of central park began faulting and cracking open like a chick hatching from the egg, until the ground split open like a volcano was hatching this monstrosity, building sized pair of claws gripping the edges of the hole as they pulled themselves out of their sleeping nests. This was the first time that Amar actually gotten a close look up at the terrifying gargantuan sized Pee – Wees, on top of their mountain like body stature with a gum drop shaped face; big and goofy with the fangs from each side sticking straight out, ripples of over skin double and even triple chinning it's face. Having the true definition of a "derp" face really the only word to perfectly describe it too, even though it had a mountain peek type body its head smoothed over like the shape of an egg, the entirety of its body was black and red splotched over each other not really having a clear or distinct pattern. That goes for the other two as well besides the rock formation shape on them they actually did have long slanderous arms, for this type of body structure that was presented to them, its legs we're already squatted and squished into position.

Taking a few lessons from their frog mentors, as they positioned their legs strikingly similar, but their feet weren't webbed but a mere reflection of the claws. As they stood their truly remarkably breath –taking stance as clumps of the street, cars, street lights, and Earth terrain was shaking off from the shoulders and top of their heads and sprinkling onto the floor. Crashing and booming against the ground almost like an oversized sumo wrestler ready to push the stick that was Amar with their iron palms, Ryker biting the side of his lip as he said more to himself than Amar "shit! Gonna be a tiny bit tricky cause we absolutely cannot let that hybrid get away! – so he can use that soul and maybe other souls to make more demonic creatures – nah that's the last thing we need – well guess we should take out those two canyons with feet first!" Ryker then began glowing a pure white luminance, Amar looking at himself to compare the radiance and he still had ways to go literally pale in comparison. Amar a creamy tan to Ryker's glowing snow even his aura became visible as it vibrated off him as noticeable as perfume being sprayed in front of them from persistent sales women at the mall, stripes of black lightning sprinkled in here and there zapping in and out appearing and disappearing at random. Ryker then said over his shoulder "I'm gonna go take down the three tons of joy there! – you go lend support to Forrest's team the soul is always the main objective!" Within half a blink of an eye Ryker was already stories high with his aura now blazing on him, the glistening white and now as sightful as fire outlined with a shining glossy black.

Tiny stripes and bolt shapes of darkness in the air as if it we're absolutely normal to be stories above the ground then a gut feeling began pulling on Amar, twisting his spiral pool – a sinking feeling that urged him forward to not do as his sensei told him just this one time. The impulse so strong it finally unleashed itself from within its cage that Amar tried to keep it in, Amar stepping forward reaching out his right hand as he shouted "wait!" Just then like his hand was some sort of summoning machine of convenience devices. A pure white splendor ivory chain big enough to shackle a full grown man to a pole looking like a magician at a children's party currently doing the endless tied hanker chief trick, this chain also looked like it was coming from Amar's sleeve as well but unlike those pretend magic casters it was coming out straight from Amar's palm like his hand was some sort of portal. The chain shot straight forward into the air more pin point than an arrow shot by Robin Hood launching all the way to the foot of Ryker wrapping itself around his leg so tight knit that Ryker just couldn't shake it off; Ryker was so concentrated on the walking dinosaur in front of him that he had no idea it was even coming, the slithering ivory chain carefully made its way to Ryker undetected not making him notice until he felt a yanking and tugging that anchored him down. Just as he was about to bolt forward – literally, strike in the speed of a lightning bolt immediately taken back at the sudden appearance of weight he followed the links with his eyes which of course lead him to a confused Amar – who knew just as much as Ryker at this point.

Just examining his hand, tapping on the chain to test its durability and realism pinching it to see if it had any connection to his nerve of pain, he shrugged as he felt nothing. Ryker with a surprised look on his face somewhat disoriented having no idea where this came from but the window of opportunity was slowly closing while his thoughts raced "where the hell did this come from? – By the look of it he probably knows less than I do! – Could this be his power? A chain or summoning? – Or maybe –"the walking tremor shook Ryker's thoughts like an egg in a shoebox. With each step forward it shifted the ground making its own miniature earthquake, standing in front of and towering over Ryker like a castle with feet; and this fortress was arming up its arsenal to launch everything at Ryker right this instant, Ryker not having a second or moment more to ponder or wonder shouting down below to his pupil "ROOK! Get your right leg ready! I **REALLY** hope your resolve is in order too because if you chicken out on me halfway then I am shipping your ass back to Safe Haven in a box!!"A bolt of nervousness surged throughout Amar's entire body for a quick moment, but Amar dismissing it as soon as he seen the urgency on Ryker's face and heard the dependence in his voice. Amar took this time to close his eyes, what was a split second for everyone around him was an eternity to find and reestablish himself so shaky and stutter some in his texture even though he was his own and only audience "I – I am not – I am not hurting something that – I – II I mean I probably am hurting it but that is not the point! – I *sigh* okay I am not a bad person because I fight these monsters! They hurt people... they are hurting my friends and fellow warriors - I mean what would I do if that was Mr. Azuru or even worse my mother... they have no remorse for who they kill and they butcher them... - but then would I be just like them if I go around killing them like it was some sort of sport?

NO! Because I am not the one who enjoys killing – I –uh... I just wish it did not have to be like this" Amar's eyes flickered open and he saw Ryker's head bobbing up and down in what seemed to be the speed of molasses he shifted his sight over to the Pee – Wee that stood between them like the mountain that Amar was just preparing to climb to meet up with Ryker at the top. Amar took a deep breath as he once again returned to the darkness of his own mind to console himself "I am a good person! I know this, others know this! I have friends, I have family! I adore and cherish life and will not stand by as they destroy it without a second thought! I will defend with my life until I can no longer move – I do not hate the creature of the darkness nor do I feel sorry for them – in fact I feel nothing towards them because I am doing what my heart desires and that is to protect the world and they stand in the way of this. So every enemy of my Father, my family, my friends and I will unfortunately meet his end because I refuse to be the one to die!" Amar's joints locked into a strong fighting stance and only shouted a compliant "ready!" Ryker then swung his right leg in such a concentrated motion like the strongest kick in kickball to ever be recorded, just booting up the air with such ferocity pretty much breaking in the poor air's teeth in. Amar torque with a force that the air was using his face as a punching bag, one second his body was firmly planted on the ground, then his stance was almost nonexistent as he was torpedoed to the beast that was bringing his right hand down over Ryker like an asteroid coming into Earth's airways.

Only got more terrifying the closer it came; a shadow began to cloud over Ryker as the building sized meaty fingers lingered overhead. Ryker not moving a single inch either, Amar seeing this as he squinted his eyes he saw clear as the cloudless sky on a perfect day; his mentor was putting his faith into his disciple to be able to come through. He is fully capable of getting out of this situation on his own but he is willing to put all of his belief on a hunch on an unstable guess on his current student even going so far as staking his own safety, possibly even his own life on the line; as the fist started to enter the yard zone only a matter of time before he literally nails Ryker into his grave Amar now not with a single ounce of nervousness in him. A determination set ablaze in his belly as he now looked at this obstacle no longer in fear and dread but as a challenge that he was more than happy to meet halfway even more so determined to overcome, as he shaped his body to missile form tucking his arms to his sides as he now spread his legs apart slowly yanking up his left leg and sharpening the spear that was his right leg in preparation. The poor Pee –Wee too dull minded to only be able to concentrate on one opponent at a time, so he was completely unaware of the incoming danger trailblazing to him; Amar using his momentum as a diving board to jump off from as he now stood up from his laid down position, his left arm being swung forward for further posturing for the perfect launch.

Looking as if Amar was leaping off one invisible rooftop to another, until the end result came in that is, Amar side swindling his right leg to the horrid beast's cheek; it was so unfair like an aluminum baseball bat going against a fine china vase. Amar's leg dug deep into the cheek of the Pee –Wee his leg might as well been a black head that's just a sample of how deeply imbedded it was smashing into the demon's face, ripple upon ripple from its fat, blubbery, loose skin bending the other side of its jaw slowly as its mouth was forced open. Just in the nick of time too, the Pee –Wee's hand was like a black cloud hanging over Ryker's head. Ryker with confidence and pride glowing off his gleaming smile "now thank you sir I don't need an umbra – ella – ella hey!" The Pee – Wee tumbled over like an ice sculpture that slipped off its pedestal, Amar then felt himself swinging back from his hand like a bungee cord once he has taken his dip just swinging in peace. Gently dangling from Ryker's foot up above, Ryker with his arms crossed over his chest victorious like he had already won "That's my student! – Knocking out a Pee – Wee first try!! – I knew it!! – I knew it! – I knew you we're gonna be special!! – That's why I picked you up – like the sad little puppy you we're - that was bound to be road kill or chow for the wolves anyway!" Amar not knowing whether to be flattered or weirded out so he did a little bit of both "umm thank you Sensei?" One thing was for sure Amar's shrine was glowing very hot and bright smiling to himself as the thought was the first thing to race through his head "I really am happy with the choice that I made" Ryker taking Amar's response as a genuine showing of appreciation and making nothing of it.

"Yes! To knock down these mountains of fat and ugly with one single hit – it was like you we're born to be on this team!! –"as Ryker began to shine brightly upon his student that seemed to be the sun that radiate upon everybody, in Ryker's eyes at this moment it completely blocked out the quaking ground that shook buildings, cars, streets, and homes all alike. Not even the howling snarling of the bestial battle cry could turn Ryker's head from his student that he was so ecstatic he took under his wing it wasn't until he began to question why he was even here in the first place again that he was lead to Forrest's team, this thought stemmed out to because they stumbled onto a trinity, and that idea branched out to 'yeah they needed help fighting three tons of fat stupid – aw shit!' Ryker looked down to see a mountain sized demon coming right for him and his chain gang buddy, it had been a while since Ryker had even see one of these guys run so it was a pretty nice reminder of how fearsome they can be mouth like a cave as it opened up wide, it's big slender arms to pound the ground and stretch itself forward good thing gorillas didn't know how to sue or these demons would be bankrupt right now. Ryker so ungraceful as he spat to his pupil "Oh hold that thought I am gonna need you to do that amazing thing of awesomeness you just did again okay? – Here we go!" Amar not able to follow completely only able to repeat the last part to himself, not as confirmation but as an echo trying to make sense "do that awesome thing again?" Ryker's grin breaking into a full blown "D" shaped smile. He responded with declaration exclaiming almost for the whole world to hear "glad to know you're with me!!!" Then with his arms spread out wing span form he then brought up the Amar carrying leg as he flipped back his entire body, spinning 360 downwards titter tottering his right leg that had Amar anchoring it down. Like a ball and a chain on an inmate, Amar completely unaware of the direction he was going as he was hurdled back like he was taking a ride in a roller coaster and it was going for a loop; but working like a clock's hands heading to midnight. Ryker being the little hand Amar being the big hand was not far behind the charging giant within lunging distance, the perfect leap within its grasp; mouth open wide like it was told from someone other than his spouse that it was **not** the father.

Big enough to fit half a city block into its mouth, Ryker then shouted "beware Pee – Wee of my most deadly attack! Rookie chain kick! Heel drop addition!!" Amar now directly over the demon and same as before he had to build up his nerve as he was traveling but as soon as he came in within his distance his vision tunneled as all he saw was the raging enemy and his body was only acting accordingly, driven by pure instinct and feeling the awkward and ungraceful Amar flailing his limbs through the air like a pigeon without any wings. But the second – no! The instant he seen the path that was carved out for him by Ryker, there was no way he was going to waste his master's trust or squander his faith he only went full force as he speared both of his legs down. The ferocious mountain with arms, legs, and teeth had Ryker within its mouth's range already able to see into like it was a humongous tunnel. All this Pee –Wee needed to do was seal the deal with a yard or two just a moment of movement for it then Ryker would be chewing gum for it, but suddenly its mouth clamped shut tight its teeth cracking some shattering and some fell out as they we're fiercely slammed by the force of the blow. The gargantuan beast plopped onto the floor and created a tidal wave of dust and debris, exploding into the air blowing like a tornado of sand; Ryker waited calmly with his arms folded over his chest as he was once again saved from the jaws of danger, he waited for the brown clouds to disperse or at least clear up. Taking a clump of moments around half a minute before Ryker's smirk once again appeared on his face, just gazing down at the defeated beast its once round and smooth egg shaped head was now pushed in with wave upon wave of ripple dented in – worse than a car collision, it resembled a dip to a skater's half pipe

In the epicenter of it all or the center of this flood of damage was Amar, with his feet more straight and firm than an arrow being put into a bow. Amar's arms over his head to further drive him deeper into the head of the beast the more he thrust himself the more cracks that faulted from the heavy load that was dropped onto the ground only getting heavier by this unleash of power, Ryker then called over to Amar "hold that pose okay!!" Amar gritting his teeth now as he gave a more mumbled "yes sir!"Ryker now flipping to the other side going upwards with both of his legs like javelins pointing forward, spiking as he dropkicked the air; Amar instantly taking off as his legs gapped a piece of the gargantuan's head. Going so fast when his chain gang buddy yanked him forward he had no time to pick up his legs so he made his own entrance, squishing down a piece of its skull like busting a budging boil. Amar then gripped his right wrist with his left hand to further control it and to steady his swaying body, pointing his legs forward locking all possible joints as he made a drill of himself; the air and wind resonating off of him acting as the spirals while his feet became the point. The unsuspecting Pee –Wee was barely getting up from his horrible fall with Forrest, picking itself up leaning on his left side so he could gently get his injured right side off the ground; using all the power it posed in its left to crane its entire tons upon tons of weight off the ground.

Ryker forming a full circle was all the momentum and trajectory that Amar needed to bullet himself forward, the belly a clear and indicate target there was no way he could miss like a blind man shooting the broad side of a barn. The Pee – Wee was completely oblivious to the five feet six inches of danger taking the shape of a missile, right now it was too busy slowly getting up to pay him any mind – which was the biggest mistake possible. Amar blitzing the gigantic bubble that was his enemy's belly, like a harpoon being shot at the world's biggest ball Amar dug deep and pointed his toes upward lifting his ankles as high as he could so he could completely change the direction that the Pee – Wee was going to be launched. In a rain of putrid sewage black blood was sent hailing down below as the Pee – Wee was bowled over and his insides rushing up and out of him, his mouth being the only available tunnel just before he lifted off from the floor like he was tied to a rocket and the long tetherous rope finally came to its end. Yanking the Pee –Wee with vicious torque sending him up, up and just kept going, Amar being the ferocious drilling force behind it tightly clenched his teeth grinding them together until they squeaked like they we're sparkly clean; letting out a growing growl of anger and the louder he got the more power was put into his driving javelin kick imploding the air around this Pee –Wee like he was letting out gas as he climbed higher into the air. More and blacker putrid blood being projectile shot from his mouth as it clumped down plummeting to the ground below.

Amar only made him climb higher and higher until he felt a yank that pulled him out of the action like a parent breaking up their child's fight. His limbs flying forward as his right arm was tugged back towards the ground, Amar confused and questioning looked at the floor to see Ryker with his leg yanked up and a ring of the chain wrapped around near his knee. Obviously Amar put two and two together that Ryker literally yanked his chain but question was why? Amar only bobbing his head up in a gendering for question expression, Ryker chuckling as he said "I cannot get over how fast you grab hold of things! – But that's good right there I don't want to have to go all the way to space to have to chase him down – he will be the alien's problem at that point! –"Ryker then put his Amar leg over the chain once again to ring it around his knee closing in the distance even more, only Amar could definitely feel the torque with this one! Wind making his mouth flap as the buffeting air pushed Amar's face in, everything a blurry sight with the forced upon squint. But it did start to settle down once he was on the crash course straight to his Sensei who simply had his hands at his sides not in the least bit worried not even a percent of panic; Amar however had to shut his eyes shut because he couldn't stand to see what was about to come next absolutely not wanting to behold the utter disaster this was going to result in. But instead of a smash in bodies, crashing on top of each other or Amar spearing Ryker with his body, Amar for some strange reason only felt a gentle tap at the back of his body like if someone was giving him a courteous pat on the back for a commending job and a whisper in the ear but by the time he turned around it seemed to not matter "you have monstrous strength, that is for sure something you got from Azuru – we're in the middle of a battle so I can't really compliment you too much but you're doing great so far just keep it up – now what I want you to do is take out that hybrid or at least help Forrest's team take it down – reclaiming that soul is the most important goal got it?! Good!"

The next moment seemed to be not even connected to what just happened, it was like a whole lecturous speech was crushed and compacted into a single frame of a millisecond and the next moment Amar felt that same weight that tapped his back earlier push down on his back rolling him forward like he was some sort of skateboard, but Amar felt as if he was going down the most slippery and fastest waterslide from hell. The whole entire area becoming blurred lines at his peripheral vision, the only thing that was as clear as Amar's face was the black silhouette that was doing gymnastic acrobatics to avoid Forrest's fireballs; then ducking and flipping behind trees to dodge all of Kayoh's signature punches even leaning, bending, and swaying from Ex's lightning – fast sword slashes just as it drew closer and closer like zooming in, in a telescope. Amar heard Ryker shout to him "retract your chain! Just think release! – You don't wanna hurt me do you?" Amar's mind frantic a scramble as he closed his eyes and began thinking "release" certainly not wanting to hurt his master or to be injured because of his clumsy novice skills. As soon as he imagined Ryker being yanked along with him and crashing incredibly worse than Amar, Amar whispered to himself "of course not" and the chain retracted from Ryker's leg as if Ryker was Faster than measuring tape with the tongue yanked out as far as it could go with this momentum change.

Amar dove forwards his hands catching him before he hit the ground somersaulting into a tuck and roll landing so swiftly so he could instantly look just what was up with his hand. Forrest hearing all this and turned to a sight that captured both Ryker and Amar, growling with discontent and just before he could spew out his rebuttal of disgust and repulsion Kayoh called him over; a cost of taking his eyes off the battlefield as he rushed over with balls of fire in his hands. Ryker looked over Amar who was now beginning to stand and was still checking his hand poking it, gripping, and flexing it as he was still trying to find out just what it was that happened. Ryker floating in the air casually as he said with such concentration and deep thought provoked "it was just as I thought I know how he works now – not too sure of what his powers are per say but I will find out soon enough" but looking back up as his attention was caught by the gurgling in the wind whistling like the birds trying to call each other to mate combined with a groaning that sounded like a crowd of diesel trucks all had some internal transmission problems. Ryker without another second of hesitation was gone within the shot of a bullet, Amar immediately looking up to try to at least catch a glimpse of his master; his powers that he barely been scratching the surface with had been stirring Amar's interest and childish curiosity like a witch stirring the spells into her cauldron.

Ryker now a speck against the falling meteor that was heading towards him that was still stories above Ryker, but Ryker treated distance like a game of hopscotch. Miles became seconds, city travel became a matter of minutes and if he wanted to he could travel the whole entire world within an hour, being able to somehow rival the speed of a lightning bolt even then Ryker truly not dipping into the potential that was the bottomless pit of speed, he then said out loud "1 face of lightning: speed!"

Ryker's aura that seemed to be just a glowing layer reflection of his soul that had his own personal tint to it; suddenly became more intense, much more thick, and became more jagged and impaling, prickly enough to lance through a metal spike. Resembling the spinning spike at the heel of cowboy boots in the old Wild West, but instead of being a copper color it was a neon glowing snow white that was getting brighter with the minutes that passed; the once glossy black as dark as shadows outlining the edges of his aura as Ryker's spread his arms forward the aura began to static around them and stuck upon them. Sparking and surging over his arms like they we're lightning rods, Ryker then wrenched both of his arms to his sides yanking them back to his waist as he then charged forward; the colossal beast shook and vibrated like the tremor that starts before the growing earthquake, Ryker's arms not even visible but he himself was in front of the gargantuan belly. Taking up half of his stomach pressing down and getting wider and wider, like a pool being constructed right into the center of his stomach or like an invisible gigantic – even for this already monumental monster wrecking ball, wrecking ball was being dropped onto his stomach and as the deeper Ryker went the bigger the dip got Ryker's arms a complete blur of lines.

Appearing and disappearing like his random lightning bolts that was also within his aura, the black blood oozing and being sprayed from the shaking Pee – Wee's mouth like a faucet that had a leak. Amar trying to concentrate harder than what his eyes we're able to capture, possibly deceiving him by what he was seeing now but no matter how hard he focused he could not see a single arm or even a single punch that was being thrown, suddenly the monumental giant was sent even higher into the air following that a bolt of black and white lightning struck the demon at the back, piercing through him. As Amar looked closer he seen that he had it completely upside down he didn't summon down a lightning bolt so strike the beast, although he could; no as Amar stared in awe of Ryker giving the winning kick goal pose but replace the ball with the Pee – Wee's back Amar finally came to realization that his master had become the lightning itself. Only adding gasoline to the blazing fire by kicking him sending all the furious electricity that surged through Ryker's entire body into the Pee –Wee, lightning coursing throughout his body exiting out through the hole that Ryker made from his stomach; hard thick steam resonated from the demon's eyes and mouth but Ryker wasn't done yet. Amar didn't even blink and Ryker had already climbed up above this gargantuan already high above him and was moving in for the devastating blow, bending his back over the demon, feet switching places with his head's usual place while he was in the air and within a snap dropped his right shin in a back flip on top of the demon's back within the quarter of a moment.

A trail of lightning followed the descending Pee –Wee down to the ground in a complete gigantic, humongous, lightning swallowed bolt. Crater - driving the ground with his colossal useless weight, wrecking an entire city just by existing at his size; cars being blown away like paper in the wind, buildings crumbling like a house of cards, smoke parties of dust leaping up into the air that covered the entire scene like a blanket. Ryker just floating looking around for his next victim glancing over his right shoulder as he heard rumbling that made the ground tremble, another gargantuan who was barely shaking off the severe spearing heel that Amar dropped onto its head as if it we're some sort of dog who got water on its fur. Even then as he tried to move he was still incredibly drowsy and dazed as it was so unbalanced to take another step, Ryker simply scoffing one second he was there the next only a white lightning bolt was left as a trail in his presence, already dissipating and fading away. Amar quick to turn his head searching for his sensei like frantic eyes searching for Waldo on every single page turning to his right to draw his attention to the ginormous beast completely due to common sense as he said to himself "that has to be his next target there is no other place for him to go!"

The beast's eyes narrowed down to the ant in comparison of size that was Amar, struck with a bolt of shivering paranoia not having a clue what to do as this thing focused on Amar then squeaking in his own mind "I reeeeeeally hope he does not remember me" the giant took a step closer to Amar and bared it's cracked and shattered teeth Amar squeaked as he was let down "yup he definitely remembers the one who made his head into a dip and made his teeth look like a shattered mirror."

As he drew closer Amar took a deep breath, letting out every single anxiety and fear then took a fighting stance as the squeaking was replaced with well paced breaths. The fear and unprepared feeling was transformed into a feeling of determination and ready to take down this ferocious beast that was reaching out its gigantic claws, even though Amar didn't have a clue on where to start he was going to burn his own path.

But then he started to notice a spotlight glow high up above the demon, it was getting brighter and bolder by each inch that gigantor over here reached out for Amar, Amar's focus slowly began shifting from the humongousaurs rex to the UFO spotlight even breaking his stances so he could gaze up at the sky; shading his face with his own hand. He squint as he tried to truly focus on this jagged, zig -zag, white and black zipper that was sparkling like a microwave full of tinfoil, discharge and electricity moving back and forth in a pulse was the only thing that was being hew like a million birds having a conversation with a fan distorting their voices. The iron dense skull of this gargantuan was not letting Amar out of his sight, the light show behind him could wait he had personal matters to handle; Amar's hawk eye vision zeroing in on the bolt in the sky, of course there was only one person who could do this that came at no surprise to Amar, but as he seen his master a speck in the middle of this whole thing, his back hunched as he cringed his fingers tightly in the air. With the look on his face, Amar knew something big was coming – unfortunately something even bigger was coming straight for him, a claw the size of a parking lot was right in front of him, all it had to do was keep on going the direction it was heading and it would run right through Amar like road kill. Just then it was as if the sky sent a miracle, a white lightning bolt line like the most clean cut blade in existence with one swift single cut the demon's hand right off. The open claw crashing around Amar a huge half circle dropping at his face, Amar instinctively shielding himself even though the only harmful thing coming his way was the dust and debris from the ground; but he was still very new, he will soon lose the hesitation factor.

Creaking his eyes open to instantly look up at Ryker, who was just spinning a full circle loading his leg back up for another one, the slow beast gripped its now nub of an arm squeezing where his forearm used to be. Roaring, shaking it's head and howling for the heavens above to hear, even managing to rumble the ground with its obnoxious thunderous vocal cords Ryker then said "SHUT UP! – THAT'S WHAT YOU GET FOR TRYING TO GET ALL TOUCHY – TOUCHY WITH MY STUDENT!!! – YOU KNOW IN SOME COUNTRIES THEY CHOP OFF YOUR HANDS IF YOU TRY TO STEAL!?! – THERE YOU GO PUNISHMENT FOR TRYING TO STEAL MY PUPIL!!"

Then like a waterfall exploding into a flood, a bolt bigger than the demon itself; glistening white and black with no pattern rhyme or reason. Completely came down full force like the demon had its own personal black cloud and this was the black cloud's last straw before tormenting him tomorrow as it exploded outwards to a dome of silver, it fried all of the demons within the area next to the Pee –Wee. Forrest his team and the hybrid all out of range but any lingering demons or reinforcements trying to slip in and help set the upper hand we're instantly reduced to frozen statues of black soot, with one touch would go flying in the wind. The people, the trees, everything around, every aspect of civilization especially Amar we're completely unharmed not even disturbed; Amar thought for sure he would conduct all that electricity because of his armor, he would be like a magnet for those bolts of lightning just clinging onto him but as he completely searched his body examining every major part, almost owl - spinning his head to do so he noticed there was not a spark on him.

Of course he would have felt it first but he absolutely wanted to be sure, turning back to the taller giant who was buzzing like a fly who mistook the bug zapper for some sort of freedom. Bolts still trickling down his body, electricity surging one line at a time at the head of everything quite literally, Ryker was standing in a crane stance one leg deeply driven into the hole that Amar had previously made. Cratered it even more as his other knee was bent up and his arms hanging above him, his right leg - the attacking leg currently was flashing like a strobe light, lightning spewing out like a thumb being put over the water hose. As much as Amar wanted to stay and watch he curiously glanced over his shoulder to see exactly how everyone was holding up, and they we're struggling;

Kayoh with full hardy swings would overshoot and miss by a long shot, this hybrid would then pat and shove her out of the way, Ex would rush to him to draw his sword and slice him in two. The hybrid would then rush to him and place, its talon like spread apart pigeon toes, onto his hand that was on his blade putting a stop to any drawing of the blade; both parties struggling as they fought for the finishing blow, the hybrid spun to the left and kicked Ex at the back sending him tumble, stumble, fumble and finally crash into a horde of trees. Kayoh back again but with her arm wrenched, her left fist pulled back as far as she could charging up a "shotgun-"the hybrid probably seeing how lethal that weapon was before and he flapped his wings using them as a spring to glide, cutting through the air before Kayoh could finish her sentence.

Kayoh with a face of distraught, but still not willing to give up charging, continued the mantra, but it was no use the hybrid drove his head into her stomach like he was a man shot out from a cannon. Launching her away the hybrid looked over its shoulder to see a furiously panting Forrest who seemed more angry than actually fatigued, giving a right left, right, jab combo that sent three balls of fire the hybrid's way; the hybrid stepping underneath them all and continued to walk forward to him, with arms widening from his sides as he spoke human language and not only that English above all "now now divine warrior! – I know you are simply flattering me by making me feel strong but play time is over, it has been for a while now... so tell your subordinates and you yourself, all to start fighting serious otherwise... I am going to take all of your souls without struggle!" Amar was utterly floored in his mind "these are elites who have been on a team way longer than I have – uh I think – and he's tossing and throwing them around – all at once! What chance do I have if I go?! -"

The hybrid clashing fists with Forrest cratering the floor underneath, the pressure of their immense power shattered the ground like it was made out of glass. Forrest grinding his teeth as this hybrid struck a grin, Forrest's words coming out like bullets from a machine gun "YOU WANT TO SEE POWER OH BELIEVE ME! I WILL SHOW YOU POWER!" Forrest then ringing his left arm around the neck of the hybrid like he was going for a bro hug, Forrest opened his mouth... so what is going on here you pull him in close and open your mouth when he is next to you?! Don't fraternize with the enemy I don't care if you're gay as long as it's not with the enemy!! Oh wait no sorry I jumped the gun on that one - he was actually gagging out a ball of green embers from deep within his throat like a hairball inside the body of a cat.

The hybrid anticipated as much tilting his head to the left for the flame to go over, his wings gusted him a few feet away giving the hybrid room for a thrusting elbow into the gut of Forrest managing to force out a cough, smashing against Forrest's spiral pool from within but also with the cough came a smirk. As Forrest grabbed the hybrid's arm holding on for dear life as he clamped down he then repeated his previous warning "I told you didn't I?! YOU WANT POWER YOU GOT POWER!!!"

Just then a ring of green fire ignited on the ground surrounding them until they we're inside the ring of fire without Johnny Cash. The fire that was a low broil to the ground leaped up like it was trying to now become the sky making a tower of ember that completely trapped them both inside this tunnel of flames; Forrest now pulling on the hybrid's arm as he chucked him like he was a simple rock across the lake. The hybrid flipping heels over head as the fire caught on him like he was showered with oil before jumping in the fire pool, a whole body suit of ember caught him as he crashed onto the ground; viciously shaking himself off but parts of the flames we're inextinguishable they we're just drawn to the evil and would not go away until it was all burned off with it, heavy steam emitting from his body as he clawed into the ground to try to recover his footing, his feet sliding into the floor to try to break his own fall. A stern and serious look on his face as he focused on the Forrest that was conquering gravity as he lingered in the air as he charged forward with his tower now facing towards the hybrid pointed at him like a gigantic cannon.

Forrest absolutely knew he had the upper hand and he shouted over in the most patronizing tone he could make "SEE THIS IS WHAT YOU GET WHEN YOU STAND UP AGAINST A REAL WARRIOR! YOU HAVE NO IDEA WHAT CALIBER I AM ON YOU ARE NOTHING BUT A BUG IN COMPARISON!!!"The hybrid able to stand up perfectly without a single hint of injury or struggle as he calmly dusted off the burning flames and responded to the man who had the equivalent to a finger on the button on a nuke. "You might be very strong even formidable... but are you stronger than BAD?" A twitching and clenching cringing overcame his face as Forrest seemed to be hit with what to him is worse than any racial slur, and not fighting words – no they're killing words "DON'T YOU EVER **EVER!** COMPARE ME TO HIM!!!! BURN IN THE STRONGEST FLAMES TO EVER EXIST!!! **BURN HIM TO A CRISP!! EVERGREEN!!!!!**"

Just as he aimed the cannon directly at the hybrid that simply stood there ready to accept his fate like a man patiently waiting to be hung. Before the entire cylinder of fire could gather the hybrid raised his hands up from the ground and a fault cracked on the floor beneath them, and not a moment later the ground split open and out poured a sea of darkness and instead of fish being the natives inside, this habitat tons and tons of demons that we're at least double the size of Forrest poured out - or more like climbed out to slide in front of their leader taking the blast like a emotionless brick wall. All emerging and not for a single second let up until the ember cannon had ran out of flame to spread out from, it was like a stop sign jumping up from the ground in front of you forcing you to brake appearing out from the ground. The sewage sludge – like liquefied darkness spreading all around the ground with demons climbing up and out like fish sprouting legs and finally being able to walk the Earth, horde upon horde of ape – sized and mammoth statured muscular, wrathful, mindless malevolent body of evil was emerging from the shadows of darkness. The shin height O demons we're in the far back, the zombified posed souls now put into the decaying body of the demonic damned souls and took up the middle, the apex predator of the fierce bodied demons double the size of Forrest we're the front line with their gigantic brother in arms in the rear back – only a quarter the size of the actual gargantuans.

Forrest gritting his teeth as he flipped back coming to a screeching halt on the ground, Kayoh and Ex merely looked at each other and that was all that needed to be said as Kayoh bouncing on her tip toes in anticipation and Ex gently bobbing his head as he fiddled his fingers on top of the hilt of his sword.

Ryker shouting down below to his student "you don't think they might need some help or something? – I mean there is an awful lot of nameless cannon fodder – it's kinda like doing a whole stack of papers you need to sign your name and date on, sure all you need to do is sign your name and the date but after 500 of them your hand starts getting tired and you start to get bor-""but what help would I even be? They seem like they are on a whole other level than me!" "*sigh* oh young grass hopper you need to believe in yourself more, you don't give yourself the benefit of even believing it is a possibility, tell you what! I will believe in you – you trust me right?! Believe in my judgment if you can't believe in yourself and with that faith, just trust that the belief will grow even if it doesn't make sense right now! Now go – go on and play with your little friends I gotta supervise you."

Amar for a second stared in amazement up at his master who had a wheel of fortune style of tones and attitude, this time he happened to land on wise beyond his years – unfortunately Amar didn't have time to reflect upon this amazing piece of advice he had to act running off towards the battlefield as the glow of his master's praise and hopes for greatness shined upon him like a beam from a magnifying glass. Ryker sitting on top of the pile of burning glistening light pile that was his beyond slain enemy, on a rooftop too far from Ryker, three shadows stuck onto the wall all different sizes we're speaking amongst themselves about the threat they had on their hands.

Their weird twitch and licks of the tongue that was their language was being tossed back and forth between them, "*sit mih tnsi retsam? Eht eno no 'sDAB maet? Rekyr?*" (*It's him isn't it master? The one on BAD's team? Ryker?*) "**SEY UOY GNIKCUF TIODI!! RETSAM ESAELP TEL EM LLIK MIH I LLIW GNIRB OUY SIH LUOS SIHT I ESIMORP!**" (*Yes you fucking idiot!!! Master please let me kill him, I will bring you his soul this I promise!*) "**MLCA SEVLESRUYO HTBO OF UYO! WE TSMU THGFI REHTEGTO HE IS AN ETLEI DO UYO KNITH HE DLUWO GO NWDO THAT YLISEA?! NO WE TSMU BE YRVE YRVE LUFERCA! EVMO NI!**" (*Calm yourselves both of you! We must fight together he is an elite do you think he would go down that easily?! No we must be very very careful! Move in!*)

Just then these shadow triplets gone like someone switching on the light in a roomful of darkness, Ryker watching Amar's cape flap in the wind as he forged on to help his fellow warriors in need; just sighing out nostalgia as he said with such heavy hopes "watching that back move into battle must be what my dad saw in me when I was just starting out – not that I'm his dad but I do expect a lot of things from that boy! – Speaking of paternal instincts –"Ryker's eyes caught a glimpse of three shadows gaining in on Amar without the novice even able to sense a tingle in the air, closing in like a frenzy of sharks with underwater twin turbo boosters. The shadow splotches now picking up off the ground, rising up like the fin of an approaching predator in the deep blue sea; but just replace the fin with a claw from each splotch of darkness, all holding razor sharp fingers that could easily shred steel like it was one – ply toilet paper. But before they could sink their points into Amar's unprotected neck, a vicious and thunderous bolt of lightning struck the floor right in between them like even Zeus himself was displeased with what was about to happen.

Amar's head creaking around to see what was going on behind his back, only to see his very own master stepping down from his shining throne made out of Pee –Wee to attend to what seemed to be personal matters. Holding all of the claws of the darkness spots in one single palm, Amar stopping for a mere moment with Ryker not even turning his head around to look Amar in the eyes as he said this such confident statement "Rook keep going! Believe me they won't even give me a hassle – remember urgency! That's how you bring out your potential – you NEED it!" Amar nodding his head in acknowledgement as he did as his sensei said, trekking forward to lend as much support and do what he could for Forrest's team, quietly speaking the mantra to himself "I neeeeeeed it! I neeeeeeeeed it!!!"

Ryker throwing their collective claws back so hard he flipped them out of their shadows and onto their feet all with their own individual design and structure of malevolent embodiment. A small but rippled body half the size of Ryker a half goat half man like some sort of demented fawn, with ram curl type horns with an all gray fur, shins that we're arched back like a primal beast's pair of legs would be, the body of a man stuck onto those pair of legs and the face of a broken and corrupted boy plastered onto the head of a simple O demon but this O demon seemed to be far more advanced than his primal and simple brethren. Next to him was a humongous mold of evil and devilish intent, being three times the size of Ryker this dark purple skinned but rough textured beast had the structure of pure mass and power, the upper body of a competitor from the world's strongest man mixed with a person who once born never skipped chest and arm day, his legs stolen straight from the lions club just vicious and fierce thighs and legs made for pouncing and chasing down its prey, a black mane of bushy hairy that completely concealed its face only leaving a pair of piercing burning yellow eyes.

Finally what seemed to be the brains of the operations and fit the position of their master, middle sized demonic figure shrouded in a black cloak this thing whatever it was seemed to be held together simply by this black hooded robe alone. Most likely this bag of human skeleton bones would fall apart like taking only one card out from a castle of cards the whole thing would come crashing down, Ryker could even see past the shade of shadows that helped cover it's umm "face?" he was able to catch a glimpse of a skeletal structure of a goat with a pair of curled horns sticking out from the sides of its head before the shadows shrouded its face as well only it's blood red glowing eyes we're left to see even though it had no eyeballs but whatever. Ryker with one hand in his pocket and proclaimed to his enemies before him "if you want to get to the boy you have to get past me!" The skeletal demon stepped forward towards his fearsome opponent feeling like it accomplished something, and Ryker was the one who was snared in a trap, let a guy dream I guess –er whatever that thing is anyways. "**WE DETNWA TO TGE UYO ENOAL! SO WE TNWE RETAF ETH YBO!! UYO LLASH TNO BRUTSDI RUO RETSMA! UYO YMA BE AN ETIEL TBU YAYTO IS ETH YDA RUYO LUSO LLWI BE SRUO!!**" (*We wanted to get you alone! So we went after the boy!! You shall not disturb our master! You maybe an elite but today is the day your soul will be ours!!*) Ryker scoffing a bit before spewing out a rebuttal in their own tongue "*ouy idd lla ttha ot tjus teg me enola?! Ouy dah a retteb echanc fi ouy dah ouyr tersam tub wrveehat! Osla! Uoy dlwou evah dah a retteb echanc fi ouy 'ditd sisp me fof by gongi rof my lppui! Ouy tnaw my lous?! Ecom teg it!*" (You did all that to just get me alone?! You had a better chance if you had your master but whatever! Also! You would have had a better chance if you didn't piss me off for going for my pupil! You want my soul? Come get it!)

The demons all dumbstruck as not even they we're advanced enough to understand their own language it seemed he was more advanced in more ways than one. Rolling his eyes as he spat on their own heritage right in front of them "geez you can't even understand your own language when it's spoken to you?! Fine I guess I'll just speak to you in English then! I basically just said come see what real hell looks like if you aren't too scared!"

Ryker cracking his neck as he threw it to the side and the demons began to take him up on his offer now forming a triangle around him, each side Ryker was surrounded but he didn't seem the least bit worried more like he was being forced to do chores he didn't want to do, like they we're just three clones of his mother. Ryker snapped his fingers and they took this as their gunshot to start the race as they all dashed to him,

Kayoh and Ex we're just waiting on their leader to give the word he stood on the opposite end of the dark army; so fidgety and jumpy lying in wait of the simple whistle that would signal an all out assault. The hybrid floating above the floor with his arms crossed over his chest seeming so comfortable now that he had his people right behind him just like a bully with his legion of followers now feeling like a king on a throne with all his loyal subjects willing to wage war for their leader. Now feeling truly confident enough to try to get Forrest even more riled up "I told you didn't I Forrest? This is a trinity do you even know how much darkness is under my control?! Seems like you're not too smart either – it is a good thing I am fighting a second rate commander like you! You're no BAD you're not even close to being a Duke either!" Forrest shaking with absolute boiling building rumbling anger that was like a teapot ready to take off the kettle that someone was just letting burn away; now the ground underneath was showing the same system of trembling as it quaked, his evergreen embers found its way out from the ground piercing out from the floor like groundhogs. Forrest could barely contain himself he was one inch from the edge when the Hybrid gave him his final push "come on show me that power of yours, roast me like a pig with the "mightiest" flame to ever exist but if you can't beat me that means you're still miles behind BAD aren't you?!"

A lion's roar erupted out from Forrest as he burned a fiery green passion, Kayoh knew they didn't have much time until they would have to move out as she was patting Ex on the shoulder for them to get ready for launch, something stumbling in among the battlefield that clearly didn't belong and definitely shattered the tension. A frantic shouting "okay I need! I neeeeed it! I neeeeeeeeeeeeeed it! Sword, chain, blaster something! Come on armor don't fail me now! – I neeeeeeed it!!!"

Kayoh slightly caught off guard as she said out loud "who or what the hell is that?" Even the demons began to turn heads in that direction but they we're entangled with the most shocking event possible, a blade slice right through the middle of their line halfway into the crowd turning instant ash upon contact, and was sucked into the edge of the blade. Only leaving a bunch of empty spaces where their bodies used to be, now in a screeching rage the demon's we're searching where to aim their wrath; but before they could even begin to start a proper search with hordes of eyes wandering all over the field, he found them. Coming out of nowhere, perfectly concealed by the trees with an entrance made for a superstar – a knee being driven into the jaw of the more brutish demons at the far left or beginning of the miniature army; the contact of this phenomenal attack converted him into a statue of ashes that was pulled into the kneecap of this shining warrior within seconds. All the rest of the demons jumping back as they tried to gauge just exactly what they we're dealing with, Kayoh giving this warrior an odd inspecting eye as she studied him he began to slowly raise from the attack he bulleted into the scene with. The hostile horde was ready to tear this man limb from limb for taking away one of their comrades, Kayoh still inspecting this man she has surely never seen him before that is something she could mark down as a fact and she knew a baby face when she seen one, despite his remarkable battle skills this had to be his first time.

Then the warrior put out his left arm to give thumbs up as he declared with confidence "go ahead and back up your captain! I can deal with them – the name is Amar I am new but you can trust me I promise!" Kayoh at that very moment received an impression of him and it was spelled all over her face with repulsion and sort of disappointment as she said to herself "a thumbs up seriously – I get it you're new but don't get any bold ideas but since this is your first time – I'll let you play hero I AM NOT NO DAMSEL THOUGH! – Gotta save my half wit of a leader anyways" – as Kayoh just gave a forced nod and tugged on Ex to follow her as Ex claimed his eager hand to draw his sword meanwhile Amar was sporting a new sword on the top of his forearm. A claymore broadsword style, pure ivory blade clumped down on top of his forearm sticking out about a foot and a half over his fist also sporting something new was the fiery look in his eyes. Burning determination, passion, and an inability to go back on his words, he said he would protect Forrest's team while they went to support him and that is exactly what he was gonna do just as the entire crowd of piercing stares pointing right at him, Amar now shaky in his fighting stances, peaking to himself to calm his on edge nerves "r-remember not to kill them but to slay them! No hate but the desire to protect and cleanse yyy-you have to protect Forrest's team so nothing is gonna get past you!"

Gulping almost immediately afterwards as Kayoh and Ex tried to circle around to make their way to the exploding Forrest who was in the air punching it forward to send balls of fire at the hybrid who would float over to the side to dodge the fearsome wrathful but blinded attacks. Forrest's eyes we're burning the same tone of evergreen as his flames that he shot out, Kayoh knew this was very bad and only getting worse as a group of the gorilla toned demons slid into their way.

Just as Kayoh thought there was no way that was going to be that easy and Amar was a newbie after all, Kayoh shaking her head in disagreement and cocked her right arm back speaking in a tone of disdain in her own mind "I knew I couldn't trust that green bean! – I should have just handled it when I had the chance!" But before Kayoh could even begin her mantra to charge up Amar was in front of her before she could even blink, it was like invisibility was another one of his skills. Driving his sword into the chest of the rampaging primate with a fearsome straight right punch, but with his range extended in the form of a sword Amar's fist stopped halfway as the sword was sticking out from its back, the primate began to crackle and fissure as his once vibrant black and red skin darkened to a cold unfeeling dreadful gray slowly coming to a standstill with its claws clutching the blade until it stiffened up and finally solidified into this pose. Now nothing more than Amar's trophy, the demon's screeching as they we're stunned with fear seeing it happen only feet away from them was completely different than catching a quick glimpse of it in the crowd

This even turning the head of the hybrid fully able to take his focus from the absolutely livid Forrest, simply lifting up his left hand to bring up a wall of liquefied darkness made from his forces to stop the burning embers. Just taking a minute to watch Amar in action but glancing over his shoulder to the shaking with fury Forrest, a demented grin began to grow as he lit up like a fire sparking onto a forest haha ironic huh? Seeing this Kayoh and Ex knew exactly what this meant the urgency just doubled! Kayoh not having time or even a chance to respond to Amar's entrance nothing other than calling over her shoulder "thanks green bean! I would commend you on your entrance or something but I gotta get going when he gets like this he gets very reckless!" Forrest a floating green baby sun in the sky that roared as far as his vocal cords could take him.

Putting both hands together with palms flat he fired a beach ball sized ball of flame straight at the hybrid – "screw this fodder army of his he brought up to be meat shields!!"

Which he was just proving was completely true as he pulled the darkness over himself to make a bubble of malevolence to protect himself. This taking the last straw and tearing it apart Forrest had, had it! He himself became the meteorite that he had been shooting this entire time, the meteor that killed the dinosaurs just a visionary dramatization I am throwing out there, as he blew the bubble like any contact that the bubble could have stumbled into; popping the hybrid right out except he had something on his hands... the skulls of his comrades he wore them like gloves, flapping his wings to back step just a foot away from the impact zone that he drilled his fist into the ground like it was his personal punching bag. Forrest quickly rebounding from this blunder as he bolted forward with both hands being stuck inside of the skulls that the hybrid was using to fight with caution; their auras like colliding tidal waves from opposite rival oceans, the pitch dark blackness was slowly being burned by the pure light the burning embers held although,

Forrest's embers we're also beginning to become a bit more damp and gray the more he held on. But Forrest wasn't about to let go anytime soon as he charged them both forward tearing up the ground beneath them and driving right through the bunches of big tall trees that they cut through like their entire bodies we're just sharp well crafted blades.

Kayoh screaming "dammit! There they go again Ex!! Why can't they just sit still so we can catch up?! You know how he gets when he is angry, he is the easiest to exploit and this hybrid isn't like the rest of no brainers we usually deal with – no I think he knows this as well as we do; that Forrest's anger is his biggest weakness!!" Ex nodding in acknowledgement as he kept his blade in place by his hip, just then the liquefied darkness that was spread all around the ground like a spill the janitor had to clean up, began to climb up and mold itself into bodies double the size of Kayoh and Ex forming a circle of cannon fodder perfectly designed to get into their way. Kayoh stomping her foot in volcanic frustration as she shouted so Safe Haven above could hear her "WHY DO THEY KEEP GETTING IN OUR WAY?!?!!? – DON'T ANSWER THAT EITHER I KNOW WHY!!!!" Just as Kayoh full of wrath and just oozing fury was about to cringe into her fighting stance she couldn't even do that as even that was taken from her, a demon thrown so fast like it was pitched by a Gatling gun. Certainly acting like a bullet as it cut right through the crowd from one side to the other taking each and every senseless demon that couldn't figure out to step to the side along with it. Kayoh turning her head to the 2 'o clock position to see an ivory blade like a javelin being speared into the ground from up above, more like a lance as it stretched into the sky, she followed it only to lead her to a silver glowing sun with a pair of arms and legs getting closer and closer the longer she stared until he was just above ground level. Straight into the fray with a spinning roundhouse to the jaw of a primate looking demon who was converted to ash as his jaw flew right off, pulling his ivory blade from the ground as he spun clockwise to slice right across the chest of another massive demon near him who transformed into a pile of ash, it screaming out in pain was acting as its last breath. Smacking another in the face with the face of his blade and another unfortunately met the back of his fist, a cloud of black ash erupted from that little spot in the huge circle as all the heads turned.

Kayoh not wasting a single second taking this as the second chance and she gained a smidge of respect for Amar as he actually was a man of his word. While the demons we're distracted tugging Ex by his arm as she looked back to see bodies flying up into the sky turning to ash as they we're up in the air and crashing to dust as they hit the ground, Kayoh turning her head back only to be reassured by seeing this glimpse of the newbie even speaking herself into a sense of tranquility "yeah he is more than enough for some basic training dummies like these! – I am just wondering… where did he get that monstrous strength from? That speed too! That isn't something a Miraclelyte gets unless it's their power from their soul, or they put Divinity into that so where did it -"

Just then Amar zipped right past Kayoh and Ex by retracting himself to his sword being like the tongue in measuring tape, as he switched his body position from his arms front to now his feet we're in front of his body and in crouching position as Amar's feet coming in like a wrecking ball without an annoying singer on top of it. Ramming his blade right into this demon, but the poor sucker was unable to be flung off like a sticky booger he was stuck too deep onto the ivory blade which was a part of Amar's plan – wow a plan already?! Just a few minutes ago he had no idea what he was doing and a little more before that he was worried about being the janitor now he is making plans! – They grow up so fast don't they?!

Using the massive bulky demon's body like a steady place for him to swing from as he split his legs knocking each demon to the side of him right in the jaw, now pulling out his sword and free in the air; slamming their heads together like two coconuts that just sent ash everywhere. To which Amar rushed out of like a bull straight out the gates to drive its horns tight into the man to dare stand its way, with a straight arrow like side kick to the gut of a demon, crossing over to a crescent sunset like right kick to knock out the dumbass who dared stand next to him, then using that momentum absolutely perfect as he flung his left leg over to slice right through the beast. He spun on the heel of his boot with the momentum he built up to slam both backsides of his fists into the dead center of both of their faces which was able to stop him in his tracks, this all happened too fast for them to even react or even know what was going on and at the same time, Kayoh seen in which demons Amar chose and why. Using their ashes like a smoke screen, both of them bulleted right through tearing through the air as they had no time to deal with these no names and Kayoh was able to catch a slight glimpse of Amar in the corner of his eye looking over his shoulder to her with a smile already cracking on his face. Kayoh giggled and said to herself "good work green bean maybe you might actually work out!"

Amar now realizing that most of these demons we're turning on their deadly switches as they began swiping at his face with claws that we're big enough to fit his ribcage in between them; but something very strange began happening, it was like Amar's body was taking over and Amar was taking a backseat in his own body as something else controlled him, knowing what motion to take just before the attack was solidified as dangerous. Amar's body was yanked back in a back step, or when a drilling stab was trying to puncture his chest he would twist to the side, no matter the number of slashing hands that we're aimed at him. He would pull his face back, bob, weave, duck, roll and pull his head out of the way going lower and lower until his legs couldn't crouch anymore.

At that point he would just tuck and roll in between their legs and was somehow able to tuck all of their collective arms under his arm pit as soon as popped back up, with them all at his mercy he pulled up and snapped all of their bones like a pile of popsicle sticks. All screeching in absolute anger and agony, Amar began to hear something soaring from above taking his eyes to the sky he spotted wingless demons from the previous circle all coming to join this party. Amar sighing as he spoke out loud "yeah I get how she is starting to feel now"

Amar tucking his feet up with him as he hopped up off the ground and spread his arms as wide as he could to place them on the shoulders of two demons as he stood on his hands upside down, then spun like a draddle slamming his boots at everyone's head inside his small circle of enemies at least once. Swiftly landing to a pile of dust as he waited for the next wave of challengers to rush at him he stiffened into his defensive stance while the first demon stumbled, but kept forging on charging to Amar he was met with a boot to the face with a straight kick,

Meanwhile on the other side of things Amar's sensei mirroring the same exact move as he kicked the smallest of the group dead center in the face he then whispered "impact 10 sec" the miniature evil package merely smacking his foot out of his face as he charged forward trying to slice and stab at Ryker like a man with a knife starving for his next meal. Ryker with hands safely in his pockets as he stepped back then to the side, then back and back then to the side again before he flipped the whole thing around in the other direction; this was very one sided game of smart mouse dumb cat. As the little idiot kept continuing to charge forward stabbing claws darting forward like a gun turret spitting out bullets to which Ryker again interrupted him, this time with an upper cutting axe kick straight to the demon's jaw that even lifted him off the floor. Once again Ryker whispered "impact" but this time with "2 sec" right afterwards.

The demon only becoming more and more angry and unstable with each useless and harmless kick that this supposed elite threw at him, the advanced O demon then used this time to get its feet back onto the floor. Then backing up to inhale all the oxygen to load his ammo as the rims around his wide mouth began to heat up and ignite with fearsome flames as it coughed up a truck sized fireball at Ryker, that Ryker simply walked through and blew all of the fierce hot air out just by his presence alone. With such an attitude of smug and boredom blended into one single tone "oh that was one of you best attacks wasn't it? Damn shame if only I was a bit weaker... and useless... maybe if I fell down the stairs... and lost my limbs... and was blind, deaf and mute... no no I think I would still beat you. Good effort though you can have a participation award if you want"

With that Ryker gently stroked the bottom of his shoe down the demon's face. Then whispered in its ear "impact 3 sec" the other two watching from a far and safe distance to observe and take notes from the big bulky muscle head seemed to eager to die "**RETSAM! ESAELP WOLLA EM OT OG DNA THGIF OOT! EREHT SI ON YAW EH NAC ELDNAH MIH NO SIH NWO!**" (*Master! Please allow me to go and fight too! There is no way he can handle him on his own!*) The hooded skeleton standing his ground against the big brute who could pull him apart and chew on his marrow like he was a chew toy "**ON! EH T'NSI DESOPPUS OT NIW I YLPMIS DEEN OT EES SIH SLLIKS! WOH HCUM REWOP EH SAH DNA TAHW EH SI ELBAPAC FO!**" (*No! he isn't supposed to win I simply need to see his skills! How much power he has, and what he is capable of!*) Just as the fun sized demon was about to make for another charge he shot back like he was launched from a cannon.

Breaking the wind quite literally as Ryker stood by watched and didn't even pick up his hands from his pockets and the demon was quite surprised so whose doing was this? He launched like a supersonic catapult had done it's designed job and full force shot him through the air and just before he could get too far as this demon before it bounced without again ever being touched or coming in contact with him, it was like Ryker and the air we're tag teaming this poor pathetic demon. Now being catapulted and shot straight up heading towards the clouds faster than an UFO not wanting to be caught on camera, before he could get out of the stratosphere it was like he was he was attached to a chain that Ryker was in control of and decided to yank him down; except he didn't he wasn't moving a single inch not even giving the demon the benefit of watching him it was like Ryker seen it all before and this was nothing special, just gently kicking rocks with the tip of his shoe as he waited for the demon to come back to meet the ground. Before his head could drill into the cold unforgiving earth that would have literally been his grave, Ryker saved him well sort of he saved him from crashing into the earth, well sort of – perfectly catching the demon's face with the top of his foot a swift kick to the face to send the speed demon body half nailed into a tree with his legs hanging limply outside the tree.

Ryker then just looked over his shoulder and with his head bobbed it up as he pointed his sight towards the big bumbling brute who seemed to be so confident he could take him all on his own. Amazed at what just happened he didn't even touch him, even when he did it was nothing but simple taps and flimsy strikes so what was it that sent their comrade through the air like that?! Just a few thoughts racing through the big brute's mind – yeah I'm surprised he could think too just as the muscular demon was about to speak his sensei cut him off "I EES OS TAHW YEHT YAS TUOBA MIH SI EURT! TI SI YLETELPMOC TNEREFFID GNIEES TI PU TNORF HGUOHT, EH NAC YALED EHT TCAPMI, ROF REVETAHW TNUOMA FO EMIT EH STNAW SA UOY TSUJ NEES! UOY DEEN OT EB YLEMERTXE LUFERAC EH SAH EROM SEITILIBA EKIL ESEHT! I LLIW TEL UOY OG TUB TIH MIH HTIW GNIHTYREVE UOY EVAH!" (*I see so what they say about him is true! It is completely different seeing it up front though, he can delay the impact, for whatever amount of time he wants as you just seen! You need to be extremely careful he has more abilities like these! I will let you go but hit him with everything you have!*)

The brutish demon now a bit hesitant not as eager as he was before as he now seen the destructive capabilities that Ryker poses, and without even trying! Ryker piercing him with his eyes and basically was pulling him apart with his eyes, like a red dot sight on an assault rifle he had him locked on and wasn't about to pull his gaze off of him; the brutish demon got what it wanted but now it was too late to go back on his desires as he slowly trekked towards Ryker, who also did the same as his frightened foe.

Then when they came within yards of one another still had some distance gaping in between them, the demon seeing this as an opportunity and lightning - dashed right to Ryker so suddenly like a gun being fired out of nowhere; a cluster stab from his fearsome iron claws missed by a couple feet as Ryker twisted his body out of the way no distress, worry, or even worked up he was still in his zone of boredom. Pulling himself closer to the demon's ear as he said to him "you think you guys know about my powers? Trust me you haven't seen anything yet! Let's see if you can keep up!" Just then Ryker hooked the left side of the gigantic demon's ribcage and the demon flinched, it merely felt like a flick on the wrists but he was expecting to go flying off afterwards he then felt two jabs at the face that also felt like nothing. What was up?! Why all of a sudden the fearsome attacks full of launching explosiveness had all but gone and nothing but love taps we're all that Ryker posed now; Ryker then screamed "don't tell me when to use my power! It's mine so I use it when I want! I don't play by your rules!!" The demon was somehow reassured by this now his hesitation factor had gone away and his claws glowed a burning red as he slashed through the air, a trail line of a red claw mark cut through the air as it made its way to Ryker but Ryker merely stepped to the side and in between the three possibly destructive energy slashes that exploded behind him, Ryker once again walking over to his thick enemy. The demon not ready to give up on its arsenal of destructive vocabulary, slamming its palms together and a blood red thunderclap beamed towards Ryker to which Ryker responded by slapping it away from his face; as he continued to stroll so casually over to the demon, who was still not ready to throw in the towel.

Pulling the air in like the cranking of a Gatling gun to get it ready for its vicious assault, its cheeks puffed up like it was storing up its food for the winter, the inside of its mouth burned a fiery red. Releasing a ring of fire right at Ryker as big as a tunnel for a truck to go in through, Ryker never stopped on his pathway towards the demon to serve him up his punishment and when the ring of fire came to swallow Ryker whole Ryker fanned the entire flame out with one single swipe from his hand. Just as easy as that, like he was trying to freshen the air when someone contaminated it with a fart, doing the trick for both occasions; the demon shaking with absolute terror how could he just swipe away one of his most fearsome attacks that could bring buildings down crumbling, is the fables about Azuru's team really true is their strength really that unprecedented? Well the demon was just about to find out as he spat out three more rings, the second ring he shot from his mouth was double the size of the first two cars would be able to fit through. The last one was big enough for a diesel truck to drive inside, Ryker simply sighing before doing or saying anything, the panting demon knew this had to at least slow Ryker down in his tracks there was no way he was going to walk away from this unscratched! Unfortunately for this foul beast that is exactly what Ryker was going to do, the action he took to combat against this was doing exactly the same he just blew a gust of air from his mouth and he blew out the entire rings of fire like they we're flimsy lit candles on top of his birthday cake.

The demon shivering and shaking at the sight of Ryker's tremendous and absolutely incomparable strength, he put as much fire he could muster from the spirit of hell he was forged in. He just blew it all away like it was a fly in his airspace, Ryker now not too far off from the demon a few more feet and he was practically rubbing his face into his chest trying to share warmth, Ryker so disappointed as he still had his hands tucked in his pockets "ya know I – wait! I am gonna give you a few more chances!! Maybe your special attacks aren't your strong suit but maybe you're really really fast!! Go! Go on try attacking me at full speed don't hold back now!"

The demon was at a loss of complete thought why was his enemy trying to mentor him and pick up his spirits didn't he know that he was just going to use that to destroy him?! But this was no time for him to question the reason either way he was going to use this chance to exploit his stupid opponent he gave him a chance he definitely shouldn't have! Jumping back to create distance between them, he disappeared in mid air zipping and zapping through the air, the sound of slicing wind was all that could be heard not a single blur was able to be visible as the ground from time to time mysteriously busted and exploded like an invisible jackhammer was doing work on the ground, or like a land mine would go off from time to time; Ryker didn't even turn his head he wasn't following him one bit, his sight was aimed towards the floor he seemed to be trying to give his enemy the benefit of a chance at least. But suddenly Ryker picked up his right leg and raised it up and pointed it in back of his position with the rest of his body twisting as well, lightning began surging from the top of his foot; aiming his leg at what seemed to be harmless air, soon materialized to be the big meaty demon with Ryker's foot a foot away from his throat, the lightning like a lion only being separated from its prey by a cage.

Ryker's smile seeming to be even sharper than the tips of his static electricity that was fizzing off his leg, as Ryker was teaching his temporary student once again another lesson "too slow! You need to amp up your speed, go ahead and try again! Second time's the charm, and don't worry I'm not going anywhere – I don't wanna make it too hard for ya"

The demon baring its fangs in absolute detestation for Ryker but even more hatred was brewing by the fact that he was realizing how many leagues he was above him. Once again the demon disappeared but was already in the air by the time Ryker put his leg down, the sound of roaring flames pulled Ryker's attention up towards the sky; looking up he saw three comets of fire heading straight for him Ryker only smiling like a child being brought to a toy store, deciding to really have fun with this demon and his resentment aimed at Ryker as he skipped away from harm's way with a trail of lightning following him like a loving and healthy puppy. As they blew up harmlessly away from Ryker the demon roaring as he dashed through the air and he was now behind Ryker who hadn't noticed because of his frilly skipping, the demon knew this was the perfect opportunity to pull his soul from his chest with his indestructible claw. As he went for the harpoon like shot of a stab aimed at the middle of Ryker's back – well I stand corrected as Ryker did notice he was in back of him, ducking right under the claw and spinning around to the demon gesturing "bring it on" ecstatically with both hands and his tongue sticking out to the side of his mouth, the demon throwing stab, slash and scratch motions with arms that seemed to sprout from out of nowhere. Eight or nine arms all swiping, clawing, and trying to drill into Ryker one way or another, Ryker popping and locking his body in a rhythmic motion, shaking and trembling so his body was always moving and alternating his movements always dodging every attack while keeping a smile and expressing his body. Even spinning to have his back to the demon and maybe give him a better chance at hitting him while his back was turned, but still all those arms and at a ten times much faster pace than Ryker's slow movement that was what the kids call the "pop and lock" oh maybe he can do a spinaroonie next – hey a guy can dream can't he?! Shut up leave me alone! Here I'm giving you ungrateful children what you want and I am going back to the story! Ryker singing in a high pitch that scraped at the bottom of his throat and almost popped his Adam's apple "try again!!!"

The demon roaring with absolute hatred and wrath for Ryker getting the hint to try to use its brute strength because its speed was useless against him, he was just too fast but maybe when it comes down to the nitty gritty of a test of strength he might fall short. The demon was willing to take this risk as it combined both of these fearsome attributes to lay upon an onslaught onto Ryker, a blurry circle dashing around Ryker as he continued to pop and lock and continued to move in whatever motion that made his body happy, this persistent embodiment of carnage and destruction just wasn't willing to accept defeat or concede to someone who was truly more superior than him. The demon lunging out for a striking slash but once upon coming close he would come to a screeching halt to bring down a smashing fist onto Ryker, to which all he did was smack it away with a sudden spike up from his right shoulder. The demon grinding his teeth together how did he not see this coming? But not letting this disturb his efforts, as he jumped over Ryker and back into the merry – go – round of blurry assault going so fast the demon didn't have to be present inside for it to keep going; Ryker now starting to shimmy and shake, his shoulders holding the most rhythmic stepping as his right shoulder continued to spike up before he would side step clapping his hands over his head. Then sliding over to the left and doing the opposite, miraculously had it timed so well every slide he did would duck under a swiping claw and every shoulder spike up would block a hook coming from the demon.

The demon fed up bringing down both fists with the knuckles intertwined inside each other in a slug, Ryker finally put his dancing on hold to shoot up one hand to catch the closing in attack able to hold the demon's attack back with the littlest effort imaginable, no sign of a struggle or effort on Ryker's face as he smiled over to the demon.

The demon on the other hand, veins we're popping out, muscles tensed, teeth we're biting down so hard in frustration and sparks we're about to fly out due to friction. But not a single inch was given, now Ryker was beginning to lift his arm higher and higher pushing both of the demon's big meaty rippled chiseled out arms; Ryker only giving a mischievous grin as he asked with what seemed like he was just trying to be polite but it was actually packed and loaded with such patronizing venom the question alone could make the demon go into a corner and cry "is that it? Can you try a little harder? I know you have more strength than that you're just going easy on me!" The demon picking up his hands that still we're crossed in each other as he slammed them on top of Ryker's hand like a very violent and passionate high five again again and again, each time cracking the ground around Ryker's feet building up the pressure from the ground but still didn't move Ryker a single centimeter. A frown slowly started to stretch across Ryker's face as he lowered his head towards the ground and let out a sigh "this is all the power you have isn't it?" Before he could try a meaningless other time Ryker then scoffed and said "okay I'm done waiting around you failed me as a demonic student!!" Ryker then smacked the demon across the jaw with a right hook that turned the demon's head and the demon wasn't hearing things when he heard "impact" right afterwards. It was followed up with a left uppercut to the body that made the demon begin to curl up but before he could fully bowl over, Ryker hit him four times in the ribcage, right, left, right, left hearing five "impacts" in total.

The demon fell onto one knee; this was the perfect chance for Ryker to kick the only leg holding him up with a sweeping right kick. Before he could even begin to descend to the ground Ryker put him back onto his feet with a fearsome uppercut, two "impacts" so far Ryker then hit that same leg again with the same lower leg kick, "impact", a left hook a millisecond afterward, "impact", then the opposite leg with a left kick, "impact", with a right hook to follow up with almost instantly, "impact", then a one two combination of a left then right straight punch, "impact impact", just as he was about to hit the demon with a no holds barred overhand right while he was already dazed. He stopped his fist inches from the demon's face dropped his arm and slipped both of his hands back into his pockets to reclaim his calm demeanor and a smile once again sparked across his face gleaming like the rising sun over the horizon "that should be enough!" stepping back a few steps and simply whistled and the demon was able to regain his head, and before he could charge forward to attack his defenseless opponent; his head violently twisted to the left almost breaking its own neck with the force of the torque, then a blow so intense lifted him off the ground as it struck him in the stomach and the demon was dropped back to the ground on one knee. Just as he was trying to come back to his normal senses and overcome the overwhelming pain that was even more devastating than the attacks that Ryker that he hit him with physically – just then the demon was hit once again by the air with smoke resonating off him and his bones cracking upon each blow that was hammered into his body, right, left, right, left the sequence that the stomach wrenching attacks came in.

Then the knee that was holding up the frail demon like only a single beam in an entire house, it was kicked at the same exact spot it had already been hit previously before but this time with enough strength to snap it in half, like a popsicle stick sword playing against a wooden baseball bat. An absolute scream of utter agony sounded off from the demon and before he could properly fall to the ground to let the pain sink in properly he was sent back onto his feet his pain intensifying as he was forced to put pressure on his freshly made wound only aggravating and worsening the condition, the same leg was sent flying away as it was kicked apart with an even brutal invisible blow. The demon screeching in complete and utter distress that he didn't even have any sound along with mouth motions, his face being smashed in like the wind was carrying a sledgehammer and just dug it into the right side of his face, bones definitely had been snapped and cracked; too much pain coming in at one time like a line with five people calling at the same time with their own separate problems that the demon had to talk them over about. With a swing gust of vicious air resonating off the only remaining leg that was keeping the demon from falling to its face in pure shame, where was all the power and strength that it was so proud of? Yet another invisible crushing blow now slammed into the other side of its face that wasn't yet scathed; now it looked like he stuck his face in the middle of a trash compacter to see what it smelled like in the second someone pressed the button. Immediately after another blow cracked the demon's neck back, hanging on by the treads of its muscles as it limply hung back and just as the demon was about to fall forward; the demon's head was sent flying off like a golf ball making a hole in one with the first shot.

Now the demon's body was given permission to falter as Ryker with a big mischievous grin said "see told you that was gonna be enough! I just love when a plan doesn't screw up when I make it up... now"– Ryker then turned around sliding only one of his hands from his pockets to point at the pet goat from the very far back who did nothing to help his comrades from being absolutely pulverized. "Looks like you're up!"

Amar was picking up more specks of black and gray dots onto his suit of armor with the more demons that were slain by his hands, back peddling as the demons coming in hordes and hordes after him, upper cutting one who snapped its jaw at him with his left fist and he vacuum sucked it into his left gauntlet. Slashing in an "X" formation into another enemy with his right hand, finally getting the hang of actual combat as he poised on the tips of his left toes spinning on these toes; spiraling his blade against every demon surrounding him reducing each and every body close to him, to nothing but a lingering cloud of ash that was sucked into his ivory blade on his forearm. Any lingering dark clouds we're quickly drained into the ivory blade like the remaining streams in a bath tub, Amar sliding back as the rest of the horde began to circle and surround him, now having to make and calculate a plan just seeing how rushing in and flailing blindly but with their pea sized brains theories and plans could come as complex as "attack him all at once or one at a time" just their level of intelligence. They need to eat other demons or soul to grow up and be a strong healthy malevolent force of darkness, Amar picked up his head to look at the stand still angry mob of demons that we're now cautiously treading not a single one of them charged; they all came up with the brilliant single plan of waiting for Amar to make the first move.

Amar pointing his sword to them, boldness shining off him as he said with such strong intense epic oozing from his voice "come on!" While under his breath he spoke to himself "I need to make sure no one interferes with Forrest and his team the faster the team gets the mission done the faster this whole thing is all over!"

Just as Amar was about to take one step towards this demonic gathering, his sword shrank back into his armor retracting back to being his regular forearm guard to never be seen again. Amar stricken with slight panic but merely coughed as he regained himself or at least tried to show that he did; his hand shaking as he demanded in a strict and stern voice "sword I **NEED** you to come out!... please?" Closing his eyes in a hopeful gesture that when he opened them it would have returned, shooting his eyes open as he began rattling his malfunctioning hand even whispering to it with the hysteria building in his voice "please come out I neeeeeed it! – I neeeeeeeeeeeed it!" The demons beginning to look puzzled and even a bit concerned as they watched Amar yell at his arm to which Amar responded "YES!

EVERYTHING IS FINE THANK YOU FOR YOUR CONCERNS!"
Going back to angrily grunting and murmuring to his hand,
Amar crouching his head down as he said with horror creeping
inside his voice "they are all waiting on me to do something
amazing I cannot let them down now! What if Forrest's team
and the hybrid are secretly watching me putting aside their
differences to poke fun at the noob who can't get his sword up!?"
Amar then shot his fist up into the sky in a pose of victory, getting
yelps of question from the demonic crowd. Amar exclaimed to
the heavens up above "I do not need a single weapon to defeat
you all! – I can vanquish each and every one of you with these two
fists... of justice!" There was complete and utter silence as dead
and cadaverous as could possibly be; on the outside Amar held
his heroic testament challenge with his arms high in the sky but
on the inside Amar's spiral pool was twisting and knotting itself.

Ringing itself out like a towel, just being prepared to be hung
out to dry, an absolute wreck on the inside "hopefully they are not
watching me and if they are I hope that they buy my statement!"

A clamor of thunderous howls from riled up demons almost
steaming mad as they wanted to rip off Amar's face and wear it
as a Halloween mask. Jumping up and down, some screeching
and howling, others were pounding the ground with the hammer
side of their fist, now the action really began with the rushing
stampede of demons; Amar's eyebrows rising up as his eyes
widening and his body stood frozen for a matter of moments,
closing his eyes while he simply stood there. But as Amar took
in calm pairs of inhales and exhales, he prepared himself, eyes
shooting open; he tightly gripped his fists as he now returned
the lashing energy. The front demon leading the pack as he was
on all fours mouth leaking fire, he then growled with intense
animalistic ferocity and just as he leaped forward lunging with
the level of an elite killing machine. Enough to make the king
of the jungle kneel before him in shame, Amar's body suddenly
surging – he could feel every single inch of his entire body on fire

skin, muscles, nerves all of it connected to a strong unbreakable flame; his body beginning to drift into a direction without him doing anything, he was practically just going along for the ride. Running forward and those menacing pairs of claws that belonged to the first opposer – half a foot from his face, his right arm slowly moved towards the gap in the middle; Amar trying to grasp this why was this happening without his say so? It is his body after all – he couldn't move his arm in any other direction it only slowly floated towards that space, Amar having no choice but to follow it as soon as he cooperated with it and flowed along with it also putting his energy into this action, real time began to move along again and his whole left side of his body automatically contorted and squeezed within the cranny instinctively without Amar doing a single thing but providing support.

All he did was follow through where ever his arm was guiding him, in the tightly balled fist Amar curved up and into an uppercut. His fist brilliantly squeezing through and giving the perfect, flawless impeccable shot of power; Amar's jaw dropped as he couldn't even wrap his mind around what just happened "w-what was that?! – It was lik –like my body was teaching me and showing me where to go – MY BODY!!" Truly a mind blowing thought, that Amar's own body was showing him the way to victory. Mentoring him in combat, instead of being sent flying with Amar's monstrous strength the demon burst into ashes like those cheap New Year's celebration poppers; full of confetti and was black holed into Amar's fist, specking his arm with further darkness that has been defeated. Without looking Amar's head was forced to duck, without his consent once again; Amar pointing his eyes to the top of his skull, desperately trying to see what was he avoiding. A claw with all the finger tips lanced forward, brushing right through Amar's gentle spikes Amar's shrine drooping down into his spiral pool as he was completely relieved, him being the newbie that he is he would have had those metal points drilled into his frame. Picking up his right arm to swing it in a half circle over and bend his chest back, his body contorting worse than a flexible gymnast but now it was Amar's turn for a counter as his eyes we're immediately drawn to the foot of the first assailant, Amar then with immense force slid out his left foot making the demon wobble and begin to timber like a building with its foundation removed as he was unbalanced mess a second stab was shot forward, aimed at Amar's shrine.

Without Amar looking, his right arm rung around this big stocky meaty claw gripping it with his bicep while he did this he slammed the descending demon's face into the ground. Smashing him as if Amar's hand we're a sledgehammer, now putting full attention the demon whose arm this belonged to; Amar quickly spun around chicken winging the demon as he folded the arm behind its back. The demon roaring in an agonizing pain before Amar lifted up the hold, popping and dislocating the arm from the shoulder, a strenuous scream was heard from the demon as it kicked and slashed the air trying to get away. There was no getting away from Amar's gridlock hold, just then he pointed his palm flat to make it like a knife and brought it down on top of the demon's shoulder and tore it off cleanly like his hand actually consisted of metal; he then dismissed the howling demon with a kick to the back before swinging around to smack a triplet of demons who we're lunging for Amar already jaws flying off in chronological with a smashing roundhouse kick that went through each and every one of them like they we're made of glass. With such a gustful burst he was able to push them all back, just with the momentum of his spin able to create his very own circle of space within the confounds of their attack force that pounced on him like roaches on crumbs of food.

Kayoh and Ex sprinting after their leader in the shadows of the flushes of hardwood sturdy trees, all they could both see was the burning ember like the light at the end of a dark tunnel only shining brighter the farther it went along; picking up from the ground both Kayoh and Ex watched on as they saw it climb up into the sky. A spiral appeared right before them both darkness and the burning evergreen intertwining in the sky, Kayoh and Ex stopped in their tracks they knew there was no reaching them now. The two strings spinning wider and wider apart from each other, colliding and crashing into each other only to wind themselves up and do it all over again, until they finally met up and slammed their hands into each other. A single energy emitting off from both of them with both of their explosive auras mixed in, suddenly Forrest pulled his hands away from the skull gloves that we're covering the hybrid's claws; only to drop both of his fists on top of his skull then aiming both hands at the descending angel of darkness, sending him down in a ball of flames like a meteorite crashing into the ground blowing up upon impact. Forrest not even close to being done to punish him for comparing him to BAD whoever that is! Flinging fireball upon fireball at the dust cloud that held a potentially still breathing hybrid, throwing one after another like a mother throwing everything into her shopping cart at the groceries store when everything is on sale; to which the fireball curved in and hooked, thunderclap after thunderclap was heard that only spurred and rose more dust up from the ground.

Forrest stopping his onslaught only to release a truly vicious and frightening roar as he screamed over to the foul beast "TELL ME NOW!! WHO IS BETTER ME OR THAT IDIOT BAD!?!?"The dust slowly began to mist and fade away to reveal the hybrid with not a single scratch on him, he also wasn't alone either a pack of his own personal varied demons from all shapes and sizes. Very smug with his evil entourage behind him the hybrid spat back "I still think you are leagues below him because he would have killed me by now!" The hybrid now gesturing for this frustrated and flustered Forrest to "bring it on" with his index claw

Amar in his prepared and conscious fighting stance saying to himself as a note "okay I am starting to get used to this... I have said this before, but for sure this time I mean it! I have the space I need I can fight as I want as well... now I am starting to understand why Mr. Azuru did all the weird vigorous training that he made me do" everything was still, low growls from the surrounding demons that we're trying to start to box Amar in; the demons he viciously tore apart and smashed in, slowly picking themselves up to stand amongst the others. So many pairs of piercing peepers, all blood toned eyes with evil just oozing out from each pair; the only thing that was moving was the leaves in the wind gently blowing by.

Amar was ready for these ungraceful clowns anytime they we're ready to charge, but they we're making progress at glacier speed not even a single move had been thought of – suddenly a humongous thunder clapping boom shattered the tension that could have been cut with a plastic spoon all the heads even Amar's turning as if they we're all obedient followers in a game of Simon says. Trying to find the source of the sonic boom that just occurred but a wave of dust then came in brushing past their waists, as a hurricane of debris slapped each and every one of them in the face; a thick blanket of brown shrouded any vision – no matter how hard Amar squinted he could not get a single speck of vision out, but like a giant swiping his hand over the entire blurry area to clear up all of the cloud of dust instantly. But there was no gigantic hand in sight the source of this sense of clarity was in the form of a tank like bullet that crashed into the huge bushes of trees like a bowling ball striking right into the pyramid of pins, just then Amar felt a hand clasp onto his shoulder.

Amar jumped back into his fighting stance as he remembered that he was on a battle zone, and no demon was going to just sit there and politely ask him "are you ready to resume the fight?" Spasming his arms to try to slap the hand that clutched his shoulder only to hear a cautious "hey hey there Rook do I look like an ugly soul stealer to you?" Amar stunned to see his master here in front of him he had already forgotten about Ryker who was on his way out following his enemy who just decided he might try out being a torpedo and see where that lead him, but seeing the masses that surrounded Amar he couldn't help but notice something "hey!... There sure are a lot of these guys much more than before... and you're taking them all on yourself?-"Amar oddly nodding to Ryker's notice he assumed this was completely obvious "because that sure is impressive for so-"suddenly cut off by his own lightning bolt that Ryker fired off from his own finger stunned the whole pack including Amar making him jump with the abrupt startle that impulsively came out of absolute nowhere. Before Amar could even question his Sensei of his actions, Ryker himself explained "sorry, sorry... sorry it's just that one looked at me weird!" Ryker pointing his index finger at now a timbering pair of legs that had more smoke emitting from it than a smoking hot stripper on fire; his white lightning borderline vaporizing the savage demon but truly showing the standard for a elite, being able to take out cannon fodder on a whim. Amar frantically responding to Ryker's reasoning "ITS EYE WAS HANGING OUT OF COURSE IT WAS GONNA LOOK AT YOU WEIRD!!! To be fair I was the one who kicked it out but that's-""well then there you go Rook it's your fault that this demon had to be euthanized, hope you're happy!"

Amar's pouting lip returned as he truly felt the weight of the loss that was all on his part, before it could sink in that it is a benefit that one of his enemies is no longer walking the face of this Earth, the ground began to shake and tremble a few "booms" and drum fires we're heard along the way as well Amar turning his head in the direction of origin. Only to see a behemoth on two feet

A mountain of muscle with more ripples in him than a pool with splashing children, on this approximately 12 footed monster besides muscle stacked upon muscle. Was the outline of his own skull double layered around his head, the chin/ jaw line, the crown of the head, cheekbones, eyes, nose all of it for some reason had an outer skeleton on top of its already rough and tough skin what was the use of having extra protection especially when the attack that launched him like a pop gun, with the string unfortunately being cut, hadn't done a single scratch to him seemed to only succeeding in making him absolutely livid it was as clear as day by the blood red boiling a glow in his twin pools. Before Amar could even ask once again Sensei knew all as Ryker wrapped his arm around Amar forcing his head underneath his armpit, thank goodness Ryker doesn't let his natural body produce its own odor; "I know what you're thinking Rook! Who is that man I never seen my handsome sensei wrestle with him before!!" "Umm yes all that except the handso-""well I shall fill in the blanks for you my lovely, curious as a dumb cat student!" "Did you just call me a dumb-""after I released you into the wild to trek on your own, fulfill your own journey! GO OUT INTO THE UNIVERSE AND MAKE YOUR MARK INTO THE WORLD!!..... These jerks showed up tried to kill you while your back was turned I was like who the hell you think you is, DAWG?! And they we're like 'raaawr! And what not' – you know they can't talk and all

Then first two of the three I wasn't even paying attention when I took out, we're only food for the pet goat – you remember pet goats right? - We just got done talking about them so I would hope you would! Well yeah anyways he ate them and gained their strength and all their individual powers added up into this big hulk – like muscles mass that is this supposedly best of both worlds. I mean I guess that is what they we're going for when they all fused together without consent – note to you Rook if you wanna fuse just ask me I will be more than willing to try – but you try to take a chomp outta me and I will put your teeth in between a curb and put my foot at the back of your head to help you get a better bite hahaha oh! Violent subtle undertones I love you almost as much as my wife – God I miss that woman!"

Amar miles behind Ryker who was running mental laps around Amar, so confused lost, dazed and disoriented he almost wanted to walk over to Ryker's opponent to ask him if he knew what was going on "so.... Are you going to make me eat a curb??" "Rook... that is what I call a joke... it is supposed to tickle the parts of your brain and cause a sensation throughout your body that forces you to share a form of joy usually it sounds like this "hahahha" "oh... haha... ha?" "Never mind no wonder Azuru didn't spend any time with you, I'm gonna remember the joke Azuru will probably think its funny! Anyways have fun with your horde of demons I gotta go take care of Ms. Universe on opposite day over there!" Amar still not able to find his way to the mental path that his master was taking, just waiving very oddly as he still couldn't grip his intelligence stature "bye Sensei" calling over as Ryker with his hands slid into his pockets, with Ryker now in sight the now revved and revamped empowered demon only reflected all his evil intent with his jagged teeth being bared as he smirked.

Vanishing like the lightning appearing to Earth's skies to give it a quick hi and bye, was already in front of Ryker trying to squish his head in between his claws that we're big enough to clutch Ryker's entire body. Ryker ducking his head like the demon's attack was a casual branch that he was strolling into while cruising through the park, bobbing his head down but while he was there; the demon was already exactly where his face was pointing towards the ground, flame leaking and oozing off the edges of his ridged teeth as the demon was actually able to lay a finger on Ryker. But Ryker not even the least bit worried or even concerned he looked like his mind was somewhere else completely, the demon actually doing better than just putting one finger on Ryker, both entire claws gripped Ryker's arms just then the now vastly superior demon spoke with its brand new intelligence "**LEEF STIURF FO YM WEN SREWOP!!**" (*Feel the fruits of my new powers!!*) a dome of flaring heat bubbled them both inside erupting like a volcano that was having erectile dysfunction, Amar full of concern was about to call over to his sensei and even rush over to his aid but he had to get a hold of himself and reclaim his composure. He would only be insulting his master if he thought that a simple attack would do him away just like that, with his sensei at the back of his mind and hopeful thoughts barely able to beat back the intrusive cognition that was getting its motor going. Finally the moment has come! All sides all charging forward, bum rushing Amar; but Amar now was in absolute still focus the perfect definition of concentration, waiting for them to close into *his* mid – range, where lunging attacks would be reachable.

Just then like a donkey when slapped on the ass - and well really any self respecting woman spun around and viciously attacked the incoming intruder, only launching one leg imbedding his boot into the dead center of the demon as he snapped it back. Combusting it into a shotgun blast of ash, immediately was pulled back in by Amar's gravitational pull; becoming one with Amar's shoe now taking the form of a black speck, as his leg was being put back down a pair of primal demons we're already slashing at his face with their razor – sharp claws. Amar simply smacking one of their hands down as if they we're an insignificant fly buzzing around, countering with a bullet right hook the instant that his hand was lowered; cracking his whole entire body into disintegration and as soon as his ashy remains began to be shepherded to Amar's armor he wasted absolutely no time going for the other one. Giving him a huge torque that treated this beast like an all steel car and Amar was the magnetic field, hooking him at the jaw as well; his fist burst through instant ash that overtook his body like an insane incurable virus, the lingering ash was thrown into the eyes of a nearby demon by the splash of Amar's destructive attack. Amar catching every action like a camera that was able to look in all directions seen this and leapt forward with his right knee might as well been a knight in a joust his mighty lance just taking the form of a knee pad, first the dark gray was able to spread to the entire body before he smashed against the floor crumbling into a heap of dust. Amar landing back into his stance, balancing on one foot as he speared his right foot into the most elegantly straight edged sidekick; hip touching thigh as his foot tore right through the demon like a rock going through a wet piece of paper, quickly pulling it out to send his gray trophy to shambles

Before Amar could set his foot down, another demon was already lunging to him, aiming for his head. Without Amar putting in effort, gently moved back to drive in between the claws; clacking heads against this unfair charger, backing him up a few hazy steps but before he could even try to shake away the stars and throbbing Amar swung a back fist and spun along with it as well. To leave this crumbling statue without a jaw, Amar then took this time to let one of his concerning thoughts hop the fence that he had on lockdown so fiercely "maybe I should check on Sensei to see how he is holding up – I really really hope he is doing okay!" Amar taking a chance on himself to disrupt his own concentration and for a mere matter of moments looked over to his sensei's previous position where the bubble from hell popped against the Earth, he was at least relived to see that Mr. Ryker was completely fine not even his clothes held a single burn on them he looked like he did a minute ago when he was checking up on Amar.

It seemed the only thing that changed was that his left leg was lifted up; the demon was now some ways off with skid marks carved into the ground and he was in complete frustration rubbing his chest with a hint of pain and sting in his primal facial expression. Lightning surged off of Ryker's leg like a static line coming up in the middle of a basic cable television, the demon now back into its fearsome stance as it exclaimed to Ryker the new form it was so proud of "**I MA YLNO GNIHCTARCS EHT EECAFRUS TAHT SI YM WEN DNUOF SREWOP!!**-"(*I am only* *scratching the surface of my new found powers!! –)* Ryker slowly putting down his leg but his interest still remained close to none as the demon continued to go on and on exasperating the villain trope. "**I EVAH EHT ELBAHCTACNU DEEPS FO EHT DECNAVDA O! EHT HTGNERTS FO EHT TSEGNORTS LAMIRP DNUORA!! DNA HTIW YM DESRUC CIGAM TAHT SI YLNO DNOCES OT YM RETSAM! REHTGOT-**"(*I have the uncatchable speed of the advanced O! The strength of the strongest primal around!!! And with my cursed magic that is only second to my master! Together-*"

Abruptly stopped like a brick wall appearing in the middle of the freeway the demon came to a screeching halt, launched up into the sky with a kick from Ryker at his gut; it came so fast he never even was able to catch Ryker move. Ryker sent him up into the sky as a bolt of lightning that he still zapped and buzzed with white and black electricity as well, even quicker than half of a split millisecond Ryker was already up in the sky behind the demon with hands never taken out from his pockets. He then whispered in the demon's ear with so much disdain and dragging almost forcing himself to tell the demon this "look! If you are going to brag about how great you are – word of advice make sure I'm either A: on the ground or B: dead... so you can **ACTUALLY** brag about your powers that you seem so proud of! Why don't you go ahead and show me!!!" Ryker then front flipped his heel on top of the skull of the demon fracturing a crack on the top of his second layer that was acting as momentary armor. Sending the demon crash down into the Earth like Zeus being displeased with the humans, before Ryker decided to zap down to the ground like he so very easily could

Deciding to look out and see what Forrest and his team we're up to squinting to see a whole other battle. Calling down below to Amar who was just about to rush to the demons to change the tide of who had the title of predator "HEY ROOK! IT'S FORREST AND HIS TEAM! THEY LOOK LIKE THEY ARE DOING OKAY...

I GUESS!" Ryker was true in this regard they we're holding their own against the growing darkness that just seemed to never let up and allow Forrest or his team to land a battle deciding blow. Kayoh guarding with her two fists parallel to her face, dashing to the group of ever growing demons and Ex bringing up the other side with him already pulling his sword out from its sheath; his thumb flicking the guard as the metal chinked alarmed the demons he was approaching but it was too late for them. In the air Forrest was trying to become the new sun by letting his rage run wild mixing in with his ferocious evergreen fire.

His aura itself was fire but spread around him like he was the burning man, only growing wider and bigger as the moments passed by. Kayoh trying to end it before this dragged on any longer she was shaking her right fist ever so slightly as she whispered "Phoenix rising, Phoenix swipe" the two unsuspecting and obviously not too intelligent either as the big Primal guards in front of a group of several push over damned souls and even flimsier Os that even with darkness backing them we're still not nearly as strong as the walking rocket launcher that was Kayoh. Flames burning gold, orange, red, and silver exploded all over her right hand as she shot her fist upward, her hand so unforgiving as her knuckles smashed the demon's chin in the second contact was made crunching the jaw into tiny bite sized bones and a screech of an eagle was heard as she sent the demon flying along with her flaming firebird that carried the demon up into the sky only to explode once spreading its wings and ash began to rain down. Before the demon could even fully comprehend what had just happened to his brother in carnage, a swift cut from Kayoh in the form of a right hook to the demon's rib cage sliced the demon torso from waist; with yet another screeching eagle sounding off as flame gathered around Kayoh's arm a huge wing of fire exploding off Kayoh's arm as she wasn't close to being finished with the dark forces.

Ex whipped his candy cane like sword into the neck of huge primate like demon, with it trying to grip the blade to pull it out scratching and clawing; too late as Ex pressing the button on his hilt and his sword now became really loose with the chain linking blades able him to whip him into the other bumbling giant. Sandwiching them together as he slammed them on the ground on top of one another, but as their bodies recoiled and bounced off the ground, Ex double tapped the button on his hilt and the whipping blades began to slide inside of each other and condense one scaling on top of another.

Slanting and pointing upwards until they all pointed forwards to one single direction, all spiraling and climbing up to one singular point, now Ex pushed his lance – like sword into the stomachs of both of these dark warriors; even his hilt now taking another shape and form. Ex pulled the hilt back to which it extended further and from there it cranked up and at now Ex had the complete set to his drill that would go as fast as he was willing to go! Immediately Ex's right arm becoming a blur, the drill having to travel ten times faster than Ex; the demons roaring out agony as a hole was being mined inside of their now shared guts. Their bodies like a pinwheel being powered by a child with asthma, very weakly picking up but still was well on its way with both of the bodies working parallel clockwork against each other now becoming like blurred blades on a fan that Ex used their bodies and his drill to spear right through the companions that we're blocking him on Ex's side. Meanwhile on Kayoh's side wings of fire emerged from her back as she was also drilling through the line that held its ground for their beloved leader, with Kayoh bodies we're either being melted, burnt to a crisp, or being tossed up into the sky like the caps at a graduation; and ask for Ex's side chunks and limbs we're being flung and slung into the air

Ex and Kayoh both closing in to the single point in the middle that seemed to be the most secure, the exact spot where the hybrid was standing. Kayoh and Ex crashing on both sides of the hybrid who only used his skull gloves to catch both destructive tools of chaos, a pulverizing and bulldozing drill that still retained his comrades on top of still spinning them around they we're just decorations at this point; and a burning fist who had wings of infernos and unbreakable tenacity and calamitous capabilities.

Somehow able to hold both of them back with darkness oozing up from the floor and even more waving up from the faults and emerging cracks in the ground. As Kayoh realized that they couldn't push through as easily she knew exactly what this meant, they we're too late turning her head up to her soaring leader to witness his flame grown even more both in size and instability; Forrest now digging his hands into his evergreen aura and Kayoh's fears had took a new life as she pleaded a scream to her captain "CAPTAIN STOP!!! DON'T TAKE OFF FIRST LAYER!!! WE BOTH KNOW WHAT WILL HAPPEN!" Forrest not able to contain himself any longer and he felt whatever this first layer was, was constricting him roaring into the sky for her to hear "I WANT HIM TO KNOW WHAT A REAL WARRIOR LOOKS LIKE BEFORE I SEND HIM TO OBLIVION!!! THIS LAYER WILL NO LONGER HOLD ME BACK!!!!"

The hybrid curiously repeating the word that they we're throwing around as common knowledge "layer?" It seemed that Forrest was prying something apart with his hands slipping through golden cracks, Ryker seeing this whole scene from afar just sighing and shaking his head in disapproval and displeasure; he zapped down right behind the demon who was barely getting to his feet still a bit groggy this is when Ryker whispered aloud "I will have to take care of this thing first so I can shut down Forrest he is going against orders." The golden layer of energy that was inside of his highly combustible evergreen aura, an egg shaped bubble that was flashing a brighter golden light the more and more Forrest fiercely ripped it apart like it was deluxe indestructible tissue paper; but Forrest tore the entire thing off of his body and not a single thread of energy was left to cover him.

Kayoh in horror and disbelief stared at her rebellious captain up in the air and with no words left to say, her attack was half halted. The hybrid completely taking advantage of this as he grabbed her fist pulled her in and aimed her towards Ex, stunned by the thinking process of the hybrid as he had to move fast. Taking his finger off the button on the hilt and the spinning lance was forced to come to an abrupt halt just in time, as the point stopped with Kayoh's chest mere hairs away from the tip of the puncturing blade; before Ex could even exhale a relieved sigh Kayoh was kicked into him and over her shoulder Ex seen an incoming blast of darkness coming their way. Ex knew that his second – in – command needed to be unharmed if he wanted this mission to be a success so he did the ultimate sacrifice that a subordinate could make, throwing her full force out of the way so the tidal wave of ominous energy would strike him instead, she fumbled and flopped against the floor looking back in concern to see

Ex trying his best to block the blast with his blade but now the hybrid used both hands to fire the dark energy from. Ex not able to hold it back, Ex slicing every ounce of malevolent energy that was fired at him as it came down the line but the force was much too strong lifting him off the ground and pushing him back with the force of a demolition truck; tearing trees in half as he speared right through them, flipping cars over, crashing right through them before he was finally able to come to a stop inside of a three storied building. The building erupting with malevolent energy like the hybrid was holding the trigger to ominous TNT and he decided when to set it off, before Kayoh could get up and check up on her fellow team mate her attention was pulled to the sky above her as a glaring light outshined the sun.

Forrest a gigantic ball of rapid building and spreading green, silver, gold and white flames; his evergreen fire emerging from his eyes, emitting from the top and lower corners of his mouth as he spoke, the ball that hosted his entire transformation was slowly evolving into a mouth with vicious teeth and Forrest being the even sharper tongue pointing down to the hybrid as he felt like the most superior being on this planet. "Now are you ready?"

A miniature street light sized tornado of darkness erupted around the hybrid, inside the hurricane of darkness we're the parts and pieces of his fallen comrades – all molding and melting inside of his body as his physique was pumping like someone had an air driver punctured into his leg, their bones gathering onto his forearms, shins, feet, abdominals and face bones from the primal demons to provide defensive coverage on his major attacking parts. With the scraps and left overs from the blended bodies of the Os and damned souls made the abdominal plate and the coverage on his nose, eyes, mouth, and cheek bones. Pointing with a whole new intensity to him like the dial for this battle just broke and they are going off of overdrive, their smiles mirror reflections of each other as Forrest yanked his arms over his chest and to his sides and his supernova bubble erupting even further growing the face of a fearsome beast who was letting everyone know who the king was by roaring and quaking the ground around them. Amar heard and felt every second of this but now did he have the time to react and take his mind off the battle? That is the real question

Amar immediately beginning to rush to the demons trying to pull the favor of battle to his side and control the pace, dashing to one primal and slid underneath its clumsy legs. He was able to hop up and snatch the back of its neck to pull it down with gravity and with Amar's frightful strength tossed him by the neck over his shoulder like a careless pitcher just trying to go home already; taking down a line of five as he bounced on his neck and other important parts of his body snapping and popping like a tire running over a pile of twigs, kept going Amar was taking out anyone and everyone not sure how he was able to read them and also not sure what they we're about to do but he knew how to counter it somehow. There we're some moves he took upon himself to do without the need for a counter and did not feel the torque from his body butting in and showing him how to properly fight, like this one for instance: Amar driving his elbow into the demon that was in front of him, the stomach was the bull's eye point Amar like the dart that shot it right on the mark. Leaving the gray miniature monument in a forever bowled over formation, Amar dropping down to a sitting position as two claws from both sides of his faces failed to drill into his brain; Amar then hopped back to balance on his hands as he drop kicked the demon's leg. Sending a puff of ash blown out from underneath as the demon slowly came crashing down to the ground, Amar now bending his legs to shoot his knees to meet the jaw of the demon; shattering the remains of this instantaneous statue, now Amar pushed down against the ground to do a backwards leap during a huge moonsault to his previous attacker. Instead of his body flopping on top of him his heel crushed down onto the skull of this demon slicing him into a gray puff of air and landing swiftly on his feet.

Amar was still very far from being out of the storm actually just entering the eye of it, every demon he slain and the more specks collects on his slowly made his armor grow black and gray polka dots on it. Dodging a slice to the face by back stepping then dodging a slash to the back by hopping forward, a fiery flurry of blurry arms coming towards him trying to poke holes into Amar's front, but Amar kept swaying, bobbing, and back stepping he was able to dodge every single attempt even bending his hip to the right as a huge stabbing lunge was made. Amar could have seen that coming a mile away though as he continued to weave through his rapid opponent, looking to have multiple arms; Amar seeing a light glowing behind the beast, glimmering very vibrant. He knew for sure that wasn't home calling him, his aura felt a sudden surge of heat before it could even come to Amar's senses; sliding to the side to dodge a massive fireball that blew up as a misfire into the crowd. Amar was sadly mistaken when he believed he could rest for a bit, as not just one but three pairs of eight dashing arms attached to three incredibly accelerated damned souls aiming to stab Amar's shrine right out from his chest; a startle running down Amar's spine as they all rushed him, Amar's body shifting into turbo or overdrive he was blurring his arms as fast as this mini brigade of rapid warriors. Not letting a single one of them touch him while sliding to the side to dodge ongoing exploding balls of fire, then also ducking as demons lunged at him, tilting his head to the side as nearby demons tried to munch his face off like beef jerky.

Amar desperately trying to focus as he thought to himself "wow! There sure are a lot of them my mind and body are going crazy trying to dodge them all! Do not know how much longer I can keep this up"

Ryker in a forest clump of trees using the thick brickets of wood as obstacles and optical illusionary diversions as he stepped to the side to take haven behind these trees that with a single slash we're broken like tooth picks; as soon as the new demon would head for that tree and knock it over Ryker would step out from behind another tree that was ways ahead and Ryker had no way of getting to. Ryker stepping back in and as soon as the intelligent beast would use his expeditious speed to get to this tree before Ryker would have a chance to leave he was already gone.

The demon getting utterly and ultimately frustrated and it certainly did not help being struck at the spine with a surging bolt of electricity dropping him to his hands and knees, as smoke resonated from his back and slowly emitting from his nose and mouth. His head and vision all shaking as he immensely struggled to try to get a sight at what direction that came from, finally aiming his sights at a laid back Ryker who had his back against a tree with one hand still unmoved from his pocket while he pointed his index finger from his left hand at the demon. Leg yanked halfway up the tree and his index finger bolting a wild static of silver electricity jumping off of his finger as Ryker not even really focused on the problem – sorry, minor inconvenience in front of him looking over his shoulder instead of at the embodiment of malice that was just gathering himself up right now.

Ryker watching his student in action, dust puffing, hands and claws flying around and limbs, chunks of bodies and demons in general we're flying around. Ryker said with an interested and intense smirk growing on his face "this is a make you or break you moment! So what's it gonna be Rook?! Come on we both know the answer to that one now!" His face instantly returning to be disappointed as he had to once again focus on his chore of an opponent instead of being able to watch his growing and blooming student, only sighing as he really just wanted to get this over with only a single white spark line was left in his place; the demon now up and at 'em just needed to look for Ryker and he for sure was dead! Until he felt a skull shaking and mind throbbing slap at the back of his head, Ryker walking out from behind the demon who was rubbing his head trying to make his pain go away Ryker then said "hey let's play a game okay? Cause the battery on my game is running on low and I need to get a little exercise, I hope you can provide that much – name of the game! My speed versus your speed!! Ready?! Let's do this"

Ryker then zipped and blurred right through the trees taking a gentle stroll right through them at the speed of a high speed super car tearing through the freeway. Just then before the demon could even react he was hit right across the jaw, black ooze spitting out to his left as it gushed out like a pimple being popped; how could this happen? Who is even capable of moving at such a fast pace?! The demon still trying to regain his head from that aluminum baseball – like strike to the side of the face, until he felt a hit to the gut that lifted the behemoth off the ground pulling all the air out of his body as well.

The world around him started to fade and haze up, all he could see was a black blurred blob moving in and out of the trees and heading straight for him. He was sent flying back against a tree his back slamming right onto the mighty oak that was able to with hold the weight almost instantly chain linked was three devastating bone crunching blows to the gut that really drew the black sewage out from him. The demon started looking around to see around the entire area of trees that they we're inside of the black blur was circling around and also zipping in between all of the trees but what blew his mind like Ryker had planted dynamite inside of his skull, was the actual sight of Ryker. Leaning up against a tree once again like the lazy bum that he was, same position and everything. But wait if he's there how can he also be circling the area and how can he also be running down each aisle of trees?? Ryker then shouted over to the demon who was beginning to lose his mind as his neck was about to break by all the directions he was looking over to, trying to track each and every Ryker that was around here. "You look very very confused, don't be! The reason why you're seeing all those visions of me is because I am a bit out of your league when it comes to speed – I am already done doing all that, your brain is barely processing all the movements – all that movement that you're seeing I did within the first millisecond that this started up!" Ryker basically shooting a bolt of lightning into the demon's brain without even having to lift a single finger he left him more shocked than any strike from electricity could have. Is this really the difference between them?? Is this really how big the gap is?? But Ryker not the type to discourage his enemies too much as he said "but don't give up buddy go ahead it's your turn now I'll go ahead and let you go!"

The demon looking over to Ryker as he thought this was some kind of sick joke, now he truly knew how his big friend, who fell before him, felt; he certainly was standing in his big shoes. Taking Ryker up on this offer as he sees this as his only glimmer of hope his only opportunity, putting both of his claws down as he was ready and set and about to go just as he made one single step forward Ryker was already gone. Being very generous to let the beast pick his foot off the ground but that's as far as he would allow, a black flash dashed right past the demon and his head turned to the left so fast you would have thought his neck was broken by whiplash; the only thing that was missing was the snap heard immediately afterward, the demon's head spinning round and round on his feeble foundation. In some instances he would see Ryker still perched up against the tree like he never really moved at all, as soon as the demon put his foot down that same black dashing shadow darted right past him back and forth three times. Every single time the demon was shaken even more and more to the core with a devastating crushing blow; finally deciding to push through the pain as he locked his vision forward, aiming for the circling shade that was going round and round the forest. The second that he leapt in the air he was met with at least four zipping attacks quicker than a drive by and Ryker was even faster than the bullets, he was able to go back and forth through the demon four times.

The demon trying to forge on through the pain that felt like a wrecking ball had managed to be harnessed into the form of a fist and each blow only doubled the damage. The demon finally able to see the stream of darkness that was the shadow Ryker was leaving behind as he traveled all around, lunging forward with every ounce of strength that he had ready to grip, then shred, then tear, then puncture, and drill his claws into the scrawny little punk. Once leaping forward the running river of shade only felt like a space of air slipping right through his hands, he didn't understand, how? How could someone be this fast? More importantly where was he now?? Looking over his shoulder to see that he had exited the plush forest area and was out in the open and in his sight that he caught when he dared look back was Ryker holding up the index and middle finger on his right hand with the biggest ear to ear smile on his goofy face. Leaning up against a tree he then said almost with joy "too slow I guess I win our little game – sorry but I have to wrap this up!"

Ryker in that same instance was within breathing space of the demon with his fist driven deep into his gut, it all happened in the same moment the demon could not believe it, there was no catching him Ryker then pulling up his knee to slam against the face of the demon; straightening him back out as he snapped his head back. Three snap jabs that bobbed the demon's head back like a pigeon, all the time Ryker was under hooking with his left leg kicking the inside of the demon's leg making him tremble double with both running a tremor coursing through him; Ryker's hand now coming out once one made contact the other would fly out and hit the demon dead center in the face, throwing an uppercut every now and then; shuffling his feet as he would switch with inside kicks outside kicks and which leg to kick with, which leg he was kicking and what part.

The demon was in absolute turmoil, a shaking, quaking, flaking, head aching, body straining, power draining, perfect aiming, never be the same, disfigured, Ryker is to blame, pulled the trigger, should remember his name, no matter if you're bigger, just fall quicker, just another lame, victim to the game, proclaiming, to differ, - I –I'm sorry I just wanted an excuse to drop my mixtape that is coming out this year. Um anyways Ryker dropping down by splitting his legs apart so smooth like a boy on the cheerleading squad (not insinuating anything I am just stunned they could do that) at the same time he also split the demon's legs apart as well kicking them open at the ankles forcing them open like flood gates. (At least take him to dinner first! Remember no means no!... I'll stop now) Ryker simply pulled both of his legs together and they clacked at the ankles as well taking the opportunity at the window as he straight kicked the demon in the face launching him back but his feet dragging in the ground was actually the only thing that kept him grounded. Looking up to only see an incoming shoe straight to the face and there was nothing he could do not even brace himself, question how do you brace yourself to be punched by a house? – Because that is exactly what it feels like whenever Ryker attacks!! Seemed that a crowd of people in a mosh pit wanted to help the cause and jumped in to help stop the spread of the evil – oh my mistake! It was actually just Ryker stomping on the demon's face so fast he might as well been a one man mosh pit!

Ending with a double stomp or more like a mid air drop kick that made the demon spin head over heels like the new wheel that they we're working on trying to be organic and not too damaging towards the environment – but yes the wheels are made of live demons. Ryker from afar just tucked his hands back into his pockets and sighed talking to himself – the only sensible person around at the moment. Sighing first and foremost and followed up by "I really hope he doesn't get back up I am getting very tired of picking on the poor dude it seems like he is really trying too!" But to Ryker's dismay of course the demon was not just going to give up to a Miraclelyte, a squeaking, groaning, and leaking mess that was just painful to watch to even *try* get to its feet.

Ryker not wanting to look over his shoulder, maybe they take a trait from dogs; if you don't pay attention to it it'll go away. No this unfortunately wasn't the case, the broken and shattered demon lunging forward only to miss; a sidestep from Ryker at the speed of a hyper old lady who had arthritis, this demon still was not about to give trying to throw another slash at Ryker's face. Wobbling right after the delivery like he was on a cruise ship with rocky waters, all Ryker had to do was step back; the demon an exhausted disaster, its hands resting on its knees while it tried to gather its energy back right in front of Ryker. Just staring into his eyes that were drowning in boredom, this creature meant nothing to him and it knew, taking this as fuel to put into its fire to motivate itself to move quicker. All the rage and wrath that boiled and bubbled up inside this dark creature finally erupted into a fearsome slash that held all the reserves of its strength; finally reaching the promise lands of Ryker's face with its dark, cold, unfeeling claws. Only thing was at the absolute last second Ryker ignited itself with a sparking silver shield of electricity that had to be some sort of offspring to be this fast, as soon as the demon's claws landed on the surface of Ryker's face it was over he was about as stunned as a man being hit by a lightning bolt on top of the head. Every muscle, every joint, every nerve had been constricted as Ryker just strolling away; whispering in his opponent's ear before taking his leave "wait for it" Ryker now began to pass the demonic statue by only being a mere spot in the background until a flash from the sky appearing only for a split of a second's blink a gray bolt of lightning hammered down on the demon leaving nothing but the impact circle of black soot. Ryker sighing to himself "I wish he could have been a bit more entertaining, after all that talk you would think right? Oh well I got something more serious to attend to anyways" that same instance he was gone only leaving a single static black line behind as his trail

Amar trying to catch a glimpse of the machine gun fingers heading to him, his body beginning to recognize the feeling of everything and he started to pick out the patterns of everyone around him. "Come on all I need – is to catch their movement I know I can do it! It is just a matter of focus!" Amar squinting his eyes while ducking, sliding to the side, tilting his head, and back stepping; picking out those bullet hands and trying to capture their movement like a photographer stalking down the most treasured bird in the world for the most absolutely perfect photo. Narrowing his eyes to a shaky, drilling, lightning - fast stab shaped claw and the more his eyes lingered on it, the less speed it posed in his eyes; slowing down more and more, so much that Amar started to see every claw coming to him. A wave surrounding him, Amar's distressed look slowly grew to a smirk of satisfaction and success as he now had the formula; he then smacked the first incoming claw of the middle opposing demon, and then with his other available opposing hand open palm pushed the side of his wrist.

An incoming fireball from behind took a second to flip back and land on his hands, kicking the fireball with his heel; sending it back as if it we're something as simple as a soccer ball. Being launched back into the mouth of the O demon that shot it like a return to sender package, choking on his own flames he fell over; quickly pushing himself back up to face his three opponents, now the demon on his left decided to go - well they we're all attempting to attack. Only in Amar's eyes could he actually see the difference in speed and who was coming with what – no particular difference in this attack, two stabs from his used to be rapid arms; two stabbing hands coming right at Amar. Blocking one by wrenching his bicep to the side, slapping the claw away with the back of his hand doing same with the other hand and claw as well. Seeing an open shot as he left him defenseless, Amar was about to go with a straight right punch but saw a much more needed opportunity to teach a lesson as he saw from out of his peripheral vision a leaping demon. He stomped his legs apart with authority on the ground as he slammed out a wrenched back fist from his left arm like a brick wall to a man riding a bike, Amar put a stop to this deadly journey leaving the demon to sink to the floor. This poor statue had Amar's fist engraved into his face as he crumbled to the floor, now turning his face back to his previous opposers; Amar finally got some difference in variation of stabbing from the demon on the far right, his right claw was already at his face with his left claw following up.

Amar already far past anticipation, and slapped them away like they we're crumpled up paper balls being thrown at him. As he heard the sound of jaws opening near his ear, Amar prioritized this minor nuisance slamming his right elbow right dead center into the demon's face; falling away and out of Amar's space, Amar now had no interference as he properly dealt with these so called "speed demons" Amar eagerly twiddling his fingers and snapped his fingers as a faint in front of the demon's faces, backing them up a couple of steps making them jolt up as he did it again and again and again. Now making them travel back all the land they forced Amar to step back in, one of the demons finally had it with these useless gags and demeaning tricks as he hooked for a slash but this is just what Amar was waiting for and with that one move that only one of the demons did, Amar was about to teach them what speed really was. Amar palm slapped the left side of the demon's elbow with his left hand then right palm slapped the left side of the wrist back with the from underneath his arm. Amar then upper palm slapped the arm snapping the bone in two and outside of the arm, the bone stuck out like a sore thumb; before the nerves could even react to it Amar was already going to put this demon out of its misery, right hooking it at its chin then coming in from the left with another hook landing straight in the middle of the demon's face. Gray barely started to spread around as the demon's mouth was opening wide to the reaction of the first brutally painful attack, but it was spreading slowly like a disease over time and Amar had already moved onto the next one.

Smashing his right fist into the gut of the middle demon but he stood there like he was waiting for the bus ever so patiently, he just hasn't felt it yet and when he does it will be too late. Amar like a shoe shining machine, but sounding like a shoe maker that was threading the sole as we speak, Amar the actual definition of a speed demon; machine gun bullets and lasers we're much more visible and had been seen plenty more times, Amar's fists like bullets piercing through a brick wall shaking the demon's body like his own personal earthquake beneath him. Amar starting from his abdominals working his way up to the upper chest, fists like climbing up a ladder so organized as they escalated up and down; finally ending his combo with a jaw splitting straight right punch as the demon's face was forced to his right regardless of time and speed before any of the reactions to any of these attacks could sink in. Amar was already onto the last and final demon, Amar shot up his right fist in a phenomenal uppercut, blasting the demon's head upward to the sky like an illegal firework on Fourth of July

Amar instantly following up with his right elbow, he smashed in the center of the demon's face. The demon's head couldn't even repel back with the devastating impact before he swung in another elbow in there as well, and again before he could even let the impact take its effect he pivoted on his toes spinning like a hurricane to thrust one last elbow. Finishing it up with his right elbow an abrupt stop to this wild twisting, corkscrew; Amar now jumping back as he wanted to give all of them a big present, slowly and carefully pulling his left arm over his chest as he gently sank down lower into his spread apart stance. His eyes like a ball in a game of ping pong panning back and forth from the left, middle, and right demon; all almost frozen in time as they slowly began to feel the reactions of all previous attacks and pain.

The gray now spreading to a somewhat major portion of their bodies, now clumping together from what started off as separate pieces, Amar now beginning to lift his right leg off of the ground like a plane taking flight from the runway and it was already on course for a nose dive crash into the jaw of the demon on Amar's far right. Amar shifting all of his weight onto his left foot, spinning on the sole of his foot sledge hammering the demon across the face with what looked like an iron girders but not ending there; Amar still continued like a crane that was carrying this iron girder was out of control smashing straight into the left side of the demon's face. Might as well have been the side of a truck, no matter of time frames or elapses was going to stop the instantaneous reaction that was his neck snapping to the right by a humongous clump of force, pushing his entire head now all that was left was the demon at the far end who was barely reacting to Amar's snapping it's elbow. Its teeth slowly turning gray as it howled towards the sky, the other available claw instinctively rushing it over to hold it tight but it was moving as if it we're being carried by a parade of snails, meanwhile Amar's foot was traveling like a shooting star to his face colliding with him like an asteroid onto the surface of Earth. Just astronomically epic, explosive, and catastrophic; getting the full momentum from pendulum build up and swing from Amar slowly pushing his jaw apart like opening gates black oozing blood just flooding out; just like water from a busted hose, contorting his neck almost to owl vision almost able to see his won back.

Both feet we're off the ground as Amar spun around mid – air, the momentum so strong he was coming back around just as a furious swing from a wrecking ball doesn't just abruptly stop after the first swing, his left leg sliding down onto the floor to slowly put a stop to his tremendous speed like a parachute on a supercar. As soon as he came to a screeching halt, now the right hand was slowly being pulled over his chest as he twisted his hips, pumped his legs then shot forward with his left leg now; a mirror image of his destructive kick immediately hitting the already critical demon who only needed a shove to beat defeated let alone a catapult – like force of a kick. His neck just a bobble head at this point so widdled down and weak, he was just a tree waiting to timber now the other side of his jaw hung loose as black ooze just poured down from his mouth; Amar barely leaving him on his feet as he moved onto the next demon rolling with the momentum of the flow. As he charged forward to the demons who we're now hesitant to charge forward to their single opponent as they seen what he reduced their brothers to right in front of them while they we're trying to intervene and assist them, but once Amar realized his true potential for speed it was over for each and every one of them there is absolutely no stopping him. Glancing over his shoulder to see the battle he was more concerned about even more so than his own, Kayoh with her hands over mouth could not believe that Forrest was breaking rules like a fine china vase; the head of a roaring fearsome creature storming to the hybrid who had darkness radiating off him like steam from a sauna.

Inviting Forrest to come at him full force, Forrest like a hot air balloon with teeth on fire coming crashing down towards the hybrid. Thrusting the thick and dense underbelly of his fist on top of the hybrid's skull, but the hybrid was just ahead of him blocking overhead with his forearm; both energies exploded and began cackling as they also did battle sounding like two televisions that we're mortal enemies that hated each other since manufacture we're doing battle. The hybrid yanking Forrest by the hand down from the air to drive his knee into his gut, Forrest cringed but pushed past the pain to try for a fierce one – two hook swing not as graceful as a boxer the hybrid proved this as he weaved his body back from both shots; but the tails of flames that we're attached to Forrest's body like a second layer of skin we're only inches from the hybrid's face, even stretching out a reach to try to get close.

Forrest jumping back as he gripped his right forearm with his left hand to steady it aiming his right hand at the hybrid like it was a magnum in his hand and in their situation it is as deadly to the hybrid as a magnum is to a normal person, so of course the hybrid treaded carefully but he wasn't as weak as a human. Like a bucket of bouncing balls put on a treadmill with the highest setting on they we're shooting out like a meteor shower at the hybrid, who flashed in between each and every fireball just as he was almost out of the dark woods that was made of evergreen embers, they all of a sudden came to an abrupt halt and just centered around the hybrid. Who even he was confused and curious at what kind of game Forrest was playing, just then Forrest snapped his fingers with a truly sadistic grin on his face; eyes widening with shock and surprise the hybrid knew exactly what this was as he hastily raised his hands up question was though, was it already too late?

A pillar of fire erupted from within their battlefield, evergreen and golden flames roared louder than a pride of lions, coloring the sky as they rose like a tidal wave retracting back before it swallowed the entire city with one swoop. But we're slashed in half by a slither of darkness chopping off the top, to reveal the hybrid's wall of darkness that came to the will of its master; but jumping right over those walls like a rebel teenager just too cool for school, Forrest wasn't about to let up with flames emitting fiercely from the edge of his elbows just as fire would exit out the tailpipe from a drag racing car. Forrest thrusting his fist right into the hybrid's face, fracturing the new bone marrow mask he was sporting; doing backwards handstands flipping head over heels against the ground until he was finally able to gather his footing again. Coming to a hard stop with the back of his heels, the only brakes available to him, Forrest pulling his personal flames over him like it was a thick blanket and that is the same coverage that he got as well

The fire only stirring up and unleashing itself even worse as its master embraced it; Welcoming him inside so that they together could make a ferocious, roaring, howling, earth rumbling, catastrophic head of a beast comprised completely out of fire. Like a bull once seeing the defenseless moron that dared step foot into the ring with it, charged forward without hesitation, second thought or mercy opening its jaws to swallow the hybrid up like he was going back to hell being welcomed by flames. The fiery beast's mouth as big as a cave the hybrid like a shark about to be munched up by a whale

As the jaws of his oblivion opened up to him, the hybrid had a big sadistic smirk on his face like he was inviting Forrest to come and try; holding something behind his back clutched tightly inside the grips of his claws. That something must be pretty big to give the hybrid a grin that big, uttering underneath the thunderous roars of fire manifesting into a body; cranking and yanking his arm back, now he played the waiting game as he abided his time to keep his eye out for the perfect moment. The closer the evergreen beast came the bigger his smile got, until the hybrid shot his arm forward pitching whatever he was holding so fast it bulleted right into the bull's eye of the storm, blowing all of the flames, with enough strength to crush a house, back to reveal a stunned Forrest who was basically naked without his flames. Much more than that he was severely injured, a darkness toned rock textured object was lodged into his chest right in front of where his shrine would be; Forrest immediately trying to pull it out but he might as well have been trying to pull out a nail that has already been hammered in out of the board with his finger nails. The hybrid, so smug as he strolled over to the struggling Forrest who now started to have golden perspiration gather amongst his forehead, his breaths we're slowly becoming heavier and much harder to get out. Dropping to one knee as he tried his absolute best to keep his eye on the blurry grayish blob that was the hybrid walking towards him.

The hybrid now a tower before the sad and pitiful excuse for a warrior, Forrest's head shaking horribly as he grinded his teeth staring up at the hybrid. To which the hybrid just crouched down to meet him at eye level mocking him, patronizing him, and metaphorically kicking Forrest while he was down "so tell me... does it hurt? Does it burn? How do you feel?? I don't care I just need to make notes to report back with – because you see what I just threw you was negative converting mal stone – didn't you think it was odd that I was provoking you so much? Or are you so thick skulled you didn't even notice? Doesn't matter really because all that matters is that it worked – we had to test it on your flame because yours is the greatest so it means Azuru and that unrelenting tramp will be putty in our hands because of this – so thank you for being an obedient little guinea pig."

This shook Forrest's core worse than anything, shivering and trembling with wrath and fury building; but all he could do was begin to fall towards the ground, his flames all turning a gray and black before truly dying out. This wasn't the end of the hybrid's onslaught either smacking Forrest right across the face like a mailbox falling victim to the unforgiving cruel baseball bat, Forrest shooting straight through the air to chop a tree in half with his body acting like a bullet before smashing against the floor coughing up his black ooze that was infecting his entire body.

The hybrid chuckled as he started to move towards the beaten and broken Forrest probably to do a bit more tests and experiments to see what results he got from him. But what stood in his path that wasn't there before, like a mountain that the hybrid now had to climb was taking the form of the beyond livid Kayoh, the ground smashed and crumbling underneath her feet; she couldn't even find the strength to look into his cold dead eyes. Her arms sparking with explosive furious flashing flames, her explosive capacity was only growing by following the stream of her anger her teeth almost stuck together as she grit them tight and hard against each other. Barely able to spew out the words she was so furious "you wanna get to him! You hav –"but the hybrid just radiating enough smugness to keep Kayoh warm from the blistering blizzards of winter intercepting her "I have to go through you? Easy enough!"

Now Kayoh snatching up some of the hybrid's smugness to use for her own smug purposes, stealing the smirk right off his face to point behind the hybrid, to which the arrogant prick did not want to even give them the benefit of a glance over the shoulder; "can you take him on too and still call it easy?!" Kayoh of course pointing to the partly injured Ex but basically using the "walk it off" method to keep on marching on, golden gleaming fluid – like trail of vitality poured out from his shoulder, his right shoulder pad and right side of his uniform was a bit torn and tattered with scratches and slashes thrown in the mix but nothing a divine warrior like him could not handle and brush off as he dove back into the wildfire begging for more severe burns. Kayoh cracked her knuckles and her whole right arm ignited cocking her arm back as she instantly dove into her fighting stance, Ex crouching down now gripping the handle of his blade and both of them ready to sandwich the devil in the middle.

Amar just slamming his foot into the face of the demon he knew to be his latest victim, crushing its facial structure like an aluminum bat smacking against a baseball at 90 miles per hour to get that grand slam. Even a thunder clap was heard upon the deafening contact; popping, snapping, cracking, all blended together in what seemed to be a mixture of sound that was instantaneous as his kick. Just kept on passing through back to where he started, where the carnage all originated the one who got it the easiest from the beginning is getting twice the damage now; Amar swinging his leg full force, it is amazing that the demon managed to stick on its feet. Wobbly and weak like a paper in the wind but on his feet still none the less, Amar's kick pushed his entire head, neck and even part of his right shoulder to the demon's left like he was almost about to tilt over and timber. A broken shell of the terrifying and petrifying beast that he once was, like Amar a ballerina in the battle frontier of war spun around immediately to face them once again; looking at the two bodies at the edges that we're already gravitating towards the floor almost a complete gray as well. Only spots and splotches of their once true skin color remained, Amar's head going from demon to damned soul to O form the demon all the way to the far right to the opposite left side, now going in for a split millisecond Amar dashed to his adoring followers.

Coming to the middle man demon amidst all of this chaos and running around, looking to be on the verge of a head butt. As he was inches from the gently loading demon, Amar split his legs in mid – air, each kicking a demon square in the face; sending down a path of utter disintegration only to end their journey to become a part of Amar's armor, now one with his boots. Amar landed perfectly in front of the middle starting demon, the primal's barely functioning mind was of course at a disadvantage as what to do next, trying to follow Amar's movements his eyes narrowing down to Amar who was blankly standing in front of him. Amar in essence was a vision of blur, a trail formed by his body followed him as the incompetent Primal just stood there, no longer even able to keep up with Amar as past actions still occurred in his sight; once again lost Amar when taking a couple of steps back then swinging his arms back, Amar did a completely flawless and perfect back flip. Both feet impaling his chin like a pointed arrow, knocking his head back and Amar's body even loosened from their stifled stand point; like a loyal steel blade holding the battle to the very end or until he landed back on the floor swiftly with both feet back on the ground just as he started. The demon's head was bursting with gray ash like an erupting volcano, until the entire body collapsed falling onto it's back and smashing into a clump of gray; not a problem as it was vacuumed up by the cleaning lady in armor, another occupant taking a room in Amar's boots, Amar began to exhale as time reverted to normal. All around him the demons still at a standstill as the reaction of what just happened was like a bad phone company they we're trying to get the message, but when they finally did they all screeched, roared and growled in astonishment.

Jumping back to widen the circle a bit and get a better inspection on just how deadly their surrounded foe was, Ryker sitting on a sturdy branch in a clump of trees clapping his hands with encouragement sparking from him like a broken circuit board "whooo! Now that's my pupil!! –"Now Ryker separated himself from what he truly thinking on the inside "It's strange he's almost as fast as we are now and he just barely started, training put aside of course, he kinda moves like Azuru if you think about it... but there's just – just something... off about him – maybe it's his style – he doesn't particularly have a fighting style but more or less a little bit of everything sprinkled inside his style – and he does go on the offensive sometimes, but he is mostly a defensive fighter, the potential really comes through when he is countering or when he swings the momentum of the enemy back at them – not bad not bad at all Rook!" Amar was looking at all the demons that still enveloped him, barricaded and boxed him in. Not a single ounce of fear was in him now, no shivers, no shakes, no doubts his body no longer rattling now as solid as titanium; his breaths flowed out so easily and smooth, head moving like a sprinkler among the area. Like a single officer with a crowd full of guns aimed at him, only thing here though that none of them had the guts to put their finger on the trigger; just as Amar was about to make his way forward into the mass of destruction and terror, he felt something drop from his hand and clank a metal chink against the floor next to his foot. Stopping momentarily to check it out, fully confident that not a single one of them would attack him or in which case it still wouldn't be out of his power to stop them.

Looking at this new object, inspecting and examining it he noticed this was the same shining ivory chain from earlier. But he wasn't in any urgency, neither did he think of it even coming to his aid; he just held it in his hands as he pondered the reason of its sudden appearance, even more odd was it had suddenly doubled in size as well and between each chain link was a huge spike that stuck out the size of two Amars pushed together width wise anyways. Amar was just stunned with his weapon's sudden transformation that was also out of his control, like it was pumped up by some outside force Amar more impressed than dumbfounded – well not going to waste someone' s kind gesture. He whipped it onto the floor, tearing up the ground upon its bare landing, now residing beside Amar; the demon's eyes collectively narrowed and zoomed into the chain and its monstrous strength, slowly bringing up their eyes back to Amar who had a determined look on his face, determined like he was going to exterminate every single entity of darkness right here and now. He moved one step forward, the whole entire circle took one step back, he took two steps forward, they took two steps back. He gently picked his foot off the ground to begin to make his way forward, they we're on their way to backtrack, but Amar fooled them setting his foot back down, as did they; Amar stood still as he looked all the way around like an imperfect owl. He had to crane his neck to look over his shoulders to get the full vision even the hybrid had his vision fixated on Amar while he dodged Kayoh' burning fists and Ex's precision blade that was only hairs off from slicing his face right off, twiddling his two fingers back and forth on top of his right bicep continuing to dodge gracefully in between these attacks. Even though his face showed how calm and collected he was, his fingers reflected his true innermost feelings, his desires, and true excitement growing the more he witnessed Amar slay one of his comrades.

Kayoh's swing overshooting spinning her around, as her own power was used against her with a simple dodge from the hybrid. Combat being her strong suit she has ran through this situation a number of times, not something uncommon for a close range fighter so her next move came as natural instinct; her feet skidding against the ground as she spread apart her legs, with her arms locked and her fists raised back up to her face now most of her weight was poised onto the top half of her feet, aching to dash back in she literally had enough fire power to back it up. On the other side Ex had his hand already on the hilt of his sword as the blade began to rear its head, like a cowboy drawing his pistol only a second was needed for that revolver to go off; both of them rushed forward and the hybrid welcoming them both with open embracing arms except I doubt that hugs we're going to be involved, having such a sly and devilish tongue there was no doubt that hell was his birthplace "wouldn't you rather save your precious leader? – No tricks! I am not going to stop you I have much better things to do – much better specimen to observe – oh and by the way the cursed venom that I infected his flames, not only is it depleting his divinity it is converting his partner "Evergreen" into a blanket of malevolent flames he will be one of us pretty soon – sorry to seem villain like by having a countdown with a glimmer of hope it is still a prototype so good luck trying to get it out!"

He then began simply walking away, like left them with only one decision; he knew exactly what they we're going to choose. Slowly dropping their stances as they looked at their agonized captain, Forrest was on his hands and knees with black ooze dripping from his mouth this black ooze was once shining Divinity that became nothing but sewage black filled with darkness. Craning his head up as he locked his gaze onto the hybrid with a stare of absolute disdain, Ex letting go the handle of his sword to rush over to aid Forrest, stopping mid – way to wait for Kayoh; who was shivering with absolute rage. Just unable to take her eyes away from the hybrid, who was taking a leisurely stroll – no worries at all, but suddenly putting his casual walk on hold as he creaked his neck over his shoulder with such an arrogant and all knowing tone "yes? – do you have something to say?!" Loosening the lid on the entire wrath she was trying to bottle in for the good of her captain. Even hearing snapping behind her, quickly looking back to see Ex signaling to her and pointing to Forrest; Kayoh was now in the fork in the road, let her anger run wild and take vengeance on this putrid creature for harming her leader and making her team look like a joke or do what a second in command should do and tend to the matter at hand.

Growling in frustration turning around and rushing over to Forrest Kayoh was grinding her teeth the whole entire time, the hybrid merely chuckling as he claimed checkmate over these pawns saying to himself "that is exactly what I thought!" Turning his head back to watch the more interesting and full of potential Amar, who was making his first move as he shot his chain forward like his hand was a harpoon launcher; wrapping around the neck of a demon collaring him, Amar then yanked him back the demon might as well have been tied to the back of a muscle car that was peeling out. But the torque would still only be half of Amar, he only giving a little tug with both hands placed on the chain and Amar pulled him head over heels to sledgehammer him on the other side of the face crushing the demon into the ground and detonating the floor around them; sending bodies inside of the crowd flying into the sky scattering like confetti being shot out from those cheap little poppers. Amar not even close to being done pulled his right arm to his right and dragged the demon's broken and battered body along the circle, tumbling, fumbling, body spasming, flopping and hopping – haha don't worry I won't have another episode like I did before.

He tore through the crowd like a battering ram knocking whatever comrades remained, to the cold hard floor, dead down the center as he was used against his own will. Until he formed half a circle, Amar actually let him rest all that was left was a contorted and broken mess lying down along with his brothers on the floor. Amar's instincts flared up as his head was jerked to the right, three fireballs double his size was heading straight for him from the side he left untouched; jumping right back into the action with his feelings leading the way for him, he wrenched his bicep for a hard tug yanking the demon off the ground and on his way to him within seconds Amar widened his right arm to a swing. Letting go once his arm reached full length the demon flying straight forward without his master to control him, firing him out like an arrow to bash skulls against one of the demons launching fireballs bodies tumbling over each other was the last sight he seen before the big balls of fire took up to his right sight of vision, Amar swiped through the middle of all three flames like his chain was a sword. Even smacking each and every demon in the jaw who unfortunately happened to be in front row, all their heads turning like Scarlet Johansson was walking in her under ware; and just before the chain could travel too far and wrap around Amar's own body, Amar used his foot like a kickstand to stop the traveling chain in its tracks; then with a minor mid – air drop, used both hands as he swung bit lower to once again cut right through the fireballs taking a massive line of heat from each humongous orb.

Now each demon's neck was slapped to the other side like Sophia Vergara happened to also be there catching a ride with Scarlet and just happened to be topless, just something anyone else would break their necks trying to see. Turning his right hand that currently had a chain being dragged out from its twisted position almost upside down, its momentum being cut in half as he placed his available hand on the edge of his right shoulder to push for support; he now went swinging diagonally up cutting the edge of the far left one off, the middle fireball was sliced completely in half just leaving two harmless floating orbs and taking off an edge from the far balls of flames on the right even knocking a couple of demons off the ground at the chin, as the chain happened to uppercut them but most of the crowd was fortunate enough to get a bit of resting time. The chain was whipped up like a dragon simply wagging its tail, coming down like a meteor to Earth; Amar putting his other hand on top of his chain hand to further stabilize his grip as he brought down onto the middle of the far right fireball, slashing it in half and happening to crush a whole row of demons in the process. Once again bodies flaring up and jumping into the sky like batons being thrown up by cheerleaders, hearing growling over his shoulder and drawing nearer must mean the previous side he attacked was rallying back to their feet; and charging, his fire problem still not solved but he had an answer to make everyone happy. Bending as far back as his spine would allow him, to lasso his chain at a level that cut the meaning single orb that was left hovering to him to be cut in two and for Amar to smack any and every demon that was within jaw cracking range.

Every single jaw line in one unison snap, bringing it back a whole full circle. Amar then ducked down like the fireball was over his head, but no it was still right there in front of him and made harmless due to the blusterous winds he made with his fellow chain. With his left hand on top of his back and his chain hand sticking forward, Amar bowed forward with his face pointed towards the ground. As he spun I a complete circle, on one foot smacking any demon in the crowd that was tough enough to still be standing in the gut like a steel spiked whip slicing each and every demon struck by it; was ashified upon contact, a cloud of dust was being sucked into the first three chain links. Amar taking the first wave of opposers out still two more waves to go to defeat this dreaded circle of darkness; Amar now coming back to the front where the orbs of fire, waiting patiently floating towards him, Amar raised his right leg as the chain link was clotheslined by his leg. Once again Amar interrupted his own momentum to go a complete clockwise and head the other way, his back now bending even more than before as he creaked his knees; he was standing parallel to the ground, just above it once again lassoing his arm so he could get the remainders in a clockwise motion.

His carnage began, the chain growing and extending to get those who weren't wise enough to jump back with each pendulum swing that formed a full circle, more and more demons fell victim to the vicious cycle, literally in this situation. The chain's spikes we're either we're able to poke them and spike them open or the slash of the chain itself, or even the raw speed and power of getting hit by that at that tremendous speed just plain and obvious. More and more trails and clouds of dust we're poofing from the once circle of demons, only a small portion that was the last wave –band of survivors remained but strangely even as they avoided danger, they we're still far from safe. They felt their bodies getting lighter and slowly but gently the weight of the ground disappeared, from beneath them as they took a slight second to look at their own feet not touching the ground; but as soon as they picked their heads back up to look forward at Amar and that this entire time a whirlpool of wind was being conjured from under their noses. The actual colorless and invisible clear wind, invisible as it lifted the entire circle off the ground wrapping itself around the entire circle in an even bigger ring, the hybrid looking very impressed as he spied on the little skirmish safely spectating from a branch he was sitting on; far enough so he wasn't caught inside all the action but close enough so he could hear the dreaded and fearful howls of his demonic brethren. An absolutely delightful sound to his eardrums that lit him up "this boy... I have never seen him or even heard of him... I want to try him out – I know I should be leaving with the report for Forrest's reaction but – I know for sure once I rip this boy's soul from his chest he will be my favorite suit in my closet... I am very curious though what kind of abilities does he hold within those powerful fists of his?"

Kayoh and Ex running over the defeated and broken bodies of those pathetic demons that dared to lay a claw onto their beloved captain. Kayoh holding his spasming and jerking tumbling body on top of her knees, as she shined her shrine onto his; she noticed how dim his light was becoming turning from gold to a dark gray. Specks of darkness we're sprinkled on as well as a growing development, Kayoh shaking her head in growing dread; this isn't good and it wasn't getting any better, by the passing moments she still kept shining on the golden rays of luminance from her shrine. Sparks and discharges sounded from

Forrest's shrine, Kayoh with a voice of climbing despair "I – I can't believe it where did this hybrid get this cursed magic? How did he even get his hands on something like that – they're advancing that's the only way! Because for cursed magic of this stature they would need a massive amount of negative energy – either way it's too strong for a regular warrior to take care of it, either we get a professional like a semi or a healer to take care of this now or we hope that Forrest can make it up to Safe Haven! The way he is looking right now it doesn't look like –"suddenly took her eyes off her fallen captain as wind howled in her ear, whistling past her face and blowing her hair in all directions.

Squinting her eyes to a crack as she tried to focus on where exactly all this was coming from, looking forward on to see a growing hurricane right in front of them. She was in disbelief, not that it was impossible but as she put the pieces together of who could be behind this typhoon, she even said to herself with complete rejection "green bean?"

Amar was twirling and swinging his chain at the eye of the storm, the ground zero him being on the ground and his chain acting like the blades of a fan that these piles of shit we're about to hit against, blusterous and catastrophic winds that whirled the circle of demons round and round like a toilet being flushed. They had as much control over their own limbs as a fly stuck on flytrap, that just cemented them inside this wall of invisible and tangible power that Amar had; complete control of and was about to use every single ounce this very moment, breaking the circular rhythm that he was race tracking his arm in. Once again let his chain loose, but after such serious spinning and whirling it was like a merry – go – round once spun full thrust then let go after a couple of whirls; now these demons we're like insects floating against their will at the command of Amar's homemade hurricane, winding his miniature tool of devastation at his side to form tiny circles as he looked at his hovering targets. A stalking predator looking up at all the free slabs of meat on the wall for the picking basically, Amar was just picking the most precise way of taking them out not wanting to squander this perfect moment he built up. His eyes shot open as he pulled his method of choice from his chaotic arsenal, he picked his chain from up off the ground. Swinging it over an oval shape to his left side but quickly bringing it up diagonally as he threw it directly into the hurricane and like a fish being thrown into the river it rode the current.

Being carried with it spiraling up wards until it hooked the foot of a demon, spiking itself on tight to the leg of a demon, as he screeched with agony and fear; Amar knew he had him exactly where he needed him he had the ultimate test for his brand new weapon. Surprisingly Amar just released it, the chain though seeming to have a mind of its own as it retracted faster than the tongue of measuring tape that was pulled out past the point of its end, heading straight for its anchored host; spearing right through him to also serpentine between more sky dwellers to reach the middle, now spinning on its own like blades in a garbage disposal. Slicing through each and every demon in its path like a merry – go – round with swords attached, smashing, crushing, and breaking through every single demon's faces, ribs, limbs, all we're broken down into the smallest of ash particles with this chain that was boomeranging itself. With the typhoon strong winds, pulling an gravitating them towards the ring of destruction until ash rained and sprinkled down to Amar with his chain also not far behind, whatever wasn't absorbed by the wrecking ball like chain was magnetized into Amar's armor. Like sand from an hour glass pouring in to form a complete hour, Amar catching his chain in his right hand and analyzing it with such a mesmerized gaze; he honestly could not believe that this ivory piece of metal that sprouted from his armor did all that.

As quickly as it came it left, shining brighter than any sun in the galaxy. Just before it vanished right before Amar going to who knows where, even Amar was looking around for it. Picking up his arms, twisting his body around and looking at the ground for it but no dice he could not find it; Amar was thankful but he did not need this and he was starting to look around for his next opponent or next victim until he heard something that made him turn his head around to see the hybrid clapping as there was not a single grain or a single particle of remains from his comrades, coming out of what seemed like nowhere just applauding and encouraging Amar in his brutality of his brethren. This had to be borderline cannibalism, so joyous as he said "marvelous! Fantastic! Glamorous! Absolutely beautiful!! You rid those weaklings of their worthless existence in such an elegant manner! You made the destruction of my pack mates look like a piece of modern art – I knew there was something different about you. Different from the other Miraclelytes, you have such a delicate touch to your abilities; it makes watching you so much more pleasurable! Maybe I shouldn't kill you and just make you my pet – and command you to kill whoever irks me and believe me when I say there are plenty of people who would be on your list!" Amar taking a step back in apprehensive caution, looking over his shoulder back at Ryker. His eyes spelling out "feed me any Intel you have on this thing!" better than returning champions at a spelling bee. Ryker chuckling a bit before cuffing his mouth to form a microphone echo "he is a hybrid!!" Amar shouting back "what is that?!" But deciding that this was going to be the last time he takes his eyes off an unknown enemy while on the battlefield, quickly cocking his body into a defensive fighting stance.

Now taking a closer look at this figure who was previously cloaked with the shadows, he recalled these features from somewhere before; the wings very wide flapping for effect behind him before folding up, a dark shadow black at the bone edges that tucked them in, the skin and flaps of the wings we're purple, there was somewhat a resemblance of a face but it still had primal animalistic features mixed and blended with in a strong jaw line, with bleeding shining red eyes red trails running from the edges of his eyes. He did have a nose but it was abnormally large and flat to be human, fangs sprouting out from the sides of his lips, he did also have black eye brows, black long wavy hair that rested on his skinny shoulders, horns tearing out from the side of his cranium, right where the sides of his brain would be. Thick built horns that just pointed forward like two miniature javelins, his entire skin color was a deep space black not even close to being any normal shade of human colored skin; the absolute darkest shade of black was his skin tone. Crusty, full of scales, rough, bumpy and crackly, texture but his hands and feet we're thick and powerful looking more like gauntlets and a pair of boots; a dark shade of purple at his claws that made them look like they we're dipped and drenched in purple. Covered with spikes on the back side, some tiny prickles and some long the size of a finger and that isn't even getting down to his razor sharp claws that could probably pierce and puncture iron girders, his feet looked like he cut them off from birds and just put a humane twist to it – yes there we're toes but that didn't take it any closer to being normal; rows of spiked blades all pointed a slick back so any contact with these legs we're going to be a wrenching gutter.

As a pull back the entire time, Amar was checking out this condensed petite muscle less mass that was this demonic entity. Almost completely overlooking the swishing tail that slendered itself out the farther it traveled from his back, Amar was appalled and in complete awe all at once; but he knew he had seen this image somewhere and since the hybrid was intelligent enough to carry a conversation might as well pick his brain a bit, "hey um excuse me!" The hybrid swishing its tail back and forth, as he twiddled his miniature blades onto the rough skin of his arm like a person patting their own arm with a dagger. The hybrid with his arms crossed over his chest was intrigued that Amar was addressing him in such a manner and decided to acknowledge him with a simple bump up from his head to show he was all ears, and Amar continued on "tell me something... did you command an O demon? Did you tell him – er it to kill a warrior?" "haha you have to be a bit more specific boy! That would be the equivalent of asking" hey did God create someone?!" in your case! I am in charge of countless demons - and a huge amount of them are disposable O demons so help me refresh my memory a bit, come on now I can feel it on the tip of my tongue!" "it was a warrior squadron that your pack of demons ambushed and was only able to take out one because he let his entire team get away!" "Aaah yes! I remember that thorn in my thigh! I had been planning to take them out for quite some time. So I had my obedient little fodder follow them like they had candy glued to their backsides – nip nip and nip at them until the mission whatever it was they we're doing until they could not even defend against my weakest squadron from there it was just cherry picking! Yes I only received one soul - but that is all that I wanted. I couldn't care less about the other no names."

The demon's eye brow rising up in suspicion, as now his eyes carried curiosity along with his tone of voice "why does it matter? Do you want his soul back? Because I have it right here along with countless others! –" Just then the demon raised his arms to the sky like he was stretching to reach for the stars, and the ground shook from underneath him, shaking, shattering and being torn open from just right behind him. A clamor and audience of moans, groans, and agonized screams erupted from behind him as this crack faulted open and out poured an ocean of gray, black, silver and white orbs with black smoky chains wrapped around and holding each and every one of these living breathing balls of life down inside of a demonic chain gang. The hybrid just guffawing at Amar's shock and awe collision right into his state of mind with a look of absolute disturbance "awwh look at him he has never seen something like this!! I can see it in your stunned eyes!! Not only are you scared you can't believe it can you?! You just cannot believe that this many people are under my control – MY DISPOSAL!! IF I WANT TO I CAN SEND THEM ALL TO OBLIVION! NEVER TO BE SEEN AGAIN!!" Amar shaking and shivering at the thought of every single one of them being thrown away without reason, forced to never see their loved ones again and fade into some sort of land of darkness named "oblivion" with gold rimming at Amar's eyes Amar cried out "NOOO!!!"

To which the hybrid only howled a bit, "Oh? Tell why I shouldn't?! Besides that being a very idiotic move – but whatever I can gather more souls nothing but a mere chore to me, but to you! To you these people have meaning, they have some sort of place in that shiny little shrine of yours don't they?! Oh I know maybe I should convert them all to demons... just like me... then you can figure out which one you want to fight first! Doesn't that sound like a great idea?! I am killing two birds with one stone, I am getting rid of a pest in a very entertaining way and converting them like I was supposed to but – you know I was dragging my feet on it and just never got around to it but now.. I think I found my motivation." The devilish grin he wore just said it all, the cruelty, sadistic thoughts, inhumane, and diabolic was as real as the ground Amar was standing on – Amar shaking, trembling huffing and puffing; Amar pulled his face up to reveal golden streams flowing down his face as he pointed at the demon and declared "you want to know what I want?! I want a deal!! Right here right now! I will put my soul on the line for all of those "useless" souls! You want me so badly well here is your chance! I know you could very easily leave if you wanted to! –""Smart boy – honestly if you didn't spice up the deal or interest me then I would have! I have everything I need – I am just here out of pure curiosity" "so what is it going to be?!"

Flipping the tables perfectly by having the decision of choosing now on the hybrid, the one who purposed the deal in the first place "hmm very well played – I think I willllll.... Take your soul to add to my collection – I suppose if I lose you get to take all of these souls back?" Amar giving a solid confirming nod to acknowledge his proposition "very well done calculating that all of their combined value is still less than your soul – more of a win for me but perfectly fine... also you never specified on the rules-"just then a red and purple aura began resonating off of the souls Amar then heard from the back of his mind "ha you reminded me of a young Azuru for a second Rook – just minus the tears, Azuru in his whole life would never cry, the tears would come out stone if anything and he would have challenged him with an ecstatic smile too" "really?! Wait who is this and how are you talking to me?!" "Look behind you" Amar recognized the voice but was just pivoting his body to look for a person near enough, until he seen in the waaaaaaaay way back Ryker feet poised up on a tree branch, ever so calm and relaxed but still his teacher as he supervised him. Giving him a salute with two fingers as his eyes burned the brightest gold from his eyes, like his brain was just a giant searchlight "I am using telepathy if you haven't figured it out – because I don't wanna shout anymore it gets tedious after a while."

Amar once again boiling over with questions, like a teapot whistling and alarming that it needed to be picked up "how are you talking in my head?!, - who is he?!, - what is he?!, - I heard you call it a him... her ... it? A hybrid – what is a hybrid?!?! How do I beat it?! Something is happening to the souls! What is happening to the souls?!" Ryker groaning in disdain as he growled back "what have I been saying about your damn questions?!?! – Stop loading them into a damn Gatling gun and shooting them at me!!!!" Amar in a voice of panic shouted back at Ryker inside of his head "are you asking me a question?!?!?" Ryker only beating Amar back with his telling stick that made Amar's ears rumble and his head shake "STOP. ASKING. QUESTIONS!!!!!" Amar now complying, barely able to murmur a "yes sir" as he tried to piece his mind back together, but the hybrid then said "I don't know who you're talking to but it's starting to make me jealous!

Bring your attention back to the deadliest creature here would you?!" While standing arms spread wide in front of a wave of ever growing darkness and the orbs of light we're unraveling as darkness began to flood and spear into them. This is when Amar truly received the opportunity to see their forms and beings, these figures of light and smoke harmonized together we're reaching out for Amar in absolute desperation and pain; as darkness surged inside them through their eyes, nose, mouth, and ears. These soulful beings we're flashing and growing into shadows; rematerializing with a more sinister, feel, intent, and figure.

Amar had no choice but to ignore the spectacle that was going on right in front of him, to refocus and reestablish his concentration, locking his gaze onto the hybrid ignoring all of his growing army behind him. Their spirits we're being molded, shaped and changed like silly putty to fit whatever the hybrid's insidious plot happened to be; Ryker began explaining to him closely trying to figure him out maybe even predict his next move "okay just to get this out of the way – I'm using telepathy! It means I can speak to you from a distance, how a person does this is a measure of their Divinity concentration. Some people can contact others from across the whole planet, so the difference varies on the person you know etcetera etcetera okay blah blah dib lee blah and onto the hybrids; the hybrids are kind of like us – scratch that! Like the demons looking like animals, the whole thought and concept of them came from us. From intense study and Intel the boys back down in lava city conducted the combination of a pure soul or a soul in general and an entity of a demonic body, which they insert into and there you go! – Instahybrid, sometimes the soul is too pure and breaks the vessel, sometimes they are more than willing to go in but no matter what the result is the same hybrids! – They're a thorn in our asses too! They are much too intellectual to be taken advantage of like the other demons that we push around, they know of the negative atmosphere and use that as an endless supply of resources. While we run on an energy source like a damn remote control that runs on batteries!"

Now as far for who is it? I have no idea you are gonna have to find out for yourself and also as for how you will defeat it... again have fun coming up with the solution on how to do that! Hahaha" Amar screaming at his own mind "that is not helpful I thought you we're supposed to be my teacher!!" "Well then I suppose you don't want my answer on what is happening to the souls! Ah hell I'll just give it to you but not because you asked for it! So I have a chance to be intellectual!! I mean it is as plain as day he even said it! He is gonna corrupt the souls and turn him into demonic creatures just like him and you can see the events taking place right before your very eyes, he is fueling them with negative and malevolent energy – sure some of them can put up a fight for quite some time being righteous souls and what not but just a matter of time until they join the others." Amar could see all this was true as these see through entities we're growing physical limbs with so much destructive capabilities, some becoming primal animals, others shrinking down to O demon size, but the lucky ones we're truly the fallen warriors who we're formerly from Safe Haven. The darkness consumed them as they became a reflection of the hybrid standing before Amar, soldiers of darkness, seekers of chaos and disorder, and now followers of the demonic force; standing alongside their master, to which Amar could not grip his head around the idea of them becoming soul less monstrosities who are willing to lay down their own lives on the line for a superior who could care less if they live or fade into oblivion.

Before the hybrid could even command his twitter - less followers he snapped his fingers and out from the ground sprouted a tiny skull. The skin catching up to coat this entire body as soon sun beamed down onto this munchkin's body, only able to come up to the hybrid's shins even with standing up straight; there was one single soul that the hybrid was unable to corrupt, unable to break and make into one of his warriors. Gravitating it to float into his claw, shooting a look to Amar now beckoning him by raising up his claw that held this floating orb like it was his trophy "this is the soul of that warrior you we're speaking of, notice how he was able to be so resilient against my dark energy a soldier of the light indeed. –"handing it down to his miniature butler that the orb almost took up its entire body, Amar's body striking into his fighting stance getting ready to shoot forward if he needed to but the demon was able to interject before Amar could even think of bolting forward "now now, you divine warriors have something that us demons do not and probably will never understand either. Sacrifice! It is virtues that I will be better off not learning thanks – but since you're new show me how you all practice it!" Just then Amar realized that the hybrid was successful in distracting Amar as the demon now burrow into the hole it once came from, Amar trying to shoot forward and make an attempt to try to reclaim the fallen soldier from their evil clutches and finally bring him home but the sound of the hybrid's devious voice once again lifted Amar's attention "now this is why I called it sacrifice! You have to let go of one measly soul to possibly save others!! So what is it gonna be hero?!"

The horde of shadows all with one voice, one thought, and one mind spoke "master!" The hybrid laughing at his own successful maniacal creation pointing at Amar as he gave them permission to rip him limb from limb "go forth my children and destroy all who oppose you!" Amar still shaking his head in disbelief as he watched the army nod their heads in acknowledgement marching towards Amar; but suddenly from pure instinct in the back of Amar's subconscious mind, just an open hand palm slap swiping from the left side of his face, Amar blinked only to see another hybrid like demon right in front of his face (just for non confusing reasons I am going to name this hybrid, hybrid jr. okay? Okay!) his iron – like claw was slapped away like an annoying fly in the air buzzing around Amar's airspace, Amar's body once again without consent took control as it turned to the side to watch hybrid jr. claw attempting to drill right into Amar's face. Amar seeing every single terrifying, intimidating inch of his steel consisted claws; Amar felt his knees become weak, all of a sudden as his legs dropped him into a crouch he heard a swipe that sounded like it hurt the air as it whistled right past overhead. Amar stumbling to his feet back peddling as he almost fell, able to catch a glimpse of yet another hybrid (dammit! Okay this one is gonna be called hybrid Jr. Jr. okay? Got it?? Good!!) both hybrid A and hybrid B stood next to each other as Amar was steadily trying to stabilize his footing, but a shock surged through his entire spine, his body jerked back and the shadow of a claw ran down Amar's face.

Amar able to watch in like a fast moving drop of maple syrup racing down the wall right in front of him, gazing upon what would have been him, the claw digging into the ground and detonating it upon contact like this demon carried TNT inside of its hands. This demonic essence pulled its arm out from the earth to rise up and stand amongst its hybrid brot- son of a bitch! That's it your name is Gilligan no if ands or buts about it! Hybrid jr., hybrid Jr. Jr. and Gilligan all stood next to one another, as they peered over so superior to their prey that they had completely outnumbered. Amar swiftly landing on his feet only to be able to see the full picture, a charging army of man eaters all rushing forward on all fours; six O demons all opened up their mouths to gag out cannon balls of vicious flames at Amar, while some of the Primal demons we're beginning to stand on their hind legs and pick up the damned souls next to them and toss them like they we're a simple foot ball going for a pass. They all lunged forward and aimed their claws front Amar, sighing as he took a deep inhale and disappeared; then reappeared in the air alongside the traveling demonic airlines, Amar then whispered to all that would hear him "please forgive me" then splitting his legs in mid air knocking both damned souls next to him at the jaw.

Flipping out of control and wildly they slammed and crashed right into Primals charging on the ground, smashing bodies and causing a pile up in two roads of this at least 12 path highway. Amar himself landing amongst the Primals, but he had a much different version of landing he shot both his feet forward straight into the face of the brutish animal, launching him back like Amar's legs we're part catapult; also knocking other bodies who we're still in the advancing back up into the air, gray ash now beginning to linger like gun smoke in a military conflict. Tuck and rolling onto the floor Amar once again in the heart of enemy lines but having some idea on how to deal with it now, rushing straight for the gut of a Primal, wrapping his arms as far around his waist as he could as he dug his face deep into his abdomen, but like an overweight full grown man trying to squeeze into a onesie he just wasn't going to make it. But as Amar began to bend back it doesn't look like he was trying to make it, like a tower bridging over his own body he drilled with a northern suplex the Primal head first into the solid ground; before Amar could take a second to even begin to pull himself away he was met to a claw coming toward his face that he was lucky to dodge, crushing the ash remains of their once comrade. Amar on the run, back step after back step through the crowd, one claw dashing right past his face, then another and another coming at every angle and missing him by mere chin hairs every single time; three fire balls loaded and shot at his back. With all the activity at the front there was absolutely no covering his backside but it wasn't something he should be worrying about, his cape flaring up like a maid making a bed and flapping the sheets to get them all nice and straight in this motion all the hot air in one single swipe.

Amar relieved in his own mind that he didn't have to feel the fiery sting of hell's fire, but not out of the woods yet Amar had to use what was available to him and if he didn't utilize it he would not walk away from this. Chop blocking all of their hits with his forearm acting like a shield, Amar's forearms came from all directions; up to interrupt down slices, right over his face to knock the claw to the side and out of harm's way, even outward to stop forward stabs. Amar might as well have had three stunt doubles with him the way his arms we're able to wave around and smack each impending doom down and outta sight, looking like a potential boy band practicing their cerography for their hit music video Amar was an absolute blur and was now planning to crank up the speed yet another notch. Finding a tiny space where time stood still, and all the arms we're still racing towards him, all crowding and entering his air space – as Amar kept his breathing steady he did it! Bobbed, weaved, pushed, pulled, craned, swung and threw his head in between each claw to start his one –two punch combination hitting the primals, at the gut, the Os at the top of the head and the damned souls dead center in the face. His fists quicker than bullets as he turned into a helicopter turret, either bowling over primal, flipping Os backwards, or launching damned souls back. Finding his ending target a pair of Primals that we're climbing over the falling bodies to lunge forward at him – Amar surprised by their speed, but no time to dawdle he rushed forward as well to meet them half way.

Amar roaring as they roared, now leaping forward as they leapt forward, cocking his arms back as they pointed their claws forward; Amar putting his hands into fate as he ducked his head down and swung with a double overhand. Smack dab in the middle of each primal's face but instead of just launching them back like a normal brutal attack from Amar's gargantuan strength, something happened that even left Amar questioning what was going on and where did this come from? Twin golden beams erupted out from Amar's gauntlets like a beam of light coming out from a flashlight inside of the shadows, burning through the two idiots who dared stand in Amar's way then made ants out of the unfortunates behind them with his fist with magnifying glass effect. Amar being pushed back by the recoil of the huge big bang he fired from his hands, everyone was stuck in silence and awe, Ryker sat up from his branch to lean forward, the grin was wiped off of the hybrid's face, and the rest of the cannon fodder except for the hybrid triplets all we're just stuck staring at what just happened still not able to comprehend what happened like a math teacher unable to figure out how the dumbass of the class managed to pass. Even Amar couldn't stop analyzing his gauntlets to see where these mysterious beams came from so he could maybe do it again, until he noticed everyone around him and shakily jumped back into his fighting stance, reminding everyone they we're all still fighting (don't know for how much longer though) the hybrid far from happy now as he was on the move taking an angry stroll forward.

Hybrid jr. smacking Gilligan on the arm pointing him to go forward, to which Gilligan responded by flapping his glorious wings and taking to the air, spiraling his way to Amar who was in the process of disarming and dismembering his comrades but still trying to figure out how he just did what he did. His body tingling a burning hot sensation just screamed for Amar to turn around to catch Gilligan who was about to push his claws into Amar's back, instead of turning around Amar ducked and was able to catch the look in Gilligan's eyes, knowing he truly messed up in his final moments as Amar shot his fist up like a rocket at Gilligan's abdominals.

Once again the light came to visit Amar munching Gilligan in half, his legs dropping to the floor as they slowly turned a gray and was sucked into Amar's gloves; Amar turning over to the hybrids with a smirk on his face, the hybrid brothers we're taken back what was his reasoning? Why was he smiling? What did he know that they didn't? All answered in the next moment when a truly dim Primal charged and tried to sink its teeth into Amar, but Amar was quick much quicker, halting the Primal by the face with his gauntlet slamming into his frontal expression.

The moments gently passed by but to the hybrids, these we're lifetimes that we're aging them, watching Amar's hand slowly glimmering a gold, brighter and brighter until it became blinding and finally shoot out a beam of light like a bullet from a gun.

Leaving nothing left not even ashes only smoke resonating offs the scorched Earth, Amar never taking his eyes away from the pair of hybrids, striking fear into them with his eyes, implanting doubt and terror without saying a single word - all action. Now began to trek towards them to which one of the hybrids retreated up into the sky – oh Jr. jr. how could you do this and disappoint your father as you leave your poor brother to be victim to Amar, who once turning his head back to the battle field once distracted by his comrade's sudden departure, only to see Amar in front of him

Stunning him by his speed that dwarfed his in comparison; Amar driving his fist into the chest of hybrid Jr. as fiercely and easily as a car would going through drywall; only after going through when he exploded his hand with a beam of light (see I could have made a fisting joke but I decided not to PROGRESS PEOPLE PROGRESS!!!) wiped away the entire body of the hybrid like an eraser doing its job, Amar taking a couple of breaths before looking up above towards the sky for his next target, when something got hold of him faster than his instincts could predict; the instant that Amar felt the touch on his skin he was shattered with a hammer of disbelief, Amar being the castle of glass. His face being slammed into the ground feeling like the bedrock punched him dead in the mouth, the haziest thing that has hit him yet at the same time the only thing that was able to land a hit on him was the ground kinda sad; Amar recognized the voice even though it sounded a bit irritated and agitated as it murmured in his ear "you're killing your fellow soldiers and the citizens that you're supposed to protect rather easy aren't we?! Also you mind sharing about that light show that you happen to do?"

Amar grunting a strained and struggling "I want Peace! I see the looks in their eyes when they are being controlled by you! They are suffering and I will not allow it any longer!! You talking about this light show by the way?!?!"

Amar pointing his arm back to aim at the hybrid's face who had his knee on Amar's spine and both hands on the back of Amar's head, as soon as Amar's hand was raised off the floor the hybrid's tail wrapped itself around Amar's hand and slammed it back down to the ground; it was like the hybrid had an extra hand, Amar cringing and gritting his teeth as he was trying to access his cape but the hybrid was sitting right on top of it. This guy knew every move Amar could possibly make now all the grunting was pure frustration and anger, Amar had to just sit there and accept his fate, the hybrid lining up his open hand with the back of Amar's skull. Just as he was about to spear it right through, a hand caught the claw by the wrist only inches from Amar's head; the hybrid not picking his head up as he bared his fangs and grinded them together, this interruption was killing him inside and the comment following didn't help either. "Wow that was pretty nice – you need to express yourself a bit more with more witty banter and one liners but yeah you're still a rookie I will let it slide – oh yeah and another thing I am finding out more and more about you by watching you but I think I am starting to get an idea on how to coach you I-"

Now Ryker interrupted by the hybrid as he opened his jaw and aimed it to him, while it glowed red and just as it was about to fire out like a cannon ball, Ryker smacked his head up by the chin and sent the ball of flame spitting out the hybrid's mouth to blow up in the sky like a decorative firework; completely harmless as Ryker continued on "well that was rude – I see how it is I interrupted you so you're gonna interrupt me?! An eye for an eye?! Okay let's play that game then!" Ryker then snapped his fingers and the hybrid's precious Jr. jr was shot out of the sky by a merciless bolt of white and black lightning bolt that fried him upon impact and left nothing of him for remains. The hybrid screeched as a rebuttal and Ryker spat back "you started this by attacking my student!" Ryker then knocked off the hybrid from on top of Amar it was so quick the hybrid couldn't even follow it and he never took his eyes off of Ryker – never even blunk the whole entire time so he wouldn't miss in specifically. All that was left for Amar to **assume** was Ryker had his right leg lifted up and the hybrid was skidded back quite some ways back – sooooo a kick?? I am guessing, Amar dusting himself off as Ryker patting him on the shoulder and said "great job Rook! Now I will be your back up finish up your fight with him!" Amar looking overwhelmed as he looked over to Ryker who he thought was joking – but nope he had a completely straight completely serious look on his face.

Amar coughing to clear his throat and ask "umm Mr. Ryker are you not you supposed to be telling me that *YOU* will take him on and I clean up the rest?... right?" Ryker's smile only doubling in size as he just thought his student's intentions and thought process was simply adorable "oh Rook do I look like a character in a movie? I am not going to hog the glory away and steal your shining moment from you! Go ahead go ahead and finish him off I know you're probably aching and itching for this fight right!?" Amar looking at Ryker like he should be placed in a psychiatric clinic "but I am not even near his strength how am I suppose –"Amar not even able to finish his argument as Ryker in back of him insisting and very persistent he pushed his pupil forward to face the toughest foe in this whole area "nonsense! You need to believe in yourself more! I believe in you so why can't you believe in yourself?!" Amar turning his head to look over his shoulder and looked at the encouraging feeling beaming from Ryker's eyes he truly believed in Amar that he could do this and make mince meat from the hybrid "really? You believe in me?" "Yeah sure whatever!" mmm maybe not well who knows maybe he wasn't trying to pressure him by telling him something as solid – Yeah I know I am the author but how am I supposed to know - shut up and read the damn passage before I end it on a cliffhanger! Ryker giving the final push that Amar stumbled forward to now stand in front of the menacing hybrid. Who was less than satisfied to be battling with a rookie, much rather fight an elite like Ryker

Amar putting his dukes up, hesitant and nervous as he stood in front of a being who was the only one able to get past his lightning fast instincts. It was like Amar was fighting against the only weakness he had, Ryker running past the match as he called over "okay you got this! I am just gonna take care of the rest of them!!" Ryker then disappeared as he ran towards the fray of enemies who we're gathering their forces together to lend support to their master. Oh definitely not today! All blitzing forward running on all fours and flames leaking from their carnivorous mouths, but above them a single strand of lightning waved over them like a torch cutting through a slab of metal. Metal had a chance of stability and was durable enough to withstand the heat, these meat bags however we're being disintegrated upon contact like they we're all touching the surface of the sun; within seconds they we're dust in the wind. Ryker in front of the entire army of darkness acting as his own army, with his right leg extended outward; Amar's jaw was hanging over the floor, he could not fathom the strength that Ryker had behind just one kick, able to take out an entire force of demons that Amar had to fight one by one. The hybrid far from happy that Amar did not have his eyes on him for their duel to the death, and at that very second he went from being in front of Amar from a far to being right in front of his face; Amar astonished that this hybrid's speed surpassed his own hopefully Amar could put his guard up in time, but it was too late even for that.

Before Amar's forearm guards we're able to cover his face, a right hook almost timbered Amar over, hazy and dizzy with his head throbbing Amar just said to himself "nope still not even close to beating Mr. Azuru!" With that Amar now fortified himself putting his guard up completely covering his face; and no matter how hard the hybrid knocked his sledgehammer – like fists against Amar's fearsome forearms. Amar taking steps forward to advance and pushing the hybrid back with each step, and each back peddle that was forced upon him he got more and more frustrated and more and more furious with his attacks, like thunder cracks smacking against Amar's armor. Amar knew this was not a golden strategy as he consoled himself "I cannot just be a walking punching bag – there has to be something else! Why did Mr. Ryker say he believed in me? What did he see that I do not?... Well whatever it is I am going to try to bring it out now this ends here!!" Amar putting down his guard and putting his hopes on himself, the hybrid didn't think much of this just fired out yet another punch; Amar getting a sudden shock to his system that made him clutch his own right fist, a blusterous wind blew right behind him at that very instant. Amar even began to feel that something was inside of his hand, a blink of his eyes revealed the hybrid's fist clutched inside, he was finally able to match his speed! The next moment Amar shot up his other hand to do the exact same and a half instant later, a fist was inside that hand as well.

This had Amar dumbstruck it was literally like a bullet, happening so quick Amar could not catch any of his movements; his body was now somehow ahead of every step the hybrid creature, like it was matching Amar's drive to stop all of this senseless violence. The hybrid now taking a very weird posture position and began pushing onto Amar, sliding back on his right foot, he then bent his right hip, pulled up his right leg and pulled down his right elbow seeming like he was trapping something. That's exactly what it had to be, the hybrid had vanished there was nothing he had to be guarding against, a split moment later Amar felt something wriggling at his hip, something trying to squeeze and slither out; he looked down to see that he captured his tail, looking back up at him with a slight hint of strain he chuckled "okay I'm guilty I tried to hit you with my tail can I have it back now?!" Amar shaking his head as he tossed up the hybrid by throwing up the tail then quickly catching it again with both hands, grabbed hold of the middle then quicker than any of the actions that have been seen so far. Amar picked the hybrid up and over his shoulder and slamming him onto the other side of where he was standing; chin hitting the ground first as he implanted himself into the dirt, Amar then said in a superior tone because he was allowed the last word "okay I'll give it back –" Amar slowly lifted the hybrid off the ground from his tail, limbs dangling while he stared back down at the floor from what seemed like skyscraper height but he came back around to finish the sentence "but in return you have to never come back along with it! – Deal?! – Deal!!"

Amar then whipped the demon to a spinning toss as he disappeared into the clump of trees, Amar immediately looking over to Ryker like a child looking over to their parent when they hit a pop flier in a little league game. Ryker seen and heard the whole thing and gave Amar a flippy floppy "eeh" sign with his hand, Amar's shoulder sinking down as he sighed in disappointment, just then like a bullet train a force stronger than a diesel truck just hit Amar with every single pound included, good thing his hands we're out to catch whatever this was that felt like a building with rocket boosters. Groaning with strain as his feet we're slowly sliding against the weight that was trying to rip him in half, not necessarily push him back, but Amar's quick time body saving him all day today; Amar's feet picking up traction while he began tearing up the floor, he then heard an arrogant "excuse me sir! You weren't fragile with my items so I had to come back for a refund!" Amar creaking his head up to see that the force he was pushing against, was the shoulders of the hybrid which completely stunned Amar; how could a pair of shoulders be this strong?! But then he heard the sound of flapping in the wind. Looking closer he saw wings unfolded and giving the hybrid a gustful boost that really began to make Amar lose in the push for dominance.

Ryker chiming back in using his telepathy like a walkie - talkie at this point "Amar you should have a counter for every situation – I have been watching you very carefully and this is something I noticed, I have no idea why you have that, but you do! Think a way out of this one – or better yet concentrate and let it come to you!" Amar then did as he was told as shut his eyes and thought of this very moment in his head, a vision played for him like demonstration video for the trainees; he quickly dropped the hold he had on the hybrid's shoulders and then dropped down completely, laying on his back as he shot his legs up for a dropkick from below hitting the hybrid in the abdomen. Sending him sky high, Amar hit with a feeling of epiphany as he knew exactly what direction to take, he then did as he was instructed by his own mind, the hybrid was flipping and stumbling in the air with no ground to roll up against or to slide upon he caught himself and had his wings be his catching system. Amar so smug as he stood up now with his finger beckoning for the hybrid to charge forward, the hybrid enraged "HOW DARE HE TRY TO BE BIGGER THAN HIM LIKE HE WAS CALLING THE SHOTS!!!"

Of course the hybrid bulleted to Amar like an arrow shot through the air to shut Amar up but before he could swipe that smug look off Amar's face a step back is all that separated them. Amar spiking up his right knee into the gut of the hybrid, paralyzed as black ooze shot out from his mouth, creaking his neck over to Amar not able to believe that this rookie this newbie packed such a powerful punch. Ironically that is exactly what Amar needed to land an even more powerful blow onto the hybrid launching him forward with a straight right punch, Amar feeling a surge of pain that rumbled in his head; Amar gripping the left side of his cranium as he groaned in pain

"So it was a success – so now you know how to harness any counter for every tight situation, only problem is that it looks like it could begin to become very strenuous if overused – it's like a muscle - I am not sure but – and definitely not sure if you should try it right now, but you should be able to see a couple steps of your enemy like the whole one step is a basic counter, using a basic amount of Divinity but if you we're to double, or triple, or even quadruple the steps you probably would be able to see said steps ahead. Drawbacks probably are that that's how much will be consumed, all depending on which one you use –" Just then the hybrid rising up from the crashed Earth, that he carved his body figure into the ground with; Ryker then feeling the urgency as he said "but yeah that's just a theory – a Ryker Valor theory! I'll let you get back to this!" Then Amar once again left alone with his own mind as he looked over to his rival, there wasn't too much wrong with Amar his aching head finally starting to calm itself; now studying the hybrid who coughed up a bit of black ooze on himself even sounding as if the confidence had been kicked out of him when he hit the ground. Also emerging from a pool of anger that Amar drove him into as he spat out at Amar "you think you're cute?! Because that is making me want to think twice about taking you as my privileged pet and more like my slave if you keep acting how you're acting!"

Dusting himself off from the dirt he had earlier rolled in as he said_"well I better kick it up a notch because I do not want to be either! But you can go ahead and mark yourself down as defeated if you want!" The hybrid now hunched over as he wrenched out the last of the loosened black ooze from his body onto the floor, pulling himself straight up from his bent over position to speak with such repulse and disgust "I was wrong! That was just adorable!!" Emphasis and growling rolling off on "adorable"

Amar already locked in his fighting stance as he waited for the hybrid to give him a gaze that he was also prepared once Amar received it, it was like a declaration of war at the very instant both of them disappeared. A shockwave imploding right in the middle man distance between them, a moment later for the human eye to finally able to catch up to speed to, an image began flashing before coming back into regular reality resolution of Amar and the hybrid slamming fists against each other; Amar's right to the hybrid's left, a thunderous clash and collision of the opposite combating auras as well. They we're like the wind forms of natural beasts, that we're born to be eternal rivals; a black shadow – like aura mist and hissed at Amar's silver and crystal glowing and illuminating like a gigantic diamond being reflected towards the sun, black lightning shooting out from the hybrid's aura and glistening rays of light pierced the darkness from Amar's aura. They both grit their teeth upon contact as they crater the ground underneath their feet, going deeper and deeper, until the hybrid yanked up his knee to Amar's jaw but Amar with full force from his right arm reaching out diagonally across slapped the knee down. Now trying to slash the hybrid in the face with his left elbow, but the hybrid ensnared it like a glove catching a baseball in a friendly game of catch, they held still for a mere moment and yanked it up even higher as Amar now switched to his right elbow to smash over the hybrid's head. The hybrid able to tuck his left forearm in between, and was able to wrench space in the middle of and push it away, seeing this as a perfect opportunity for a straight left punch he suddenly felt a hammer hit his chest; as the air flew out of him, making the hybrid slip back as he pressed his claw on top of it like a person having a heart attack, Amar capitalizing dashing to him to climbing off his knee that was extended outward to slam his shin at the side of the hybrid's face.

The hybrid stumbled back as Amar swiftly caught himself with his hand and lifted himself onto his feet, the onslaught did not stop there due to the hybrid's hazy vision and throbbing head ache Amar was able to rush him confidently striking him with a right hook, but the last millisecond the hybrid's killer instinct returned and gave him the power needed to duck and roll underneath, even bobbing under a left hook as well. Amar now going for a body blow with a kidney – aimed right, the hybrid was able to catch it; with his hand pulled all the way back of his hip then slamming his elbow to the side of Amar's face, definitely brought a few stars to Amar's vision. Before he could connect with a second one, Amar stuck his left arm in the air like he was asking a question to cut the elbow off before it reached its destination, then rolling right over it to tuck it under his armpit; now both opponents we're armless, Amar quickly without a second thought went for the upper thigh of the right leg then following up with a kick to the side of the knee that buckled the hybrid's stance a bit. Before Amar could go for the final stomp on his toes, the hybrid interrupted Amar's leg with his foot holding the bottom of his boot with his dagger -like toes; they struggled in the middle and the hybrid smirking as he realized Amar was holding onto him. Letting him hold all of his weight he began barraging with a wave of kicks, stamping Amar in the chest like a playful child kicking and peddling their feet struggling to get out of their feety pajamas.

His avian – like feet just tapping Amar's armor furiously, his chest plate chinked like someone was running with change in their pocket soon enough the hybrid was able to loosen his arm; Amar brought both of his forearms up to block the onslaught. Now the hybrid used his hands to swipe at Amar's face, but every time his fearsome claws swiped at Amar they only scratched the surface of Amar's fortress of defense that was his unbreakable wrist guards. Amar was not going to take a second more of abuse, he needed to make a move and fast he quickly spun around as the quickest instinctive thought naturally snapped into the hybrid's head that he left his back open as soon as he went for the pouncing piercing from his deadly claws; he felt a slash himself, his body jerking inches back to pull his face from receiving anymore damage but all he saw was his own shining reflection from Amar's spotless, sheen cape. Flapping in the wind he noticed the edge and tail of the cape we're crisp straight and sharper than a steel blade, even seeing the spot that marked his blood; bits of splattered black ooze on what seemed to be the world's greatest spotless glowing mirror. The next thing he seen coming to him was Amar's boot, coming out from under the cape like every single child crawling out from the covers of their comfortable bed, pounding him so hard he back flipped in the air shaking his head to regain his composure. His wings spread out like a sail to keep him afloat, but he could even completely put his head back together an image of Amar trying to join him in the sky filled his widened blood red eyes, barely managing to catch Amar's knee as he cuffed both hands as his abdomen; cushioning Amar's destructive knee like a sleepy head on a pillow, but now there was nothing blocking his face.

The hybrid just realizing this as Amar pulled both of his arms up a blur of rights and lefts just smashing into the hybrid's unfortunate face, hooking his head from side to side, the hybrid's entire body shaking and shivering with Amar's quaking blows. The hybrid flapped his wings furiously to try to blow him off, but it was going to take more that a blustering wind to get Amar off now; he was like a cat digging its claws into its victim, good luck trying to get them without a nail clipper. The hybrid's wings finally cut into the middle of the carnage and took a few blows before flapping outwards, just shooting Amar off launching him off the hybrid completely; ruining the vicious assault, he was currently unleashing. Instantly thinking in his head as he saw the hybrid once again, shaking his head clear, spitting out a bit of black ooze from his mouth wiping off the trail of black discharge from the corner of his mouth "I need to get back up there" Then Amar felt a warm glow from his chest and he looked down to where his shrine is, he only watched as it glistened brighter and brighter until his ivory chain returned! Shooting out from the middle of his chest to both Amar's and the hybrid's surprises.

The ivory chain perfectly on course with the hybrid, at the last moment snapping himself out of his amazement attempting to fly away; but it was only a minor problem for the chain, that was aimed at the hybrid's chest to lasso around the hybrid. A misfire due to the hybrid able to climb too high into the sky during his escape route, this was also fine as it wrapped itself tight onto the hybrid's leg as just as Amar's thought "did it just –" he was torque like the demons he was tossing around earlier. Limbs flailing in back of him peering down to his chest to see the chain getting shorter and shorter; it was like he was the big prize fish being reeled in, but again Amar thought to himself "oh well make lemonade I guess!" Wrenching his right arm forward fighting against the resistance of the wind before he could even get close to fighting the hybrid, able to crank it to his shoulder length by the time he got to an approaching distance; the hybrid no longer trying to run either. Only taking them higher and higher in the sky, by doing this he turned his focus down to the climbing Amar even the Amar also cocked his fist while waiting for Amar's arrival; an explosive contact came between them once meeting each other, both fists driven deep into each other's faces in a cross counter. A boom equal to a seismic wave bubbled and rumbled in the sky roaring to shake the floor beneath them while scattering wind like free fliers, Growls and frustrated groans coming from both parties as neither wanted to show the amount of damage that was dealt, in some instances the hybrid just looked like a black blob that had its droopy, fingerless single flab pushed deep into Amar's face. On the opposite side of things, the gray cracking virus was spreading from Amar's fist slowly growing on the hybrid's cheek; taking a bit longer to turn him into a statue like all the others because unlike the others this thing wasn't a pushover demonic entity.

This was an entire different elite league of his own, both of his piercing eyes met and locked onto one another, their gazes only burning brighter and brighter as their teeth began grinding at the same instant. Before they started it all off again, with opposite hands from each combatant repeatedly ramming into each other's cheeks, Amar's left viciously thrust into the hybrid's right cheek and the hybrid's right fist was driven deep into Amar's left cheek. A booming clap of air popped off the second their fists met their destination, once again each of their punches met a wrench in each of their well oiled beings; putting their locomotive engines to an absolute stop, as they both groaned and growled even louder in building and climbing frustration. They we're both well aware of their current stalemate, both of their bodies creaked and squeaked as inch by inch they got their next move ready once again, being sound off by the contact of their eyes; first than any other this time not a single invisible firework – audio of a flare up was heard but a whole series like pop rocks. Crackling, sizzling, and combusting claps in the sky, every single sonic boom having enough wind force to blow up clouds of dust from the ground all the way from where they brawled in the sky. Ripping and disintegrating clouds as they blew up the air like running on top of land mines, with the collision of their fists too fast to be seen with a naked eye anyways

Amar was cross firing, colliding, smashing, parrying, carrying over and countering with the hybrid it was like two helicopters both shooting their machine gun turrets but the bullets we're the punches in this high speed battle. Amar currently cracked his fist against the hybrid's both fists crunching and melting together as yet another shockwave squeezed out from the middle of this, Amar curving around with his left hand for a kidney hook; it connected and spasmed the hybrid's body, sliding over his right fist on top of Amar's forearm that slammed right into Amar's chin that you would think would crack because glass is oh so fragile but he clenched down his teeth to show that steel lied behind this glass wall. What even I the all powerful story manipulator thought was made of fine china chipped away to show it was actually made of iron, Amar using this as an opportunity bringing in a left hook, then a right hook, then pulling up his knee to test the durability of the hybrid's chin.

Not nearly as strong as Amar's chin as he was sent flying back, only to be tugged back in by Amar's chain that was still wrapped around his foot Amar already having his hand armed, loaded and wrenched with fist clenched and balled up tight. This feeling no longer new to him so he did the same as well with his left hand clenching, balling of the fist and tucking to his side, by the time those two came close enough for a clash their vices we're already swinging going back and forth like a tennis game amongst the tennis gods, like two machine guns and amongst the two tidal waves of bullets, not a single one made it through.

Every bullet on both sides mashed and molted against each other that is exactly what this was, both parties arms we're an absolute blurry flurry but when they did have their instances of clear sight a collection of eight arms, take or leave some. Colliding fist against fist was the only help that you could get the auras just as blazing and burning as they now clashed along with their owners; the hybrid's ominous smoke screen, black toxic gas with lightning zapping and discharging all over like it was a storm cloud. While Amar's army of rising diamond dust showers spraying off from him like Amar was the nozzle to the hose, the beams of glistening and sparkling light shot through the darkness leaving bullet hole sized punctures inside it. It was gonna take much much more than that to completely banish it away, the storm of two spiritual forces began to swirl around their respective owners as they entangled in one another; Amar and the hybrid we're completely engulfed in a whole other battle that put the two auras in their place back in the minor leagues. Picking up as at first they slowly rotated around each other like the hands of a clock, with each full spin not only did the speed of their circular tempo and rotation quicken but the speed and intensity of their hands as well

Sparks beginning to fly as they went faster faster faster and faster, tremendous speeds that no manufactured weapon could reach. It was like the hurricane reappearing as their auras expanded along with their growing fighting spirits, Ryker with a hint of nostalgia as he sat upon of a burning steaming hot pile of burned enemies shaking his head and chuckling "give him hell and all the demons along with your fists! Who would have thought you would be taking on a hybrid and be going toe to toe with it – that is an achievement that might even raise Azuru's eyebrow... but he will remember he is Azuru and there is nothing more impressive than himself... but still this match is coming to an end soon enough – I am pulling for ya Rook but I'll be here just –" not wanting to even finish the remainder of that sentence as he watched on observing those two growing rivals climbing higher and higher into the sky. Their intensity and ferocity on par with their growing power punches, still not have slowed down one bit; more like a locomotive engine turbine, only going quicker as it traveled Amar thinking at the back of his mind speaking frantically to himself "I have to be faster than him! – I have no other choice – I know exactly what move he is gonna make that is obvious but I need to know what move I should make in order to put this vicious cycle to rest! –"Amar then dug deep into the subconscious of his mind for answers, digging all the while his fists working overtime, bending over backwards and loading themselves in overdrive so Amar could find a helpful thought; eyes shooting open with an epiphany stricken expression as he mouthed the words "I found it" was all the hybrid saw off of Amar's face this setting off a tingle of apprehension down the hybrid's spine, rushing down like fire fighters down a pole to go do what they do best

Still not in a position to swerve from what was keeping him afloat so he increased the tempo, his hands already invisible now picking up the revs like the poor tire of a sports car going up another gear. He began to notice the absence of Amar's hands not smashing along with his hands anymore, slowly pulling away for some strange reason; no matter how much force no matter how much power or effort he just kept slowing down. Like his hands we're being curved off and the speed was just being robbed from them, he felt his hands flopping and misfiring and at the midst of all this the hybrid looked straight at Amar's calm but yet determined face, narrowing his eyes down he could clear as day see his hands that we're there and that is when it hit the hybrid smack in the face like sledgehammer sticking out the window as it drove by and clothslined him. When he seen Amar no longer trying to compete with the tide by trading blows, he was riding this upcoming wave to use against him, Amar was parrying so precise so calm like water coming up naturally from the beach; he flipped one hand with his backhand at times, and at others he flipped them one over another crossing them. Reducing momentum by cutting down their speed, until not only could the hybrid feel his own hands slow down he could see them right before his very eyes losing their blur; their formidability just seemed to vanish right before him, Amar had the hybrid's own hands crossed over leaving him in an utterly helpless state for a mere moment and a mere moment was exactly all Amar needed.

The ivory chain then tugged on itself giving away some loose elbow room to stretch around in, swinging up from the hybrid's leg the hybrid watched as he seen the chain loop around him that split second. Amar then drove his knee deep into the abdomen of the hybrid as he bowled over, Amar released his arms and the ivory chain wrapped itself around the hybrid constricting like a python around him; making sure he was as uncomfortable as possible. The chain locked down onto him Amar then rolling over to his side while in mid – air twisting twice over to drop his shin right at the back of his skull and anchored him into a cannonball – like shot that made the hybrid seem like he was heavier than an anvil shooting up a geyser of dust. The chain breaking itself like it had a mind of its own and even it could see that is not something it wanted to be a part of leaving Amar to slowly float himself down to the ground now beginning to breathe easy, now that for sure known that he was on top but then once again his head rattled and throbbed; stumbling a bit as he swiftly landed on the ground, but this head ache felt like one of the hybrid's mean slugs to the mind Amar having no other choice but to shake it away, groaning a bit as he said to himself with caution "okay it feels worse than before – I –I – just for safety reason sake I will only have one more hindsight left in me and I'm gonna save it because I felt the weight behind that kick – with that guy's tenacity and strength – I am going to need it" the dust cleared from the well shaped hole that Amar did the most excellent job of drilling the hybrid inside of, but focused on it and ever so patiently waited, he finally got what he wanted but now came into question if he really wanted it.

Claws grabbing the hinges as he slowly pulled himself out, tugging his entire body slithering out of that hole, dusting himself off and trying to mask the fact that Amar was now sitting in the dominant seat. Not even bothering to wipe away the flowing river of black ooze coming down the middle of his forehead no smirk, no words to say, no arrogance, nope! None of that, Amar wiped it all of that clean like a house keeper taking care of the dust. But mysteriously just before Amar was about was about to rush to him like a line backer seeing just the jersey of the other team, he noticed something; something shining that he hadn't picked up on before. A ball of light sparkled and glistened at the left side of the hybrid's hip, Amar even rubbed his eyes thoroughly thinking something was wrong with him – I mean clearly not the strangest thing he had seen all day whatever boats his float I'm not judging – well at least not now anyways. Once he took his hands away from his eyes he was now wondering why it was still there, just as the hybrid was about to engage Amar and rip him apart limb from limb; he noticed Amar's sudden abrupt stop in his tracks, Amar's spaced out focus being poured in a pin – point piece of his body, his left side even taking a shocked double take at that. Until it snapped to him, he just remembered what was there.

He stood perfectly still as well as he put his left hand at his waist and patiently waited then whistled, beckoning for something to come to him like it belonged to him. Just then Amar followed the uninterrupted glowing ball of light as it passed right through the hybrid's wall of skin that was his left hip, as if it we're nonexistent, floating all the way to sit over his hand like some sort of well trained pet. Bobbing up and down over the hybrid's dark palm gently bouncing it, the hybrid so smug as soon as he started speaking he pulled Amar's eyes from the illuminating ball like his voice had magnetic properties to Amar's iron clad vision. "Ha so you noticed my little trophy did you?! Very keen eye my friend – very keen! Not just an average can sense light that has been swallowed whole by darkness! –"Right in the middle of the hybrid's proud boasting, Amar began to hear a voice echo in his head like someone yelling inside of a tunnel he assumed it might have been Ryker fooling around trying to disguise his voice and scare Amar because he was starting to get bored. Paying close attention "y-ou – you! Ahve – the power USE IT!!!" Amar not completely understanding what was saying to him even externally speaking aloud "huh?" The hybrid of course taking this as directed to him, answering Amar's confusion anyways "oh nothing I was just saying how I don't know who you are but you have managed to put up a very entertaining fight so far. All fun and games must come to an end sometime, so now I must crush your skull – oh I have also mentioned something about this little prize being the soul I stole today to lure Forrest and his team to this site in the first place. But hey I still took it fair and square! I had to put it away while I was "fighting" them so they couldn't snatch it back but enough talk!"

Amar not fazed by the hybrid's sudden regain in confidence and threats in the least, what concerned him the most was the message of distortion what did it say? What did it mean? Now the hybrid began dominantly walking over to Amar with shoulders strutting forward as he squeezed the bright ball in between his left claws like it was his anger management squeaky toys. Just then Amar heard with a bit more pain and strain in the hint of the bodiless voice that came from everywhere in Amar's head "OW – NOW – UNG – Yu – UONG ONE! – SS-SSES – Posses the power – use USE – USE – USE it!" Amar so lost in his sea of distraught as he now had frustration building up inside of him "WHAT POWER?!" Still not even a drop of sweat worried about the menacing hybrid, who was looking to want to erase Amar's existence right here like he was the butt of a pencil. No amount of sky scream or self exclamation was gonna stop him either, Amar's right hand began glowing white a vibrant circle of light was rippling and ringing off his hand as it grew warmer and warmer. Like he was trying to put the lid on top of the sun, Amar pulled his hand up to his face looking as if he was trying to see if it was bigger than his face; flipping it over on its sides until it fully colored itself in a blinding light.

His instincts once again ringing in as they told him to lift up his hand and to hold it towards the lambent ball; as his hand trembled and shook he started to notice his target that was being aimed at, first a cold shiver boiling up to an erupting volcano of quaking. Even making the lost in concentration hybrid, glance down at his hand to see what was shaking, shifting, and ruffling, and as soon as he did it shot right through the middle gap in his claws like a rubber bouncy ball being squeezed down upon between two fingers. On its way to its new master, who was greeting it with a shocked face and widened eyes; not even knowing how to respond or accept this, but as it was halfway in the air and Amar was losing his mind the hybrid appeared right in front of him to shoulder shock him to the ground. With his left shoulder like a brick wall crashing into Amar's chest smashing against the ground like an anvil dropping from the sky; the hybrid appearing right in front of the orb standing in its path like an ominous road block, just boasting again like it was his only known language "you see – you might have a nice pretty nifty trick even I will hand that to you - but there is one thing that hunted down prey will never forget! -" Looking down at the calm flowing floating ball that gently breezed towards the hybrid's open palm. Picking right back up as he was about to close it "they always know who the predet-"feeling a yanking at his left hand as he was just about to clamp down onto the orb leaving him unbalanced for mere moments, looking forward to see Amar on a single knee. Refusing to let this light fall into darkness, his ivory chain tightly wrapped around his dangerously deadly claws; his sadistic eyes narrowing onto Amar's pair of bold peepers, and not for a single moment did each of them turn away a challenge was made without words at that very moment!

Amar then began reeling in the chain but the hybrid violently grunting as he held down his ground, sliding against the terrain and dirty gravel refusing to give Amar even a single inch. Amar just smirked as he picked his feet off the ground and the hybrid once again wobbled with unbalance, his vision struggling to reach a equilibrium as soon as he was back on solid ground for his eyes and for his feet; he was met right in the face with a pair of metal boots using his face to catch them, a dropkick slammed his head back but did not drop him. Amar now changing his footing, being on his right side with his left leg closer to the ground as he lied down in mid – air, kicking the hybrid in the gut with the left then the throat with his right, leaving the hybrid out of breath and unable to gasp for air; making him jerk and spasm with the gut – throat, gut –throat, gut –throat, gut – throat, gut – throat, gut – throat, gut – gut – gut, THROAT!!! Combo he was pulling the final kick launched the hybrid forward like no cannon in the world could. That was when Amar swiftly slid against the ground gripping his right hand with his left hand for a steady guided arm as he began to reel in his chain gang buddy who further stretched out the chain, Amar then started spinning the ball of his foot as he began to rotate like clockwork hands on crack.

Turning the hybrid's body into a blotchy blur, lifting up the dirt off the ground to even form the shape of a clock then releasing him at 3' o clock sending him gliding over the floor; he headed towards the bush of trees, Amar now tended to some much needed investigation, taking a few steps toward the floating ball which bubbled up with joy, somehow? As Amar came closer and closer towards it, but being buffeted and punched by fierce winds, the hybrid was not letting Amar walk away with the prize he worked so hard to keep. Creaking his head up from its lied down position fighting hard against the wind, was like trying to pick up his head with big, stocky, bulky, team of beefy football players we're sitting right on top of his neck; he was able to get the much needed glimpse he so desperately needed, Amar's hand just over the orb just about to place it down on the top. Until the hybrid tucked in his wings, and although he flied faster like he turned himself into a torpedo, he wasn't the main concern right now as he flapped them back out with a slapping motion gusting his own flurry of winds toward Amar; who picked up his arms to block the invisible fury, but not able to secure the ball of light in time. It flew away like a flimsy straw hat in a typhoon, Amar then pulled his arms down to lock gazes with the hybrid as he broke the gustful winds that previously had him pinned down, panting a bit as that maneuver wasn't so simple, same goes for Amar's attacks but they both stared each other down then their vision turned to the floating prize that seemed to be bouncing away. Forrest's team catching sight of this and exclaimed "there it is! It's the soul he had captive let's get it before he does!!" Just as Kayoh we're going to momentarily leave their captain for the mission objective as they we're about to sprint off a black and white lightning bolt struck the ground before them.

Kayoh and Ex of course came to a screeching halt due to their keen instincts, after the flashing explosion and dazzling moments of miraculous timing a back was being shown right in front of them. Kayoh and Ex brought their hands down from shielding their faces to see electricity slightly discharge from glossy and glistening illuminating aura, arms crossed over his chest from the front but from the back it was obvious to tell that this man was in deep concentration as he instructed them "stay out of this! Rook has to do this! I know for a fact he will be the one to grab that soul! – Besides I still need to see more of his skills and abilities" Kayoh absolutely flipping out just losing her lid on her cranium as she exclaimed "are you serious?! What if he messes up – this is not a game you know!! We cannot afford to take any risks we need to reclaim the soul if the opportunity is in sight!" Ryker looked over his shoulder only to glance at her furious expression, then turned back to resume his spectator mode of this fight "that's why I am here – and you would be so easily willing to abandon your captain? –"Kayoh caught off guard with the realization of the error she just made, looking back at her wounded leader who was roaring in pain. Ryker continued his lecture "just give the green bean a chance! He does show a lot of promise for his first mission!"

Kayoh forced to grit her teeth to this one, not being left with a lot of options here, going back to the heated battle that for the moment was like they we're treading on egg shells. So cautious of the other person's move so they could counter, then counter that counter, then counter that counter of a counter, then counter that countering counter of a counterment... I guess – the hybrid floating off the ground with his wings flapping in the air as often as people blink; Amar about to get whiplash as he kept turning his neck to check up on the floating soul like a balloon in the sky. Trying to conjure up a plan for how he will react to the hybrid, and it finally coming to him Amar pulled out the plan like a rabbit from a hat, crossing his arms over his chest and giving the hybrid a welcoming gesture. Ryker chuckling up a storm as he said dripping enthusiasm "oh cannot wait to see this! Rook got confidence now!!" The hybrid not seeing any other way out of this stalemate either, he then pulled up towards the sky with his wings like propellers or like a sling shot shooting him up to the soul in a straight path, but on this path of course the hybrid treaded carefully with all ears and eyes open, he was not about to be doped into the newbie's plan. He knew it was here somewhere it was just waiting for him the right time to show up, and he even started to hear a metal chinking beginning to reel in sounding like it was rapidly being wound up; just as he was pouncing towards the soul ready to grasp it in between his claws, now that metal chinking sounding like it was being pulled in right next to his ear. The hybrid knew his careful tip toe nature to his approach was spot on, he knew there was no way Amar would let him do something without any strings attached.

Putting the whip crème on the Sunday that he was using the same chain whip move he has been burning out their entire fight. He would have to be a complete dolt to not know or not have it down by now, quickly swinging down to slap the head of the chain with his left hand but the hybrid's triumphant smirk was crushed by the sight and realization that what he slapped was not the head of the chain. Defiantly something attached to it but not the object in question, disbursing into the air around him like his hand was the rock that shattered the glass house it was thrown into, spreading these miniature spiked ivory balls that seemed to be made of metal all over circling around him in the sky as the soul directionless bounced higher and higher into the sky; and like someone throwing a match into a pool of gasoline the whole thing went off worse than the most expensive pack of illegal fireworks. A flower explosion in the sky booming and crackling with a bright white dust cloud, meanwhile the chain was flailing over to the soul with the direction that the hybrid fiercely smacked it; then fell into the middle of the soul and stuck to it like Velcro, slowly dragging it down from the sky weighing and dropping it down from its height like unnecessary band members.

Amar reeled the ivory chain in towards him, but out of the lingering glistening cloud the hybrid jet right out with his black sewage blood like high marked side burns and spewing from his mouth as well. Roaring furiously before spitting out an even more humongous dark green fireball the size of a tunnel for a train, heading right to the soul on a chain Amar was pretty sure his chain would still be intact but he didn't want to take a chance on someone else's safety. So he hugged the chain in between his chest and began reeling in a bit but the opposite began happening as he pulled up into the air and very rapidly like he was climbing an imaginary ladder, just in time to leap up with a swinging round house kick rolling over to send the big ball of embers away; but Amar was nowhere near from being out of the woods, as the hybrid speared right through Amar's successful attack driving his shoulder right into Amar's gut. No amount of armor was going to stop Amar from feeling that steel bat like shot at his abs, even a spit of silver Divinity slipped out from his mouth as it quickly shifted to black before hitting the ground, his arms and legs dangled helplessly forward what Amar was most worried about was his chain shaking with the soul at the end. Amar biting his lip on this one not really wanting to resort to this being so close to the finish line and all, but again running out of choices; a knife slid out from the sleeve of his hand. Glistening like the sun with its ivory glow, also concealed his hand underneath, the hybrid immediately bracing for impact, having the upper hand he wasn't about to let go of his chance. But when he heard a metal chink and felt no stinging sensation he shot his eyes open and looked over his shoulder to see a chain slithering away in the wind like the string to a lost balloon in the air.

Continuing to sink towards the ground and the spine – length slice of chain was drifting away in the air with the soul, the hybrid hissing with exhausted irritation and Amar only retaliated with a smile. Then a stab from the mighty knife, right into the hybrid's wing screeching and screaming as the hole burned into the now punctured wing; the hybrid only able to fold his wing in to dive faster to the ground. Dust popping up to stand and touch the sky when Amar and the hybrid came in for a surprise visit to the ground, the hybrid instantly blowing away the smoke that lingered crater that was their battleground; a thunderous left was the first shot fired from the hybrid laying into Amar's face, the agonizing pain waking him from his dazed phase. Immediately bringing up his forearm guards to try to buy himself some time, so he could at least *try* to recover, each powerful left and devastating right blew the dust around them even further from them; quaking the ground and shaking Amar's body like the epicenter, feeling like a truck being dropped on top of him again again and again. Not a single scratch marked Amar's armor though, he took a few panting breaths before he lunged forward to hold the hybrid's arms in with a tight compressing hug, the hybrid grunted as he tried to wriggle loose but then screamed in agony and fiercely, desperately, severely tried to shake himself out of Amar's grip.

Spikes as big as Amar's forearm shot out from every inch of his armor, puncturing every spot that was available soft tissue, Amar losing power in his clamp he had on the hybrid released him not able to hold him any longer. The spikes then sank back in, put away like he sheathed his sword, the hybrid running off like a man of thirst who spotted a drop of water dropping onto the floor and gripped his throbbing, stabbing leaking body. Amar slowly pulled himself up from the ground, patting the dirt off from his body even saying to himself "that torpedo dive really knocked the breath out of me I will admit it was a desperate move but I could not keep whaling on me. Eventually something had to give" looking over his shoulder, due to a bloodthirsty roar sounding off and shooting into the air from the drenched hybrid, Amar letting out an exhaled sigh as he commented to himself "I am kind of running on E here I really got to lay off the flashy moves and just let him fight my fight for me... orrrrr" Amar looked up at the soul balloon with the chain string floating up overhead. Leaping back three good leaps worth, never taking his eyes from the sky only to look down at the spot where he was standing but before whatever he was doing could truly come into fruition the hybrid was done and not having it. Roaring "I'VE HAD IT WITH YOU!!!" Trying to go for a slash to the face, but of course Amar slapped it down at the wrist as he turned his face and body to the side, already making the next move, as he shot the back of his left fist forward to block the incoming claw before it could even travel halfway. Amar spinning around smacked the right claw down with a back palm and holding the hybrid's left claw with Amar's left hand driving his right elbow into the middle of the hybrid's face

Then quickly curled his bicep up to hit the hybrid with the back of his fist, Amar leaping off the ground for a back kick from his right to the gut of the hybrid like he was being poled with a blunt javelin, sliding back and fighting as hard as he could to keep his ground the hybrid gave out a low growl. Never taking his eyes from Amar but Amar was standing up in an exhausted stance, arms drooping down about to hunch over and place his hands onto his knees; only thing stopping him was the fact that he knew the hybrid would shred him like a paper shredder if he we're to let his guard down, so he fought against himself as he also fought against the unrelenting hybrid. Who now looked past his blinding rage to devise a plan, he then hocked a loogie out at Amar, out of pure repulse Amar pulled his right leg up to dodge it; he didn't even know or to think if it had deadly properties – again it was just instincts, but he jumped back as he heard the ground dissolve. Sizzling like good brand bacon, decaying and dying away like water in a drought, before Amar could fully begin to question and react to this science experiment; his face was forced to the right with a straight right fist his body reacting as he still tried to get his head together. Smacking away the incoming left fist, ducking his head down then swung around to try to shake the haziness away like water stuck in his ears – now backing up as the pace was worked against him all he could do was block and get some slap shots when the chance sprung up like gofers; smacking down an incoming stabbing right with his left, swinging his right fist back to slam the incoming five fingered comet away.

Amar as quick as the tire of a sports car from an over privileged rich kid trying to burn rubber to impress the no named gold diggers. Spiraling on one foot slamming the hybrid with an unadulterated, raw, no holds barred spinning back fist that cracked the hybrid's head as it snapped it to the side. Still not even close to putting a stop to the crushing right fist right in the middle of Amar's fist, lifting him off the ground for a bit only for Amar to set his own body back down; once shaking away the stinging throbbing pain, falling back to the formation smacking both of the hybrid's incoming claws with vicious hands that we're like meteors hailing onto Earth. Lightning crackling even sounding off as they made contact upon the hybrid's hands, quick as lightning too Amar hit him with a one – two straight combo that did virtually no effect against this driven monstrosity. Driving his head down like a submarine submerging, but before he could even try to switch – aroo on the hybrid, the hybrid was waiting with a left claw already piercing the air to get to him; Amar fired off a right jab that stalled the claw so he could set his footing, stretching out his right leg to further steady him then swinging up to the crown of the hybrid's head. Dodging a little too late as Amar's misfire was able to land right on the jaw like an aluminum pole slid up the hybrid's belly and made its way to stab right into his jaw, swinging his head back. Amar recollected memories of him standing up and slamming his poor skull into the draur on top of him.

He had no time to dwell on his current pain, he then gave two fearsome thunderous! Wide body shots that connected to both of the hips that shook the body of the hybrid; Amar just knowing that he felt those there was no instinct needed to tell how much pain he just drilled into him, pulling his right arm back possibly taking steps forward towards the hybrid to switch up the battle control or who is currently wearing the battle pants in this battle relationship. Amar prepared for him to rear his ugly head once it sprung back for the slightest millisecond, Amar snapped his neck back and sent his body along with it as he slid back now Amar was the pursuer, rushing to the hybrid. Opening with a swinging mid – kick that crumbled the hybrid's left hip, Amar immediately following up with in split seconds a smashing diagonal left punch that pointed the hybrid's jaw down; a momentary pause came in between them like a referee to check if the hybrid knew how many fingers he was holding up, within this short pause Amar tried to grab his breath. Then setting up and unleashed a rocket straight right, but it was miraculously caught by the hybrid's mighty and quite livid palm, Amar taken back like a student showing up to chemistry expecting to know how to set up the Pythagorean theory; his resiliency set Amar's mind back a bit but honestly didn't surprise him as he now caught the hybrid's straight left punch. He then wildly swung the arm that had Amar's arm gripped in and with the wild out lash Amar pendulum swayed the side of his elbow and clipped the bottom of his jaw, he then felt a strong kick behind the calf that almost made him buckle.

With this distraction he didn't see the other elbow coming from the hybrid, continuing the very wild swinging with the arm that Amar had gripping control on. Hitting him at the same exact spot, opposite side the moment of haziness the hybrid already knew was going to be there, he took advantage of. Shaking away Amar's grip, he now had free hands that blitzed all over Amar like a shotgun blast replacing the bullets with fists of blazing fury; blurring all over Amar's body as he rattled with recoil and shook him like the tail of one of the most deadliest snakes. The hybrid then spewed up a fireball and definitely created space between each other to say the least, Amar sliding out from the smoke and ash with steam hissing off from his forearms. Panting now as the hits started to sink in, he couldn't take much more looking over his shoulder to see a creepy crawler behind him with his right claw yanked up, aimed to slash through Amar like he was a training dummy for samurais. Amar barely able to dive his head at the last second and with more precautions wanting to be taken, Amar leaped back as far as he could but as Amar slowly drifted in the air about to come up on his landing site pretty soon, he noticed the disappearance of the hybrid and he more than anyone else knew that was extremely troublesome. Just as his feet we're in hopping distance off the ground a shadow essence was already waiting for him exactly at his destination like a security guard about to ask for I.D.

There was no way that Amar could maneuver or try to drive away from the full utter force of the straight right punch that skidded Amar's body to the ground. Attempting to get back up but falling back down to bed of dirt, exhaustion proving to be too much even his instincts had reached their limits, not knowing it's properties and how to be used productively also being put into an even more complicated predicament burning Divinity even quicker this way and tuckered himself out to the point where he couldn't use his instinctive countering skills. He was huffing and puffing calmly as he creaked his head up to stare at the victor who defeated him, casting a shadow over Amar as he stood in absolute superiority over him; shaking his head the warrior he once admired now looked so pitiful and worthless. Kayoh, Ryker, and Ex all seen this unbelievable sight, Kayoh had her hands pressed over her mouth as she turned to the calm and collected Ryker who didn't even flinch at all the explosive blows that we're exchanged like trading cards. His sight glued to the battle and he didn't look like he was about to take affirmative action either; which meant that he had some trust in Amar, or maybe seen the whole picture that everyone was blind to.

The hybrid walked closer and closer towards Amar he pulled his left claw up as he prepared to rip Amar's throat form his body to show it to him in his last existing moments. Amar as he lied on the plush floor he spread his arms out to feel a gap to the left of him, quickly turning to see this was the acid pool that the hybrid made before; Amar now staring oddly hard at it, a very weird thing to be excited about but now Amar was pushing himself up by arching his elbows, he put his right hand out to the hybrid almost as a friendly handshake or a peaceful testament of friendship, maybe this was Amar's way of surrendering and begging for mercy since he had no energy left; either way the hybrid couldn't care less, his left claw getting the right pin point distance right to loom over Amar's face. Staring right inside his widened and speechless eyes not really able to grasp that these we're going to be his last moments with his new life, his new chance, and new body all squandered on this powerful demon. The way the hybrid was just savoring it all like taking a bite into his favorite burger, taking in the desperation, distress, and defeat lingering in the air as he stared deep into those pleaful brown twin pools of his enemy. The hybrid only licking his lips with satisfaction this was truly a great hunt for the apex predator, he hasn't faced such a challenge to push him to the brink of his existence like this so he was going to at least give Amar the benefit of groveling and begging that he was doing so excellently with his right hand put out like he was asking for spare change, now his eyes shut tight and whispered so very low toned to himself "please please please!" But sadly all of this meant nothing, no matter how satisfying the hunt was he was not going to spare Amar's life. He was after his soul after all but time was up, no pleading or begging was going to save him now! The hybrid's left began to stab through the air on its way to Amar moving like a missile targeted onto another's land.

The hybrid's body abruptly jerked forward completely sending his own hand off course, blood gushing into the air like someone jumping onto a bottle of lotion. An arrogant smirk broke right across Amar's face as he put down his right hand even murmuring to himself with relief "I was hoping it would work! It was just a theory but I am so so so SO glad it worked like I pictured it. Thank goodness it was spot on I would have been done otherwise!" Amar's vision trailing up to the ivory white chain that pierced right through the hybrid's chest, the soul at the butt of the chain just hovering over the hybrid's body. What was once a blunt object had suddenly became a spear on the will of Amar, coming to him as soon as he called it home, the hybrid beginning to lose balance as his growing weak legs began wobbling, more and more black ooze of his sewage blood thrown up by the gallon from the hybrid's faucet like mouth; pretty soon spread over his throat and chest as he struggled and strained violently to pick his head up at the elaborate Amar. With eyes of both astonishment and detest even rumbling a weak and weary "h-how d-did –did –" Amar cutting him off like the misfit branch on the perfect tree "let me stop you right there so you do not have to strain yourself in your last moments. I began to notice that you were getting angrier and angrier – so you completely let it slip by you that I was just getting into position for this! Funny part is that even I am surprised that it worked! – It is my first time in battle so I am just finding out what I can and cannot do. So I was not 100% sure but thank goodness it pulled through for me – you know if you would have kept a cool head you could have avoided this! I will admit your anger and rage completely overpowered me and you towered over me in strength but sometimes – especially with me strength is not always the winner".

Huffing, puffing and growling began sounding off from the hybrid as he struggled and so desperately strained to push his legs back into action. Gripping the ivory chain, squeezing as hard as possible trying so hard with so much desperation to make his way to Amar, just roaring furiously at him "DON'T THINK YOU WON YOU SMUG SHIT I AM STILL BREATHING!!! NEVER THINK YOU'VE WON UNTIL THERE ISN'T A SINGLE CELL OF ME LEFT!!! – YOUR SOUL WILL BE MINE!!" The hybrid hobbled and inched his way toward Amar, brutally sliding himself down Amar's ivory chain. The most agonizing and gruesome determination that Amar has ever seen, but Amar then said with confidence rising in his voice "you should not speak that way... to people who control your fate!" Amar then beckoned his right hand forward with the "come on" signal. Taking this as a taunt, only poured gasoline on the burning demon, but the hybrid felt his entire back cave in, which is what finally put a stop to him; moving at speeding glacier velocity, immediately in one motion actually tore a hole through his chest like a car going right through a tunnel. A soul being the speeding car that drilled right through the hybrid's crusty body, was at the end of the chain now right in front of Amar and was not alone anymore either.

Once treated as a trophy as a prize, a trophy awarded to him because of the amazing hunt, treating the body that did not belong to him like food. This was ironically his downfall, the completely fitting end for him but looking like a train on its tracks was not just one orb of light but now two. The hybrid faintly stretching out his left hand to try to catch the one that just fled from his chest becoming drained without it as he called out "m –my soul" a gaping hole in the middle of him decaying and rotting him away, he began to blow away in the wind bit by bit little by little as he watched it run on to Amar, who never took his eyes away from the hybrid and said with a hint of disgust in his stern tone "do not get it wrong! This is not your soul!! This is a soul of an innocent you stole! You were combined with it, it acting like your beating heart in the land of flames!! It was never yours it was given to you look how gray you made it!! –"Amar holding up the shining ball of gray to further heckle and humiliate the hybrid giving his final words as he goes on his way to oblivion "you do not deserve something so precious as a human's soul! So what?! You can have the life and energy you need to take away the lives of others?! No! Your terror stops now! "Your soul" can finally rest in its rightful place!"

Amar stood up with a wobble, stumbling and almost fumbling as he held both of the souls in his hands, the bright glowing white one and the soft glow of the gray one that only illuminated brighter in Amar's presence. Amar then heard the voice ring in again but much more clearly still shouting at him "why didn't you use us?!" Amar simply answered back respectfully in his head as he tucked one of the souls under his arm "because you are not weapons you are people!"

He then yanked his chain from the almost frozen body of the hybrid, tearing a new rip from the circular gap that was basically his body. He now fell over with the huge tug, and his chain slid back into his hand like a retractable cord to a vacuum cleaner, now another voice popped into Amar's head as he began walking away "excuse me I am new but – to my fresh knowledge that I gathered off of the vibrations I feel that are screaming of f of you its telling me that your armor is actually built to take in souls and empower them as they fight by your side."

Amar a bit taken back as he looked down at the glowing orb in his hand, his expression on his face said it all the soul even followed up with "it's the truth I swear it on my grave where ever it might be!!" Amar only able to respond with a "really?" The first soul to ever speak to Amar shouted again "tis true!! I first felt this when I –"trailing off, Amar or the new souls he carried we're completely unaware that when the hybrid's now hollow body fell over he did not simply blow off into the wind. As Amar rode off into the sunset, to live happily ever after roll credits, oh now he began belting and molding inside the ground going inside of the ground like water sinking in the grain of the dirt; Amar was left totally in the dark about this, Kayoh and Ex letting out a relieving exhale as Kayoh said "geez that broke down to the nitty gritty didn't it?! What kind of show you putting green bean?!"

Amar walking up with both souls handing them over to Ryker as he said "here sensei I retrieved both of them from the hybrid, one of theme was the soul that was infused with the hybrid." Ryker nodded his head in acknowledgement as he spoke "impressive, very impressive usually we would have to absorb all of the ashes from the defeated and slain demons in the area and dig out the surviving souls ourselves. But you you're not only able to sense them you pulled them out yourself Rook!"

Just before this comment would completely register with Amar as weird and unusual, he was yanked by his collar almost enough to give him whiplash as Kayoh with or without consent lead him to Forrest. Their leader groaning in pain with hands over her mouth she pointed to him, no words we're said but plenty of information was fed to him more than enough for Amar to get the hint as he started moving towards Forrest; Forrest lashed out at him "NO! NO! YOU STAY AWAY FROM ME YOU OMEGA PIECE OF SHIT!!" Amar pulled back, not really sure what he was talking about. He thought at first he was just hallucinating maybe he was seeing Amar as a demon of some sort trying to cause further harm to him, Amar patting down the air with both hands in a gesture he came in peace. Even with a soft and harmless tone "hey hey you do not have to worry I am not going to hurt you"

Forrest once again lashing out like a pit-bull on a chain, chomping at the air right next to his face "OF COURSE I KNOW THAT I'M NOT SUPID! I WOULD JUST RATHER DIE THAN LET A STUPID OMEGA TAKE THE GLORY OVER ME TO SAY THAT THEY "SAVED ME!" Amar completely lost as he shouted back "first off, what is an Omega?! Second if I can at least try to help why will you deny it?! You are a leader start acting like it!" "OH FOR LORD'S SAKE HE DOESN'T EVEN KNOW WHAT OMEGA IS!! – IS THIS REALLY WHO THEY THINK IS "GOOD"

ENOUGH TO BE ON OMEGA?! – AND LSITEN YOU FRESH TURD DON'T TELL ME HOW TO RUN MY TEAM ALRIGHT?!" Kayoh tapping Amar on the shoulder as she stepped forward and inserted herself "Omega is the team you are currently on, it happens to be the highest of the elite three. The Omega or Divine Intervention which ever you would like to go by, is at the top, then us at Alpha, Beta below us and he is very unintelligently insisting that he will NOT ACCEPT HELP FROM ANYONE ON THAT TEAM! – WHAT THE HELL IS WRONG WITH YOU LET IT GO!! What green bean was saying was right! YOU ARE A LEADER AND YOU NEED TO ACT LIKE IT!!" Forrest just shaking his head with absolute disdain and disgust as his body shook and spasms with jolts of black lightning zapping his body as he could not believe the words that we're coming out from his comrade's mouth, Amar was repeating to himself in stunned amazement "I – I am in the top elite team??" Just then Ryker slung his arm over Amar's neck as he jumped in on Amar's personal thoughts "that's right Rook! What's wrong surprised? Come on now have faith in yourself – I think I am starting to grasp why you we're seated in that spot and not put in the lower ranks -"

Amar creaking his neck so his curiosity could be fed "and why was I put on this team?" Ryker only answering with a superior chuckle first response "I'm pretty sure I know but that would completely ruin your journey of self discovery. – I mean you still haven't taken the first step – you're still in denial that maybe you could be just that amazing, once you get past that the rest is a cake walk – kind of!" Ryker jumping off Amar's shoulder to hop over to Forrest's agonized body leaving Amar to drown in his own thoughts. "Self denial?" Looking at his own hands and the armor on his body, he even admit to himself this all came as tsunami of events that he never believed was possible, just bending reality like it was a simple rule. Ryker crouching down a couple feet away from Forrest's feet as he said in such a lecture filled tone "so you have a disease – your team needs you! – This army needs you! – Father needs you! It's not like we don't have the antidote I know for a fact my pupil could help you! – You're just refusing the help – "and I mean that's on you" is something I would say if you weren't in such a powerful position. You have lives dangling in your hands and you're willing to throw that all away for some stupid grudge you have against us?!"

Forrest turning his face from Ryker as he grumbled "don't you dare lecture me Ryker! You aren't my superior and I doubt that kid could do it! – WHAT MAKES HIM SO GREAT?! JUST LIKE THAT HE STEPS IN AND CLAIMS A SPOT JUST LIKE THAT?!?! – He doesn't even know what team he's on and you expect me to trust him just like that? No thanks I'll pass" " no you're right I'm not your superior I'm a Miraclelyte of a male just like you, and one Miraclelyte of a male to another. Sometimes we are faced with things we absolutely hate doing, I mean we aren't in Heaven yet! Your pride shouldn't swallow the welfare of your teammates their feelings, ambitions, and more importantly their lives! I know this from watching my own leader in action playing role model right before my very own eyes. So you cannot say that I do not know what it takes to be a leader, I might not be one but I sure as hell know what a true leader looks like! – I seriously would not doubt this kid, putting Rook down would probably be one of the biggest mistakes you could make and another thing he didn't pic-"

As Ryker was talking, Amar walked over to Forrest's body, face aimed down as his shoulders we're strutting forward in a dominant fashion. Making Amar completely stick out enough to capture Ryker's attention as he was telling Forrest what goes up and what goes down; but now he was shushing himself to see exactly what was about to happen. Forrest's vision curved up as he stared up at Amar, who was creepily standing in front of Forrest without words, shade concealing his facial expression so anything right now was basically a wild card at this point. Forrest groaning out a very irritated and bitter "yes?! W-wha- ah- what do you want green bean?" Amar then pressed one of his knees on top of Forrest's chest as he gripped him by the shoulders, now it was as clear as a cloudless sky with the sun shining bright overhead.

The passion burning bright in his eyes, his teeth clenched together and the anger that was building up in Amar's voice "you have people that care for you! – That need you! That want to make sure you are okay and you are just going to slap them in their face with rejection just because "you do not like certain people?!" You lost your privileges to choose!! You are cared for and I am not going to let you throw away your life because of some stupid misguided pride!!" Amar then pushed his fists into Forrest's chest and an orb like shape of light bubbled around them, encasing them inside a glowing radiance that only became blinding within moments like a one percenter of the actual sun. With the piercing beams that sprinkled in all directions, everyone turning their faces until the burning bright lights became dull and safe for their eyes to once again look in that direction. Only to see all the blackness had vanished from Forrest's body, his face no longer pale, his glowing essence of his body remaining still and no longer spasming or jerking with pain and agony; all the darkness that enslaved Forrest was in Amar's hands, dripping from his gauntlets like he stuck his hands in paint. Little by little as the moments passed by all of the darkness began sticking and merging with Amar's gauntlets almost making some sort of design.

His once white pure shining armor now had a bit of gray spots and blotches on his armor, all of the evil and darkness just clung to him like a magnet among metal. Amar was just cleaning up house at this point like a vacuum he took all the darkness away, he slowly took his knee off from Forrest's chest as he stood over the prideful Forrest who hated every second that Amar helped him, he would rather be screeching in agony as they drag him back to Safe Haven but Amar just wasn't having it. His expression still as fierce as when he leaped on top of Forrest like a deranged starving cannibal, looking Forrest dead in the eyes as he said "I do not care about your stupid vendetta! What really matters to me is the feelings of your friends, that is what made me do what I did – because they should not suffer all for a selfish move that you wanted to do – you are free to do what you want now!"

Forrest now sitting up he arched one knee and extended one out, examining himself, Ryker was inspecting Amar with a keen eye as he even smirked only speaking a side note to himself "I see it! The reason why Azuru took this kid on as a disciple in the first place – this kid is like a freakin' onion peeling back each layer to show me what he's made of – I know he said Azuru didn't spend much time with him but he certainly rubbed off on him you could tell he came from his dojo." Forrest getting up from the ground, slowly and carefully still a bit sore as he dusted himself off and looked at Amar straight in the eye "thanks" then scoffing away; Amar's face brightening up a smile as he responded with a "you are welcome" Forrest now severing the formalities pointing to Amar and shouting out "as the pride of a man – I 'm in your debt! I will do whatever I can as quickly as possible to get out of this – yea' it's one thing to be in debt but to be in debt to an Omega burns just burns me so if you're not watching your back in battle guarantee I am"

Amar with his hands pushed up near his face in discern as he said "hey it is not a big deal really you do not have to pay me back its fine we are on the same team right?!" Now Forrest's eyes looked as if he had just spot an enemy, cricking his neck with a prepared to leap type of stare as he asked incredibly curiously "are you disrespecting my pride as a warrior?"

Amar frozen both in both mind and in position, was caught and he had no idea how to get out thank goodness that Ryker came over as he tossed the two souls that Amar passed him earlier. Amar in confusion looked at both of them as they hovered in his hands and before he could even open his mouth to ask, Ryker pointed over to the field that Amar just fought at as he said "oh yeah I forgot! That guy you thought you killed, turned out you didn't really after all. Because the shell of negative energy that he was infused with sunk into the area – because yeah! No one thought it was a good idea to cleanse the area and yeah so being the only smart one here, he sunk into the ground to absorb all the negative energy in the area – long story short he's bigger badder and probably ten times more stronger than he was before – so remember to duck use those hooks and protect your privates at all times – oh and use those souls or you stand zero to no chance against this guy!" All of the information coming so fast feeling like he was just slammed with ten exams and had five minutes to finish them all.

Amar shouted at his incompetent master as a panicked rage was built up inside of Amar "why did you not tell me earlier?!" To which Ryker batted it back like a tennis racket "umm what we're the first two words I said "I forgot!" EXACTLY!! Anyways just use the damn souls already! They we're telling me how you could use them to enhance your battle skills – they also told me all of your juicy secrets haha someone has a crush on Zandra oooo!"Even Kayoh oooooing as she joined in, Ex couldn't ooooo but he was cuffing his mouth like he was screaming it louder above everyone else; Amar's face brighter than the most valuable priceless stack of gold. Through panic surged through his entire body – "DO NOT TELL HER!!" Ryker just rasberrying a scoff "bro I used to be young too – I've kissed my fair share of girls and had my crushes the bro thing to do would be to help you out and I will be sure to do that – oh yeah stop viewing them as weapons! That is really what offends them they are your partners in battle and should be treated as such they fight alongside you, give you strength as you fight for their freedom so when you turn them away you're throwing their act of bravery right in their face" Amar didn't think about it that way, he barely even gripped the concept but quickly wanting to fix his error without a moment of hesitation. Amar with determination shouting out from his voice "so how do I do it sensei?" "What you want to do is put the soul at the place where you put your little buddy Camarada" "my shrine?" "That's exactly the spot just hold it there, and I promise you the soul will do the rest of the work" just then the ground began quaking and shifting underneath their feet.

The field that was the coliseum for Amar's battle was now the epicenter of the entire wave of the ground and even beginning to glow a red circle from where the hybrid's body was left defeated and broken. A fearsome, stocky, meaty arm with shredding claws just pierced right through the ground, this startling Amar as he got a move on with the process; looking back and forth between the souls, they looked completely similar to the naked eye both glistening, bright, shining perfectly cylinder balls of light. Amar could tell which one was which though, one was the soul that was suffering within the embodiment of the hybrid and the other was the soul that was being held up like some sort of prize that both sides we're going for, finally choosing between the two Amar gently pulled the soul on his left hand to the center of his chest clinking against his armor chest plate. It seemed that the soul was burning through Amar's armor as a huge hole of light that opened up big enough for the soul to enter, revealing Amar's shrine, it slowly drifted and hovered inside and the hole of entrance closed shut like a gate that wasn't accepting visitors at the moment. The dullness returned to Amar's chest as his chest plate also came back as well, Amar began examining himself to see if anything remarkable had been attached, popped up, slid out, enforced or clipped onto his body. Swinging his neck from one side to the other as he twisted each limb and scanned up and down

Ryker doing the same, looking all over as well Kayoh turning her neck from side to side even the ball of light was floating all around Amar in a spiral, searching for change like it was a lost puppy. Ryker then said as he began spinning Amar himself as he looked for a pattern shift in Amar's armor or something as he curiously asked "do you feel any different?" Amar said very weakly growing more and fainter "dizzy!" Ryker sighed as he replied "sheesh kid I swung you in a damn tornado not too long ago and you didn't complain then!" Kayoh then grabbed Amar by the shoulders to halt him as she then assured "open your mouth" Amar did as he was commanded from him to show nothing but a normal tongue, rows of teeth, a pink walls of skin and a dark roof nothing changed or exciting. She said from her speculations "hmm minty smell but no fire, lightning, or light exerts" she then shut Amar's mouth herself and pulled on the bottom of her eyelids to see if anything would beam out from them, but all she saw was the normal burning ball of light behind the shield that was behind his eye, again just another normal quality of a Miraclelyte. She let Amar's eyelids slap back onto the shields that we're his eyes, Amar groaned in pain as he rubbed his eyes but Kayoh moved his hands to begin scrambling his face as she started to configure ideas of her own "maybe if I move his face a certain way it will activate something – I am pulling out any idea I can think of because everything else is obvious! Oh green bean, think of something maybe you have telekinetic thoughts!!"

Amar closed his eyes as Kayoh washed his face like it was a dirty dish that only got more violent as the moments passed and an excited and anxious Kayoh oozing curiosity pondered out loud "so what did you think of green bean?!" Amar barely able to respond as her palms rubbed over his mouth "a restraining order!" But it was just then Amar's body truly began to shiver and shake on its own accord, Kayoh backing up a bit to give him some room while a voice clearly not Amar's spoke out loud it was very old and very jaded. Sounding like the old man who lives at the corner block who yells at you for stepping on his grass – well someone gave him a microphone as his voice echoed off of Amar's body in a single vibration "transcendental armor activate!! Also sorry for the late start up I'm an old soul so it takes me a bit to get around! This place is like museum I should tell Ingrid about this place it would be a nice place to visit... what was I doing again? – Wow this place is huge! – I should tell Ingrid about th-"Amar began knocking on his own chest plate as he politely inserted "umm excuse me sir - yes you could tell Ms. Ingrid about my – uhh body later – right now could you please continue with the transformation and please could you give it a better name?" "Oh thank you young one what do they call you – Omar?! – Yes well thank you for jogging my memory and I really don't have combative properties per say! But what I did was bring your potential out to its maximum, bringing out all the power in your armor it could be a taster of what is to come if you train yourself to hone your abilities – and you're right young one! – I shall call this form Ultra transcendence!! ... Of heroism, better?"

Amar not wanting to hurt the poor old soul's feelings, withholding the true feelings as he masked his response "yeeeeah thank you for that" Amar's attention now being dragged away from something insignificant as his name, now looking on and watched his own arms as he held them up in front of his face. The normal, harmless thin fabric that was his clothes that he wore underneath each shielded appendage began to waver then point forward; as the creases we're ironed out to become as straight as a blade, and any wrinkle in it was razor sharp. Leveling up to the rest of his armor instead of being underneath, looking down at his thighs and knees as they violently shook looking like the dance fever was passing through Amar like ghosts faze through walls. The neon white pants that glowed brighter than a thousand Christmas lights, had begun clumping together to make jagged plates and protection that was separated by only a thin line that a fingernail would struggle to fit into. His gauntlets already large only solidified their size and strength as they doubled not goofy or clunky as they took this shape looking like now he could crush boulders with a single grip, mysteriously a hole appeared on each of the knuckle on both gauntlets. Spikes showing themselves on Amar's knees, a single hill big enough to put a demon's eye out with a precision flying knee, Amar's abdomen if it wasn't bad enough it was engraved and carved out before, now it was glistening, glowing, and just sparkling. His shoulders bared the ivory chain that came out from one end and wrapped itself comfortably around Amar's neck like a simple scarf; then dug into the other shoulder pad, Amar's collar that was around his neck started to rise from the front of his face, while Amar was left without a helmet but in this form seriously doubting he would need it, the way his eyes we're blazing out like shining cannons of sparkling silver starting to look like all he needed to do would be to stare hard enough.

Meanwhile at the same exact time his armor clanked a hard metal shut as it melted together like construction doors that took heavy duty machine operated tools to pry open. Rising all the way above the bridge of his nose to flawlessly, just then the former metal collar turned battle mouth – guard had six miniature vents three rows on each side. That began to slide open and with each breath that Amar took, Divinity like diamond dust as it leaked out; just then, Amar's eyes like suns burning through the air like paper and began to glow out to blind everyone who raising their hands to shade their faces as they looked at Amar up and down as they "oooooed" and "aaaaahed" so it was basically an audience of two Ryker and Kayoh, but Ex was right alongside them with his eyes almost popped out of his skull. Forrest with his arms crossed over his chest and his back turned away as he pretended not to care, Ryker then said "I heard that old soul tell you that he helped bring out all the power inside you – so this is what it would look like huh?! Noted!!"

Even Kayoh had an eyebrow raised with impress as she said "very nice green bean! You actually pretty manly if I didn't know you, I'll admit – I would walk on the other street if I saw you!" Ex just gave his thumbs up of approval and Amar just scratched the back of his head in embarrassment and said "thanks guys" instantly stopping to recognize his own voice that sounded like it had been dipped inside a pool of madness and swam in the ocean of masculinities with a metallic and iron background Ryker chuckled as he inserted, "Wow you even went through puberty with that transformation! That really does deserve the title of "Ultra transcendence"... of 'heroism."

Amar just shaking his head in disagreement trying to ignore his masters heckling now knocking on the lowest abdomen and it slid out like a drawer and the other floating soul hovered over to Amar's hand in exclamation of discovery that Amar's amazing powers never seemed to end. Ryker then said "your abs are drawers?!?! Dude you have candy drawer! Give it some thought it makes sense!!" Amar staring at Ryker with an odd eye as he gently dropped the soul into his drawer for safe keeping then sliding it shut before he could pick his eyes up to see the progress of his villainous rival, Forrest already beat him to the punch "Hey you might want to get your ass in gear! Because it looks like your best buddy is ready for round two don't screw it up!" Amar stepped forward to investigate just how much the hybrid had transformed or grew in strength, he was still pushing his upper body out from the ground like he was climbing out from a well, big beefy stocked with rippling and shredding muscles, pushing further as his iron clad abdominals now crawled out of the burning tunnel that now started to shoot darkness in the air like it was some sort of volcano the more he climbed up and out the more leaked out.

Amar couldn't believe that, this poor soul that was inside his abdominals, was the heart of that beast; even more unbelievable was how much he reverted into a beast that is exactly what he is now a beast, no longer a combination of two different concoctions. A gray line that tight roped between the two worlds he slipped and was engulfed by the animalistic side, his fangs that merely jabbed out the corner of his mouth were just as big as saber tooth tiger fangs, his wings were somewhat graceful as they were perfectly fit for the body of that caliber like the wings on a bird they were particularly small for that petite sized warrior but now they looked like two bazookas folded right in back of the beast his clause no longer simple claws but sharp and deadly daggers his biceps were big enough to choke a baby elephant his chest like semi deflated balloons that puffed forward matching the size of his hill like shoulders his jet black horns retaining their unicorn straight shot shape but now his jet black hair was much more messy his eyes crying blood, in fact his whole entire twin eye sockets were just pools of liquid scarlet his pupils were burning suns that radiated infernos.

His face now having a more ferocious lion texture to it, the flat double sized nose was kept, but the wide cheek bones, thick jaw line, razor sharp – jagged teeth, and ripples of scrunches now that was new. Completely different from the delicate frame that the hybrid once had, as the beast pushed itself more and more out Amar stated to realize just how much about him had changed; the space black darkness that was his rough, rugged, and raunchy skin tone along with his texture had also converted, changing over to a more natural feel. It was still a beast, but this was the skin he was forged in and now the color that the beast sported was a wrathful dark red, carvings looking to be bladed all over his muscular and defined body; even his legs taking on a more beastly presentation, snapping back at the shin to a more aggressive arch. Still keeping the bat feet format, placing both of them on the ground as he finally stepped out from the hole he dug himself from the crust of Earth, holding nothing but darkness inside and Amar was clearly on this beast's mind, having a hunched back rising up from the ground the first thing he did when reentering on fresh soil was to physically point all of his anger and hatred to Amar. Forrest, Ryker, Kayoh and Ex all stepping to the side to stay out of this cooking beef, even Ryker's attention was caught enough for him to mention something of it "ooooo I think he likes you Rook! – Go give him a hug!"

Amar's attention was not side tracked or taken away from his walking problem who was trekking towards them, Ryker seeing that he was being ignored grew bored as he said "eh I am gonna cut off the sewage of darkness and purify the area, anyone wanna come with?" Forrest began walking to it with his arms crossed over his chest, Kayoh declining the offer as she enthusiastically said "you guys go on ahead and do the boring grunge work I am gonna get a good branch to watch this slugfest" Ex nodding his head as he chased after her, in the sky within moments everyone had gone their own separate ways. Now it was only Amar and the beast left in the bridge of destruction, Amar began strutting his shoulders as he marched forward, he heard a weak voice echo from his head "I was inside that? – Or that was me?!" Amar sternly and so confidently responded "yes that was you – but do not worry, give me a minute or two and you will not ever have to lay eyes upon him ever again!" Amar's confidence was like a fire burning through a forest, staring down the at least ten foot monster that was heading to him slowly. Licking its long twisted and jagged teeth with its slender tongue as the black ooze drooled from alongside of the corners of its mouth.

Amar puffing out a golden cloud that glimmered from the slots in his mask, like Amar was miraculous enough to find the golden hemp tree (420 blaze it all day every day legalize!!) as he took a few steps at a time, but with every blink that the beast took Amar became extremely close, like Amar would freeze time every time he would instinctively shut his eyes. Amar was traveling too fast for time or sight to capture and hold back, dashing in a blur trail of zig zags until he came up to the humongous meat tower he was half the size of; just about to drill an absolutely thunderous right into the stomach of the beast. Amar was sure he would bring him screeching to his knees, he looked up to see the beast's eyes were focused up on the hill that Amar started at, but suddenly narrowed down to him as he also caught Amar's tiny in comparison fist within its grasp and yanked him up to eye level. Only to mock in its own twisted and spurred up language **"T'NDO KNITH I MA SA WISO SA I ECON SWA!!"** (*don't think I am as slow as I once was!!*) Just as he was about to slam Amar against the ground like a sledgehammer into a boulder to reduce it to pebbles, Amar with one single spike speared right through onto the other side of the demon's palm, receiving a growl from the ferocious beast; Amar then began to descend as the beast was forced to release him, that is when Amar sent a boot straight to the nose of the beast that slid him back like a crowd of people pushing him back to get to their deals to black Friday. Before his blurred vision could become clear Amar was already rushing to the beast with the ivory chain spiraled around his arm, all the way to the tips of his gauntlet, Amar driving it straight to the gut; just digging his fist into the huge abdomen of the beast. Half of Amar's arm sunk in to the beast and as was sent launching forward, gliding above ground.

Around his belly glowed a bright white ring that started to detail and define out the farther and farther he flew. Until the ivory chain reappeared to wrap itself around the waist of the beast, the beast's entire body snapped forward as it abruptly stopped mid – air; limbs still attempting to go that direction, but whatever the torso says, **GOES,** Amar was sliding right leg to the outside as he responded **"DAN UYO DLUWO EB HSILOFO OT KNITH YM REWPO DENIAMRE ETH EMSA!!"** (*and you would be foolish to think my power remained the same!!*) Widening the beast's pools of blood and flames that gave him sight as he gravitated the beast towards him, it was like an entire city was in the back of that chain and just before the beast could enter into Amar's personal space Amar leaped up and spun, having enough time before climbing up the tower that was the demon's chin for a slamming spinning right roundhouse. The ivory chain exploded a further impact shockwave, a boom that spat the beast forward as he torpedoed right through a sea of trees like the we're merely paper, groaning a painful squeak he shouted "**WHO OD UYO WONK YM EVITNA EUGNTO?!**"(*How do you know my native tongue?!*) Amar already walking over to him he had time to squeeze out an explanation in his own language so he could understand "**I EVHA A ROTALSNTR THAT SKAESP LEVEL EON – EH DEKCPI TI PU NEWH EH SWA EDISIN UYO!!**" (*I have a translator that speaks level one – he picked it up when he was inside you!!*)

One second Amar was half a mile away from the beast the next he was hovering over him, his cape waving back and forth with the wind, the beast did have to readjust his eyes to figure out and understand exactly where or what was happening before him; Amar's cape was liquefying right beneath his feet. Every inch of his boots we're now covered by metallic toned liquid, Amar's legs turned to huge metallic spikes that we're driving towards the beast ready to impale him, but the beast gripping the tips at the last second before they could take a dip in the scarlet blood pools. The beast's body tensed up as he held those spikes at that exact spot but it was like sliding silly putty as it slipped through his fingers, slandering and slithering along his shoulders curving out so there we're perfect shots on either side. All the beast could do was hold the other body in his hands for some strange reason as he watched and waited for the incoming pain, spearing right into the mountain peaks that we're his shoulders, like two bullet trains crashing into the side of a rocky mountain . The beast groaned as he squeezed his body in tighter but now gripped a higher and different place of the moldable spikes, he then whipped Amar from the air down to the ground; lashing his back to slam and crush against the ground, now it was the beast's turn to go on the offensive as he rushed to Amar with the spikes still drilled into his shoulders. Amar's spikes like a tube with liquid traveling through it or more like a fuse that was lit on its way home to TNT, a bright white luminance was trailing down to the points of the spikes, pops of white explosions we're snapping and bursting off the beast's body.

It kept on merely sprinting as if it we're just background explosion effect, to make him look more intimidating and it was working. Amar was the only thing on his mind, unfortunately for him Amar had thoughts traveling like high speed chases through his mind and 90% of them we're the next step; he took his feet out from the cape like it was just a simple blanket that wasn't at all covering his legs. Now morphing them, he then rolled over backwards and his cape whipped down obediently over his back, and guess who was still attached to the cape. The two spikes embedded in the beast's body lashed the beast sky high over Amar, slamming him into another miniature blanket of trees and green life the spikes now pulling themselves out and retracted back to master; to mold back into the straightest edge, Amar looking back over to the crash site fully knowing he was never going to go down that easy, especially with all that hatred and negative energy like fuel running through his veins. Amar now adding a bit of energy to the pile as he was hating that he was right, a full sized tree flew through the air like it was a beach ball being tossed around by girls in bikinis, just as Amar reached to the back of his cape pulling it over his arm matador style. His hand fiercely throbbed and vibrated as he let go of his cape to hold his wrist with his left hand, he heard a magazine chink and ammunition rattle he then nodded his head in confirmation as he said "okay!"

He then gripped his right wrist with his left hand as he aimed it like a pistol at the tree, which would be target practice at this point. Thunder clapped off his hand as he shot a burning ball of light from the hole in his index knuckle, pushing his arm up with some serious firepower recoil; it might as well have been an RPG missile shot from Amar's fist, it was as visible as one and it left as many chunks and pieces as a regular one would. Ash rained and trickled down as he watched the cloud of smoke linger slightly, he slowly took his head back down to where the beast was last seen, readjusting his aim because there is no way the tree jumped out of there with free will. Sure enough the beast incarnate charging out from the smoke a determined man on a mission, as soon as he was visible Amar fired out a shot from his middle knuckle that curved perfectly for a momentum hook shot, straight to the chest. Shoving his chest back some ways and slowing his speed for a minor moment but this wasn't going to slow him down in the least, regaining himself as he continued to wound up dashing to Amar like an everything must go store; Amar firing another shot then trailing a shot from his pinky knuckle immediately after, the beast dodged the ring knuckle shot by weaving his head but the pinky knuckle shot was a tricky one aiming very low as it side - swiped the edge of his left knee making him hobble a bit. Definitely halting his speed like traffic due to a crash and at that very moment Amar already repositioned his arm, but this time his hand gave out a sonic boom texture as he fired all four shots at the beast that created an explosion in of itself, a hurricane of light and flames twisted and towered up into the sky.

Amar trying to catch his own arm that was blown back by the power shot, holding his hand down and to his side not sure what to think, of course he wanted to be prepared but that was one hell of a blast if Amar was able to admit. Even as it continued to spiral upward roaring such furious and fierce flames made of light, suddenly it was all blown out like a birthday candle as the beast with burned and charred skin from the blistering light still actively ablaze on his body charged forward to Amar. Leaving the flame behind him to wither and die as he ripped out a chunk of its energy, Amar letting go of his wrist as he brought up both fists with thumbs under his palms, his hands held like dual weld side by side clicking ready to go; Amar gave him not a second more to prepare himself as he released a storm of zooming bullets made from pure golden light, hands shaking so fast like a bobble head during an Earth quake. A good 40% of them actually hit their mark most just zoomed right past him leaving burn scratches and graze marks as they shot right past him but harmlessly disappearing into thin air with their loss, the beast's body convulsed with each appendage that did take damage, his left arm flopped around for a couple of second when a ball of light blew up on it at the shoulder socket before the beast snapped and popped it back in. A gross disgusting pulse was heard as he reconnected it, then hit at the right knee he hopped until he could force himself back into a sprint

His torso being the biggest piece target, the broad side of a barn in this case, taking the most hits beating it like a pair of bongos. Some exploded upon contact covering his chest with flames for a few seconds before blowing off, some shot through his body like a real bullet piercing through that bulky stock of muscle he dare call skin, some even bounced off the trampoline of tight knit muscle that was his body. His head had to be the most painful as it cracked back with every single hit like the dart of light had the strength of a bull in each blast enough to snap his neck like a twig but somehow didn't, not even masked his face with fire or even revealed what his bones looked like. Finally reaching the promise land that was Amar's face already getting his chunk of meat that was his iron girder –like arm, sticking it straight out as he rushed forward to clothsline Amar's neck, Amar firing as many blasts as he could between them, flashes like strobe lights in a midnight rave popped up between them and still nothing did any effect. Amar had to abandon his plan of bringing him down with this maneuver, and move onto the next one ducking under, both of them spun around but when Amar came full circle he was already ready with his arm past the locked and loaded stage and was heading towards the beast's body. The index knuckle on Amar's right hand began to glow in between the beast's right shin and Amar's gauntlet exploding inches from them, Amar listened closely and he could hear a snap he knows he got him with this one, as the beast roared out a screech in complete utter agony before the beast could bring his head down to catch sight of the puny bug that broke off a piece of him.

Amar was already at the other leg with his left fist, this time a huge glow sparkling and erupting between the two, a shockwave imploded inside of the beast's leg as it crumbled. However the beast was not about to stumble but his knees did buckle, and that is exactly what Amar was going for as he leaped up in front of the beast that was heavily occupied with managing the pain, trying to keep it as internal as possible. Both of Amar's arms we're now slung back as far as he could go with his fists glowing from every inch like the world's brightest pair of light bulbs – the view from space anyway, his illuminating pair of gloves that shined from the beast's frightened, desperate, and fearful eyes but as he trembled with terror he also began to smirk a truly devilish smile. Yanking his mouth wide open to spew out a river of darkness, lightning mixed with blackened air and a dark smog all shot from the beast's open gap of a mouth, just before it could directly touch Amar who already knew it would be trouble; Amar used his finisher against this pitiful surprise attack that land mined right in front of him against the dark forces. Only able to cut the river of darkness in half, taking Amar back like he was caught in a flood, sliding and skidding him against the floor.

Heavy steam radiating off Amar's body as he had his forearms up to block the entire onslaught, now his whole limbs we're gray and black instead of dots or splotches. Amar lowered his arms, the way his chest was moving in and out looked like he was panting that last attack actually inflicted serious damage against him; the beast now speaking in a superior tone as he said "**I THGUOTH OS! RUYO ROMAR SBROSAB SSENKRDA!! – ELIWH UYO DEYASL YM SREHTOBR!!! I SWA GNIKNIHT FO A YWA OT EUS TAWH I DNUOF! WNO HSIRPE!!**"(*I thought so! Your armor absorbs darkness!! – while you slain my brothers!!! I was thinking of a way to use what I found! Now perish!!*) The beast then stabbed his own claw into the ground and like a man who struck oil, darkness streamed out he drank from it just as a dog slobbers from a fountain and in all the pierced holes, broken bones, and burned skin closed up, snapped back together and molted back to its original tone. He then swiped it at Amar, a river of blackness was dragon charging at Amar, but of course his speed is unmatched by the time the beast could realize he dodged it Amar was already behind him; with his right hand aimed at the beast, and his left hand gripping his wrist for steady support but the beast only gave a cocky smirk as he glanced over his shoulder and before light could glisten or twinkle inside of Amar's middle knuckle. A tower of darkness shot up, spearing up to try to drive right through him but Amar's speed was not going to be touched, Amar already sliding back with caution as he used his left hand to break his heavy momentum but before Amar could even begin to execute his counter measure, the ground beneath him began to crack and as he looked at it he took his eye off the prize and the beast swung forward for Amar's face.

Amar's lightning instincts pulled his face back with a quick step back but underneath him the dragon of darkness drilled through the ground; all Amar could do was quickly pull his cape over his arms as a shield. A brigade was made to barricade the darkness from coming any further shooting Amar up into the air like a ball of flame launched from a catapult to invade the enemies walls, curving over until he smashed and was drilled into the ground. A crater cracking the Earth as he was continued to be pounded and pulverized into the dirt, his shield a perfect protector but the darkness began to spread onto it slowly like a growing plague; and from underneath him Amar heard a creaking cracking as he saw darkness breaking through the crevices of Earth. Amar kept looking back and forth like a paranoid schizophrenic psychopath – what to do what to do?! Amar surely knew as he shot a sonic boom volume explosion of light from his cape, sliding back on his feet as he tried to look for another vantage point, putting his cape down as he seen the humongous stain of darkness upon it like it was dipped right in a jet black paint bucket. Throwing his cape down, Amar was brutally and mercilessly rushed from the beast who shot up from ground in the middle of the crater in the Earth; Amar made, the beast's waist was swimming inside of the pool of darkness that became a fearsome stream whenever it was directed at Amar,

He grabbed Amar by the neck and dug his claws into Amar's armor, no good it wouldn't pierce through his divine plate of protection – but no matter the beast just tossed Amar forward as he hit him with a fearsome right that cut through the air as it made its way across Amar's jaw. Rattling his head inside of his facemask like a car that was flipping over during a car crash, immediately swinging back with a left hook to twist Amar's head in that direction; but then coming down from below with an uppercut that rocked his chin, his armor feeling paper thin as all these shots rocked his head to the left, then right, then up, then down, left, right, left, right, up, right, left, start yes! I finally got the infinity lives mode!! Oh yeah back to that guy – the darkness itself shot through the beast like a torpedo, blasting Amar forward as he was dug into the ground and driven deeper by the river of blackness that was pushing him in deeper like a stick at this point. Until a golden bubble blew the stick off like an invisible karate man cut in and flawlessly chopped it in two, deep inside the now cleared out circle of what used to be trees, Amar with one arm hanging down low his left had to be dislocated; a good gash chipped off a piece of his facemask on his right side ripping up to the side of his cape that covered his face. His own Divinity was splattered on the side of his face, losing its glow as it slowly faded to darkness revealing the side of his mouth that showed the edge of his lip, huffing and puffing as he looked at the levitating beast dead in the eye as orbs of darkness floated near him all around him pillars of darkness tore through the ground to entrap Amar in a clockwork shape of towers of pure negative energy.

Amar was looking at his own armor to see on top of being dislocated his entire left arm was dripping blackness, a big pentagram was halfway splotched onto his chest plate. Black holes we're being burned in his cape and polka dots of darkness we're showing up in his armor, there were no words that needed to be said that arrogant smirk on the beast's face said everything; Amar just sighed as he shut his eyes tight, the beast then waved forward for his horde of darkness to charge, the towers bent over to curve perfectly on top of Amar, the beast's orbs of darkness all bulleting towards Amar. Just as he heard the roars of darkness and the flames that darkness created, Amar heard a chime like something as innocent and delicate as a wind chime, cracking one eye open to look for the source only to see a pure silver ring sweep away all the darkness like it was dust bunnies under the couch; putting out the blackened flames, wiping away the black lightning, the beast was absolutely lost in confusion and to be honest so was Amar who was looking around for some explanation or answer. Ryker floating in overhead with a not interested Forrest by his side as he exclaimed "UH! JUST SHUT GOT CHECKED LIKE A MARK BIZNATCH! – Also that's my student you're roughing up there, go Rook! You have to show him what you're made of, that's the last push I am giving you by the way!"

The attention being brought back down to Amar as the beast landed swiftly on the ground and exclaimed "**I EVHA HGUONE SSE NKRDA NI YM YDBO OT YORTSDE UYO LAL!!!**"(*I have enough darkness to destroy you all!!!*) Amar standing up straight as he said "I need you desperately now!" A cloud of darkness was being formed right in front of their eyes as the beast sprouted out his power like steam from a hot shower, just exuberating energy. On Amar's side his lowest abdomen drawer just slid open and he reached in to pull out some tiny stick shaped object that was big enough to stick out from Amar's hand as he held it, seeming to be dropped in a can of gold paint before Amar picked it up all it needed was diamonds encrusted on it to be really blinged out, Amar now shaking this mysterious object that he somehow had and with panic building up like the beast was building up his final attack "I got this when I was finished with my training but I – what do I do with it?! Is it a sword?! A Gun?! I do not even know what it is supposed to do but I am out of options here!!"Amar struck his stance with his right hand only able to grip onto this hilt object, a dragon monsoon of darkness munched Amar whole like an eagle swallowing a fly in one foul swoop. Ryker made a dramatic and sort of "glad I'm not that guy" expression, Ryker then heard in the back of his mind "how's he doing?"

Ryker hesitant to answer, but a delay is all the answer this mysterious voice needed "hmm that's all I needed to hear, intervene if you need to but if you think he has even a slim chance, then let him fight for it. I didn't train that marshmallow for nothing" silence the only thing that was now occupying Ryker's mind now, whispering to himself "yes sir"

Following the call back to the location a somewhat anxious Azuru was just taking his hand off of his sun – illuminating chest, letting out a sigh that instantly drew concern out from Emily who was in the same white room that Ryker and Amar beamed downed from. She waited patiently along with Duke by her side, Azuru expressing his thoughts "I know he can do it! I know for a fact he has it in him there is no way he doesn't; he's just still adjusting, he's thinking too much!" Emily giggling she very rarely sees Azuru this flustered "awh just look who cares deeply about his student!""He's making me look bad!! Now the demons are gonna think I just train anyone!! My name will be drug through the mud!"

Emily shaking her head in disappointment, of course this was the actual reason that he is concerned. Duke now tipping his hat to remove the shade from his face "so Azuru, in all seriousness;

how long do you think the kid has?" Azuru picking his head to look Duke dead in the eyes, the urgency now showing clear through his blue lagoons. "If he really has the talent that I believe he does, he should begin to make his comeback right about now... if my opinions and thoughts about him are wrong and hell does freeze over; then Ryker should be saving him in about fifth - teen seconds. That is around the amount of damage he can take, I just didn't think he would be taking on a hybrid his first mission out – you're supposed to build up to those things!" Duke breaking out a smile, "don't worry A –man I think he'll do fine, just have a bit of faith" Azuru still with his deadly serious look keeping the sight deadlocked onto Duke "I'll give him fifth - teen seconds instead"

Amar sinking deeper and deeper into darkness like his armor was made of anchor metal and this sea of shadows was pulling him in as well Amar just forgot to wear his cinderblock shoes, hearing a voice that sounded so distant and growing farther "I know what it does Amar! AMAR!! AM-a! Amar!" It was too late Amar was already too far gone like a person who swallowed up the ocean into their lungs.

His armor, piece by piece being torn off like the darkness itself was clawing and scraping off the divine metal, only to become scrap as it fell to the deep depths of the dark floor. The voice in his head regardless if Amar was conscious or not spoke to him again "I will not let this happen to you Amar! You need to hold on though! AMAR AMAR!!!" The hilt gave off one final glow of desperation and hope, just as an animal who was caught by its prey gives one final struggle before accepting its fate. Ryker, Kayoh, Ex, and Forrest now standing over with a golden light radiating off of their feet as they all watched this vortex of twilight spread out, flood and overtake the whole entire forest, swarming in between the trees, covering the ground and now moving outwards toward the civilians who were pushed to the outskirts of the park for safe keeping. Ryker then noting out loud "I gave Rook enough time to retaliate I am not going to jeopardize the lives of the people, they are what we have been fighting for this whole time, so I' m gonna have to move in soon" Kayoh and Ex's face just oozed concern and they desperately wanted to believe in Amar a second more but they knew this was the right decision but a rumbling and ground pounding started quaking behind them, looking over their shoulder all their eyes became wide as surprise blew their minds, except Forrest who grinded his teeth and mumbled to himself in irritation "are you serious?!"

Amar left to float around in the sea of ever long and growing abyss that was the shadows, creaking his eyes open as he kept hearing something that pounded on his eardrums, the more he squinted his eyes open the more he could clearly hear it. Opening his eyes to see a glimmering ball of light in this surf of murk, Amar lifting and stretching his hand out to his circular friend as he aid to himself in his mind "g-et get out oo-f here! You will not survive here" apparently on the same channel as Amar was able to hear him as the floating gray ball replied back "I told you I wasn't going to let this happen to you!! Now I am going to save you like you saved me!!!" Amar thinking that the light was coming for both of them was gravely mistaken, seeing a bubble from outside this shadow world that was clouding his vision that was only getting bigger and bigger this beam of white light. Finally piercing through the darkness straight to the soul and Amar to which the soul screamed out to Amar "HOLD OUT YOUR SWORD!!!" Amar barely able to do that as with his last remainder of strength pushed his hilt forward and like vacuum for all the dust in the world the laser of condensed and stream of souls all shot into. A shockwave able to burn the darkness away only leaving the beast himself with his personal ring of shadows, as Amar now back on his feet with his entire left side of his armor torn completely off to the point skin was revealed, his mask was gashed off, more rips and tears we're spread out throughout his armor even dents, holes, and crush marks but still Amar was able to valiantly stand with his what was now a complete and invincible sword in his hand, with a skinny golden cross guard and a white blade that moved like flames emitting white, crystal, silver and black smoke.

The beast was taken aback by how much of his force was obliterated by a mere sword showing up into Amar's hands, however this wasn't even going to blemish his plan or his resolve to pulverize Amar, with darkness gathering to his hands and shoulders like blood gathering to the brain by standing on your head the beast was ready to give his final attack – no more games, the ground shattering underneath him while the darkness that has been burrowed underground for months maybe even years rearing its ugly mug by shooting out like geysers in back of him. The beast then covering himself in a ball of darkness and malevolent spiritual energy proclaiming to the world "DEMONIC WORLD DARKNESS PLUNGE!!!" Amar surprised by him speaking English must be a special occasion, Amar then heard an echoing tranquil but unified voice speak to him as it said "do not be frightened Amar, you have all the power you will ever need in your hands, we will also be beside you every step of the way now go forth and show him the power of the light!" Amar holding his claymore broadsword sized sword now with two hands as the spiritual essence of the sword resonated and trailed off of Amar's body, Amar ran forward with his blade at his side and his two hands firmly clutching his one last chance. The demon not having it, finally firing off his gigantic city sized, demonic head of the beast that had all the malevolent energy gathered and mashed together inside ready to swallow Amar up again but this time it would chew before letting him go any further.

Amar kept charging forward not an ounce of fear or a hint of doubt in him and leaping to the jaws that we're the size of buildings of this vicious head shouting over as he sliced down his blade "HEAVEN'S STRIKE!!!" His sword hitting its growth spurt that very second, extending to the size for a giant to be swinging it around slicing the demonic entity in half like a harmless tomato, with waves of blinding and blustering light spreading it apart even further with a thunderous crashing only moments later burning it all away to the point not even a crispy speck remained. Out in the very middle, the eye of the storm, the epicenter of chaos was the beast, who now held the blade dead center in his brain, slowly and gently slicing down his body like it was made out of bread; finally shrinking down to its claymore self once the beast was now two separate beings that we're slowly incinerating from the bottom up like lighting fire to a dollar. Amar picked up his blade full of souls and as soon as they seen that the beast had been slain they seen that their duty had been done, now breaking apart from the smoky sword, they all flew upwards to form a cloud overhead Amar, the cross guard disappearing only leaving the hilt in Amar's hands to which Amar smirked and said "thank you guys I could not have done it without you" Ryker and Forrest watching on while Kayoh and Ex had to catch their jaws before it hit the ground, while Ryker had his hands casually pocketed, Forrest was clutching his fists at his sides in ferocity both jealousy and amazement as he caught a glimpse of what was lying dormant inside this slab of fresh meat, this green bean. Now he started to realize these feeling surged up and down his spine this is the level of power he was capable of all this and he wasn't even properly introduced to this world or even himself and his capabilities.

On the outside of this Ryker was simply nodding his head, bobbing it up and down as a golden grin gleamed off his face that just shouted out his proud feelings for his student but inside of his head he was speculating and pondering "so this is him... this is the one who will replace Ambrose... and this is why he was chosen, maybe that is why Azuru told him to keep that little secret under wraps but I wonder why"

Back up in a land high above Earth, Azuru with arms crossed over his chest while gently bobbing his head the whole entire waiting, patiently – I might add! Indeed very very strange to behold on Azuru's behalf, of course this didn't last too long when a smirk broke across Azuru's face. His typical arrogance and smugness bleeding out from it, Emily taking a second to prep herself "okay Azuru what is it now? Did you contact Ryker to see how Amar is doing?" Azuru's smile getting wider by the passing moments, now finally deciding to elaborate "nope, don't need to. It's been longer than fifth – teen seconds" Emily and Duke curiously looking at each other with the same exact idea branching out from their combined minds asking in unison "so do you think he's okay?" Azuru barely able to hold back his growing enthrallment "I think he's better than okay... but when he gets here... I have a few choice words for him"

TO BE CONTINUED?